K9 MINE

BY

SHANNON MACLEOD

979-8-9879920-2-9 K9 Mine (Print)

979-8-9879920-3-6 K9 Mine (Kindle)

Contents

DEDICATION

"Most people are like sheep. Nice, harmless creatures who want nothing more than to be left alone so they can graze. But then of course there are wolves. Who want nothing more than to eat the sheep. But there's a third kind of person. The sheepdog. Sheepdogs have fangs like wolves. But their instinct isn't predation. It's protection. All they want, what they live for, is to protect the flock."

— Barry Eisler, Livia Lone

With much love and deepest gratitude, I dedicate this to those courageous

Sheepdogs—both two-legged and four—who answered the call.

ACKNOWLEDGMENTS

To Taylor and Corporal Nolan, the two halves of my heart.

To Angela, who is always there, always supportive, and has put her hand over my mouth to stop me from talking more times than I can count.

To Brigadier General Dan Hickman for his assistance with military terminology and procedures, gardening tips, and big brotherly advice.

To Corporal Thomas Stevenson and K9 Thor for his vast knowledge of law enforcement and K9 training, and for knowing where the best sushi is.

To Senior Special Agent Robert vonLoewenfeldt and K9 Ollie for their many years of dedicated law enforcement service in the military and on the police force. Ollie's toys are still off limits.

To Officer Edward Ratliff and K9 Ace for indulging me with random questions about *a day in the life*, tips on K9 handling, and for great working doggo memes.

To Sergeant Mark Tappan and K9 Mattis, for their service above and beyond, a wealth of great TikTok videos, their incredible book, _A Dog Called Mattis_, and for being an overall inspiration.

To Renee Rocco for the fantastic cover, her wonderful dark romances, and for keeping me on the right track.

To Ray and Gail for cheering me on, their delicious cooking, and spoiling my dog rotten.

To Mitch, Vanessa, Candy, Donna, Jimmy, Maria, Danielle, Alex, Bob, Kerry, Matt, Guilene, Tim, Julie, and Stephanie for helping me understand, making me laugh on the daily, and being the best tribe I could ever hope for.

K9 Viking, EOW 11-7-2021

K9 Axel, EOW 2-14-2025

And to G., always.

PROLOGUE

Ireland, AD 512

Brú na Bóinne

FIRE!"

The roar of the engulfing flames, the crashing as wooden buildings collapsed, and the chorus of panicked screams behind her began to fade as she ran—a welcome thing. Acrid black smoke choking the air burned her lungs. Her legs, unused to so much activity, screamed in protest. This dark, forbidding forest had no clear path in the hours before dawn, and her thin, shapeless gown caught the grasping hands of each branch and bramble. Her dirty, bare feet, she was sure, found every sharp thorn, splinter, and acorn littering the ground. There would be bruising later from the many falls and blows, but later would be time enough to worry about it. At this moment, she had much greater troubles.

Those poor wretches she thought of as sisters refused to flee when the opportunity presented itself. She last saw them huddling together like frightened sheep, watching their dwelling house burn with dull, despairing eyes.

"One is missing—find it!"

One deep voice rang above the chaos—*Ansgar*. Younger than the other druids, he had been a warrior first and still had a strong, robust body under his elder robes. Soul-numbing terror made her push harder, for his chances of catching her were greater than any of the others. And he was known to be crueler than most when encountering what he considered disobedience.

While dreams of escape had been constant, the opportunities were few. Her first thought—her only plan—was to somehow reach the portal she had seen the brothers use. She knew not the sacred words to recite before entering, but made a wish that her heart's intent would be enough. She no longer prayed to their gods; they had proven deaf to her pleas ages ago.

Faster.

The heavy *lunula* collar banged against her collarbones with each jarring step. The binding spell prevented removal, inflicting excruciating pain upon the wearer until released. She had ceased trying to take it off some years past but vowed to find a way once she gained her freedom or die in the attempt.

Faster, faster.

The heavy footfalls behind her drew closer as she burst into the moonlit clearing. She raced toward the stone circle in the middle of the field with a speed she never knew she possessed. Inside the ring stood a massive dolmen, dwarfing the smaller stones. She did not know their true purpose, but as the grand seasonal rituals took place here, she knew it must be a site of great power.

The forest shuddered in anger, and she glanced back in time to see the large shape explode from the line of trees. Ansgar's gaze swept around the field before coming to rest on her, and he bellowed like an enraged bull, then continued the chase.

Faster, faster, faster. Her heart slammed against her chest, fluttering like a bird's wings. She reached the first of the standing stones and scrambled to the center as his rhythmic chant reached her ears. *Raising energy,* she knew. *Must not let him... someone... save me...*

She dared a last glance back, but this time toward the only home she had ever known. 'I will return for you,' she vowed, 'I swear it.' With one great leap, she dove into the shimmering space beneath the table stone of the great dolmen. With no clear destination in mind and escape born of desperation as her sole intent, she tumbled headfirst into the infinite blackness.

PART I

CHAPTER 1

Modern Day

Summer in the Deep South

C orporal Travis Ewan McLean of the Cherry Grove Police Department considered himself an overall happy guy—just not today.
He groaned into the pillow as his phone's snooze alarm went off for the umpteenth time. He needed to get up, throw on some clothes, and head home. That was what he *had* to do. The disappointment from this trip hit him harder than usual, and he wasn't interested in getting out of the cozy, if somewhat lumpy, motel bed.

Figuring he couldn't put it off any longer, he resigned himself to getting up. He fumbled for his phone to silence the alarm but, still stalling, paused to check his messages. He went by lots of names—Trav to his friends, McLean at the precinct, and a plethora of colorful obscenities from the people he arrested. After hearing the ranting, rambling voicemail from his now ex-girlfriend, he added *coldhearted, obsessive asshole* to the list.

We are DONE, Travis. You hear me? D-O-N-E.

Disentangling himself from the sheet and throwing back the covers, he walked naked to the bathroom. Even though they had dated on and off for the last year, he wasn't too broken up about the relationship ending. Lori Ann was sweet when she wasn't all riled up, but he'd figured out quickly that the beautiful blonde was what his brothers in blue called a badge bunny—drawn to the uniform first and the man second. Still hot, though. He'd give her that. Years of collegiate tennis and beach volleyball competitions had done wondrous things for that woman's body.

He twisted the transparent plastic knob, lifted the button to turn on the shower, and dangled his hand into the spray, waiting for the water to get hot. Her demands on his time had increased over the last couple of months, and he suspected she had commitment on her mind. He snorted with amusement at the thought. *I'd rather reenlist and go back to Bagram—better odds of survival.*

He grabbed a fast shower and shaved. With one of the thin motel towels tied precariously around his lean hips, he quickly swept the modest but comfortable room, stuffing his belongings into a worn army duffel bag. Cold air conditioning hit the moisture still clinging to his exposed skin, and he hastened into his jeans and a clean polo shirt.

Heaving another deep sigh, he plopped down on the single overstuffed chair to tug on his short boots. Suddenly, the jarring ringtone of "Dirty Deeds Done Dirt Cheap" filled the small room. Travis grinned, seeing his cousin/best friend's name on the caller ID.

"Hey, cuz." He pressed *speaker* and tossed the phone onto the bed to finish getting dressed.

"Where are you?" Mike demanded without preamble. "I just went by your house."

"Motel outside Columbia off I-20. I told you I was driving up to look at puppies this weekend."

"Yeah, I forgot. You alone? Is it one of those rent-by-the-hour no-tell motels?"

Travis laughed. "Yes, I'm alone, and no, it's a fine, upstanding establishment."

"I don't hear any yapping, so I'm guessing you didn't get one. How come you didn't take Lori Ann with you?"

"Jesus. Say that again, but this time, hear yourself," he said with a snorting laugh. "She left me a screaming breakup voicemail last night."

Mike's tone changed to one of concern. "You good?"

"Oh, one hundred percent," he assured him. "She's been dropping hints lately about taking it to the next level. I've been eyeing the door for a while, but I'd rather let her think that ending it was her idea."

"You don't owe her that. She'll drag your name through the mud every chance she gets."

Travis snickered. "She won't be the first one to try that. And you know the good girls can't resist the challenge of setting a bad boy on the path to righteousness." He took the phone into the bathroom and towel-dried his wet hair. "Anyway, what you got going on today?"

"We're all going to watch the game and shoot pool at Rocket's, wanted to see if you're in the mood to lose some cash. And I need my wingman—the new Dispatch trainees said they'd be there," he said, his voice taking on a teasing note.

"Hell no—if there's money involved, I'd rather face you on the firing range than over a pool table. I know you couldn't hit water if you fell out of a boat. You don't practice enough."

"Asshole—I'm getting better." Mike laughed. "But I can still whup you on the par three."

"You can hit a golf ball three hundred yards. I can hit a golf ball *at* three hundred yards. We are not the same."

"Alright, you got me there. But you're right; my pool skills are on point."

Travis finger-combed his hair into a slightly ruffled look, tilting his head to ensure he didn't miss any spots. "Parting a tourist from his hard-earned money isn't a good look, Detective Reynolds. Hustling coworkers isn't nearly as frowned upon unless it's me. Anyway, I can't—I've still got a three-hour drive to get home, and I switched shifts with

Carter. My ass has to be in the seat for roll call by oh seven hundred."

"Jesus, you patrol guys and your crack o'dawn schedules," Mike complained. "If you change your mind, that's where we'll be."

"Make good choices. And be careful with those trainees. I saw them this week—I'd say better than half look like they're ready to fill their plates at the badge buffet."

"Path to righteousness. Got it."

As a group, police officers tend to be superstitious, wearing lucky items or engaging in rituals for protection known only to them. Travis was no exception. He picked up the plain beaded chain next to his phone on the nightstand, rubbing his thumb absently over the raised letters on the dog tags. He paused to read his parents' names before slipping it on, wearing their love as his invisible suit of armor.

I could sure use some of their insight right about now. His mother had the gift of seeing straight through to a dog's soul, knowing at first glance which pups would find joy and purpose in working and which would be happier as couch potatoes. His dad used training techniques he had never seen before or since, and the results were nothing short of astonishing. Travis learned them all. He knew he was ready for a working dog of his own.

Lately, he had spent all his weeknights searching online and his weekends scouring every breeder east of the Mississippi for that perfect pup. He had seen hundreds but hadn't found the one he clicked with. Hence, he supposed, Lori Ann's exit.

Not much loss there, he mused. He never lacked feminine companionship, and when absent, it was by his own choice. He grinned at himself in the mirror, the dimples preserving a boyish charm in his otherwise ruggedly handsome face. *Now, who would've thought my perfect girl was a four-legged brunette?*

What an awful stench.

Her first impression upon waking was the horrible assault on her nose. She cracked one eye open and found herself flat in the dirt behind an immense metal box. Dark green and filthy, it appeared full of stinking refuse, spilling over the sides and into the area where she lay. Pulling herself into a sitting position, she scanned the unfamiliar surroundings but sensed no immediate threat.

Soaking wet, her skin prickled with glistening bits of ice that melted at once under the bright sunlight. Her metal collar gave an unnatural shudder, followed by an unpleasant tingling. Sucking in a fortifying breath, she grabbed the collar with both hands and ripped it from her neck, braced for the blinding pain. When none came, she breathed a relieved sigh. She turned it over to view the strange markings, but they made no sense. Drawing back, she threw it as far as she could into the woods with a small sense of satisfaction. *Free. FREE.* She smiled.

A male voice laughed and spoke in a strange language she did not understand.

She whirled at the sound with a soft hiss and moved into a defensive crouch, her fingers curling into claws. The elderly man put both hands up in surrender and smiled. He lowered his voice and spoke again more softly, as if reassuring a scared child.

"Where am I?" she asked in the common tongue. "Was I followed?"

He gave her a quizzical look and scratched his head, ruffling the shock of thinning gray hair. She thought to *sip* his *knowing*, something she heard those like her could do, but the spelled necklace had prevented it. The simple charm would do him no injury, but if successful, would give her the local language along with other valuable bits of information. She gave him what she hoped he would see as a trusting smile and offered her hand. He took it without hesitation and tugged her to her feet.

The violent shock from the flow of his knowledge into her made her weak body tremble. "Sorry, I didn't mean to scare ya," he said, his voice warm and kind.

"It is of no import," she said stiffly, her voice still scratchy from the smoke but pleased that the old tale proved true.

He whistled low. "Looks like you've had one heck of a time," he remarked, his gaze giving her a once-over. "You must have gotten caught out in that summer squall. What's your name, Miss?"

Now *that* was a question. She thought hard, trying to remember. Did the brothers ever use a name for her? "I know not," she said honestly. "I do not think I ever had one."

The man's eyes narrowed. "Well, where did you come from, and what are you up to behind my dumpster?"

This foul-smelling metal box, she reasoned. She paused and then tried assimilating his speech pattern to put him at ease. "I don't remember much," she lied. "And I only just woke, so I have not had time to get up to anything yet."

He chuckled at that, and she beamed, pleased she had amused him. "Well, if you pardon my saying, looks to me like you're wearing a dirty feedsack, and you're not big enough to shake a stick at. And barefoot to boot," he added, looking down and pointing. "There's broken glass all over the place back here, so mind your step. Do you want us to call someone for you?"

"I have no one," she said, shrugging her shoulders. In all her dreams of being free, thoughts of what she would do with that freedom never once occurred.

"Well, we can't just leave you out here all by yourself—there's homeless folk, raccoons, and rats sometimes. Even saw a black bear looking for his dinner once. Come on inside," he said, sweeping his arm toward a long, single-story dwelling and indicating she should follow. "My wife just made lunch, and it looks like you could sure use a bite. We got a big box of clothes people leave behind in their rooms after checking out. I bet if we looked, we could find you something clean that fits. Might even be some shoes." He gave her a wink.

Hot tears immediately stung her eyes. Overcome with gratitude, she struggled to speak. "Thank you, my lord. All those things would be most welcome."

"Oh, *pshaw*," the man said, flushing pink as he waved her off. She followed him to the head of the dwelling, where a glass door was marked with lettering and strange symbols. The bells jangled when he tugged it open and stepped back for her to enter first. "Name's Horace, by the way. Most folks call me Bud. Virginia!" he called out.

A plump older woman appeared, her face crinkling into a warm smile as she wiped her hands on her apron. "What we got here?"

Bud explained how they met, her lack of a name or memory of how she got there, and his promise of clothing. "Bud, sometimes you ain't got a lick of sense about women. Come on, sugar," she said, extending her hand. "I wash everything that gets left before it goes in the box, and we've got a couple of empty rooms. How would you like a nice, hot shower before you put those clean clothes on? I just fried up a whole pan of chicken, cooked a mess of butterbeans, rice, stewed okra and tomatoes, and a fresh peach cobbler, too. There's biscuits ready to go in the oven, so don't think you're running off without eating first."

The female couldn't help it; she burst into tears, covering her face with her hands. "I am sorry; kindness is new to me."

Crooning softly, Virginia led her away, giving Bud an uneasy glance over her shoulder.

A short while later, in the private chambers attached to the office, the female sat with the couple at their table, eating the most wonderful food she had ever tasted. The shower had been a revelation, the first time she had ever washed all of herself at the same time without using a bucket and rag. And the soap! It had a wonderful, flowery, clean smell that she adored. The woman applied some stinging ointment to her deeper wounds and put on sticky bandages that stayed on all by themselves.

The new clothes felt both strange and comfortable. They were tighter than she was accustomed to, stretching to fit her slight frame. She loved the bright-colored slippers with springy soles and long laces. Virginia had helped with her freshly shampooed hair, pulling the matted clumps apart and combing it until it hung shiny and straight past her waist. Oddly, the air inside the dwelling seemed much cooler than the oppressive heat outdoors.

The kind woman had smeared a creamy liquid on her face, neck, and hands, massaging it in. "You gotta start moisturizing when you're young so that when you're old like me, you're not covered up in wrinkles," she said with a chuckle. The tiny triskelions marking her as *other* stood out against her pale skin. "Don't know that I've ever seen tattoos on the face before," she murmured, then catching herself, added, "but they're mighty pretty on you."

Once dressed, Virginia led her into the modest kitchen. "You just have a seat right there and I'll fix you a plate, sweetie," she said, gesturing toward their small table. She slid the pan containing the biscuits into the preheated oven and began pulling plates out of the cabinet. "It's so nice to have you here for lunch," she said conversationally as she began setting the table. "Our children are all grown up and living in Columbia, but we get to see them and the grandchildren a few times a week. The kids come stay with us pretty regular during the summer. They think living in the motel is exciting." She laughed and shook her head, wiping her hands on the dishtowel. "Oh, to be six years old again."

The girl was unsure how to respond, so she just sat and listened, hands folded in her lap. Whenever Virginia looked her way, she smiled brightly and nodded. Her mouth watered at the heavenly aromas.

Bud wandered into the kitchen in time to pull the biscuits out while Virginia dished out three plates of food and placed them on the table. When they both took their seats, they clasped their hands and reached for hers. "The blessing," he explained before reciting the short prayer.

The girl nodded as if she understood and mimicked their actions, bowing her head. They each squeezed her hand before releasing it. "Go ahead and start; don't wait on us. You look hungry," Bud directed.

She nodded, picking up her fork as he did. Not recognizing any of the foods, she decided to work her way around the plate and speared several pieces of the delectable okra. The flavor exploded on her tongue, and she sighed with pleasure. "It is sweet and very good," she said, making short work of the plate's contents, followed by seconds on everything.

When she could not eat another bite, she gave a tiny, embarrassed burp. "That was very fine," she sighed. "Thank you for—"

She froze mid-sentence, the blood draining from her face as she shuddered violently. She sucked in several deep breaths before she could speak. "H—he's here—fo—for me. An—Ansgar's here," she stammered. Reaching across the table, she grabbed the couple's hands. "You have not seen me," she warned, then rushed to add, "I have broken no laws; I want only my freedom."

Virginia's eyes went wide. "I knew it," she said to Bud. "This poor child has been trafficked like you hear about on the news."

She shook her head, knowing she had precious little time to make these kind people understand the dire threat they faced. "This man is dangerous beyond your understanding. Rid your mind of any thought of me and tell him you know nothing. You will not place your lives in peril on my behalf."

The bells rattled harshly in the next room as the front door opened.

CHAPTER 2

"I'll get it." Bud rose slowly from his seat. He glanced uncertainly at the two women, their heads bent together in a frantic but hushed conversation.

At his first glimpse of the imposing stranger, he took a deep breath and said a silent prayer before stepping out behind the front desk. "Good afternoon, sir," he said, keeping his tone genial and businesslike. "Check-in isn't until 3:00 p.m., but I can go ahead and get your information now if you like. By yourself today?"

The tall, powerfully built man glanced around the room as if memorizing it. His tangled and dirty black hair reached his waist, parts of it braided with pieces of bone, feathers, and beads. The planes of his face were hard, his flinty eyes even harder. Deep frown lines appeared chiseled into skin weathered from outdoor life. An old scar ran from his right temple and down his cheek, disappearing under the scraggly salt-and-pepper beard. The long robe hid much of his body, but he moved with the arrogance of a man accustomed to having his orders obeyed without question.

The heavy smell of wood smoke clung to the stranger. He strode to the office counter, thin lips curving into an insincere smile. "I have no need of lodging. I seek a young woman in my care, but she has gone missing," he said imperiously, his strangely accented words slicing through the air between them. "Small, somewhat thin, dark hair. Markings by her eyes. Have you seen anyone such as she?"

Bud pursed his lips as if thinking. "Nope, can't say as I have. Haven't seen anybody since church early this morning."

"Are you certain?" The man frowned, his eyes narrowing in suspicion. "I am prepared to reward you handsomely for her safe return."

"Sounds like someone I'd remember, but still can't say as I've seen her." He lifted both shoulders in a shrug. "There's a couple gas stations and a McDonald's down the road; you might try there, Mr.... sorry, I didn't get your name."

The big man moved in a blur, grabbing Bud by the throat with one hand and hoisting him off the ground, leaving his toes to dangle. "My name is Ansgar, but you may address me as My Lord, if at all," he snarled, dropping the golden collar he held with his other hand onto the desk. "I seek the woman who wore this. And doubt it not, I will kill whoever thinks to hide her from me. I smell your fear, old man, and I know you lie. I will ask you but once more—where is she?"

"I saw her," Virginia cried, bursting into the room. "She was out back behind the motel."

Bud made a strangled noise as Ansgar tightened his grip on the struggling man. He turned to give her a chilling smile. "And where is she now, woman?"

"I thought I was seeing things," she said, her voice shaking. "I saw this poor girl wandering around and went to speak to her, but..."

Ansgar ground his impatience into a single word. "Where?"

"There's no other way to say it, sir. She turned into one of them pretty red birds and flew off. I ain't never seen anything like it; I thought my eyes were playing tricks on me. I didn't see which way she went, but she's long gone. Now you put my man down right this minute," she ordered.

The loud bells announced another visitor. Ansgar released his hold, allowing Bud's feet to touch the floor again. He gave a menacing growl in warning, then whirled to assess the newcomer. A tall, clean-shaven young man entered, wearing a CGPD ball cap over dark hair cut short but stylish. The dark blue polo shirt stretched tight across his broad chest, and a pair of aviator Ray-Ban sunglasses dangled from the V. Both muscular arms bore full Celtic tattoo sleeves. A silver badge sat at the waistband of his tight, faded jeans, next to the belt straps of the drop leg holster holding a 40 mm Glock. In his right hand, he carried a duffel bag.

Ansgar's rapid gaze swept over him, landing on the firearm. He straightened to his full height and seemed to grow even larger. The air thickened with apprehension as if the walls held their breath, waiting for the impending violence to erupt.

Travis picked up on the subtle changes at once and shifted the bag to his left hand. His sharp expression tightened as he strode across the lobby and stopped at the desk, dropping it to the floor beside him. It landed with a heavy *whomp*, masking the soft sound of thumbing open the holster with his right hand. "Morning, just letting y'all know I'm checking out. Always a pleasure staying with you and the missus," he said, purposefully not using their names as he placed his room key on the counter and slid it over to Bud. His eyes narrowed as his gaze darted back and forth between the two men, but he kept his tone conversational. "Is there a problem here?"

"Mind your own," Ansgar snapped. "This does not concern you."

"Wasn't talking to you," Travis snapped in a slow drawl, looking to Bud for confirmation.

It took a minute before Bud was able to answer. His shaking hand rose to his throat, where the last fading fingermarks were still visible. "Uh... no. He said he's looking for a girl that's gone missing, but I already told him she ain't here."

"She turned into a bird and flew off," Virginia added quickly.

"Bird, huh?" Travis gave her a quizzical look but shrugged, refocusing on the strange man. "Sounds like you've learned all you can here, then. Maybe you best be on your way to keep searching. Or if she's a missing person, we could call County police and get them involved. Your choice."

"That will not be necessary," Ansgar said, snatching the collar from the counter. He glared at Bud. "Mayhap I will call on you again if perchance she should return."

Travis turned with raised eyebrows, questioning. The older man shook his head slightly and smiled. "I think we have everything in hand here, Officer. 'Preciate you, though. Any luck this time?"

"Wait just a second," Virginia said simultaneously, darting to the back room. She returned shortly, handing Travis a brown paper grocery bag with little dots of grease visible. "I packed you a little something for the road."

Travis beamed, accepting the welcome gift. "Y'all take such good care of me. Thank you, ma'am." He answered Bud's question with a quick shake of his head. "Not this time, but you know I'll keep looking. I'll likely be back in a few weeks, but I'll call first to let you know when I'm coming." He gave the robed man a last once-over. "Gandalf," he said as he nodded, tapping the brim of his hat respectfully. He bent to retrieve his bag, slung the straps over one shoulder, and headed for the parking lot.

Travis dialed the non-emergency number for the sheriff's office as he walked quickly, pressing send as soon as he closed his car door. He gave Dispatch a cursory explanation about sketchy vagrants at the motel and requested a welfare check. The dark-tinted windows cast the cabin interior in shadow, but he put on his sunglasses and pretended to study some random paperwork piled in the passenger seat while watching the office door. The stranger stalked out a minute or two later, a menacing scowl twisting his face. He shielded his eyes with one hand, his gaze sweeping the parking lot before coming to rest on Travis's car. He stared for a long, tension-filled moment, then turned and stalked toward the rear of the building. He circled the dumpster as if searching and then disappeared into the woods.

Travis waited a bit to ensure the weird man wasn't coming back before hopping out of the car. Locking his car with the remote, he jogged to the lobby door. The old man stood behind the counter, head jerking in alarm at the harsh sound as he burst in. "What was all that about?" Travis asked, jerking a thumb toward the door.

Bud glanced around nervously, as if to ensure Ansgar was gone. "I found this little slip of a girl hiding behind the dumpster, barefoot, wearing what looked like a dirty pillowcase. We brought her inside and cleaned her up, gave her some clothes out of the lost and found. We had just finished eating when that guy showed up looking for her. She called him Ansgar. Acted like she was terrified of him."

Travis nodded and turned to Virginia, who had joined Bud behind the desk. "What's this about a bird?"

"That's the honest-to-God truth, Travis. When Bud went out to talk to the man, she told me to say she turned into a bird and flew off. I thought she meant like that little girl in the Forrest Gump movie. But then she got all... fuzzy. Next thing I knew, she vanished into thin air. The clothes she had on just fell in a heap on the floor. Hold on," she said, disappearing into the kitchen area again. She returned with an armload of clothes, some new-looking running shoes, and another paper grocery bag folded under her arm. "This is what she had on when Bud found her, and when she disappeared." Snapping the bag open, she stuffed the shoes and clothing into it.

"What did she look like?" he asked.

Bud opened his mouth to speak, but Virginia answered first. "Pretty as a picture, maybe twenty or thereabouts. Covered from head to toe in cuts and bruises, bless her heart. Close to my height but skinny as a rail. Long black hair with a bit of curl in it."

"Did you happen to notice her eye color?"

"Gold. I've never seen that color before. Oh," she added, tapping a fingertip near her temples to illustrate, "and she had swirly tattoos the same color right here."

"Next to her eyes?" he clarified. "Huh. That's different."

"They're tiny, and they looked like..." She glanced around the room, her gaze finally focusing on his tattoos. "Like that," she said, pointing to one of the triskelions on his forearm.

Not wanting to appear skeptical, Travis nodded in understanding. "Twenty-something, about five feet two inches, slight build, pretty, long black hair with tattoos next to her eyes. Did you notice anything else about her, maybe some other markings or piercings?"

"Her ears weren't pierced. That's unusual these days, what with everybody putting earrings on their babies soon as they're born. And she acted like she had never seen a shower before."

He nodded. "Anything else?"

Virginia shook her head no. "There was something real odd about the way she talked, all formal," Bud added, jumping in. "At first, she didn't sound like she was from around here, but then she did."

"Here's what we're going to do." Travis pulled a business card out of his wallet, grabbed a pen from the counter, and jotted his personal cell number on the back before handing it to Bud. "That guy could be dangerous. If he shows up here again, I want you to call 911, then me, understand? Anytime, day or night. I can't get here right away, but I have people who can." He jerked his head toward the register. "I also know you have something hid on that shelf down there. Call the police first; let them handle it. And," he added with a wink, "I'm sure it's not that old sawed-off shotgun because you know those are illegal, right?"

Bud flushed pink, and the couple nodded in understanding. Virginia thrust the full bag of clothing into his arms. "This is what all she had on. Maybe you could do some of them DNA tests to find out who she is."

Travis gave her an indulgent smile, accepting the bag. "That's a very smart idea, Mrs. Virginia; I'll see what I can do." He opened the door to leave but paused before stepping outside. "Remember now. You see him, you call 911 right then. Don't wait around to see what he's going to do, okay?"

"We sure will," they assured him, waving goodbye.

Waiting inside his car, Travis lingered until the county cruiser turned into the motel driveway, then headed out. He stopped for gas and topped off the tank in his late-model muscle car before merging onto I-20 and heading home to Cherry Grove, the northernmost point of the sprawling Grand Strand and Myrtle Beach, South Carolina. His duffel bag, the paper sack of clothes, and the one containing what he hoped was fried chicken rode in the backseat. Even with his favorite *Music to Haul Ass By* playlist blasting, the boring interstate trip seemed to take forever. Once he reached his exit and started driving what he thought of as regular roads again, the view became more varied and colorful.

August heat shimmered off the two-lane highway like a desert mirage loomed just ahead. Fluffy white clouds floated across the azure sky, although the oppressive heat and high humidity suggested rain later in the evening. Many old country frame houses sat far back from the road, with packed dirt driveways and folks on the front porch swings or rockers fanning themselves. The fancier houses had crushed coquina drives that crunched under tires, announcing a visitor's arrival before the dogs could.

Looks like it's going to be a good cotton year, he thought as he passed fields of prickly bolls, along with corn and soybeans. Cows and horses clustered in the meager shade found under the sprawling pecan and pear trees in their pastures. Since it was Sunday, he didn't see anyone plowing or working in the garden. He did spy an ATV or two streaking across open fields, kicking up rooster tails of dust in their wake.

Makeshift stands dotted the roadside, selling boiled peanuts, fresh vegetables, or watermelons. Most still had the "honor system," meaning that if you took something while the owner wasn't there, you simply dropped your money in the lockbox—typical of a sleepy Sunday afternoon in the Deep South. What few businesses he saw, mostly small and family-run, had their closed signs visible, respecting the commandment not to toil on the Sabbath.

It differed within the city limits, or *in town,* as the locals would say. Not much honor system to be found there. Travis's precinct stayed busy, especially during the chaotic summer months when the weekly influx of tourists more than quadrupled the number of year-round residents. As he drew closer home, the roadside stands gave way to beachwear stores offering three souvenir t-shirts for ten dollars, saltwater taffy, reduced-price attraction tickets, and hermit crabs. Pancake houses were everywhere, many open twenty-four hours a day, seven days a week. He often enjoyed meals in those: the local police always knew which ones had the freshest coffee and the fastest omelets.

Waving to a neighbor out washing his car, he pulled into his driveway several rows back from Ocean Boulevard in the late afternoon. Even though he had grown up here, he struggled to think of it as his house. The spirits of his parents still lingered in every room. His father had been home on leave, discussing retirement, when a freak auto accident claimed their lives and that of their two working dogs almost three years ago. He had not done much to change it. His dog, Reno, had crossed over the Rainbow Bridge from kidney disease the previous year, so the house that greeted him after his shift each day sat silent as a tomb. Remodeling was high on his *When I Get Around To It* list.

With four bedrooms, three and a half baths, and an attached garage on a double lot, his modest ranch-style home was not close enough to the ocean to need the high, wooden stilts, but you could still be waist-deep in waves inside of ten minutes. And the best part—a huge backyard surrounded by a taller-than-average privacy fence. The area realtors had been at him for over a year, urging him to sell, as it was *way too much house* for a bachelor. One even went so far as to bestow motherly advice, telling him if he was set on keeping the house, he needed to think about settling down and starting a family. He never bothered to tell them about the house's best feature, that the entire backyard had been transformed into a professional-level K9 training area with all kinds of hurdles, teeters, tubes, crawlers, and ladders. If they made it, he had it. There were even a couple of mounted car and SUV doors. Other kids had swing sets growing up—Travis had swinging tunnels. And he loved every minute of it.

The Hellcat coasted past his parked patrol car and into the garage. Pressing the overhead button, he lowered the door and grabbed his bags from the rear seat. He juggled the paper sacks, freeing his hand to punch the passcode on the alarm system keypad beside the door.

The welcome blast of cool air hit him as he stepped into the spacious kitchen. He dropped the duffel to the floor, tossed the bag of clothes onto the table, and, after clearing out a space, put the food in the refrigerator for later. Grabbing a cold beer, he popped it open and headed for the large den. A brief search found the remote between the couch cushions, and he turned on the second afternoon game in time to catch the kickoff. He removed his badge and belt, then stripped the lower Velcro straps on his holster. After checking the safety, he placed everything on the coffee table next to the beer. The boots came off next, and with a contented sigh, Travis fell back onto the long sectional for some late Sunday afternoon relaxation.

That first beer went down smoothly, so he helped himself to another. At the start of the second beer and quarter, Travis closed his eyes for a minute and fell soundly asleep.

The halftime commentary on the evening game gave him a general idea of the time when he opened his eyes again. He lay still and listened for any out-of-place sound, wondering what caused him to jerk into this level of alert wakefulness. The entire property and house had a professional-grade security system that he had designed himself, but he didn't remember arming it when he got home. The only light in the dark house came from the TV screen. An unfamiliar noise had woken him. He just had to locate the source.

It didn't take long. The refrigerator door closed with a muffled *thump*, a breakfast nook chair squeaked, and a paper bag rustled. Whoever was in the kitchen was trying to be quiet. Never a good sign, in his experience. He moved soundlessly and slid his firearm from its holster, easing off the couch. Staying low, with eyes trained on the kitchen doorway, he moved around the room's perimeter. Taking a deep breath, he reached around the corner and threw all the switches, bathing the room in a blinding fluorescent light.

"Police," he bellowed from where he leaned against the wall, "identify yourself." When no answer came, he raised his Glock and peered around the corner.

CHAPTER 3

She sat at his kitchen table, eyes rounded with alarm, frozen like a deer in the headlights. A wild mane of inky black hair framed her face, loose waves disappearing behind her shoulders. Well, most of it was black. Under the bright light, it almost looked like she had dark streaks of forest green. She had an otherworldly, waif-like air that reminded him of a young Kate Bush.

Sitting cross-legged, she wore a retro black AC/DC tour shirt, floral yoga pants, and leather running shoes with neon socks, one yellow and one orange. The paper bag with the motel clothes lay empty on the floor beside her chair. She clutched a fried chicken leg with a missing bite with both hands. He scanned the area but did not see anyone else. "Who are you, and why are you in here eating my chicken in the dark?" he asked, struggling to keep his tone firm and professional.

"I was hungry," she said in a tiny voice.

Damn, she's gorgeous, he thought, briefly forgetting her *unknown intruder* status. He shook it off. "How did you get here?"

"I came with you."

"No, ma'am, I'm pretty sure I would've remembered inviting you in. Being as I just got home a few hours ago, how long have you been in my house?"

"I came with you," she repeated patiently. "I was with..." She paused to think, then brightened. "Bud and Virginia. They gave me clothes and food. Then he came"—she shuddered—"but then you came, and I left with you. So now I am here, wherever here is. Please, may I finish this?" she asked, gesturing with the chicken leg. "I really am very hungry."

Travis lowered his gun and stared at her, taking a step closer. His breath caught as he saw the tattoos beside her large, golden eyes. "You're that woman he was looking for."

Apparently deciding she had waited long enough for an answer, she took two huge bites and nodded, chewing vigorously.

Procedure. Stick to Procedure. "Do you have any weapons on you? Drugs, anything sharp that will stab or stick me?"

She slowly shook her head, mumbling through a mouthful of chicken. The grease slicked her lips, giving them an almost hypnotic shine. "I do not, but if you wish me to remove this clothing to show I speak true, I will do—"

"No—Jesus—no! Keep your clothes on!" The words burst out before he could stop them. *Jesus H Christ, McLean.* Travis pointed a finger at her. "Do not move from

45

that chair," he ordered sternly. He turned, flipping on the lights as he ran from room to room in a fast perimeter search, but did not see anyone else, anything missing, or out of place.

After a minute, he returned to the kitchen. The woman sat as still as a rock, taking his order not to move literally. As he strode toward the table, the way she shrank down in her chair like a child about to be punished pained him a little. Slowing his pace, he stuck his handgun into a front pocket and put his hands up. "I'm not going to hurt you," he assured her, taking the chair across from her. He forced his shoulders to relax, hoping to put her more at ease.

"I know," she said matter-of-factly. "You are my champion, my hero. Few would stand against Ansgar and live to tell the story. You have kind eyes and a courageous heart, so you must be very brave."

"Ansgar? That's the wizard guy?"

"He is a druid, one of the Elders." Pursing her full lips thoughtfully, she added, "I do not believe he is a wizard, but I cannot say for certain. What is that?" she asked, gesturing toward his pocket.

He blinked and glanced in the direction she was pointing, noting her unusual interest. *She's looking at it like she's never seen one before.* "My service weapon. I'm a police officer; my badge and holster are in the next room. What is your name, ma'am?"

"I do not believe I have one," she said, shrugging. "The brothers only called me girl. Sometimes It."

"It?"

She nodded. "As in, It needs to be fed, It needs to be taken outdoors. They called all of us the same."

Travis's quick mind seized on that. "*All* of you? Wait—were you held captive somewhere?"

Delicately slanted eyebrows bunched as she frowned. "I do not know that word." She extended her hand and smiled shyly. "Please, may I touch you, my lord?"

My lord? Good Lord is about right. Woman, you keep smiling at me like that, and you can touch whatever you want. He shoved those dangerous thoughts back and offered his hand. She clutched it in her smaller one with a surprisingly firm grip for such a little woman. Something like a millisecond burst of static electricity shocked him; gone before it even registered.

She trembled, then smiled before pulling her hand back. "Yes, I and others like me were held captive," she said.

"You want to tell me what just happened there?" he snapped, looking at his hand as if it had grown extra fingers in front of him.

She gave him an impish smile. "I sipped your knowledge," she explained. "Now I know what you know. Well, not everything, of course, but a good bit. You have not been harmed, and I am wiser than before. Some of your words are strange to me. This helps me communicate with you." She straightened. "I mean, talk better," she said, mimicking his Southern accent.

Travis stared at her for a long while before he spoke again. "I think we're going to need to start at the beginning. First, though, I can't keep calling you ma'am, and you said you don't have a name. What would you like me to call you?"

When she gave him a blank look, he tried again. "Do you know where you're from?"

That much she did know. "Brú na Bóinne."

Okay, not a local girl. He didn't have the first clue where that was. Pulling up a browser on his phone, he began searching, and after a few spelling variations, he got it. The first words, World Heritage Site and Neolithic, jumped out at him. *What the actual hell? How did you wind up here?* "Okay, this says Bru, uh, what you said is in Ireland. If you want, we can start with Irish names and see if there is one you can live with."

Another search yielded an international baby names website. He rattled off some of the more popular ones before she made her decision. "Saoirse," she announced. "It means freedom, so I think it most fitting."

"Me too," he agreed, slapping his hands on his thighs. "All right then, Miss Saoirse—why don't I pour us a glass of tea while you tell me your story?"

Recounting her life to date took the better part of an hour. At first, Travis sat across from her motionless, giving her an indulgent smile while trying to process everything he had just heard. It was too fantastic, too Hollywood movie magic to be real. He picked up his long teaspoon and spun it around with his fingers. "Do me a favor, please," he asked, holding the handle up. "I want you to follow this with your eyes only. Don't turn your head. Can you do that?"

When she nodded, he moved the spoon from side to side, carefully watching her eye movement. After a moment, he set the spoon down and sighed.

"Did I pass?" she asked, her expression worried.

He gave her a sharp look. "Pass what?"

She frowned in concentration. "The..." her voice trailed off as she tried to pronounce the strange words. "The hor-iz-on-tal gaze nis... na... nystagmus test." She beamed. "Did I say it right?"

She did, but he wasn't going to tell her that. A small part of him had hoped she was high on something, making everything a lot easier if he could get a medical unit involved. He scrubbed his face with his hand. "So, let me see if I have all this straight," he said calmly, staring at the tabletop. "You are from some place in Ireland whose name I can't pronounce. You don't have a name—"

"Saoirse. You just said so," she corrected with a bright smile.

"Okay, you have a name, but you don't know how old you are. You can turn into any animal you want. You and other women like you were captured by druids who wanted to breed with you because they wanted to turn into animals, too. You set fire to one of their buildings, escaped the druid chasing you by jumping through some standing stones, and wound up behind the dumpster at the Palmetto Sunset Motel. And you read minds."

"Yes."

He decided to play along until all this made more sense. "Are you an alien from outer space?" he said, meaning it as a joke.

She nibbled her lower lip as she considered her answer. "No."

"How about human?"

"No."

Wait—what? "All right, then," he said slowly. "What are you? You look pretty human to me."

"The brothers say we are *púca,* but I do not think that accurate. We are perchance related, though."

He opened yet another browser window and searched. "You're a faery?" *This keeps getting better and better*, he thought. *Looks like we're going to need psych after all.*

Saoirse pondered that for a moment, shrugged, then nodded yes. "I am Tuatha Dé." At his puzzled expression, she added, "Seelie, the light court. Most *púca* are dark fae. Unseelie."

He closed the browser window and carefully laid the phone on the table. Clasping his hands together, he steepled his fingers and tapped the tips to his chin while he thought. Finally, he lowered his hands and raised his gaze to meet hers. "Ma'am, do you not hear yourself? If you tell that fantasy story to anyone else, they'll lock you up in a padded—hey, where do you think you're going?"

She rose from the table and stepped back a few feet, holding up one finger for him to wait. As he watched, her outline blurred, and a gold shimmer rippled down the length of her body. Her empty clothes collapsed in a heap, and Travis swore loudly, glancing around to see where she had fled. A slight movement near her shoes caught his eye. He watched in disbelief as a small gray mouse crawled out from under the pile of clothing. It stopped, sat up, and began cleaning its whiskers.

Feeling like the biggest idiot ever born, Travis leaned down. "Saoirse?"

The mouse looked up, and if he didn't know better, he would say it smiled. He held out his hand, and the mouse vaulted onto his palm, curling her tail around her body. He lifted her to eye level, cradling her tiny body in both hands. "If that's you, roll over on your back."

When the mouse did as he asked, he almost fainted away. "Raise your hand—paw," he amended.

Left paw up.

"Now the other one."

Both paws up.

"You can understand me," he said, awestruck.

A tiny voice responded, "Yes."

Travis nodded, crediting his years of police experience handling the weird, wild, and wonderful in a resort town as the only reason his heart had not stopped. "What else can you turn into?" he asked, genuinely curious.

She shimmered again, and he shoved away, forced to drop her. A shaggy, caramel-brown Highland cow lowing noisily suddenly filled the kitchen. More sparkles, and a bright blue and yellow songbird perched on the back of her chair, chirping a happy song.

"How about a..." His thoughts took off in full stampede mode, trying to imagine the most outrageous thing possible. "A velociraptor. Can you do one of those?"

The trilling serenade stopped as she tilted her head in question. He recognized the problem at once. "You've never seen one. Hang on," he said, grabbing his phone. He found a short YouTube video of the Jurassic Park kitchen raptors and held the screen up for the bird to see. "It's a dinosaur that went extinct millions of years ago."

The blue tit's head cocked from side to side, and although Travis would deny it to his dying day, he screamed like a little girl as he fell back into the wall and slumped to the floor. In his kitchen—his fucking KITCHEN—stood the seven-foot reptile, complete with a million razor-sharp teeth and extra-long tapping toenails. Grinning. At HIM. "Ch-change back," he gasped, holding his hand out as if that alone could stop her from coming closer.

When he blinked again, the raptor was gone, leaving Saoirse standing there completely naked. "Clothes on," he barked, turning his head away, but not fast enough. That mental image would be seared into his brain forever. Long legs, slim hips, a tiny waist that he was sure he could encircle with both hands, and have mercy, those full breasts. He wasn't going to sleep a wink tonight; he just knew it. Her long hair reached down to her ass in shiny waves. He put a hand over his eyes, making it even worse. "Are you dressed yet?"

"I am, my lord," Saoirse replied, taking her seat across from him at the table.

He shook his head. "Please don't call me that," he begged. "My name is Travis McLean. Just—Travis is fine."

She looked skeptical. "I am permitted to address you by your given name?"

"Give me a minute; I've got to think through this." He went silent, staring at her. After a moment, he jumped up and began pacing as he talked to himself. "We can't go to the police; she's technically not a missing person, and Lord knows we are not equipped to deal with something like this at the station. Same for any kind of shelter or hospital. She can't fend for herself, not here." He stopped pacing. "Do you think that druid guy will keep looking for you?"

"Ansgar will never stop until he finds me," she warned, her words filled with quiet resignation. "He plans to give me to Pendaran Dyfed, the highest of all druids. I fled because I learned they expect his arrival in the coming weeks. I suppose it is meant to be an honor, but I did not see it as such. Ansgar does it to win favor as he desires power above all things."

"Given? Like married?"

Saoirse looked away. "Given like a gift. For his use."

"Then we have to hide you; you're not going back to that," Travis growled, slapping his hands on the table. "Putting you back in that situation is not an option."

Her shoulders sagged. "Ansgar is ruthless and will kill anyone in his way. He is a fierce warrior and adept at working magicks. By sheltering me, you place yourself in grave peril."

He gave her what he hoped was a confident yet reassuring smile. "Won't be the first time, and I doubt it'll be the last."

"Oh, my," she gasped, eyes rounded. A pink flush stained her cheeks, and she gave him a shy smile. "You are very handsome when you smile."

Don't do it. Don't do it. "Thank you, ma'am. And if anyone hasn't told you, you are very beautiful when *you* smile." He grinned at her, then added, "Just not while you're a dinosaur. That's going to give me nightmares for a week."

Saoirse opened her mouth to speak, but yawned instead. "I grow weary," she announced, pointing to the floor near the corner. "May I sleep here?"

He frowned. "On the kitchen tile?" When she nodded, he shook his head. "I have extra bedrooms; you can take one of those. I'll see what I've got that you can sleep in, maybe a t-shirt or something. C'mon." He waved for her to follow.

He led her to his old bedroom, the first door in the hallway across from the bathroom. The panel door swung open with a whisper, and he inhaled the musty yet familiar smell. A few remnants of his childhood remained: wrestling trophies and framed varsity letters from high school, music posters, a few worn paperback books, and ticket stubs stuck in the dresser's mirror frame served as a reminder of his former life before enlisting. With his parents gone, he had moved most of his things into the master bedroom. He turned on the overhead light and peeked in, satisfied that it was neat and had been dusted sometime in the last month. "You can sleep here until we can figure something out," he said, waving toward the double bed. He began pawing through drawers, searching for anything that would pass as sleepwear. When he glanced back over his shoulder, Saoirse stood motionless in the doorway, looking pale and stricken. "Something wrong?" he asked.

"I have never slept on a bed before," she whispered, awe creeping into her voice.

He found the oversized shirt he was looking for and shook it out with a snap. "It hasn't been worn in a while, but it's clean," he explained sheepishly, handing it to her. "And I get the feeling you're going to have a bunch of firsts while you're here."

Her entire face lit up when she smiled, stealing his breath away. "Where do you sleep?" she asked.

Jesus, take the wheel. I am in so much trouble here. "In a different room," he said swiftly. "Let me show you where things are in case you need something." He took her on a short tour of the house, skipping his bedroom, that door thankfully closed. He had been so rushed to leave on Saturday morning that he knew it must look like a crime scene.

Another brief search yielded a new, unopened toothbrush. He placed it on the sink in the adjacent bathroom, along with a full tube of toothpaste and what he assumed was one of Lori Ann's hairbrushes. "Just help yourself to whatever you need, or if you're hungry or thirsty.

Just promise me—if you don't know how something works, come get me before trying it on your own." When he got her nod of agreement, he smiled and then yawned. "I don't normally do first watch. I switched with a friend tomorrow so he could do something with his kids. There's no way I can call off, or else I would. I've got to get some sleep, so I'll just say good night, Saoirse. Sweet dreams."

She gave him a radiant smile. "Sleep well and good night, my... Travis."

Yessir, this here is trouble just looking for a place to happen.

Ansgar stepped out from underneath the table stone, shaking off the light dusting of ice. Traveling through the standing stones without correct preparations and precautions had been risky, even for him, but he dared not let the rebellious fae escape. The fact that she had gnawed at him fiercely, but he vowed her freedom would be short-lived.

He wondered how much time had elapsed as smoke and the smell of charred wood still permeated the air, but the shouts of alarm had dwindled. He would have been missed had he stayed longer in that strange place, but he had no desire to explain a lengthy absence to those self-important fools in his order. No, he would return to his quarters and prepare for a lengthier journey from which he would return with the girl.

He patted the inner pocket of his robe, satisfied that her lunula still rested within. *She cannot travel fast or far on foot. That world is strange to her, and she does not know the extent of her abilities. There is some time*, he reasoned, *although not in abundance.* He threw back his shoulders and strode through the clearing and into the forest, making his way back to Brú na Bóinne.

CHAPTER 4

I *have a name. Saoirse. My name is Saoirse.*
Far too excited to sleep, she lay awake long after Travis had turned off the lights. So many new things in her world. It was still hard to believe she had gained her freedom. Even more unreal was how kind everyone had been to her. She was afraid to close her eyes, not wanting to wake and find this all a dream. It did not feel like a dream, though. The *léine* he gave her to wear was so soft and smelled like him. And the bed! Never before had she lain on anything so comfortable—no bits of chaff pricking her skin through the bedding if she turned in the night.

She hugged herself, almost afraid to believe in her good fortune. *Travis McLean,* she thought, turning his name over in her mind. Such a kind soul to give her these many wonderful things. He was, without doubt, the most handsome man she had ever seen.

She did not see evidence that he had a lady wife, nor did she detect any fresh smells indicating that others shared his dwelling. No slaves or servants either; odd in such a grand palace. Perhaps this was something she could offer in return for her shelter. She had no skills but was willing to learn and decided to ask when she saw him again. Her last thoughts before sleep claimed her were of his greenish-brown eyes and the way his smile made her stomach feel strange yet wonderful.

To his surprise, Travis made it to roll call early the next morning. After the sergeant completed the rundown of announcements and assignments, they were dismissed to get out on the roadways. On his way to the parking lot, he noticed Captain Bellamy's door ajar and decided to give it another try. He knocked twice and stuck his head inside the office. "Could I have a word, sir?" he asked.

"Come in, McLean. I don't usually see you at this time of day." Captain Bellamy's voice boomed in the small office. "Close the door."

"Carter's kid had a thing at school today. He wanted to be there, so we switched." Travis pulled up a chair across the desk. "So what I wanted to ask—"

"Have you thought any more about my recommendations?"

"Sir?" He hadn't but thought fast and remembered their last meeting. "You mean going to SWAT?"

"You got your daddy's size plus some, you're a crack shot, and I know you can hold your own in a fight. What sets you apart is your ability to stay calm under pressure. I think you'd excel as a crisis negotiator. We don't have too many of those calls, thank God, but we're getting more than we did five years ago. There's a promotion in that too, you know. More money in your pocket."

"Yes, sir. It sounds like a solid career path. I will seriously consider it." He had no intentions of it, but figured it couldn't hurt to appease his superior officer.

The captain nodded, narrowing his eyes. "You're looking more like your mother every day," he commented with a sad smile. "Did she ever tell you how hard I tried to get her and your daddy to join the department? Nepotism be damned—I know good cops when I see them." He removed his glasses and scratched his eyelid before putting them back on. "You've had some big shoes to fill, but everything I've thrown at you, you've kicked ass and thrown it back." He chuckled but then sobered again. "Hard to believe it's been nearly three years since they passed."

"It is," Travis agreed, bowing his head in respect. "In a way, that's what I wanted to talk to you about."

"If this is about reactivating the K9 unit, we don't have the money. You know a decent single-purpose dog will run twenty, twenty-five thousand dollars. Even more if it's imported or dual." Their agency had a K9 unit before, but their one single-purpose German Shepherd Dog, Viking, and his handler had retired the year before after long, successful careers. The department still had the tricked-out cruiser with the K9 kennel transport system, complete with remote door pops, cooling fans, and the HOT-N-POP® heat alarm needed for the sweltering South Carolina summers.

"Tell you what," Travis offered. "If I find the right dog, outfit it with my own money, train it myself, and get it certified, will you put us both to work?"

"Sold," the captain said without hesitation. "You do all that, and you're in. You looking for another Shepherd?"

He was braced and ready for this part of the pitch. "A GSD or Dutchie would be okay, but I've got my heart set on a Mal."

Captain Bellamy gave him a skeptical look and sighed. "You know those dogs are batshit crazy. They call them *maligators* for a reason. SLED had a bomb Mal once. I heard he bit a former president for trying to take his Kong. You could pet him nine times out of ten, but on the tenth, you'd wind up at the ER getting stitched. The problem was that his trigger number changed daily. That dog had one hell of a nose, though. Watched his handler like a jealous girlfriend. You think you could train a dog like that?"

Travis struggled not to grin, that sigh telling him he had won the battle, if not the war. "I am aware, sir. But I'm confident in my ability to train a good working dog. Plus, if I have to haul a dog up and down stairs, I for damn sure would rather have a sixty-pound Mal on my shoulder than a ninety-pound Shepherd. Lord, Viking got up to over a hundred pounds."

"That's because he mooched food off everybody in the precinct." The captain grunted, his gaze flickering toward the drawer Travis knew for a fact was still filled with doggie treats the older man denied owning.

"No, sir—won't be any mooching on my watch," Travis said solemnly.

"You see to it there's not."

Saoirse knew not how long she slept, but it was well past dawn before she awoke. She stretched and yawned, enjoying the feel of the smooth sheets against her naked legs. The house was silent, and she remembered that Travis had said he might return home later to eat his midday meal. She hoped so, eager to see him again. In the meantime, he had said she could explore the house but not go outside for any reason. He explained that she was free to come and go as she pleased, worried only that she would get lost or injured until she became more accustomed to her new surroundings.

Throwing off the bedding, she headed for the privy across the hall. The fixtures kept her busy for a time, turning the faucets, shower, and lights on and off. She brushed her teeth as he had shown her, amazed at how fresh and clean her mouth felt. Dragging the brush through her thick hair, the long bristles scratched her scalp, a delicious experience. She gazed at her reflection in the looking glass for what seemed like hours. When her stomach rumbled, she wondered if there was any chicken left, or if not, what else there was to eat in his larder.

Saoirse first heard the clicking sounds when she entered the large room where the—she struggled for the word, then remembered *teevee*—hung suspended on the wall. On instant alert, she shrank back against the wall, inhaling deeply and listening. Travis had said he would return, but this scent was unfamiliar. Not him. A female.

"Travis?" a voice called out from the kitchen. "Honey, you home? Your car is in the garage, but I didn't see the cruiser." There was a rustle of bags as the refrigerator door banged closed. Cabinets and drawers opened then shut with soft thumps. The voice grew closer, still talking. "Look, I'm sorry about yesterday. Maybe I shouldn't have yelled at you like that, but it's like you're ignoring me. It's been a month or better since we went out for dinner or a movie. I have needs, too, you know. If you spent half the time on me that you spend searching the damn internet for—who the hell are you, and what are you doing in my boyfriend's house?"

A tall, striking blonde appeared from the kitchen doorway, glaring daggers with her bright pink lipsticked mouth open in shock. Saoirse stared back and froze, searching for the appropriate response. The heavy, perfumed smell transformed into a sharp combination of anger and fear.

"I asked you a question—who are you and what are you doing in here?" she said again, her voice becoming louder and more strident. Dropping the plastic grocery bags she still held, she stormed toward Saoirse, a scowl marring her pretty features. "And why are you wearing his clothes?" she demanded. "Did you sleep with him? Answer me!"

Saoirse's fight-or-flight instinct kicked into overdrive. Without a word, she whirled and darted back down the darkened hallway. The woman yelled for her to stop, then gave chase.

Travis groaned aloud when he spied Lori Ann's white SUV parked in front of his house. He had no desire to deal with her drama—or her—today, after the weekend he had just had. *Maybe she'll leave when she sees I'm not...* His heart slammed to a halt. *Saoirse. FUCK.* He floored it, whipping into his driveway next to her car. He jumped out and ran through the open garage, just in time to hear the blood-curdling feminine scream from inside.

Travis burst through the kitchen archway into the great room a millisecond before Lori Ann plowed into him at full speed like a linebacker, knocking them both to the floor. "It's back there, back there," she screamed again, sobbing and gesturing wildly toward his bedroom. She shoved him hard in that general direction, then scrambled back crablike. "Sh—shoot it! It's trying to kill me!"

"What's trying to kill you?" he asked, keeping his tone calm. Halting her backward flight, he grasped her by the shoulders and gave a gentle shake. "Lori Ann—talk to me. What's back there?"

With her hand shaking wildly, she pointed at the hallway. "W—w—wo..." she stammered before screaming again. "Shoot it!"

He tried a reassuring smile, realizing she was too deep in panic mode to give him any helpful information. "You wait here and work on your breathing. I'm going to go take a look."

He began to rise, but Lori Ann suddenly lunged and grabbed his arm, tumbling him back to the floor. Like a drowning woman with the last ring buoy, she clawed and clutched at his vest. "Don't leave me out here all by myself," she wailed.

"Look," he said firmly. "I need to see what's going on back there. If you want to leave, now's your chance. I can't stay here with you and go see what the problem is at the same time."

She glared but nodded and released him. "I'll wait here to make sure you're okay," she sniffed, swiping at the tears and smearing her eyeliner. The sobs evolved into sniffling hiccups.

"Uh-huh." Trying his best not to sound sarcastic, he rose to his feet, held his hand up for quiet, and listened intently. *Nothing.* Saoirse was nowhere in sight. Having no idea what to expect, he placed a hand on his unsnapped firearm and moved slowly toward the darkened hallway. The spare bedroom door near the end of the hall was ajar. The room inside was pitch black, courtesy of the heavy blackout curtains. He frowned and blinked. *Something moving in there?*

Withdrawing the heavy flashlight from his duty belt, he clicked it on and raised it to shoulder height. He directed the bright beam at the suspicious room, where a pair of wide-set yellow eyes reflected. He took another step forward and flipped on the hall lights with the back of his hand, exchanging the flashlight for his collapsible baton. A long snout poked out of the crack in the door, nudging it open. The shaggy head that followed was attached to the most enormous black wolf Travis had ever seen. It eased into the hallway, padding silently toward him. The mouth spread wide in a toothy grin as the long tongue lolled to one side. It stopped about ten feet away and sat back on its narrow haunches, waiting.

He blew out a long exhalation of relief. "Saoirse," he breathed, trying and failing not to grin back.

The wolf flopped onto her back, its large feet sticking up comically. He crossed the remaining distance and knelt, his hand moving automatically to scratch the proffered belly. Saoirse made a happy chuffing noise, her back leg bicycling frantically. "You scared her half to death," he mock-scolded in a whisper.

The wolf snorted, then sneezed with a loud *ah-oof.* "She scared me first," she whispered back in a deep, rumbly voice.

"Travis? Are you okay? What's going on?" Lori Ann called.

I am never getting used to this, he thought, running a hand through his hair. "Stay back here and out of sight." He scratched under her chin, then rose and stood still for a minute, deliberating. It didn't take long for him to reach the only real conclusion—he couldn't explain any of this. A weird shudder ran down his spine at the thought of news crews, scientists, or the military storming his house, intent on snatching his faery away for further exploitation. *Not on my watch.* After a moment, he added *and not my faery.*

"Everything's fine," he answered, raising his voice. He turned and strode back to the den, turning the hall lights out again as he passed. Lori Ann still cowered on the floor near the kitchen archway. He sucked in a deep breath. "No problems."

"No problems?" she screeched. "What the hell was that thing? Who is that girl wearing your t-shirt, and as far as I could tell, nothing else?" She rose to her knees and pointed an accusing finger at him. "I know what I saw. It looked like a wolf, Travis."

"You need to simmer down. I'm not going to talk over you screaming at me like that," he said, keeping his tone even.

"Don't you *cop voice* me," she snapped, scrambling to her feet. She braced her fists on her hips. "Who is that woman, and what is she doing in your house?"

"I—"

She didn't give him a chance to finish. "I stopped and got stuff to make you lunch to say sorry for yesterday, and this is what I find when I get here. I swear, Travis, maybe I need to rethink our relationship." She looked at him expectantly, her foot tapping with impatience.

"*Maybe* you need to rethink? According to your voicemail yesterday, you already did that and decided you were—what were your words?" His voice rose in a girlish falsetto. "D-O-N-E done with Y-O-U."

"Now you know I didn't mean any—"

He cut her off with a wave. "If you'd stop your yammering a minute, you might notice I'm not fighting you on that point. I also didn't expect you to turn up here again without giving me some kind of warning first."

"Obviously," she snapped, scowling. "That means you're sleeping with her then. Sure didn't take you long. And where did that hell beast come from?"

He knew better, but he did feel obligated to defend his honor a little. "Even though it's none of your business, I'm not sleeping with her. And the dog is hers."

"Dog, my ass. I know a wolf when I see one."

"That hallway is dark. What you saw was a dog. A big, shaggy dog. And she's very friendly."

"You're missing the point, Travis. Where is she? I want to meet her. I want to look her in the eyes while she tells me she's not sleeping with you."

"You've already made an impression. She's not interested in meeting you."

Lori Ann looked past him toward the hallway. "Are you having sex with my boyfriend?" she demanded, a shrill fingernails-on-chalkboard note creeping into her voice.

Pretty sure his heart just stopped again, Travis whirled to see Saoirse standing close behind him, fully dressed. "My name is Saoirse," she said simply.

"Saoirse what?" Lori Ann spat out.

"Just Saoirse," he answered quickly. "Saoirse, this is Lori Ann, and I'm not her boyfriend. Up until yesterday, I suppose you could say she was my girlfriend."

"Up until yesterday?" she screeched again. "One mad voicemail and suddenly it—"

"I am honored to meet a friend of Travis," Saoirse said sweetly, breezing past him to stand before the raging woman. He reached out to grab her arm, but she did some weird NFL sideways juke move and left him holding a handful of nothing.

"I'm more than just his friend, sweetie," Lori Ann sneered down at the smaller woman. "As a matter of fact, I'm—" A sudden blank look crossed her face, and she stopped talking.

"You did not see me or a wolf. You were not here," Saoirse murmured, her voice soft as velvet.

Lori Ann sounded very far away. "Wasn't here," she echoed.

"You will leave now. You will not return until My Lord Travis requests your presence." She paused, then as an afterthought added, "And you will leave behind the food you brought."

"I should go." With that, Lori Ann spun on her heel and fled through the open kitchen door. Moments later, her car engine revved, but the sound faded quickly as she sped off.

"I wonder what this is," Saoirse remarked, kneeling to inspect the abandoned groceries. "It smells good, and I am very hungry."

Travis knew he must look pretty stupid, standing there with his mouth hanging open, but powerless to close it. "H—how did you do that?"

She lifted one shoulder in a casual shrug. "I did not know if it would work. The brothers call it *voice*, a compulsion charm. I watched them practicing on the slaves," she called back before disappearing into the kitchen with the bags. "I myself have never tried it before, but she seemed very open to suggestion. She is unharmed, if that is your concern."

He stood frozen for a moment before following her, rounding the corner just in time to see her cute little butt wiggle as she bent over to rummage through his fridge. Those spandex yoga pants hugged every square inch of her narrow hips and long legs, molding like a second skin to the lean muscle beneath. "We've got to get you some more clothes," he blurted out.

Saoirse's concerned frown popped up over the open refrigerator door. "Are the ones I now wear not acceptable?" she asked. "They do not appear dirty or torn."

"No, they're fine," he assured her. "You need more than one outfit, though, probably some other, ah... girl stuff, too. We'll go to Target or someplace after my shift and pick you up a few things, okay?"

Her initial excitement dimmed. "I have no coin," she said, her eyes downcast.

"I know you don't," he soothed, "but I do, so don't worry about it."

Her face lit into a ball of blinding sunshine, stealing what common sense he had left. "You would do this? For me?" she asked, a note of awe in her voice.

"Of course I would," he scoffed. "At this point, I feel..." His voice trailed off, as he wasn't entirely sure what he felt. "I mean, you're here and I'm..." He tried again. "You're my responsibility until we can get all this sorted out."

Her light dimmed, and he hated his choice of words, not meaning to sound so cruel. "I don't mean it like that. I *want* to help you, keep you safe from Ansgar and the other people chasing you. You're..." He hesitated, searching for the right words. "You've had a rough life, and I don't like seeing people being hurt or taken advantage of. It's why I became a cop." Reaching behind her, he grabbed a soda from the fridge door, handed it to her, and got one for himself.

"Cop," Saoirse murmured, the word unfamiliar. "Lawkeeper?" She examined the cold metal thing in her hands, unsure what to do with it.

He nodded, popping the tab on the can. "Yeah. I don't make the laws, though, I enforce them."

"Ah," she said, mimicking his actions and taking a long drink of the fizzy liquid. Her eyes flew open, and she began coughing, scrubbing frantically at her nose. "Oh—oh—oh—OH!"

Travis burst into laughter. "I'm sorry—you probably haven't had one of these before. Just breathe, it'll pass."

She nodded uncertainly right before a loud burp erupted. Her expression turned sheepish as she covered her mouth with her hand and pinkened with embarrassment. "I beg pardon, my—Travis," she corrected automatically.

"It's my fault. I should have warned you." Something else occurred to him. "It's got caffeine, a drug that gives you energy. Be careful until you know how it affects you, okay?"

She nodded again and ventured another sip before turning the can to inspect the label. "Die it D R Pep-per?" she asked.

"D and R are short for doctor, so Dr Pepper," he corrected. "The diet means there is an artificial sweetener like fake sugar in it." He patted his flat stomach. "I don't need extra calories packing on weight."

"I think your body is very pleasing to look upon." She tried to hide her smile as she turned away, blushing furiously.

It was his turn to color at the compliment, and he refused to think about how his *pleasing body* tingled with anticipation at her innocent words. "Well, be that as it may, do you see anything in there you'd like to have for lunch?" He gestured weakly at the fridge.

When she gave him a blank look, he gently nudged past her and gathered bags and jars. She leaned over to watch as he spread the sandwich makings on the counter, grabbed two small plates from the cabinet, and retrieved a knife from the drawer. He explained the process as he went, giving her a taste of the spicy brown mustard (a big yes) and the mayonnaise (hard pass, but with a cute nose wrinkle that he wouldn't mind seeing again). Shaved turkey and slices of smoked cheddar layered on whole grain wheat bread, topped with crunchy romaine lettuce and a ripe red tomato cut into thick, meaty slices. Grabbing the refrigerated containers to put them back, he shook the mustard bottle, which was almost empty. "Aria," he called toward the ceiling, "add brown mustard to the grocery list."

"Brown mustard added to grocery," came the disembodied female response.

Grabbing a bag of baked salt and vinegar potato chips from the countertop, he shook out a generous portion onto each plate. He turned, only to get smacked across the face with hair as her head whipped back and forth, searching. "What's wrong?" he demanded.

"Where is she?" Saoirse whispered, eyes rounded in fear. "I see her not. Is it a spirit with whom you speak?"

It took him a moment to understand, and he struggled not to laugh. "She's not a real person—it's a little computer called a virtual assistant," he explained, taking the plates to the table. "She adjusts the temperature, tells me about the weather, things like that."

She brought the sodas, and they sat across from each other at the kitchen table. "Does this vir-tu-al assistant always listen?"

"I think so," he said, popping a chip into his mouth. "But she doesn't say anything back unless you say her name first."

She frowned. "That is very strange, but so many things I have seen in your world are. It would seem I have much to learn."

He nudged her plate toward her. "Then start with lunch. Eat."

Her eyes closed in sheer ecstasy on her first bite, and she made a soft purring sound. "Good?" Travis asked.

"Aye. 'Tis the most wondrous thing ever have I tasted," she murmured.

He wolfed down several quick bites, dabbing the mayo from the corner of his lips with a paper napkin. "If I could make a suggestion to help you blend in," he said carefully, not wanting to offend her. "Your English is a bit too perfect for this time and area. Maybe you could learn more from watching TV." One of the officers at his precinct, Ralph, immigrated to the United States as a young German child named Rolf. He often joked that he learned the language by watching Bugs Bunny cartoons and, in fact, did incredible impressions of the Warner Brothers characters. "Maybe not the Spanish channels yet, though. Let's get your English down first, then you can tackle another language if you want."

She nodded eagerly, cheeks bulging.

They ate in silence, awkwardness dragging the minutes out. "Do you already speak any other languages?" he finally asked, sipping his drink.

She rattled off several that he had never heard of, but *Pictish* caught his immediate attention. He watched the History Channel occasionally, enough to know that language died out thousands of years ago.

With no small amount of hesitation, he asked the million-dollar question, knowing he didn't want to hear the answer. "Do you know what year you escaped?" Having discovered the chips were to her liking, they were all in her mouth, crunching noisily. He added *table manners* to the growing list of things they needed to discuss. "Slow down, honey—nobody's gonna take it away from you."

She swallowed, washing it down with a more cautious sip of soda. "Five hundred twelve. The sun disappeared from the sky at midday, a very powerful omen. It turned full black, and we were all very frightened. I remember hearing the brothers discuss recording the event in their books."

"The year five hundred and twelve? Like in the sixth century?" *You asked for it.* Travis stared until she became uncomfortable and squirmed in her chair. "I'm sorry," he said, shaking his head. "I guess that caught me a little off guard. You're a lot older than you look. We're in the twenty-first century now, so that's like what, fifteen hundred years?"

"I believe," she began stiffly, "I am around twenty or twenty-one of your human winters, based on the blood. I am *not* old."

Comprehension came slowly as to what she meant. Like many men, the particulars of women's periods were something he chose to stay blissfully ignorant of unless it directly involved him. He had the basic knowledge, of course, but zero desire to learn any more than that. Doing a fast mental inventory of the bathrooms, he tried to remember seeing any boxes of women's products Lori Ann might have left. "Are you having that now? The, ah... blood?"

Shaking her head, she popped the last bite of the sandwich into her mouth. A drop of the spicy mustard clung to the corner of her lips, and the tip of her pink tongue darted out to catch it.

This woman is so far off limits you'd need a map to find her, his inner voice warned. No circumstance or situation existed in which he could wake up with her in his bed and not feel like the biggest asshole that ever drew breath for taking advantage of her trusting nature.

She raised her hand with the back toward her face, apparently intending to wipe her mouth. With a sudden frown of concentration, she lowered it and picked up her napkin instead, gently dabbing at her mouth as she had seen Travis do. "Is this right?" she asked.

At his slow nod, she beamed with happiness.

He smiled back even as he heaved a big sigh internally. *I am so freaking screwed.*

CHAPTER 5

After showing her how the remote worked, he left her channel surfing with firm instructions not to answer the door or go outside. His last glance confirmed her sitting cross-legged on the couch, wrapped in a plush throw, solemnly watching as she clicked through the channels. The open bag of chips and her soda waited within arm's reach on the coffee table. This image colored his thoughts most of the afternoon as he struggled not to think about her.

He replayed the remarkable events of his last twenty-four hours over and over, hoping to get some sort of plan in place. His parents even chimed in with their opinions, much to his growing bewilderment. *Sweetie, you can't just keep her like she's a puppy you found on the side of the road,* his mother warned. On the other hand, his father reminded him, *she picked you to rescue her, so she's your responsibility.*

In all honesty, he wasn't just in—he was drowning under those proverbial uncharted waters. Up until last night, he knew without a doubt that shapeshifters, fairies, and wizards were all make-believe. Harry Potter stuff. Up until the dinosaur in his kitchen, anyway.

First responders know the one word never said aloud when describing a current shift is *quiet*. Saying something as simple as, "Quiet night, huh?" all but guarantees the universe will ask you to hold their beer, accept that challenge, and unleash unmitigated chaos. Travis preferred something in the middle—less crazy than spring break Friday night but more exciting than a wintery Tuesday afternoon.

He was absolutely not, under any circumstances, going to think about the strange woman at his house.

His day plodded along while he drove one of his regular routes. That afternoon, most of the tourists seemed to be of the law-abiding variety. Inexhaustible patience had never made the short list of his positive attributes. Still, between the *Hurry Up and Wait* Army and long hours spent patrolling, it had improved slightly to exhaustible—a work in progress, like everything else.

He backed the cruiser into one of his favorite alleys off the Boulevard, between a beachwear store and the ice cream shop that sold the best smoothies on the strand. It took a moment to finish his last report and radio his status to Dispatch. "842—I'm gonna be 10-7 for a few."

The new voice made him wince. "Copy, 842. Getting some ice cream?"

"Hey, Daisy," he said, making a concerted effort not to add *Crazy* in front of her name. He had broken one of his cardinal rules by asking a coworker out on a date in the first place. Over dinner, she had asked what baby names he liked. Sensing danger, he ran, not walked, to the nearest exit. Later, he had added "D1" after her name in his contacts for "DefCon 1 = imminent threat." Mike had christened her "Crazy Daisy," and the name just stuck. "Smoothie. They're good here."

"I've never been. You'll have to take me there sometime," came the coy reply.

He closed his eyes and shook his head. "Yes, ma'am, I'll be right back." Hopping out of the patrol car, he locked it with the remote and straightened his vest before stepping out of the alley. He quickly surveyed the surroundings—cars cruising bumper to bumper, clusters of strolling tourists, college students, couples, and teenagers filled the wide sidewalks. Nothing out of the ordinary, just a Monday afternoon during peak season.

He pushed open the door of the ice cream shop, enjoying the rush of cold air. A chorus of "Hi, Officer Travis" greeted him from behind the counter. "The usual?"

"Yes, please," he said and nodded, gesturing toward the restroom door marked with a large hand-lettered sign that read "For Our Customers Only." By the time he finished washing up, his order was ready. He grabbed the plastic cup and a few napkins, then handed the teenage girl behind the counter a ten-dollar bill. "Thank you—put the change in your nursing school fund," he said, grinning.

Four college girls walked in, smelling of bronzing oil and bad choices. Sharing a joke, they laughed and chattered in neutral Midwest accents. "I am so moving here—their cops are *hot*," one of them called out, giving Travis an appreciative once-over.

"I'm pretty sure I'm hiding something dangerous if you want to search me, Officer," another one piped up, while a third added, "Bring your cuffs—I'm into that."

"Ladies," he drawled with a respectful nod, tapping the brim of his ball cap. He moved around them and reached for the door. Smiling, he couldn't help offering a little advice and let his natural accent thicken. "Y'all have fun, but be smart out there, y'hear? Y'all are way too pretty to wind up in jail."

They clutched each other and squealed. "Oh my God— that accent! Honey, I'd pay to hear you read the phone book. Can we get your number?"

He gave them a cheeky grin and winked. "Yes, ma'am— it's 911."

Back in the cruiser, he sucked on the smoothie straw and tried again not to think about Saoirse. He spent some time people-watching while finishing overdue paperwork, noting it crept along like elephants swimming in molasses. He resolved to ignore the clock, but when he checked in on the elephants an hour later, only five minutes had passed. "You gotta be kidding me," he groaned.

"10-9, 842? Did not copy." A different dispatcher's voice crackled inside the car.

Shit. "Just talking to myself," he hurried to explain, adjusting his seat so as not to lean on the mic button again.

"842, 10-26 in progress..." Dispatch gave the address, but he didn't need to plug it into the GPS. He knew the mega beachwear store and the excitable owner/manager who made multiple suspected shoplifting calls daily. Still, the timing proved perfect. By the time he got his guy cuffed, stuffed, and processed, it would be the end of his shift, and he could get back home to... He shook his head violently, not wanting even to start that line of thinking.

It was a short trip down the street. Travis rolled up to the curb and stopped in the No Parking strip, nodding to acknowledge the Middle Eastern man standing by the door waiting for him. "Afternoon, Mr. Amiri. What's going on today?"

"A young man. I want him arrested. He is in the vape section now, stuffing his pockets like he thinks no one sees.

Jeans and a red T-shirt, dark hair. A girl is with him, but I did not see her take anything."

Nodding, Travis walked inside and made the guy at once. He approached from behind and tapped him on the shoulder. "We need to take this outside. Come on."

"I didn't steal nothing," the man griped. The girl took off in the opposite direction, and he twitched like he was going to cut and run, too.

"Don't even think about it. It's too hot out to be chasing your ass." On closer inspection, Travis realized this was a kid, not a grown man. "Funny—I never said anything about stealing." Taking him by the upper arm, he walked him to the patrol car, where the owner met them.

"I wish to press charges," Mr. Amiri said, his tone lofty and formal.

The apprehension had been going smoothly, right up until the culprit spied the shiny handcuffs out and open for business. The kid turned into a Tasmanian devil whirlwind of flailing fists and feet. Travis caught a glancing blow on his cheek, earning the shoplifter a felony battery on a LEO charge on top of his misdemeanor theft. He also won an up-close and personal view of the sidewalk when Travis easily put him on the ground.

Once the cuffs were on, he patted the kid down and emptied his pockets of several hundred dollars in about-to-be stolen merchandise. "Anything else on you? They're going to search you again at the jail. If they find something you don't want found, that'll be another charge."

"No, sir," the kid said, a little more respectful now. Mr. Amiri snatched up his property and stalked back into the shop, nose high in the air, muttering to himself in his native language.

Travis opened the back door of the patrol car and assisted his prisoner in, placing a hand on top of the kid's head to protect it. As he closed the door, he glanced back to see the girl watching him from a few cars away and waved her over.

She approached him like a stray cat, nervous and ready to bolt. "Where you taking him?" she asked.

"Cherry Grove Police Department." He got a good look at her, and his heart softened a little. "How old are you, Miss?"

The girl's chin tilted upward in a small show of defiance. "Ain't your business, but I'm eighteen."

No way, Travis thought, *fourteen or fifteen at the most.* "Are y'all locals or here on vacation?"

She jerked her head to flip the dirty blonde hair out of her eyes. "That ain't your business either," she snapped. The girl was thin, with bony arms that she hugged around herself. Her dirty and wrinkled clothes looked as if she had been sleeping in them.

He fished a business card out of his wallet and handed it to her. "The station address is on the card. Right next door is a shelter where you can get something to eat and a safe place to sleep tonight. Show them my card and tell them Officer Travis sent you. They'll take good care of you." He hesitated, realizing the station was almost ten miles away, and she wouldn't be safe alone on the street after dark. "You got a ride?"

Her reddened eyes filled with tears as she took the card and shook her head, mumbling her thanks.

"Look—we aren't supposed to do this, but you can ride with me if you want. I have to cuff you and pat you down first, though."

"I don't have anything on me," she insisted, eyes widening with alarm as she took a step back.

"It's policy. You want a ride, you get cuffed and searched. Not negotiable."

With a reluctant nod, she followed Travis around to the front of the car so that the cruiser's camera would also record video, in addition to his body cam. He did a brief search using the backs of his hands and confirmed she wasn't carrying any weapons. As he snapped the cuffs on her skinny wrists, he glimpsed the beginnings of track marks and groaned inwardly. The beach resort town attracted runaways like flies, and more often than not, it didn't end well for them.

He held the door open for her to scoot into the back, next to her friend. Pulling away from the curb, he remembered his mother's story about saving a single starfish from hundreds stranded on the beach. *I can't save them all, but I can make a difference for this one.* He looked up into the rearview mirror. Both teens sat quietly, shoulders slumped in defeat.

Back at the precinct, he opened the girl's door first and uncuffed her, pointing toward the homeless shelter. He watched until she disappeared safely inside the building, releasing his starfish back into the wild.

CHAPTER 6

Travis had already decided that once home, he would change out of his uniform and take her over to Target or Ross for clothes and necessities, then maybe stop somewhere to eat. Saoirse seemed thinner than her height suggested. The image of her naked body flashed in his mind, and rather than blink it away as he should have done, he paused for a closer look. Visible ribs and sharp outlines of the delicate bones confirmed his suspicions that kindness and a comfortable bed weren't the only things she had been shorted on. The way she inhaled her food should have been his first clue. *Extra groceries too, then. Put some roses back in her cheeks and get her healthy.*

After parking the patrol car in the driveway, he grabbed his mailbox contents, rifling through the junk mail on his way through the garage. He punched in the security code, making a mental note to change it and the garage door programming before Lori Ann dropped by unannounced again. The kitchen door swung open, and he paused to listen, hearing only the sound of the TV in the next room. He tossed his keys into the nearest above-counter cabinet and popped the Velcro releases on his vest before he noticed the single golden eye peeking around the kitchen archway. He smiled inwardly at the childlike gesture. "Hi, Saoirse. You can come out; it's just me."

She edged around the corner and sagged, her back pressed against the wall. Her pale skin appeared almost translucent, making the tattoos near her eyes stand out in stark relief. "Please, my lord—may I go out?" she asked faintly. "I need to touch—I need—earth—I—"

Alarmed, Travis rushed forward and caught her in his arms as she collapsed. She weighed almost nothing. "Outside, you mean?" he asked, brows drawing together in concern.

When she weakly nodded and then went limp, he swept her up, holding her tight against his hammering chest. He bolted through the kitchen door into the mudroom and rushed to unlock the rear door, muscling his way into the backyard. Moving as gently as he could, he lay her down on one of the few grassy patches and knelt beside her, brushing a long lock of hair away from her eyes. She faced up toward the sun, her slight body pressed against the ground, eyes closed against the bright glare.

As he watched, a most remarkable change happened. Healthy color began creeping back into her skin, transforming into a peaches-and-cream complexion. Her black hair lightened several shades to a dark chocolate brown. Rosy spots of pink blossomed high on her cheekbones, and her lips plumped to the color of ripe cherries. The lines on her oval face softened and smoothed. Almond-shaped eyes slanted near the delicate tattoos, the long, sooty black eyelashes sweeping her cheeks.

Travis watched all this with his lips pressed tight together, not trusting himself to speak. For the first time since their unconventional meeting, he allowed himself to study her delicate features. *She is, without a doubt, the most beautiful woman I have ever laid eyes on.* Another thought slammed into him on the heels of that revelation. *She's not really a woman, though, is she?*

At that moment, he decided he didn't care and leaned forward, intent on pressing a kiss to those sweet lips, just parted in waiting for his—

He stopped short just in time before making a fool of himself. Her eyes fluttered open, widening with surprise at him hovering over her. "Are you okay? What just happened?" he demanded, disconcerted at his uncharacteristic lapse of self-control.

She blinked again and stretched, a delicious smile curving her lips. What that innocent movement did to her breasts under that t-shirt... he shook his head, determined to get this all back on track. "Are you okay?"

"I am now. You have my thanks," she replied, her gold eyes smiling up at him. "I mayhap should have mentioned that I need contact with the earth each day. Without it, I would wither and die."

"Don't let yourself get this sick again," he warned. "You can go in the backyard and do... whatever that was anytime you want." He added *Look for a Faery Care for Dummies book* to his growing mental to-do list. *Do they even have those?* He stood and offered his hands. Accepting his help, she rose to her feet, brushing a few stray grass clippings from her shirt. He winked at her. "C'mon, let's go shopping. We need to make one short stop first, though. I've got a surprise for you."

She frowned, then brushed her fingertips across the darkening mark on his cheek. "You are hurt," she murmured.

Travis shook his head and laughed. "Nah, just a little dust-up at work. Nothing to wo—"

Her soft hand cupped his face, and she began to sing softly, the chiming notes rising and falling in a hypnotic rhythm. His skin grew warm, then hot under her touch. The thought occurred that he should step away from the well-meaning but too intimate gesture, but he found he had lost all ability to move. A few heartbeats later, she lowered her hand and nodded. "That is better."

He worked his jaw back and forth, tenderly probing the bruised area with a fingertip to find no lingering discomfort. "What did you do?"

"I sent the pain away," she said, stepping back toward the door. She tripped but caught herself before falling. "What is that? It is part of a cart?" she asked, pointing to the cumbersome oddity that caught her heel.

"I'm sorry; I didn't put that away. It goes with the weight bench on the porch." He touched her arm to move her aside as she bent to retrieve it. "No, let me. It's heavier than it looks. Those discs weigh—"

She lifted the bar with one hand, carried it back to the stand, and dropped it onto the rack with a loud clatter. "It goes here, yes?"

"—two hundred fifty pounds," he finished in amazement. "You lifted that with one hand. That's insane, you're so tiny—how did you do that?"

"I am stronger than I appear," she said, giving him a noncommittal shrug and grinning. "Now, what is this surprise you promised?"

"No peeking, now." Standing close behind her, Travis placed his hands over her smaller ones and guided her away from the car. The light ocean breeze ruffled his hair and lifted her own to tangle around their wrists. He lowered his hands while she still held hers tightly over her eyes, but her chin tilted upward as she scented the air, dancing from foot to foot with excitement. He stepped back. "Open your eyes."

In that one single moment he would remember for the rest of his life, his heart shattered with the sheer beauty of her. Her gaze swept the beach and waves, her lips curved into a silent "oh," and a slender hand placed over her heart as her entire body trembled. She stood transfixed for a long while, watching seagulls wheel and swoop in the vast, cloudless sky, her sharp gaze darting to the sudden movement when a fish jumped. Tiny fiddler crabs ran along the foamy line where the incoming tides met the hard, packed sand. Warm tide pools dotted the beach, some empty, waiting to be filled again. The wind made a *woosshhh*ing sound, rippling through the sea oats and tall grass near the rolling dunes.

"It's the Atlantic Ocean," he explained, pointing slightly northeast. "You're in Cherry Grove right now. Ireland is just over 3,700 miles that way. I looked it up."

When she finally spoke, her voice sounded far away. "'Tis the most beautiful thing I have ever seen," she said, staring out over the crashing waves.

"I think so, too," he murmured, hoping she did not notice that he wasn't looking at the water. His fingers grazed her arm to get her attention. "Take off your shoes and socks," he suggested, removing his own and rolling up his jeans. She watched him with rapt attention, then eagerly mimicked his actions, wiggling her bare toes in the hot white sand. He extended his hand to her in invitation. "Not too far in now; we're not dressed for it," he warned. "We can come back after we get you a swimsuit, uh...outside clothing." With a jolt, he realized he did not think that one through at all. *Maybe one of those old-timey ones that cover you head to toe*, he thought, refusing to visualize her in a bikini. *One of those Sports Illustrated ones that looked like strings. With a gold belly chain...* He shook his head to derail that runaway train of wishful thinking.

With a shy smile, she slipped her hand into his. Together, they walked down to the waterline, wading in about ankle-deep. Saoirse gasped, then giggled as the first wave tickled her slender ankles. "It is warmer than I expected," she noted.

Travis laughed. "We're near the end of summer, so this is the warmest it gets. I never understood the early tourists who go swimming in the spring. The water in my fridge is warmer."

She stood motionless, staring down at their feet as they disappeared and reappeared underneath the softer sand being moved about by the tides. A broken shell swirled and rolled toward her with an incoming wave, and she stooped to retrieve it. She turned it back and forth, studying it. Before Travis could explain, she said, "This was once a creature's home, but she moved to a larger one."

He gave a start, never having thought of the delicious snails as being male or female. "That's right, a conch. How did you know that? Have you seen these before?"

"No," she admitted, smoothing a finger over the jagged edges. "They are lower creatures and do not think as you and I. I sense... images that remain. Several used it before it became broken." She tossed the misshapen piece back into the water and again entwined her wet fingers with his.

As they began to walk, he told her about the area, pointing to people fishing or playing volleyball, some packing up after a day of sunbathing. They crossed beneath the pier, pausing for her to inspect the barnacles on the massive wooden legs, and kept walking until they reached the end of the strand at Cherry Grove Point. "That's Hog Island right there," he said, directing her gaze. "I come out here to run sometimes in the early morning before the beach fills up."

She glanced up, a look of alarm on her face. "What do you run from?"

He laughed. "Call it my keen sense of observation, but I'm getting the impression my world is very different from yours. We're going to have lots to talk about. But first," he said, turning them back toward the car, "we've got to get you some clothes."

She made a happy chirping sound and bounced as they walked. "Is it far, this place we must travel to?"

"Not far," he assured her before adding something so bizarre that it didn't even seem real. "When you're out in public—where other people can see you—it's best you don't turn into anything else. People don't do things like that here. Ever."

"Oh." She seemed crestfallen for a moment before brightening again. "But I can do this in front of you?"

"Yeah," he agreed with a laugh. "Just warn me first. The human brain has limits, and I'm pretty sure mine draws the line at surprise dinosaurs in my kitchen."

Shopping with an ancient faery turned out to be every bit the bizarre thrill ride he anticipated. They started with women's clothing, guessing at the sizes. Saoirse began to enjoy herself, chirping with excitement as she held up tops and pants next to her body for his approval. They had yet to find a color she didn't like or one that did not look good on her. For the time being, he stuck to sportswear and casual, things he reasoned would be most comfortable for her.

They had much more help than usual; he assumed there must be new hire training because of the sheer number of sales associates offering her their unsolicited aid. Travis couldn't decide how he felt about that—grateful for the help, of course, but not so much for the unsettling amount of attention lavished on Saoirse. Shopping on his own, he had never had even one employee ask if he needed help, much less the dozen or so following them around now. He spent more than he intended, but watching her face glow with delight at everything he suggested turned out to be an addictive drug.

Before long, the cart was full, and Saoirse's shopping was almost complete. He bought several full changes of clothing, socks, another pair of shoes, and a pair of flip-flops he couldn't resist after watching her try to walk in them. He was grateful for the motherly female employee who, seeing his discomfort, swooped in to help her select pajamas, bras, and panties, then led her over to the swimwear racks. With the authority of a seasoned army drill sergeant, the woman pointed to a row of chairs where he could wait and ordered him to sit. He could not help but be a little apprehensive when they disappeared into the dressing rooms with an armload of swimsuits on hangers, but the kind saleswoman had clearly taken Saoirse under her wing. After that, they stopped by the health and beauty aids section to pick up shampoo, scented soap, toiletries, and the feminine products she would soon need.

"Let's swing by the grocery store on the way home and pick up something for dinner," he suggested as he loaded their bags into the trunk, discarding the earlier plan of eating out in his haste to get her back home again.

"Whatever most pleases you," she nodded, caught up in sightseeing again.

If only he could take back those words.

CHAPTER 7

"Captain, ma'am," he blurted out in surprise as he pushed their full cart around the end cap at the grocery store, into the next aisle, and the older couple's stationary cart.

Captain Bellamy and his wife stood in front of the coffee bean grinders. Mrs. Bellamy held two in her hands, comparing. "McLean! Watch where you're driving that thing," he boomed. At the same time, his wife smiled and said, "Well, hello, Travis!"

Travis slapped on his best blank look but knew questions would be unavoidable. He opted for the quickest diversion. "I have that one, and it works great," he said, pointing to the green box Mrs. Bellamy held.

Captain Bellamy glanced sideways at Travis, then turned to Saoirse, giving her a warm smile. "And who might this be?"

Clutching a large jar of sweet gherkins to her chest, she smiled back but did not answer, looking up at Travis with uncertainty.

"Uh, this is Saoirse," he said. "Saoirse, this is my supervisor, Captain Bellamy, and his wife, Helen."

"I am pleased to meet you," Saoirse said. At the same time, the captain asked, "Saoirse, what?"

Without answering, she released her grasp on the pickles. The heavy glass jar hit the floor with a loud *crack* like a gunshot, exploding into a million pieces and spraying both her and Travis with spicy brine. The captain and his wife jumped back in time to avoid being soaked. "Are you okay? Are you cut?" Travis rushed to ask, lifting her hands to look for himself.

Her expressionless face tilted up, devoid of any emotion except for the questioning look in her eyes. The overhead intercom blared the message *Clean up aisle eight* as if right on cue.

The captain pulled his cart away from the spreading pool and nodded once at Travis. "Sounds like help is on the way," he said, returning his focus to Saoirse. "Pleasure meeting you, Miss Saoirse. See you back at the station, Travis. Next time you're on, how's about you stop by my office for a minute before you head out."

"Yessir," Travis agreed, his stomach sinking. The captain had been in law enforcement for more years than Travis had been alive, and without a doubt recognized a diversionary tactic when he saw one. *The real question is, how did Saoirse know?* Dying for an answer, he'd have to wait until they got home to ask. Or maybe in the car. Out of the store, at the very least.

The older couple waved and headed up the aisle, Mrs. Bellamy still holding the grinder in the green box. When they disappeared around the corner, a teenage boy, armed with a cleanup cart, arrived and began sweeping up the broken glass before mopping the soiled area.

Travis placed his hands on Saoirse's thin shoulders and gently tugged her out of the way. "Sorry about that," he apologized.

"No worries, man. Accidents happen, ya know?" Head down and focused on his job, the young man waved him off as he cleaned. Sweeping up the last of the glass shards, he turned to empty them and froze. The poor kid stared openly at Saoirse, mouth agape, his gaze softening right before he dropped the dustpan, scattering wet glass fragments everywhere. A flood of embarrassing color crept up his neck as he gave her a shy but hopeful smile. "Are you okay, ma'am?"

If Travis did not know better, he would say the boy looked lovestruck. "She's fine," he snapped with an unfamiliar surge of territoriality. *If this doesn't stop soon, I'm going to start pissing on things for sure.*

The teenager stared a few beats longer before shaking his head as if waking from a daydream. Facing the floor again, he bent to his task. The glass and ruined pickles soon disappeared into a brown trash bag. "Y'all have a good day," he said, pushing his cart back to the stockroom area without a backward glance.

"Guess he's never seen a faery before," Travis muttered. In the next moment, the prettiest sound he had ever heard caressed his ears, and when it stopped, he craved more. He shot his shopping companion a side-eyed glance, her hand still over her mouth as she tried to stifle a second giggle.

They maneuvered the rest of the grocery store without incident, and their shopping excursion came to an end. Saoirse had nonstop questions as he drove home, a trait Travis found more endearing than he would have thought possible. Even buckled in securely, she still managed to squirm around in her seat, trying to see everything all at once.

"So much color," she marveled. "It is all so beautiful. And so many people! I have never seen this many in one place. What is Cal-a-bash? They have all you can eat sea... food." She gestured to the billboard advertising the buffet. "Look at all the food! Do they mean that? I do not think I have ever had so much that I could not eat more."

Travis glanced over and smiled. He had never been to one of the colossal buffets. The seafood tended to be lower in quality, meant for tourists who didn't know what a good fried shrimp was supposed to taste like. Locals steered clear of them, preferring the smaller Mom and Pop restaurants. "They do, but there are better places to eat."

His arm rested on the center console, fingertips grazing the gear shift. She grabbed his hand in both of hers and squeezed. "If it pleases you, I should like to try this food from the sea."

Yup. Travis got that tiny, now familiar charge of electrical energy and, to his surprise, made no effort to pull his hand away.

A sporty red coupe blew past them in the left lane, traveling too fast. At once, a loud, screaming noise assaulted their ears. She covered them with both hands, curling into her seat. "What is that terrible noise?" she gasped out.

Travis did not answer, focused more on the pursuing silver, black, and blue car with bright flashing lights on top. "Hold on," he said, whipping his car into the lane behind them. He hit the gas and stayed a car length or two behind, following them into a strip mall parking lot. Both cars had stopped, the silver vehicle a short distance behind the red. Travis coasted in behind the cruiser and shifted into *park.*

By then, the horrible racket had ceased, so Saoirse ventured a peek at the strange activity. The young officer exited the vehicle and hitched up his duty belt. He walked up to the red car, casually touching the trunk and taillight as he passed, then stepped back and spoke to the driver. Saoirse strained to listen, tugging on Travis's sleeve. "What happens here?" she whispered.

He held up one finger for her to wait, his unwavering focus on the other policeman. When the officer nodded and began walking back to his car, he looked up and saw them. A wide smile split his face, and he raised his hand in greeting, which turned into a thumbs-up gesture. Travis grinned back and gave a small salute. Glancing down, he shifted into reverse, backed up, and headed back onto the roadway.

"Is he another friend?" Saoirse asked.

He nodded. "That's Bennett—we work together in the same unit," he explained. "When he hit his lights, I saw he didn't have a partner with him. Traffic stops can be dangerous sometimes." His Southern accent turned slow and thick. "Like a box of chocolates, you never know what you're gonna get." He chuckled at his own joke but sobered quickly. "Yeah, I doubt you saw that movie."

Her eyes went wide. "You watch over him?"

A frown creased his brow. "Not so much that. Just hanging around in case there's a problem. I've had other officers do that for me. It means a lot to know there is backup nearby in case things go sideways."

Saoirse fell silent for a long while. When she finally spoke, he leaned over to hear her soft voice. "You are like the shepherd watching over his flock."

He gave a dismissive shrug. "It's my job, Saoirse. Those of us doing this type of work look out for each other. I'm not out here trying to save the world, okay?"

She nodded but said nothing until another billboard caught her eye. "What does Rip-ley's Be... lieve It or Not mean?"

CHAPTER 8

Doubling his mother's family recipe, Travis decided on a meatloaf for dinner. Saoirse perched on a barstool near the counter, watching him mix the ingredients with his hands and press them into the greased pans for baking. "I don't much like cooking, so when I do, I always make extra to have leftovers for the next day or freeze," he explained. A stray thought struck him, and he voiced it aloud. "Have you ever cooked before?"

She shook her head, a confused look flitting across her face. "What food we had was brought to us. I have never before seen it prepared."

He fell silent as he finished the prep work. He scrubbed his hands in the sink before sliding the heavy pans into the oven. "I think we need to talk," he finally said, twisting the rooster-shaped kitchen timer to set it for an hour. "I mean, about what your plans are and all."

"My... plans?"

"You know—where you want to go, what you want to do with your life now that you're, um... free." He did not look at her, busying himself with rinsing off the dirty bowl and utensils.

Saoirse tilted her head to the side, puzzled. "May I not stay here with you?"

"Of course," he rushed out, wiping his hands on the dishtowel. "For as long as you need to—want to. I just wondered what ideas you had."

"I confess I did not think of anything past escaping. I suppose I never thought it possible. It still seems as a dream to me." The flash of an idea crossed her face, and she clasped her hands together earnestly. "Why have you no servants or slaves?"

Travis let out a bark of laughter. "We don't have slaves in this day and time. Servants sort of, but only if they're paid for their work. They're called staff now. I'd just as soon save the money and do for myself, anyway. Why? Do you think I need some?"

"I am thinking of ways I may repay your many kindnesses. Were you to show me what to do, I would be happy to serve you. I am a quick learner," she insisted.

He did not know how to respond without saying something he would later regret. He turned away and shuffled jars around in the refrigerator door, pretending to look for something. "That isn't necessary," he said over his shoulder, a sudden wave of desire making his voice rougher than he intended.

"Then I shall have to think of something else."

Desperate to change the subject, he remembered his earlier question. "When we met the captain and his wife in the grocery store, I think you dropped that pickle jar on purpose. Why?"

She gave a dismissive shrug. "Your scent changed."

"My what?"

"You were calm, but then you became anxious when he asked about me," she explained. "I wanted to shift his attention from you. Everyone has their own smell, of course." She turned a becoming shade of pink and ducked her head. "Yours is very pleasing, like the salt in the air and sunshine. Male. Clean. You wear perfume sometimes, but not overmuch like that white-haired woman."

Not human. Funny how he kept forgetting that. "It's cologne. Men don't wear perfume," he corrected. Captain Bellamy's voice echoed in his head, and he shoved the random thought away. *SLED had a bomb Mal. Hell of a nose.* "Ready to make some salad?"

She straightened on her stool and beamed with excitement. "I know not what that is, but yes—I am ready."

Ansgar sat at the library table, surrounded by piles of books on astronomy. Using quill and ink, he made notes and calculations. *It was late summer there, perhaps August or*

September, he reasoned, *so the time of their year parallels ours.* He scratched through one column of numbers and began another. Traveling through the stones was much easier, not to mention less dangerous, when one held the destination and date firmly in mind. He had taken a monumental risk, jumping in to follow the rebellious fae, but he was not about to let the stubborn little chit best him.

He slammed his current book closed, startling some apprentices studying nearby. Picking up a different book and a fresh sheet of vellum, he dipped the pen in the ink and began another series of notes. When his mind kept wandering from the task, he angrily slammed the quill down. "Damn her," he muttered under his breath. By far the most beautiful of the current group, she was also the most troublesome, pushing the boundaries at every opportunity. He dared not make an example of her, unwilling to break that wild spirit or spoil her ethereal beauty, tempting though it may be.

Ansgar grew hard beneath his robe and shifted in his chair to relieve the unwelcome pressure. *Maybe I will keep this one for myself and allow her to grace my bed instead,* he thought, laughing inwardly with delight. *Such a feral and unpredictable creature would surely strain that old fool Pendaran's heart. I am more than up to the task. And when I am High Druid, she will help me gain my—*

"P-please excuse m-m-me, my lord," a young boy stammered, interrupting his daydream. "I have a m-message for y-you, my lord."

"And?" Ansgar snapped. When no answer came, he gave the youth a shove hard enough to make him stagger. "Speak or get ye gone, boy."

The boy reached into a pouch on his belt and withdrew a small scroll tied neatly with dark thread. He ducked his head respectfully and, with both hands, presented it to the seated man.

"Give me that." He snatched it away and yanked on the thread, smoothing the single page on the tabletop. He read the single-page missive once, then again:

I am delayed. One moon, possibly two, before I arrive at Brú na Bóinne.

Pendaran Dyfed
Ard-druí Érenn

He noted the pompous use of his official title in the signature and snorted with amusement. *You are the High Druid of Ireland for now, old man, but not for very much longer.* His mouth twisted into a sly smirk as he folded the parchment into a neat square and pocketed it. He would have plenty of time to hunt and bring his rebellious fae to heel before putting his plans in motion.

CHAPTER 9

The following week passed without incident, as did the week after. Travis had managed to dodge questions about Saoirse from Captain Bellamy, shrugging her off as a "Miss Right Now." Not entirely sure the older man bought that, but at least it bought him time to come up with a more believable backstory. The trouble was that none existed.

When Saoirse said she learned quickly, she meant it. In no time at all, she had the basics down. Things he never gave a second thought to, such as using silverware, had been unfamiliar to her. The security system and metal door locks were bewildering and alien. For some bizarre reason, the washer, dryer, and dishwasher came naturally, and she took over those duties with gusto. One day, as she put in a load of towels to be washed, he asked why she thought that might be.

"I do not know," she answered thoughtfully, "but I have only ever seen clothing washed in buckets. This is a kind of magick, is it not?"

A few boundaries were set, but she accepted those without question. Things related to his profession, such as his duty belt or other equipment he might leave lying around, were off-limits. The same applied to his gun safe and any of the firearms hidden around the house. Once he explained what they were, how they worked, and that it was for her safety, she gave them a wide berth.

She seemed curious about his laptop, but he sensed she was not quite ready for that technological jump. He spent an hour or so each evening scouring breeder sites, often with her watching silently over his shoulder. Her language skills improved, and she applied herself to learning to read better, albeit at a slower pace than everything else.

While he was out on patrol, she spent much of her time watching TV, assimilating the language, mannerisms, and social mores. He had not realized how much she had learned until returning home early one morning to find her already up and doing laundry. The chirpy "Hey, babe—is that you?" that greeted him from the little mud room between the kitchen and backyard had been a healing balm to his soul after a tense evening.

They ate together whenever they could, and a whole new world opened up for Travis as he questioned her about her former life. Saoirse had many questions for him as well, so they agreed to take turns. Seated across from each other at the kitchen table, they passed a large conch shell back and forth to determine whose turn it was to ask a question. Saoirse took full credit for that process, having gotten the idea from TV.

One night, Travis pulled the conch over toward him. "When you become an animal, do you also have whatever abilities they have? Like how a squirrel can jump or how fast a cheetah runs?" At her frown, he added, "A cheetah is a big cat, the fastest land animal in our world." *The phrase "in our world"* sounded so strange to say aloud.

"Yes and no. As a squirrel, I can climb trees and jump from branch to branch with ease. The body I assume must eat and sleep and—" She pinkened with embarrassment. "—and use the bathroom. You would see no difference between me and a real squirrel. But even though I am female, I could not have baby squirrels. Do you see?"

He exploded into uproarious laughter. At her alarmed expression, he hurried to explain. "I just had this visual of you with an armload of kits."

She joined in his laughter, then snatched the conch back to her side of the table. "It is my turn," she announced. "Why have you no lady? You seem past an age when a man would take a wife." Belatedly realizing how accusatory her question sounded, she covered her mouth with her hand as if trying to recapture the words. "Truly, I meant no offense; I just wondered, is all."

"No offense taken." Sobering at once, he cleared his throat before speaking. "Guess I haven't found the right lady yet," he said, suddenly uncomfortable. "I've had my mind on other things, work mostly."

"Are you a warrior as well as lawkeeper?" She tilted her head in that way he was coming to regard as adorable.

"I enlisted in the army right out of high school. That's our military, soldiers." At her nod of understanding, he continued. "I did four years, then joined the police force after my discharge." He conceded, making an *I guess so* gesture.

She opened her mouth as if to ask another question, but he grabbed the shell first. "I hope this doesn't come out sounding strange, but... is there something you do that makes men..." He faltered, not quite knowing how to proceed without offending her. "Like the sales guys in Target, or—or that boy in the grocery store—he got all moony-eyed when he saw you. Do you give off... I don't know... vibes or a signal or... *Eau de Faery* or something that attracts men to you?"

She looked thoughtful and paused before answering. "I have heard that is so. The lunula we wore—"

"The what?" he interrupted.

"The lunula—a collar made of gold, spelled so that none of our magicks worked, and we could not change into *other*. I am still learning what abilities I have." She folded her arms on the table and leaned toward him, her eyes slanted up in a smile, soft lips slightly parted. "Do you think me attractive?" she asked in a breathy Marilyn Monroe whisper.

WANTSEXHUNGERLUSTDESIRE

NAKEDNEEDNOWNOWNOW

Out of nowhere, an avalanche of fierce and tumultuous emotion overwhelmed him. Before the thought of what he was doing even registered, he caught himself rising from his chair, reaching for her. "T... tu... turn it off," he rasped, his voice hoarse as he fought to distance himself. When his out-of-control id settled back down, he fell back and sighed with relief. "Yes, ma'am. I think you're very attractive. But let's not do that again, okay?" He snatched the conch back before she could ask another question, still trying to catch his breath and lose the painful hard-on her simple words had aroused. "So," he said, redirecting that conversation, "do you remember anything before you were captured, your family, maybe?"

"I was very young," she explained, eyes downcast. "I know not what became of my mother. I do not remember my father. I have never seen a male like me. I suspect they hunt only females."

Travis's heart cracked right down the middle at the forlorn tone of her soft voice. "Well, you're free now, and that's what matters, right?" he said, seeking to cheer her up again.

"Yes, I am free," she murmured.

He was not convinced. *She should be happy*, he thought. *It's not like she can do anything about their situation.* Still, he knew how he would feel in the same circumstance—honor-bound to rescue those he considered his brothers and sisters. But as Cherry Grove appeared to have a distinct shortage of standing stones, he did not see any way for her to jump back through time to save the day.

CHAPTER 10

Shaking off the ice crystals from his journey, Ansgar glanced around to get his bearings. The motel from his first visit stood about fifty yards away. He closed his eyes and sent out mental feelers in every direction, but as he suspected, she was long gone. He had known this one would cause him problems from the moment he first laid eyes on her, always questioning, always pushing his patience to the brink. But what a beauty she had grown up to be! By far the most wild-spirited of the lot, he could only imagine the ride she would give once trained to respect his hand.

He squatted down to inspect his bag, filled with food and pouches of ale. He would need modern clothing and footwear quickly to blend in, but those should be easy enough to find. He did not relish the idea of walking in his primitive boots, so perhaps a means of faster travel could also be found.

Concerned that the motel owners might catch sight of him and cause tiresome delays, he decided against rummaging through their dumpster for anything usable and moved further away into the woods.

Pulling her collar from his robe pocket, he whispered a few words and then held it out like a divining rod. He turned in a slow circle, stopping when it suddenly tingled. *There you are*, he thought, and set off in her direction at a determined pace.

Saoirse's new favorite activity—laundry day—found her musing over the current situation. She knew Travis had not been looking for a roommate (an unfamiliar word), but he seemed to accept the changes in his life with grace. He had been so kind and good to her, much more than she deserved. *I wish I could repay him.* From what she had seen, her unexpected arrival had turned his life upside down.

She pulled his sheets out of the dryer, pressing them to her face and breast, reveling in both his male scent and the heat radiating from them. Folding the fitted sheet proved to be an exercise in futility. She did the best she could, tucking the parts sticking out under the parts that weren't. The flat sheet cooperated, and she smoothed it briskly. She expected his arrival home any minute and wanted him to be pleased with her labors.

She had to lean far into the dryer's cooling warmth to reach the pillowcases. At once, a freezing chill enveloped her, and her entire body convulsed with a great shudder.

The floor rushed up to greet her as she fell to her knees, banging her head hard on the dryer door, drawing a gasp of pain. *Magick... Ansgar... searching.* Shocked that she had even for a moment lost sight of being his unwilling quarry, she hid the only way she knew how and shifted into the gray mouse.

The painful cold disappeared at once, and the trembling stopped as she scampered behind the dryer to hide. Rubbing tiny pink paws together, she smoothed her whiskers nervously and listened. Gravel crunched in the driveway as if from far away, and the garage door rumbled open. She tilted her head, listening, then ventured a peek at the door through the narrow space under the dryer. A car door slammed. She held her breath, waiting.

Five muffled tones from the alarm keypad beeped before the kitchen door swung open. Heavy footsteps sounded in the kitchen, and his keys jangled when he tucked them away in the cabinet. She sat up on her hind feet and sniffed the air, squeaking excitedly at the familiar scent.

"Saoirse?" Travis called out. His voice faded in and out as he moved through the house. At last, he stuck his head in the laundry room, saw the back door still locked, and frowned. Spying the small pile of clothes on the floor in front of the open dryer, his gaze darted around uncertainly. "Saoirse? Are you..." His voice trailed off as he appeared to choose his words carefully. "Something else right now?"

"I'm here, I'm here," she squeaked excitedly as she ran out to greet him. His head cocked, listening. When he did not see her right away, she hopped onto the vamp of his boot. She considered shifting back to human but decided against it, remembering that her nakedness upset him. Holding onto the Velcro straps for support, she bounced up and down on his boot to get his attention. "I'm here," she called again.

He glanced down, and his eyes widened in alarm before he grinned at her. "Hello there, Miss Mouse," he boomed, his voice thunderous to her tiny ears.

Grabbing hold with tiny claws, she scampered up his leg, abdomen, and chest to perch on one of those broad shoulders. "I am glad you are home," she chirped.

He offered his hand palm up, and she hopped onto it. "I don't think I'll ever get used to this," he laughed, raising her to face level. "I'm kinda feeling like Dr. Doolittle here. Good thing I'm not scared of mice, huh?"

At that, she closed her eyes and placed a tiny paw over her heart. She staggered a bit, then fell onto her back, her legs sticking straight up as if she were dead. Her laughter came as quiet chittering.

"Yeah, just like that," he chuckled. He knelt, placing the back of his hand gently on the floor. She hopped off and scampered over to her pile of discarded clothing. Rising onto her hind legs, she gazed up at him with shiny black eyes.

He flushed a charming shade of pink. "Right," he said, "mice need their privacy. I'll... uh, go... change clothes now." He rose and strode to the kitchen archway before glancing back at her. When the shimmer began, he bolted out of sight.

By the time he returned barefoot in soft sweatpants and a baggy T-shirt, she had dressed and finished stacking the rest of the folded linens. "I am happy you are returned," she said hesitantly, meeting him in the kitchen. "Much of what I see on your TV tells me yours is a dangerous job."

Travis snagged an apple from a ceramic bowl on the counter. "It can be sometimes," he admitted, taking a large bite. He frowned. "Why were you a mouse when I got home?"

She looked away with a shrug. When she opened her mouth to speak, no words came out. Her lips pressed together into a thin line. Clutching the sheets to her chest, she ducked past him as if to put them away.

He set the apple down and placed his large hands on her shoulders to stop her, turning her to face him. "Why did you shift?" he asked again. "You're trembling. Tell me what happened."

Saoirse would not meet his piercing gaze. "I did not wish to worry you. Ansgar uses his magick to search for me, but I believe he cannot sense me while I am in another form."

"Is he nearby?" he asked in a calm voice that masked his growing alarm.

"Closer than when I first arrived here, but not very close. That is confusing. Do you see?"

"I understand," he assured her, prying the squashed linens from her hands and placing them on the counter. "You don't worry about that now. I have the mother of all alarm systems with backup security installed all the way around the house, inside and out. He's not getting in without my knowing about it. And you need to understand I will protect you with everything I have." At her nod, he pulled her close and put his arms around her in a tight embrace. "I will keep you safe," he whispered against her hair.

She tensed, every muscle coiled to run. "What is this?" she gasped.

Travis blinked in surprise. "Hugging you. Hasn't anybody ever done that before?" At her violent head shake, he forced his body to relax but did not release her. "I'm not going to hurt you. Just breathe."

"This is strange to me," she whispered.

"Might as well get used to it," he said with a low chuckle. "You're in the South now, and we are a hugging people."

Bit by bit, her body unclenched and softened in his arms. Her fluttering heartbeat slowed. He held on until her breaths no longer came out in short pants. When she began to relax, he pulled her in tighter against him and laid his head against hers. "I *will* protect you, Saoirse," he promised. When her arms crept up to encircle his waist and tighten in return, he wondered if it were possible for a heart to explode with joy. If not, his might be the first ever.

They stood entwined in the kitchen for a long while, Travis gently swaying her back and forth and crooning wordlessly in his deep voice. After a few minutes, her muffled voice pierced the fog in his head, and he relaxed his hold just a little. "I'm sorry. I guess that was a little tight," he apologized.

"I find this most pleasing." She sighed against his chest. Although he could not see her face, he heard the smile. "I have not been touched so before. I did not know it would be pleasurable." Pulling away just a little, she tilted her head to gaze up at him and inhaled deeply. "Do we mate now?" she asked, her voice dreamy.

As if doused with a bucket of ice water, Travis released her and jumped back against the counter. "I'm sorry—do what?"

"Mating. Is this not what happens at the beginning? I have never seen the actual act, but I overheard slaves speak of it, and this is how it always starts on TV."

"No! Yes! Well, sometimes," he stammered, flustered. "But not now." Happy that his oversized t-shirt hid the now rock-hard bulge in his sweats, he drew in a huge breath and straightened his shoulders. "A hug can mean any number of things, depending on who is doing the hugging. For example, a grandmother hugging a child is much different from a man and a woman, or whatever your preference is. I mean, it *can* lead up to making love, or sex—we don't call it mating—but it doesn't have to." He blew out a deep sigh. "I don't think I'm explaining it very well."

"I think I understand," she said slowly. "It depends on how you feel about the one you are hugging. Your scent changed several times with me."

He cocked an eyebrow and tilted his head as he put two and two together. "It did? What makes you think that?"

"Oh, yes," she assured him. "At first, it was tranquil. Then it changed into contentment, like a warm blanket wrapped around me. Then it became one I do not know. I have only smelled it a few times since being here with you." A slight wrinkle appeared between her delicate eyebrows as she frowned in concentration. "It is a wild scent, like an animal, yet clean. Spicy, male. I like it very much. It makes my body feel strange and wonderful and tingly, all at the same time."

I think the word you are looking for is pheromone, he thought miserably, wondering if there was any way in hell to turn his off.

CHAPTER 11

The email that changed everything came on a Thursday night. Saoirse sat cross-legged on the sectional couch, munching on popcorn, engrossed in a Discovery Channel documentary on the Celtic Isles. Travis sat beside her, close enough to feel the heat from her body but not quite touching. With the laptop balanced on his thighs, he scanned through the unread email. He punched the air with a whoop of joy, startling her into a shriek of alarm. Popcorn flew in every direction, showering them both in buttery snow.

He burst out laughing at the sheer absurdity. "I'm sorry, I didn't mean to scare you," he apologized. "It's just—I've been waiting for this email for a long time."

She shook a few puffy kernels out of her hair. "It must be something important to give you such joy."

He nodded, excited. "This breeder promised to email when they had another litter." He paused to read, then continued. "He says they'll be ready to go in about six weeks."

She looked confused. "Litter of what?" she asked, leaning over to scoop up the pieces that had fallen under the coffee table.

He caught her hand before she could pop them in her mouth. "Don't eat those, they've been on the floor. We can pop another bag," he scolded. "And a litter of puppies. Six weeks until they're ready. I've been waiting forever for this guy to email me."

With her lower lip pushed out in protest, she reluctantly opened her hand and dropped the dirty popcorn onto the table. "You want a pet?"

"Not a pet," he clarified quickly, "a partner." He had mentioned his dream of training a dog for duty before, but now he added the why. "My father and mother both were K9 handlers in the army. When Mom got pregnant with me, she traded in her uniform for mom duty and took a discharge. But after I came along, she couldn't stay away—started her own private training business right here at home." He laughed, jerking a thumb toward the rear of the house. "She used to teach classes in the backyard with me strapped into a backpack. As soon as I could walk, I was part of the team."

"That had to be quite a sight," Saoirse said, giggling.

"Mom always said I would make a great handler because I got my dad's head and her heart. I wanted to make them proud, you know?" His gaze drifted to the great room wall, where their lifetime of achievements still hung in silent tribute. Travis had carefully rearranged everything to make room for the large shadowbox holding their folded flags and a smaller one displaying the collars and vests of their working dogs. "I thought they'd always be here," he murmured, his voice soft. "But I guess now they're watching from heaven."

Her head tilted in plain confusion. "And this is truly where your heart lies?"

Her random question caught him off guard, and for a moment, he could not answer. "Yeah," he finally said, nodding. "It's what I've always wanted to do."

At her prompting, he gave the condensed version of what a K9 officer could do once the training and certification processes were complete. "My partner will stay busy sniffing out drugs, helping me arrest bad people, and watching my back in the field."

"How do you teach this dog to find drugs?" she asked, showing an unusual interest.

"Hang on." He raised a finger, signaling her to wait, and disappeared into the unused bedroom. A few muffled thumps came from within before he reappeared, triumphantly clutching a square, molded plastic suitcase. Without ceremony, he swept the coffee table clean with a forearm, sending popcorn skittering back to the floor, and dropped the case with a thud.

Snapping open the latches, he lifted the lid to reveal rows of small glass jars nestled snugly in foam. "Each one contains the scent of a different illegal drug or explosive," he announced in a tone half science teacher and half carnival barker. "You start with one and add others when the dog gets his nose for it." He removed one of the jars, unscrewed the lid, and held it out for her. "Here, take a whiff—this one's cocaine."

She inhaled deeply, wrinkling her nose. "It is a most memorable smell. Show me more."

He jumped at the opportunity; such was his excitement over sharing his passion. Eventually, he opened all the jars, allowing her to smell each one. He had them arranged alphabetically: carfentanil, cocaine, methamphetamine, fentanyl, heroin, marijuana, MDMA, and common opioids. One row held the explosive scents: gunpowder, HMTD, TATP, ammonium nitrate, and C4.

"Show me this dog you seek," she urged, pointing to his phone.

Travis did not hesitate. He had a screenshot saved of the most beautiful Malinois he had ever seen, coming from a breeder in the Netherlands. The coloring was exquisite, the mahogany deep and rich against the requisite black mask. He looked up from the photo to find Saoirse beaming at him, vibrating with excitement. "What?" he asked, afraid of her response but suddenly happy in a weird sort of way.

"I know how to repay your kindness," she murmured, and with a whisper of fabric hitting the floor, she turned into the Belgian Malinois.

CHAPTER 12

Travis sat transfixed for far longer than he probably should have. His mind raced in a hundred different directions at once, the possibilities coming so fast that he could not process them all. "You are gorgeous, that's for sure. Are you still able to understand me?"

"Yeeeesss." Her silky voice reminded him of the crafty Siamese cats in the old Disney movie. She pawed at the open scent case, breaking him out of his frozen stare.

"Oh Lord in Heaven," he breathed, finally seeing the biggest picture of all. "Can you show me which of these is cocaine?"

Saoirse rose to all fours and leaned down to sniff the jars. After a moment of deliberation, she placed one paw squarely on the correct bottle lid.

"You wait right here and don't look," he ordered, snatching up one of the bottles, loosening the jar lid as he tore off down the hall. He returned less than a minute later. "Go find it."

With a graceful leap, she sailed over the open case lid on the coffee table and bounded away. In less time than he would have thought possible, she proudly trotted back, her head high, the jar held gently in her teeth. She dropped it into his open hands and sat back with a derpy Mal grin.

The silence was deafening as Travis stared down at the jar. His movements were slow and deliberate as he secured it in the case, closing and latching the lid. "I'm going to put this away. Please, uh... change back and get dressed." He rose from the couch, grabbed the case, and walked away without looking back.

Saoirse shifted and rushed to dress, confused at his sudden change of demeanor. *I thought he would be so happy. Well, he began happy, but then he became sad. I do not understand him at all.* She snorted, yanking her clothes and fuzzy socks back on. Sitting back, she folded her arms and waited for his return. And waited. And waited. When the time stretched beyond her patience level, she jumped up and went to look for him.

He sat on the edge of the bed in the spare bedroom, his elbows on his knees, his head bowed, and his back to the door. She slipped into the room, careful not to make a sound, but he heard her anyway. He glanced back over his shoulder and gave her a crooked smile. "It's getting pretty late," he said, standing up and stretching, "I should probably go to—"

"What is wrong?" she demanded.

He sighed, a deep, bone-weary exhalation. "Nothing's wrong."

As he tried to slip past her, she touched his arm tentatively. "Please," she said. "I have made you sad, but I do not know why. Help me understand."

Travis sighed again and held out his hand, indicating she should sit on the bed. He sat beside her and took one of her hands in his. "I appreciate you wanting to do this for me, shows just how sweet you are. But I can't accept your offer. We don't talk much about what I do, and that's been on purpose for my part." He shrugged both shoulders and looked away. "As it is now, my job is dangerous *sometimes*. You start working with me in a K9 unit and that *sometimes* changes to *most times*. The people selling these drugs aren't just bad; they give zero fu—uh, they don't care who they hurt or kill to make their paper—money."

Saoirse frowned. "What has that to do with me?"

"It means they won't hesitate to shoot or stab you if they think you'll find their drugs. And I couldn't live with myself if anything happened to you, knowing it was my fault you were there in the first place."

"I could wear the armor like you," she argued. "I have seen you watch movies where the dogs all have armor and helmets with the camera and goggles and…"

"The answer is no, Saoirse. I'm not going to let you risk your life just because you feel obligated." He slapped his thighs and rose. "Good night, sweet dreams."

She leaped to her feet and stood to face him, arms akimbo and fists braced against those slender hips. "So you think you could find a better partner than I? Smarter, faster?"

"Doubt such a dog even exists. Answer's still no."

"But—"

"NO. Good night, Saoirse."

She stared at his back as he walked out and flinched when his bedroom door closed behind him with a firm *thunk*. Snorting in frustration, she rubbed her temples. *Stubborn*, she mentally complained. *Refusing my help. What am I to do with myself all day while he is away? There is only so much laundry and cleaning to be done, and I weary of the TV. I would make the best partner. I know I would.* She had a fleeting thought of seeking real employment, but quickly dismissed it, certain Travis would not approve. Besides, what could she even do to earn coin? Her complete list of skills in this world included washing clothes and cleaning, and she was not convinced she did either well enough to be paid for her labors.

Vowing to think on it more tomorrow, she went into the bathroom to get ready for bed. She flipped on the strip of globe lights and grabbed her hairbrush. In a fit of pique, she began yanking it through her hair. Moments passed before she noticed the large, rectangular mirror mounted on the wall behind the vanity. Steam fogged almost every square inch, as if someone had just finished a long, hot shower. No fine mist of moisture lingered in the air. The bathroom felt as cool as the rest of the house.

Even as her mind began to register how strange this was, she bent to reach beneath the sink for window cleaner and paper towels. Straightening, she aimed the spray nozzle at the center of the mirror, but seeing how fast the fog began to dissipate, she lowered it again, confused. A dark shape moved behind the remaining condensation, and she squinted, trying to make out what it could be.

With no warning, a large hole opened in the middle of the steamed mirror and a face swam into view.

"There you are, little one," Ansgar purred.

Travis punched his pillow into submission, finally collapsing back on it with a deep sigh. *There is no way to let her...* he stopped, cringing at how awful and derogatory *be my dog* sounded. He did not want her in harm's way, period.

She sure made a gorgeous Mal, though. DAMN. His thoughts bounced all over but kept coming back to Saoirse. *She said the wizard is still hunting for her, but he can't sense her when she's... not her. How long would it take him to get here on foot, maybe a couple weeks? And that's if he knew exactly where to go.* He felt confident that if Bud or Virginia caught sight of him skulking around, they would call. Still, he made a mental note to contact them first thing in the morning to check in.

What are you going to do about her, though? He had tried not to think about their situation, hoping some phenomenal idea would present itself at the right time. The perfect plan in which everyone got the best outcome remained elusive. After his parents died, coming home to the empty house had bordered on painful. He refused to admit that his heart gave a little jump every time he pulled into the driveway, knowing she would be happy to see him. He would not think of that perfect body, now soft, healthy, and filled out in all the right places. Or those big golden eyes gazing up at him with adoration, such an unusual color with tiny rainbow flecks throughout. Or that glorious mass of shiny, long hair his fingers itched to...

He swore as the blood raced south of the border under his pajama bottoms. Yet another raging hard-on, all dressed up and nowhere to go. He got those increasingly around her, and it became harder to hide each time. *It's like being fourteen all over again.* That Saoirse remained unaware of his interest was a good thing. He snorted, at once recognizing the lie for what it was. Forget any vague hints—she could smell when he was turned on. *Damn pheromones.*

My bunny club policy made me lazy, he thought, shaking his head. Even in high school, he never had to put forth much effort or guard his feelings before, never had to worry about subtle innuendo or getting emotionally entangled. Out of bed, many of the bunnies had all the depth of a shallow puddle and couldn't hold up their end of the conversation with a broom handle. In bed was another story, but one couldn't stay there twenty-four hours a day.

Lori Ann had been an exception, lasting longer than most because she didn't push him for a commitment. He never understood women who equated fighting with love and made it their mission to intentionally piss him off so they could convince themselves he cared.

Maybe I really am *an inconsiderate asshole.* For the first time, a twinge of guilt and remorse over his cavalier attitude crept over him. His mother would be appalled at what she would refer to as his *moral deterioration* since her passing. He remembered one of the last conversations he had with her, sitting at the kitchen table. *Thirty years old is on your horizon, Travis, and forty comes about ten minutes after that. You change girls like some people change underwear. It's time you settled down with one good woman.*

I settle down with a good woman almost every night, he had joked back like Joe Pesci in Goodfellas. Decorated combat veteran and badass police corporal notwithstanding, his mama had still boxed his ears like he was ten.

Travis focused on his career, advancing in rank, finding the right dog, and joining the K9 unit, in that order. He absolutely did not have the time or the desire to deal with a demanding woman who wanted a real relationship.

Saoirse had changed all that.

He began to doze but suddenly bolted upright. He waited a beat, then heard the eerie, hushed sound again—a sort of whimper—not good. He flung open the bedroom door, saw light spilling into the hallway from Saoirse's bathroom, and heard the deep male voice. That whimper came again, followed by an inhuman cry that made the hair on his neck stand at attention. Travis charged toward the open door and rounded the threshold into the bathroom.

"NO!" Saoirse flattened herself against the glass block shower, hand thrown out to stop him. "Come no closer!"

For a moment, Travis just stood and blinked in amazement. A long arm and part of a man's shoulder protruded from the mirror, stretching toward the terrified woman. "Is that him?" he mouthed.

She nodded violently, white with terror.

"Ah, that must be your savior. Come forward so I may thank you properly for taking such good care of what is mine," Ansgar said, his voice silky smooth.

Travis worked through the problem with lightning speed. *He doesn't know who I am or where she is. If he sees my face, he'll recognize me and go to Bud and Virginia for my address.*

"Come here." Ansgar's voice sounded weird and trippy.

He automatically began to step into the bathroom, then broke the trance, spun, and retreated into the hall. He held up one finger where she could see him—*wait*—before running to the great room. His duty belt was still on the coffee table. He snatched up the belt and a throw pillow without slowing and rushed back to the bathroom, flicking his wrist to expand the collapsible baton.

He waved to get her attention. "Saoirse—shift!" he mouthed.

She stared vacantly at the mirror, like his words had never reached her. No longer cowering at the wall, her dragging steps had taken her to the center of the large bathroom, closer and closer to the outstretched hand.

"Saoirse—shift now!" he said again, louder.

When she still did not respond, he wound up and threw the pillow, striking her hard in the face. The glazed look vanished, and she glared daggers at him.

"SHIFT!" he bellowed. At once, her clothes fluttered down in an empty pile. At the same time, Travis swung around into the bathroom, using the threshold frame as an anchor. With his left hand holding the baton, he struck the mirror twice, putting everything he had into it. The glass exploded, spraying millions of tiny reflective pieces on the bathroom floor. With a mingled roar of outrage and pain, the arm retreated and vanished altogether, leaving behind an expanse of unpainted wall.

The silence that followed bordered on deafening, broken only by the tinkling of falling glass from what remained of the mirror. Travis bent over, resting his hands on his knees, gulping in deep lungfuls of air. "I think he's gone, Saoirse. I don't know where you are, but don't move," he rasped. "There's glass everywhere."

Everything happened all at once, spinning his brain out of control. Saoirse winked into view, completely naked. Arms outstretched, she leaped over the broken shards, and he caught her against his chest. Without a word, she wrapped arms and legs around him, then pressed her lips to his. They fell back against the wall in a tangle of soft cotton and skin. With a deep growl, he answered, crushing his lips to hers and pulling her closer.

He dropped the baton and ran one large forearm under her bottom to support her. His other hand crept into her glorious mass of hair, luxuriating in the softness. Clutching a silken fistful, he tilted her head back and deepened the kiss, slipping his tongue into her open mouth and teasing hers into the age-old mating dance. Hardened peaks cushioned by full, high breasts pressed into his naked chest.

She squirmed against him, all soft whimpers and sighs. He groaned, certain his cock would explode any minute. He couldn't remember ever being harder, more ready, more frenzied, more out of his mind with desire. All he could think about, the only image playing on a nonstop loop in his imagination, was driving into her until they both screamed and reducing his bed frame to a smoking pile of splinters.

The tastes of her—lingering sweetness from the kettle corn and another, more elusive, that he could not name. Even as he laid siege to her mouth, his mind tried to pinpoint that honeyed flavor. His subconscious answered, but the words were slow to penetrate his lust-fogged brain. *That's inexperience. She's never been touched by a man before. What the hell are you doing, McLean?*

Falling into a pool filled with ice water could not have had a more cooling effect on his raging ardor. He gently disentangled himself and smiled weakly down at her. "We can't do this," he murmured, resting his forehead against hers.

The only sign she heard was a low whimper and more squirming as she rubbed catlike against him. "Saoirse, sweetheart—we can't," he said a little louder, holding her out at arm's length.

"But why?" she cried. "Do I not please you?" She gasped and staggered back. "That is the reason—you do not think me attractive enough to mate with. You say you do, but you are not being truthful." Splotches of pink appeared high on her cheeks, and to his abject horror, her bottom lip began to quiver. "I know not how or what to do. More fool I to think I could please a great man such as you." This last was delivered in an increasing wail.

"Honey, you know not a bit of that is true," he said in a soothing voice, moving closer to embrace her and offer comfort. "And I don't know where you got this *great man* idea from. Most days just being okay is a struggle."

"It IS true, or you would want me. I see the words on..." She gestured around wildly, sobbing.

"Writing on the wall," he automatically corrected, then flinched, wishing he had kept his big mouth shut.

"And stupid as well as an ugly, useless burden to you," she wailed, tears streaming down her cheeks.

"Now you hold your horses, I never said anything of the sort and—"

She shimmered and vanished. Travis glanced around wildly, expecting to see the mouse, but he stood alone. "Please, sweetheart—can we just talk about this?" he cajoled.

Silence.

"Pretty please? Saoirse?"

Nothing.

He leaned against the wall and slid down to the floor, wrists dangling on his raised knees. *Well, if we were looking for concrete proof that I am a complete ass, I believe this is it.* "I'm sorry, Saoirse," he said. "I don't know whether you can hear me or not, but I am sorry. Truth is that you're the most beautiful woman I've ever laid eyes on, and you are so smart. You'd have to be to pick up on the way our world works as fast as you have. You are funny and sweet as the day is long, and you are so trusting and caring. I would never do anything to hurt you. I know you don't have a lot of experience touching and being touched, and that is okay, but I don't want you to look back at this moment one day and think it was a mistake; that I took advantage of you."

Travis figured he was talking to himself at this point, but what the hell, might as well get it all out. "If we ever were to... you call it mating, I call it lovemaking. If that... were to happen, it would be because you understood all the whats and whys of it. When it's done right, it's not just bodies involved. It's your mind, and your heart, too. It's, well... it's everything."

Like you'd know, his conscience warned.

Shut up, he shot back.

"After everything you've been through, you deserve to be treated like a princess. Your first time should be special— rose petals on the bed, champagne, chocolates, and strawberries, that kind of thing. And with someone you love. You're not a casual sex kind of girl."

Now that's something you do *know about,* the little voice chided. *Dude, she deserves so much better than anything you have to offer.*

The silence stretched out. "I truly am sorry, Saoirse," he said, his voice soft. "Tell me how to make this right so you'll give me another chance."

"I accept your apology."

He glanced around but still did not see anything. "Where are you?"

She materialized kneeling between his raised knees, of all godawful places. He *oofed* in surprise but caught her before she bumped him in the worst place possible. *Hard- on = reengaged.* She threw her arms around his neck and gave him a self-satisfied grin. "When do we start?"

That now familiar sense of impending doom settled over him, and at once he knew he had just stepped into a well-laid, well-played trap. "Start what?"

Saoirse giggled. "Teaching me to be your partner, of course."

CHAPTER 13

"Okay, let's run through them again," Travis said, reading from his printed list. "*Revir*."

"Search for something, right?"

He nodded. "How about *zustan*?"

She frowned, a tiny wrinkle creasing in between her brows. "Do not move?"

"Yes, stay. *Pozor*?"

Saoirse dropped her voice to imitate his. "Be on the lookout," she said, very gruff and serious.

He smothered a grin. "That's BOLO. *Pozor* is to be on guard, ready to act fast. *Drz*?"

She opened her mouth as if to speak, then snapped her teeth together twice, followed at once by an attack of wiggling giggles.

He laughed at her obvious enjoyment. "Correct. How about a break? We've been at this for hours. I could use something to drink and a snack." He set his binder aside and gave her a sidelong glance. "I sure hope you don't have to bite anybody. Those teeth of yours look lethal."

Training had been a breeze. The number of things you could teach a dog was amazing when it understood every word and offered feedback on training methods. Saoirse proved to be a quick study, anticipating and executing the commands before Travis could speak them aloud.

He knew she held back when they trained with the bite suit, and he cautioned her not to do that when it counted. The one time he instructed her to give it everything she had, she knocked him off his feet and sank her teeth through the sleeve. The result was a rapid swelling mass of bruises and tooth-shaped cuts on his arm. She fretted and fussed like a mother hen while she tended to his injury, and he did his best to soothe her. In truth, it hurt like hell, but he would never tell her that. To misquote Mr. T, he pitied the fool who caught an unpadded bite from that mouth.

Travis had completed his handler training while in the military, but still read over her shoulder as a refresher while she studied. He quizzed her often, and she never failed to astonish him with her quick answers. She committed the NAPWDA K9 certification guidelines and requirements to memory, making notes if she ran across something she did not understand. They practiced for hours in the backyard, which became as much play as work. When she asked what types of places they could be called to, he opted to show rather than tell so she could become more accustomed to moving around in unfamiliar environments. They made numerous trips out in public, visiting Broadway at the Beach and the Boardwalk, abandoned warehouses, retail stores, the malls, public restrooms, movie theaters, and the airport—anywhere they might have to go as a working team.

During one trip to Broadway, they met an elderly woman pushing a stroller that carried an even older Chihuahua, weighing five pounds. The tiny dog barked and snarled, spittle flying as she lunged against the padded harness holding her in place. "It's okay, Shuggie," her owner soothed, attempting to calm the enraged animal. "That big, scary dog isn't going to get you."

For her part, Saoirse did very well in ignoring the unprovoked outburst. She did not even look in the little dog's direction, dividing her attention between Travis and the moving crowds of people. Travis knelt to retie a bootlace when they were out of earshot. "What did that dog say to you?"

Saoirse stretched into a play bow. "I shall not repeat it, but the nasty little beast did not want us in her presence and showed in no uncertain terms how hard she would bite should we draw closer."

Travis nodded. "It's that little dog energy. The smaller the dog, the greater the chance of getting bit."

They visited nightclubs, local bars, and restaurants, ranging from fast-food drive-throughs to sit-down dining. Saoirse placed her orders in advance, opting to eat later. At least once a week, they stopped by the nearby Chinese restaurant for her favorite vegetable stir-fry and noodles. She even learned how to use chopsticks at home, but the slow process always had her switching to a fork halfway through her meal. The pair became a common sight and a big hit with tourists visiting the area.

"Do they not see the signs?" she whined from the backseat after a trip to one of the tall bank buildings downtown for elevator and stair practice. "I could be dangerous."

Travis blinked in confusion. "Signs?" he echoed, navigating his car through a tight construction area.

"My patches. They say *Do Not Pet*, yet parents allow their children to come so near. Why is that?"

He gave a noncommittal shrug. "I couldn't tell you. My parents taught me from day one that you don't just run up on a strange dog. And the thing is, if that happened, and you bit a child—"

"I would never do such a thing," she interrupted.

"I know you wouldn't. But for argument's sake, say you did. They would demand you be put to sleep. I'd be charged with not controlling a dangerous animal instead of the kid's parents taking responsibility for not teaching their child basic manners and common sense."

She tilted her head. "Put to sleep?"

He cleared his throat uncomfortably. "That's when the vet gives you a shot, and you go to sleep but never wake up." At her confused expression, he added, "It kills you."

The silence in the backseat stretched while she worked that out. "And they do this to dogs who bite?"

"Yeah. The dog is almost always the one punished instead of the instigators."

A low growl rumbled through the cabin. "Yet you teach me to bite. Tell me in truth—do you seek to be rid of me?"

At once, Travis threw on a turn signal and pulled over onto the shoulder of the roadway. Once the car rolled to a complete stop, he turned and propped his elbow on the passenger seat. "Absolutely not. You'll be a police officer; that's completely different from a regular pet. You know to bite only when told to, and biting is the next-to-last resort when you're trying to stop a criminal." He lowered his gaze and flushed pink as he gave her an affectionate scratch behind her ear. "And I would miss you a whole bunch."

The furred face glowed with adoration. Eyes closed, she pressed her face into his hand. "I would miss you, too."

CHAPTER 14

At long last, the day Travis dreamed about, longed for, and worked hard toward arrived. He would be the first to admit he was scared out of his wits. Taking a deep, fortifying breath, he rapped twice on Captain Bellamy's office door, then stuck his head in. "Got a moment, sir? I'd like you to meet my new girl."

Over the desktop littered with stacks of the week's reports, the captain's bushy eyebrows lifted in surprise and interest. "Come in, McLean. I can spare you a minute or two."

Travis pushed the door open and stepped aside. Saoirse pranced in, head high and proud in her new Kevlar vest with the morale patches. She picked out several herself and liked the ones that said *FUR MISSILE* and *#FAFO* best of all.

A devoted dog lover at heart, Captain Bellamy's face lit up like a neon sign. "And who is this pretty girl?" he asked, pushing away from the desk. He reached out a hand for her to sniff and ventured a hesitant scratch under her chin.

Travis's life flashed before his eyes as time ground to a screeching halt. *How could I have forgotten something as simple as... why the hell did I not think of a name?* He thought fast and came up with the closest thing possible. "Her name... is... ah...Search. Yeah, Search. I thought maybe if we got a second dog later, we could call it Seizure."

"Mal." There was a whole lot of unspoken packed into that one word.

"She's stable and very friendly, sir. Only bites when she's told. Right, girl?" he said, looking down at her.

Saoirse wagged her tail in agreement, then ran around the desk to woo the captain. She sat back on her haunches, placed one dainty paw on his knee, and gazed up with those soulful, chocolate-brown eyes. The charmed man melted on the spot. "Well, now—she looks awfully sweet to me. Is she ready to work?" He directed the question to her. "How about it, Search? Think you could find some drugs for us?"

At the mention of drugs, she stood, her body vibrating with excitement, tail whipping back and forth in a blur. Her wide, toothy grin said she was *very* ready.

"What's she trained on?"

"Everything, sir. Narcotics, explosives, apprehension, tracking—you name it."

"Huh." Captain punched an extension on his desk phone and put it on *speaker*. "Prather, do me a favor real quick—pull a pouch of narcotic scent and a distractor out of the K9 training aid kit and hide them separately, somewhere good in the locker room. Let me know when that's done—

we're testing a new dog. Maybe," he added, casting a narrowed glance at Travis.

"Yes, sir," Prather responded. A few minutes passed before his phone rang. "All done, Captain," she reported.

Captain Bellamy stood and gestured toward the office door. "Let's go see how good a handler you are."

The three walked to the rear of the precinct, stopping at the locker room door. Word travels fast, so by the time they arrived, a small crowd of officers, dispatchers, and administrative assistants had gathered to watch, adding to the already suspense-filled moment. Travis squared his shoulders and looked down at Saoirse. "Okay, Search— ready to work?" He pushed the door open and glanced around. A few officers who had already changed in or out of uniform sat on benches between rows of metal lockers. He unclipped her lead and swept his hand toward the room. Taking a deep breath, he gave the Czech command word for a narcotics search. *"Drogy."*

She darted in and began sweeping row by row, giving the seated officers an impersonal appraisal. She paused by one locker, snuffled at the closed door several times, then continued searching. Within seconds, they all heard the loud rattle of one of the closed metal doors near the back. Travis ran toward the sound, finding her in the last row, yipping and pawing at the closed door. He lifted the handle and tugged it open. Some of the smelly contents tumbled onto the floor, the locker having been stuffed full of dirty clothes and towels. He looked down at her and grinned. "Show me," he ordered.

Saoirse began bouncing straight up and down, high enough to look him directly in the eyes. "Up top?" he asked, crossing mental fingers that she remembered not to speak where anyone could hear her. When she continued jumping, he felt around on the top shelf. He pulled out a pair of dirty running shoes, which he upended and shook. The duck cloth pouch fell out of the left shoe, hitting the floor with a soft *plop*.

A cheer went up, along with a rousing round of applause. Travis knelt and scratched her shoulders. "Good job, sweetheart," he whispered. She said nothing but lunged forward and enthusiastically gave his face a thorough licking.

Travis and Search basked in the shower of applause and congratulations as they walked back to the office. Captain Bellamy nodded his approval. "Get her certified fast as you can; that's one hell of a nose she's got there." Dropping his voice to a near whisper, he added, "Damn good job, Travis. I'm impressed. Your mom and daddy would be proud."

"Thank you, sir," he answered, flushing with pride.

Still off-leash, Saoirse ran ahead and made a beeline for his desk. She plopped down in front of the bottom right drawer, pawed at it once, and then looked up at the captain with the obvious question in her eyes.

"I reckon you've earned it," he grudgingly conceded, opening that drawer to reveal at least a dozen different bags of treats. He pulled a big venison jerky strip from one and tossed it to her. She didn't hesitate, gobbling it in midair.

"Uh—"

"One word comes out of your mouth about this drawer, McLean, and I'll have you running jail transports to J. Reuben for a month."

It was a monumental struggle, but Travis held a straight face. "Wouldn't dream of it, sir."

The certification process, trials, and exams went off without a hitch. Saoirse even made a few minor missteps to avoid suspicion, but she aced the pass/fail test and completed her certification.

True to his word, Captain Bellamy did not hesitate to put them both into service—after first announcing it at the precinct, at a press conference, on all the social media accounts, and in the local newspaper. Travis took all the well-meaning congratulations in stride, but the victory at achieving what he thought of as his life's goal was surprisingly hollow. That nagging thought at the back of his mind would not shut up, playing *you couldn't have done this without her* on an endless loop. He knew his training techniques were effective, but he also knew he could not take all the credit for her stellar performance.

As they drove home from their last media appearance, Saoirse was unusually quiet. Lost in his own thoughts, Travis did not notice until she finally spoke up, startling him. "I'm sorry, do what now?"

"I asked why you are sad," she said, her voice small.

"Who said I was sad?"

"You forget I can tell these things. You smile and pretend you are happy, yet you are not. Why is this?"

"I'm fine." He shrugged. "Aren't you happy and excited?"

She fell silent, and several miles passed before she spoke again. Her words cut through all the emotional detritus and went straight into his heart. "You are not your parents."

"I have no idea what you're talking about."

"Yes, you do," she insisted. "They gave you the best of themselves, but their path is not yours. This is not what they wanted for you."

Travis whipped the cruiser into the first available parking lot and slammed it into *park*. "How could you possibly know what my parents did or didn't want?" he snapped. His knuckles turned white where they clutched the steering wheel, but he did not turn around. "You have no right to say that."

"I know this," Saoirse whispered, "because I can sense the images imprinted on your home. And the love... so much love. They wished you to find happiness in whatever path you chose."

He inhaled and forced his body to relax before he spoke. "They always thought I—"

"Travis, honey, you know you can be anything you want when you grow up." His mother's voice coming from the backseat raised the hair on his neck. "Now, whether that's a dog handler, an astronaut, a farmer, a movie star, or even a juggler in the circus—it is up to you to find where your heart is. Your daddy and I will always be proud of you, no matter what."

"That's not fair," he said in a broken whisper. "Th... this is what I want." When she did not say anything, he tried again. "It's what I've been working for." He sucked in a deep breath and nodded once. "It's what I want," he said again firmly.

The answering voice was once again Saoirse's. "It is not I you must convince."

With a jerk, he threw the car back into gear and pulled out onto the roadway. They did not speak again as they drove home. Travis told himself everything was going according to plan, but his inner voice called out the elephant in the room—*is it, though?* And for once, Travis did not have that immediate, reassuring answer.

CHAPTER 15

"**A**re we there yet?" the small voice from the back cabin whined.

"Just arrived." Travis rolled to a stop at the rear of a half dozen parked police cars. With their lights flashing, the berries and cherries created a weird strobe effect on the abandoned house and the surrounding woods. Still adjusting to the K9 Unit cruiser, he fiddled with the buttons before tugging on a fresh pair of latex gloves. "It's showtime. Are you ready for your first real deployment?" he asked in a low voice.

"Just let me at him," Saoirse giggled, snapping her teeth in a fast, staccato motion.

"Oh Jesus, I've created a little monster," he said with a chuckle. "Don't forget—biting is the next-to-last resort. We do not need any lawsuits, and I'm not trying to go to jail."

The voice from the rear transport bordered on pouty. "I understand."

Suddenly nervous, he drew in a sharp breath, held it for a long moment, and then exhaled slowly before getting out. He slammed his door a little harder than intended. Wincing, he opened the rear door for Saoirse. He grabbed her harness, snapping on the lead before moving aside to let her bound out. He took a knee, pretending to adjust her prong collar.

"This thing feels strange," she whispered, "but it is much better loosened."

"Part of the uniform. Now remember what we talked about," Travis murmured near her ear. "Do NOT get yourself hurt, understand?"

Exasperated, she rolled her eyes. "I promise," she whispered back.

"Let's show 'em how to do this." Aware of the many eyes watching them, he gave her a firm pat on the shoulder and stood up. He took two steps before he realized Saoirse was not beside him. He turned to find her sitting beside the cruiser, a pensive frown on her furry face.

He moved back and squatted in front of her, adjusting her collar again. "Nervous?"

The frown deepened. "No. I have to..." She faltered and then completed her sentence. "...you know."

"One of the best things about being a dog is that you can go almost anywhere. Do what you gotta do and let's get to work."

"You are *looking* at me," she whispered. "I cannot with you watching. Turn around, please."

Struggling not to smile, he turned his back and inspected the items on his duty belt until the quiet trickle subsided. "Ready now?"

"Ready."

Saoirse began yelping with excitement as the crowd of officers around the dilapidated porch stepped aside to let them through. Without a word, Travis waved to the sides of the house, confirming cover for the windows and back door before mounting the steps. He pounded on the front door with the flat of his fist, sending the old paint chips fluttering like dirty snowflakes. "Police K9—If you are inside this building, make yourself known. Come out now with your hands up, or you're gonna get bit," he bellowed. Saoirse kept up the energy, barking and chattering her teeth with excitement.

No answer.

He repeated the same order a second time, then a third. When there was still no response, he took a step back. One of the officers used a pry bar to force open the locked door, cracking the frame. Holding Saoirse by the harness handle, he unclasped her lead. "Police K9—last chance—come out now or you *will* get bit!"

He waited another full minute before leaning down. "*Revir*," he commanded, releasing her.

The flashing lights pulsed on the dirty, yellowed walls, illuminating the room in short bursts. The thin carpet had been beige, but time and misuse left only patches of the former color in between spreading stains and burns. This house had been abandoned for some time, and for a moment, he feared she wouldn't be able to pick up the target's scent. The gloomy interior reeked of cigarette and marijuana smoke layered over the overpowering stench of unwashed bodies, urine, mold, and human feces. He raised his flashlight to his shoulder, pointing the beam upward to light as much of the area as possible.

Saoirse dropped her nose to the ground and took off running, disappearing into the ominous darkness. Travis kept her in sight, giving her a comfortable space as she darted from room to room. Nearing the back of the house, she slowed in the narrow hallway where the bedrooms were. She scentcasted the air and raised a paw, indicating the last room on the left, the only one with a closed door.

Travis paused to listen, then turned the knob and nudged the hollow-core veneer door open. Ducking, he peeked through the crack. Once assured no ambush awaited them, he waved her ahead.

Before he could even blink, Saoirse darted inside. Her sharp gaze swept the room, which was empty save for a foul-smelling mattress, trash strewn about, and piles of discarded clothing. The louvered doors hung askew, revealing an oversized walk-in closet. The broken window allowed enough light in to illuminate the one possible hiding place.

She poked her head inside the closet and sniffed loudly. The filthy, ragged man crouched in the corner, a challenging smirk of tobacco-stained teeth peeking through his greasy beard. A boxcutter glinted in one hand, and he beckoned her closer with the other. "C'mere, bitch—I ain't afraid of you."

She tilted her head and grinned, showing every sharp tooth. "Oh? How about now?"

The officers clustered outside around each door and window, listening. Suddenly, screams of bone-chilling terror erupted from inside the house, raising the hair on the back of every neck within earshot. The shrieking man exploded through the hole in the window glass, landing flat on his face. Then, to everyone's shock, he scrambled to his feet and stumbled toward the nearest officer, dropped the razor, and held out his wrists. "Arrest me, save me," he blubbered. When the officer hesitated in disbelief, the man glanced back toward the window with wild eyes and wailed again, even louder. "IT'S COMING!"

"Clear," Travis called into his shoulder mic. The waiting officers swarmed the hysterical man to cuff and Mirandize him. He screamed and babbled all the way to the cruiser and, although muffled after the car door slammed shut, continued his unhinged howling.

Flicking his body camera off, Travis peered out the window at the spectacle just as the grinning velociraptor stuck her head out. "Little over the top, but effective," he said, chuckling.

"That man reeked of methamphetamine and was not at all nice," she retorted with a haughty sniff. "He said he did not fear the dog. I but gave him something he could be afraid of."

"Major tweaker—scared him straight, I bet," he whispered, bending to retrieve her vest as the sparkling preceded her shift back to Search. "Why didn't you take him down when he ran past you?"

"Your companions are waiting just outside, so he could not go far without being caught. Also, I do not know what a law... suit is, other than something you do not desire. You must explain so I do not err and bring one upon you."

"I can do that." He grinned as he strapped her vest back on and reattached the lead. "I am so proud of you. Ready to go mingle with your fans?"

As they stepped out onto the porch, they were met with some desperately needed fresh air and enthusiastic applause. "Good job, Search," several called out while others said, "Way to go, McLean."

He nodded his thanks and patted the victorious K9 on her shoulder. "It's all my girl here. I'm just the idiot holding the lead."

As Saoirse bounded down the steps, the prisoner in the back of the cruiser stared at the dog in wide-eyed horror. She deliberately turned her head to look straight at him and grinned from ear to ear. The terrified man began kicking the seat, banging his head against the window, and bawling his eyes out. One of the nearby officers shrugged. "He got hold of something bad, been yelling some shit about dinosaurs after him. Hey, anybody got a helmet?" he called out.

"Dinosaurs, huh?" Travis kept his face deliberately blank. "Well, he'll sober up quick enough in lockdown."

The gathered officers exploded with laughter. "That one doesn't need a jail cell—he needs a padded cell and one of them pretty white jackets with the extra-long sleeves."

CHAPTER 16

Travis stuck his head into the captain's office. "You wanted to see me, sir?"

"Uh... yeah," Captain Bellamy said, distracted. He began shuffling through drawers, at last finding the envelope he needed. "Here."

With a sinking feeling, he approached the desk to stand before it, accepting the envelope with his name handwritten on the front. "What is this, sir?"

"Tickets to the police fundraiser at the convention center. Fancy dress and all. I had hoped to get out of it, but once the missus heard about it on the radio, my goose was cooked." He shrugged and gave Travis a big smile. "We need to have our department represented there, even if we are small. And you clean up nice, from what I'm told. I imagine you'll be taking Lori Ann?"

Travis got all tangled up with the visual of Saoirse in a formal gown and was slow to answer. "Um, no. She and I called it quits a while back."

"Shame—she's a pretty girl," the captain mused. "Looks a little on the high-maintenance side, though."

He nodded solemnly. "You have no idea. I hear she's dating one of the jump-out boys now. She's all about those badges."

Captain grunted in response and craned his neck to look over his desk. "Where's your girl?"

"She's keeping the nice ladies over in Dispatch company. They're throwing the Kong for her, so I imagine they're all best friends by now."

"They better not be feeding her," the captain muttered darkly.

"Should I not mention you feeding her?" Travis asked, eyes rounded in innocence.

"I'm guessing you enjoy your job, so I would say that's a negative, Corporal."

Travis managed to tear Saoirse away from the doting dispatchers and stopped by the precinct front desk before leaving. The low, deep-throated growl startled him as he talked with the officer behind the counter.

"Hey, stranger!" Lori Ann's bright voice snapped him to attention. "I was so hoping I'd run into you here. How have you been? Seems like I haven't talked to you in *forever*—"

"Well, this is where I work, so..."

She didn't miss a beat. "—and I just wanted to stop by to see how you're doing. I've been thinking about you a lot lately. I didn't like how we left things between us, you know?" She moved in too close, and he fought the urge to step back. "I thought we could maybe get together for dinner or coffee sometime soon, just to, you know... talk?" From her husky tone, talking was the last thing on her mind.

The soft growling increased in volume. Travis glanced down and gave Saoirse a little scratch behind the ears. "Friendly," he whispered.

"Doesn't sound like it," Lori Ann said, her tone skeptical.

"Wasn't talking to you," he replied. "I'm telling her that *you're* friendly. She's very protective."

With a stern glare at the dog, she dropped her Louis Vuitton hobo knockoff to the floor with a soft *plop*. "Anyway, about dinner. I'd like that if you have time." She stepped closer to pick an imaginary bit of lint off his vest. "I've missed you."

Saoirse moved lest she be caught in the middle. Travis wondered at her sudden docility, but as social subterfuge was unfamiliar territory for her, he doubted she understood Lori Ann's true motives. "Thought you were dating Kendricks over in SWAT. Doubt he'd take kindly to that."

"Oh, him." She gave a dismissive wave and sighed. "We aren't seeing each other anymore. I guess I can't get over you."

"Uh-huh." He nodded, looking around for his exit. "Well, it was nice seeing you and—"

She moved even closer and lowered her voice. "He gave me his tickets to that police thing at the convention center, said he wasn't interested in dressing up. Are you planning to go?"

Some uniformed officers had gathered at the other end of the counter for a water cooler chat with the detectives. Before Travis could reply, a burst of uproarious laughter made every head turn to the source. He could not have asked for a better disruption. "Yeah, but I already have a date," he said, moving toward the door as a group of boisterous college students pushed their way in. "Better get to work; I'm running late. C'mon, Search," he called over the noise, patting his leg.

"McLean!" the captain barked from the doorway of his office. "Glad I caught you! Need you back here for a minute."

"Yes, sir," Travis said, moving toward the office with Saoirse trotting alongside. The captain's impeccable timing ensured the determined woman would not follow him into the parking lot. God only knew what would happen without an audience looking on.

"Let me know if anything changes—you still have my number, right?" Lori Ann called after him.

He threw up a hand in a half-hearted wave but did not turn around. The captain had questions about an open assignment, which were answered promptly. As he turned to leave, he scanned the lobby and parking lot. He exhaled with relief, seeing Lori Ann and her car nowhere in sight. He clipped Saoirse's biothane lead to her vest and headed for the front door.

"Your girl sure is jealous, McLean," the same group of officers called out to him. "You know, hell hath no fury and all that. You better watch your step."

"Lori Ann's not my girl, so—" he explained patiently, but was interrupted by more hilarity.

"We aren't talking about her."

He walked closer so they were not yelling at each other across the lobby. "Don't keep me in suspense. Who are we talking about?"

They all pointed, hooting and wheezing with raucous guffaws. "Your partner—Search."

Puzzled, Travis glanced down, but she appeared uninterested in the conversation. "You heard her growling all the way over here?"

"You turned and looked. You didn't see what happened?"

When Travis's head sliced left once in negation, Mike stepped up, struggling to get the words out as he slung an arm around his friend's shoulders. "My brother in Christ—I would be expecting another screaming voicemail in your immediate future. Search took a piss in Lori Ann's purse."

He closed his eyes and groaned. "Are you sure?"

"Yep—we watched her. Stepped right over it and squatted, looked deliberate as hell to me. I don't think she much cared for Lori Ann sidling up to you like that."

He looked down into the expressive brown eyes gazing up at him with adoration. "Did you do that?"

She yawned and looked away.

Travis shook his head with mock regret. "Not one single ounce of remorse." He struggled not to smile, but he knew they all heard it in his voice. "I appreciate the heads up on that call."

He pushed the lobby door open for her, and they headed for the cruiser. Saoirse looked back to ensure she would not be overheard. "I do not like that woman."

"So I gathered. Once she finds the present you left, I don't think she will like you, either."

She chattered, her teeth snapping together like castanets. "I care not. I could bite her, and then she would leave you alone."

If I didn't know better, I would think that's jealousy talking. "Damn—almost forgot," he said, deftly changing the subject as they reached the car. "I have doughnuts for Dispatch."

"Had."

He opened the door for her to hop into the back cabin. "What do you mean—had?"

"Had," she repeated. "Past tense of have, meaning to own or possess." She tilted her head as if questioning his intelligence.

"Are you kidding me right..." Travis got in and shook the suspiciously light bakery box. He lifted the lid and sighed. "You ate all but one of these?"

"Don't like the maple kind." She let out a hearty burp. "I like the round ones with the cream and that cinnamon spice rolled up in a spiral." When he continued to stare, she added, "You left me alone in the car for hours and hours. I saw the Specter of Death reaching for me—"

"You're immortal."

"—and knew I was caught up in the clutches of starvation. Had I not eaten those, you would have found my skeletal remains and be consumed by soul-crushing guilt for leaving me to die alone. I thought to save you that heartache."

"That's a little dramatic. I got those for the ladies in Dispatch," he repeated. "And I stopped at Circle K to grab some coffee and a cruller for you. Less than five minutes tops. Not hours."

"Felt like hours," she muttered.

He smiled and blew her a kiss in the rearview mirror. "I miss you when we're apart, too."

CHAPTER 17

When the doorbell rang once, Saoirse raced down the hallway toward Travis's bedroom. Steam rolled out of the cracked bathroom door, and both the shower and classic rock from the overhead speaker ran full blast. "Travis?" she called, but did not get a response. She tried again. "Someone is at the front door. What should I do?" When he still did not answer, she ran back to peek at the visitor through the narrow sidelight window. The clean-shaven young man in mesh basketball shorts, a t-shirt, and half-laced high-top sneakers turned and glanced around the yard before pushing the doorbell multiple times in succession. In one hand, he carried a brightly colored box.

She did not recall the name but recognized him as a friend from work, another officer. They talked often, and he had been over several times; Travis seemed to hold him in high regard. They did not frequently have visitors, but Travis always answered the door when they did. On those occasions, she became Search to avoid undue scrutiny and stayed in the back of the house. Just as the thought that she should shift occurred, she was alarmed to find the young man staring directly into her eyes. He smiled and waved with his free hand, then raised his eyebrows and tilted his head, indicating the doorknob.

Oh dear, oh dear, oh dear, he is going to be furious with me. Saoirse worried her lower lip with her teeth even as she unlocked the door and cracked it open anyway, eyeing him cautiously through the narrow slit.

"Well, hello there—call it my keen sense of observation, but *you* are not Travis," the man said with a wide grin. "He's expecting me."

She did not sense an immediate threat. Still nibbling her lip in indecision, she thought about running to Travis again but shook her head against the idea, not wanting him to think her afraid of her own shadow. Against her better judgment, she opened the door wider to allow him entry. His sharp gaze swept around the foyer before stepping inside, frowning at the large mirror covered by dark bed sheets, their edges secured by duct tape. "He *is* here, right?"

"Yes, he is bathing," Saoirse said, stepping backward toward the hall, keeping the man in sight. She glanced back over her shoulder. "He should be finished any moment. I shall announce your arrival and let him know you wish to speak with him, Mr...."

He raised a hand to halt her flight. "Hold on now, you don't have to scamper off yet. I'm Mike Reynolds, Travis's cousin. We work at the same precinct. What is *your* name?

I don't believe we've met before. I am sure I would have remembered you."

She flushed pink under his keen scrutiny. "I am Saoirse."

He winked at her and grinned. "What you are, Miss Saoirse," he said in a conspiratorial tone, "is a very well-kept secret. You are a mighty beautiful woman, so I can see why he would want to keep you all to himself." He joggled his package from one hand to the other, pretending to stagger under the weight. "If you don't mind my coming all the way inside, I'll stick these in the fridge before they get warm."

With a solemn nod, she stepped back for him to pass. He headed straight for the kitchen, opened the refrigerator, and shuffled things around on the shelves to make room for the suitcase of beer. "I'm going to help myself to one of his until these get cold again," he laughed, popping the tab on the can. "So, how long have y'all been dating?"

That question blindsided her, and she forgot all about alerting Travis to the man's arrival. Unsure what to say, she picked up a dishcloth and began wiping the spotless counter. After regaining her composure, she answered, "I do not believe we are dating."

Mike's piercing blue gaze sharpened with interest, his eyes crinkling at the outer edges as his rapidly widening smile spread. "You must be another cousin, then."

"We are not related, no."

"Just friends?" he pressed.

"I, um... I should go and see how much longer Travis will be. He will want to know you are here, Mr. Reynolds."

"I don't mean to pry," he rushed out, "and I'm sorry if I offended you, ma'am. Force of habit, I guess." His soft Southern drawl became a little more pronounced. "And Mr. Reynolds is my dad. Call me Mike, please."

Travis opened his bedroom door and padded barefoot up the hall. Hearing the voices, he briefly wondered what TV channel Saoirse had on. That last sentence, "Call me Mike, please," came from the kitchen. He ran the remaining steps and burst through the archway.

"See—speak of the devil, and he always turns up." Mike laughed, raising his beer in a toast.

"Hey, Mike... ah, good to see you," Travis said, startled. "What brings you here?"

Mike shifted his sad gaze to Saoirse. "See, this is what happens when you start getting old—memory lapses. There's other stuff too, but I forget what."

When she giggled at the corny joke, Travis rolled his eyes. "Uh-huh," he said. "So, what's up?"

"You make my soul hurt," Mike moaned, placing a hand over his heart in mock anguish. "Every year for the last, I don't know, hundred or so, we have joined together in male camaraderie to watch—"

"The Carolina/Clemson game! That's today?" Travis appeared shocked.

"Yes, that's today," Mike mimicked in a high falsetto, glancing around. "Where's Search? I expected your fur missile to meet me at the door, not a gorgeous woman."

"Uh—groomers. Let me grab a beer, and we can get settled in."

"No need to rush. We've got a few minutes before kickoff. I was just getting to know your pretty little friend here." And because Saoirse could not see him, he waggled his eyebrows suggestively.

He put too much emphasis on *friend* for Travis's peace of mind. Without a word, he threw open the fridge door, grabbed a beer, and waved for Mike to join him as he stalked out of the kitchen.

Mike followed close behind. "Hey, did somebody die?" he whispered.

Travis shook his head, puzzled. "Nobody I know of. Why?"

"Just wondering, covered mirrors and all."

Travis offered no further explanation as they plopped down next to each other on the sectional. Mike kicked his sneakers off, leaned back, and sighed with satisfaction. "I've been looking so forward to this. Y'all bougie roosters have a major ass whup coming."

"Watch your mouth, alley cat," Travis shot back good-naturedly, more relaxed now that Saoirse wasn't nearby. He puzzled over that for a moment but dismissed the idea of jealousy. *No way, I don't have any right...* Rights or not, he one hundred percent did not like what he felt at seeing his friend flirting with his... other friend. *She's more than that, though. Not just a friend. But what is she?*

The national anthem began. Trying to focus on the starting game, Travis planned to think more about that later. By the end of the song, he swore off planning altogether. What he planned versus what ended up happening were fast becoming two completely different things.

The stream of truck and beer commercials between the anthem and kickoff had barely begun before Mike blurted out, "So who is she?"

Travis groaned inwardly at the expected question. "Saoirse, you mean?" he answered, his voice mild. He gestured toward the screen in hopes of distraction. "I hope y'all got more running game than you had last year."

Like a dog with a juicy bone, Mike would not be deterred. "Yes, her. Who is she to you?"

"That's an excellent question," Travis replied. "Still working on that part, Detective."

"She said you two aren't dating. Does that mean she's avail—"

"NO," he snapped.

"Where does she live?" When Travis did not answer, Mike's bear-trap mind went to work, piecing it all together in record time. "She answered the door while you were in the shower, which indicates familiarity. Both of you are barefoot, so you're comfortable here. I made her nervous, and she started wiping the kitchen down, a familiar, repetitive action for her." His gaze darted around the immaculate room. "And your house is the cleanest it's been since your mom passed. She lives with you, doesn't she? Yeah, she does. Dude, how could you *not* tell me about her? I am *crushed*. Where is she from? How did you meet?"

Travis did not answer, instead taking a long swig of beer. He shrugged and took another drink, his gaze locked on the TV.

Mike stared hard at his lifelong friend when the unnatural silence stretched into minutes. "Something about this is wrong, and it's got you all kinds of twisted up. What the hell, Trav?"

"I'm sorry about forgetting the game. I've had a lot on my mind."

"I can see that. Now answer the question."

Travis drew a deep breath and lowered his voice so it would not carry. "You and I have been friends since we were basically eggs, right?" When Mike nodded, he continued. "I've been thinking about this a lot lately, and well... our jobs are dangerous, and much as I hate the thought of not returning home after work one day, I can't say the possibility isn't there. I need your absolute hand to God word that you won't tell anybody what I'm about to tell you. And I need you to mean it. It could be life or death if you don't."

Mike frowned, his eyebrows drawing together. "Damn it, Trav—you haven't gotten yourself into something shady, have you?"

"Oh no, nothing like that. I need, uh... in case something happened to me, she's got to be protected."

He jerked his head toward the kitchen. "Her?" he mouthed.

Travis nodded, his shoulders stiffening with resolve. "Saoirse? Could you come out here, please, ma'am?"

She popped up at once, drying her hands with the dishtowel. He patted the couch next to him for her to sit. Her nostrils flared, and her gaze darted between the two men as she did. "What is happening?" she asked. Outwardly, she looked relaxed, but he could feel her muscles vibrating in anticipation.

Travis took one of her hands in his. "Do you trust me?" When she gave him an uncertain look and nodded, he continued. "I've thought about this long and hard, and I've decided we need to tell one other person about you, just in case—well, in the worst-case scenario. I've known Mike here my whole life, and I trust him with it. So—I guess today is as good a day as any to share the crazy."

Saoirse reached for Mike with her other hand. Taking it, he yelped at the crackle of static electricity. "He is worthy of your trust. You are his brother, and he loves you," she agreed solemnly.

"What the hell—"

"Hold your questions until the end—it'll go faster that way." Travis laughed as he stood, tugging her to her feet. He led her around in front of the mounted TV and placed her in front of Mike. "She told me about it first, and I almost called the psych unit on her. This is the only way I could believe it for myself, and I still struggle with it daily." He sucked in a deep breath. "Search, please."

She shot him an incredulous look. "What do you ask of me?"

"Show him."

She shook her head furiously. "You said never, never, ever where anyone can see."

"This is different," he said, giving her a nod of encouragement.

"As you wish." She shrugged, shimmered, and shook off the pile of discarded clothing. With one big leap over the coffee table, she landed beside Mike on the couch and offered her paw for a shake. "I am K9 Search; pleased to meet you."

Moments later, Saoirse hovered anxiously while Travis waved an ammonia inhalant under the nose of his unconscious friend. "He wakes," she said in a hushed whisper, tugging her clothes back on.

Mike's eyes fluttered open, his eyes dull and glazed. "Da hell... wha... what happened?" His voice took on an accusing note. "What did y'all do to me?"

Grinning, Travis peered down at his face. "Can't say I wasn't dying to see your reaction. Never had you figured for the fainting type, though. First time I saw it, I just screamed and hit the floor."

Mike scrubbed at his face to clear the fog, then eased himself into a sitting position. His alarmed gaze darted back and forth between the couple. "I need an explanation, and I mean *right now*."

"Simmer down," Travis admonished. "So, what had happened was..." He gave him the backstory of how they met, how she became his partner, and ended with their dilemma of hiding her from Ansgar. Then he sat back to watch the fun, arms folded across his chest.

"So you're a faery." Mike's voice held no trace of question. "A real, live faery princess who does magic. Right here in Cherry Grove." He shook his head in disbelief. "Hold up—aren't all fairies supposed to have wings?"

Her answer came fast. "Do all humans have red hair?"

"You gotta admit that's a valid point, Mike," Travis said.

"I am Fae," she corrected, "but I am not a princess. I have never seen our Queen, but I have heard she is the most beautiful of all." She frowned, a cute little wrinkle forming between the delicately arched eyebrows.

Mike fixed Travis with a stern look. "Faery—uh, Fae. Non-royal variety."

"Uh-huh. Go figure."

"And this wizard dude is hunting her."

"Yup."

"And Dumbledore held her hostage for some wizardy breeding program. That's human trafficking." He gave a start, correcting himself. "Faery—Fae trafficking." He closed his eyes and groaned. "I can't even say that with a straight face."

"Sounds like it to me. And that's your area of expertise, as I understand it."

Mike fell silent for a long while, mental wheels turning. "I know this girl in the Criminal Justice program over at Tech," he finally said, turning to Saoirse. "She is studying to be a sketch artist. Would you mind talking to her? She is always looking to practice, putting her portfolio together. I'm thinking if we got a picture of this guy, we could post it and say he is wanted for questioning." He cut a sideways glance at Travis. "You know, get some more eyes out there looking for him."

Travis shook his head. "No. I can talk to her; I got a good look at him." To Saoirse, he explained, "Mike is a detective, different from what you and I do. He specializes in investigation."

She nodded in understanding. "Like Rossi."

The two men looked at each other in confusion until the proverbial light went on over Mike's head. "Not quite. Rossi is an FBI profiler; that's way above my pay grade. Would be fascinating work, though." He chuckled and gestured toward the TV. "Criminal Minds, Trav. Try to keep up."

Travis ignored that. "I think it's a good idea. I won't have to give her specific details about the case, correct?"

"We don't discuss that at all. You just describe the person of interest, and Geena recreates the face. I think you'll get a better rendering if you both talk to her. Men and women tend to notice different things. This better work. It'll cost me dinner out, ya know."

"You do not mind. She is pretty and clever. You like her very much," Saoirse remarked.

"How could you even know that?" Mike blurted, then lightly smacked his forehead. "Oh yeah, the electric thing." He narrowed his eyes and gave her a speculative look. "Do you have a last name, or haven't you gotten that far?"

She turned to Travis with a confused expression. "I need another name?"

"A surname, it's called. It tells people what family you come from. For example, my first name is Travis. My last name is McLean. My parents were Dylan and Caroline McLean. Mike's last name is Reynolds, and so on. I guess you could pick out any one you like."

Raising a finger to her lips, she considered her options and came to a swift conclusion. "Kardashian," she said brightly, rolling the r. "I like the way that sounds very much."

Both men shook their heads, struggling not to laugh. "That is a little too high-profile. Something less conspicuous would be better," Travis explained.

"The surname tells who your family is," she repeated, giving him a shy smile. "Saoirse... McLean? You are the only family I have."

Mike shot to his feet with a hand clamped over his mouth to stifle the outburst of laughter. "I definitely need another beer now. Anybody want anything?" he called back over his shoulder on the way to the kitchen.

Travis shot him a murderous glare, which triggered another bout of snickering. "What is amusing?" Saoirse demanded.

"Nothing. He's an idiot," he muttered, lost in the sudden vision of her wearing his ring and a lacy, white wedding dress. *And me helping her get that dress off...*

The insistent tapping on his leg snapped him back into the moment. "Then what name may I have?"

"Let's worry about that later, after you've had a chance to think about it. We're missing the game, and Carolina is already up two touchdowns." That last was delivered in a louder voice, directed toward the kitchen. The resounding clatter of a can hitting the floor and the muffled stream of cursing that followed was music to his ears.

"Then I shall go outside to be with the earth and think, if that pleases you," she said.

Travis dropped his voice to a whisper. "Don't worry about pleasing me. You work on pleasing yourself, okay?" He patted the hand he had just noticed still resting on his thigh. "You've been through a lot; take some time for yourself."

Saoirse nodded, rose, and skipped to her bedroom, calling back over her shoulder. "I shall wear the new outside clothing you purchased for me, my—Travis."

He opened his mouth to speak but only nodded, praying Mike had not heard that.

Of course, Mike heard that. "My Travis?" he mouthed, returning with two full beers and sitting beside him on the couch.

"Trying to get her out of that habit. The druids forced her to call them my lord whenever she said anything."

"So all this is real," Mike mused in a low voice, serious now. "For a second, I thought y'all slipped me some shrooms or something. What in the world are you going to do with her, Trav?"

"I have no idea," he admitted. "I am waiting for inspiration to strike. And I'm open to suggestions, if you have any."

They silently watched the game for a while, settling back into the overstuffed sofa. Travis leaned over to ask a question, only to see Mike's mouth open in astonishment as he gaped toward the hallway. He followed the gaze, and his heart stopped, seeing Saoirse in the new outside clothing that he for damn sure did not pick out.

There was hardly enough fabric even to call it a bikini. Delicate chains on the sides secured the three minuscule triangles in front. For a moment, he was terrified she would turn around, but at the same time, hopeful she would. His thoughts shot off in multiple directions, trying to remember where they bought the shiny gold material he thought might be underwear. Not something to be seen by the general public, and definitely not a swimsuit that showed off every single one of her—*Jesus*—assets.

"Have mercy," Mike whispered under his breath.

Saoirse turned from side to side and spun around, modeling. "I told the saleswoman that you said I needed specific clothes to wear near the sea. She brought me lots to try on but said this would be your favorite. It did not seem like much of a covering to me. I asked if she were sure, but she was positive you would think it perfect."

"Perfect," Mike echoed, his voice faint.

Travis growled at his friend. He sucked in a deep breath, then exhaled slowly. "It is very pretty. Is, ah... is there something you're supposed to wear over it?" he asked hopefully through gritted teeth.

"Oh, yes." She beamed, shaking out the fistful of gauze he had not noticed. Slipping on the sheer wrapper, she tied it at the waist, turning this way and that to show it off. The diaphanous fabric barely reached her upper thighs and did a poor job of hiding anything beneath. "Does it please you?"

"It's very nice," Travis choked out, flapping his hand in dismissal. "It's supposed to rain later. You should go now before it starts clouding up."

She bobbed in a quick curtsey, then darted for the back door, closing it behind her with a firm *click*. He fell back against the couch, tilted his head toward the ceiling, and closed his eyes. "Not one single word," he warned.

"Soooo... is she available or—"

Eyes still closed, Travis did not let him finish. "I know how to make you disappear without a trace. I'll even organize a search party and help look for your sorry ass while I'm writing your eulogy and wiping away the tears. NO, she is *not* available."

All Mike could do was laugh.

The next hour passed quickly. The football game long forgotten, Mike plied him with question after question. "I'd love to see the raptor sometime," he admitted, laughing when Travis told him about that first evening. As yet another idea occurred to him, he asked enthusiastically, "Have you shown her Game of Thrones yet? Man, flying over the ocean on a real dragon would be—"

"Stop. It." He tried to keep his face blank, but he had to admit that the idea was beyond intriguing and could not hold back a broad grin. "Riding my girlf—faery—Saoirse is out of the question."

"Do you think she could talk to Bo, maybe tell him to stop digging infantry foxholes in my backyard? It looks like we're under siege or something."

"It's a dog thing. He is gonna dig whether you like it or not. You should set him up a designated area."

Waving that idea away, Mike pressed on. "And she can talk to you while she's an animal. No wonder y'all are getting famous."

Travis went still. "Famous?"

"Dude, I hear about you all the time from other units around the state singing your praises. One of the SLED guys even asked if I thought you would consider transferring."

He frowned. "I'm not sure famous is good, considering I'm trying to hide her."

Mike did not seem to notice his dilemma. "You know, your hostess skills leave a lot to be desired. I require sustenance. Pizza good with you?" Without waiting for an answer, he unlocked his phone and scanned his contacts.

"Sure," Travis replied faintly.

Mike called in an order for several pies and then headed for the kitchen, asking over his shoulder, "Want a bottle of water?" The refrigerator door opened and thumped closed, followed by an ominous silence. "Hey, Martha Stewart—you got somebody new doing the landscaping in your backyard?"

Travis snorted with laughter. "Wiseass. So many dogs have pissed back there, I don't think the grass will ever—" Belatedly recognizing the ulterior motive, he leapt to his feet and raced to the kitchen, suddenly afraid Saoirse had removed her *outside clothing* to get more sun.

Mike stood before the kitchen window, staring outside with his mouth agape and eyes rounded like saucers.

Travis glanced out the window, and his own jaw hit the floor. "What th—"

The packed dirt and anemic yellow patches were gone, replaced with a lush, verdant carpet of Bermuda grass. As they watched, thick vines bearing heavy, exotic flowers in a riot of color slithered up and coiled around the equipment like rainforest snakes in snarls of dark green. Travis could smell the sultry blooms all the way from the kitchen; intoxicating floral and spicy scents that filled his nostrils, doing funny things to his insides. The bumblebees had already arrived, moving eagerly between bright petals, collecting their nectar.

"Look at that," Mike murmured, pointing to the far corner of the yard. As they watched, a small twig pushed itself up from the last remaining bald patch, growing taller by the moment. It rose higher, sprouting branches, then leaves. When it reached the fifteen-foot mark, tiny buds began popping out, and within seconds, they ripened into fat, red fruit.

Saoirse lay face up on the thick grass, her arms flung out wide, eyes closed, and a sweet smile curving her lips. Tiny wildflowers sprouted and blossomed around her still, prone figure. A kaleidoscope of butterflies flitted around her like courtiers near their queen, swooping close and then winging away. Some were the familiar bright-colored swallowtail and monarchs, even the little white dusters so common in the South. Others were blue or purple, and a few in shades he had never seen before. She threw her arms over her head and stretched languorously, putting a dangerous strain on those bits of fabric covering her generous breasts.

Mike exhaled in a soft moan, ending in an *oof* when Travis thumped him hard on the chest.

That. Was. It. He threw open the back door and burst into the backyard, Mike hot on his heels. "Saoirse?" he called.

"I am here." She gave him a serene smile as she sat up, shading her eyes with her hand. "Is it not a most beautiful day?"

"Uh-huh," Mike mumbled.

Ignoring his besotted cousin, Travis focused on the woman damaging his calm. He swept his hand around the backyard. "Is all this you?"

She blinked, seeing the flowers as if for the first time. Grabbing her wrapper, she slipped it on and scrambled to her feet, scattering the butterflies. "Our kind affects nature in ways consistent with our season. I am Springborn, which means growing things respond to my mood. I am happy, so..." Spying the tree with its branches bowing under the weight of its bounty, she burst into merry laughter, and more blooms opened in answer to the joyous sound.

"Can she come over and catch some rays in my garden?" Mike whispered. "I'm having one hell of a time getting anything to—"

"Are you *trying* to die?" Travis snapped, then softened his voice as he turned back to Saoirse. "It's fine, just a little startling. Could you not do trees, though? The neighbors can see those, and I can't explain a full-grown fruit tree that just popped up out of nowhere."

She gave him a solemn nod. "I shall do my best." Without waiting for an answer, she ran to the tree and picked several low-hanging fruits, cradling them as she returned and presented them to Travis. "These are delicious, but I do not know your word for them."

He scratched his head as he took one, turning it over in his hand. "I think they're pomegranates," he said, pulling out his pocketknife. The sweet red juice dripped as he cut around the diameter and then twisted it apart.

Mike eagerly took a piece and popped several jeweled arils into his mouth. "Yeah, I love these. What are they called in... ah... your language?"

She smiled and made a tinkling sound like a music box. At their startled expressions, she continued speaking in her native tongue, the chiming notes rising and falling in a hypnotic melody. The spell broke when Mike swayed dangerously, a tranquil smile on his face. Travis dove to catch his friend, easing him to the ground. "Turn it off," he whispered.

Wide-eyed, Saoirse clapped her hand over her mouth. Mike's glazed expression sharpened at once, and his gaze narrowed at Travis. "What just happened?"

"She throws off this faery ecstasy vibe that turns your brain into oatmeal," he explained. "I'm still learning, but I think it's like hypnotism. Shopping with her is an experiment in terror; she attracts salespeople like flies to honey."

Ignoring them both, she shaded her eyes again and glanced up into the sky. "The storm will be here very soon."

Mike looked skeptical, seeing nothing but blue skies and feathery cirrus clouds. "I thought it wasn't supposed to rain until late tonight."

"Do you not smell the water and lightning?" Even as she spoke, a low rumble of thunder sounded far off in the distance. She cast an uneasy glance toward the west and sniffed. "There is more than storm on this wind," she murmured.

Travis did not like the sound of that. "Is it him?"

"I cannot be certain, but I have seen him command the weather when it suits him."

Unthinking, he held his arm out in a protective gesture, and Saoirse moved into the shelter it provided. "Maybe we should go back inside now," he suggested, turning them both toward the back door.

Mike fell into step behind them with an aggrieved snort. "Friends, my ass. Yeah, y'all are dating whether you want to admit it or not," he added with a quiet chuckle.

Travis asked Saoirse to change clothes for his own peace of mind and join them. The pizzas arrived soon after, and they polished them off while watching the rest of the game. It ran into overtime—the Gamecocks pulled out a last-minute Hail Mary victory, leaving Travis whooping with joy, Saoirse confused, and Mike in an exaggerated sulk. "It's a good thing those refs are Gamecock fans, or y'all would never have won," he grumbled.

A sharp clap of thunder made them all jump. "Storm's getting close," Travis murmured.

Mike rose to his feet and stretched, winking at Saoirse. "I'm going to head for home before the rain starts. I can't have all this hotness melting." He struck a heroic pose, thrusting his chin up comically.

When she giggled in response, Travis could not keep the mischievous spark out of his eyes. "You're just encouraging him, you know."

Mike broached the earlier subject as they walked to the front door. "I meant that about my garden. My tomatoes are tragic. It's like the hornworms are running an all-you-can-eat buffet before they even get ripe," he moaned. "I hate the little bastards, but I'm not down with the idea of putting poison out. Bo likes a good tomato right off the vine now and then."

"I should very much like to see your garden," Saoirse said. "If I can help it heal, I would be pleased to do so."

"We'll just have to figure a way to sneak you out, so your watchdog doesn't get his boxers in a bunch," Mike's voice dropped to a stage whisper.

Travis shot him with a warning look before bursting into laughter. "We'll talk about it another day if you live that long." He smiled and offered his hand. When Mike clasped it, Travis pulled him into a bear hug. "Thanks, man. I appreciate you," he whispered near his ear. "I knew I could count on you to have my back. Means a lot."

Mike's chest rumbled with laughter. "I know you'd do the same for me. And I can't wait to see how all this plays out." With a quick smile at Saoirse, he waved and began whistling a jaunty tune as he turned to leave.

Despite his reputation as a no-nonsense detective, Mike had a secret soft spot for Disney animated movies, often playing them at home on loop for background noise. Travis sat through more than his share over the years while hanging out at Mike's. He recognized the tune from one of those films and burst into laughter at the image of Saoirse as the big, blue genie:

Come on, whisper what it is you want—you ain't never had a friend like me!

CHAPTER 18

They stood at the front door waving as Mike backed out of the driveway, honked twice, and sped off. "What are your plans now?" he asked as they went back inside.

"If there is nothing you require, I thought I might clean up a bit, then perhaps read."

Travis shook his head. "Nope, you're not the maid here." He marched her back into the great room and directed her to the couch. "I've got a little tinkering I want to do in the garage, so you just sit back, relax, and read or watch some TV, okay?"

She nodded solemnly, touching the remote to turn off the TV. "Is there aught I can do to help you?" Picking up her current read, an old history textbook with lots of pictures, she cradled it against her chest.

He shook his head. "Nah, I got it. Thank you, though." He turned and disappeared down the hallway, reappearing moments later in a pair of baggy, paint-splattered sweatpants, and a muscle tee. He paused at the kitchen entrance, an unreadable expression on his face. "I need to move the car out, but I'm not going anywhere. I'll be in the garage if you need anything."

Smiling, Saoirse nodded as he left. She laid the open book on the table when she heard the rumble of the garage door opening, followed by the car engine turning over. With a furtive glance toward the kitchen, she dropped to her knees and stuck her arm under the couch, feeling around until she found the stack of magazines hidden there. Her head cocked sideways, listening. When faint music started playing, she grabbed several off the top and scrambled back onto the couch. Sitting cross-legged, she spread the glossy magazine across her lap. The monthly editions of Cosmopolitan, Vogue, and Allure had been rescued from the garage, fished out of the tied stacks of old newspapers bound for the recycling center. Addressed to Travis's mother, they were years old, but she reasoned they may still have valuable information to offer.

She frowned at some of the images, confused. Things were so much simpler in her time, but try as she might, she did not recall ever seeing a fine lady in the dwellings or at any of the rituals. From what she had read so far, being a desirable woman in this day and age required much more toil and planning than she first thought. Disheartened, she did not know where to begin. The only woman she had met once held Travis's affection, so she started there. Saoirse had never seen a woman so tall or with hair so yellow that it was almost white.

She closed her eyes to get the mental picture. The woman had paint around her eyes, a sort of kohl that lined and darkened her lashes. Her cheeks were an unnatural pink, so those had been painted, too. She had a bright, shiny lip gloss that caught the light. The perfume she wore would have been pleasant had she not bathed in it. Having no paints or scents such as those, she hesitated to ask Travis to purchase them for her. Of a certain, they were costly and worth coin better spent elsewhere. Saoirse gave an inward sigh, vowing to make the best of what few womanly gifts she had.

She had gotten through one magazine and reached for the next when it thundered again. The first fat raindrops struck the windowpanes, leaving sparkling water trails as they streamed down. Closing her eyes, she relaxed into the soothing pitter-patter of the summer storm and weaved a small fantasy, imagining herself as Travis's lady and seeing him smile just for her.

For a long while, the garage had been silent except for muffled music. Her curiosity quickly overcame her desire to learn. Stuffing the magazines back into their hiding place, she tiptoed through the kitchen to investigate.

The metal garage door was open to the front yard, a light breeze ruffling Travis's hair as he knelt with his back to her near a large machine. It lay on its side, a layer of newspapers underneath protecting the concrete. Saoirse eased in, watching with fascination as he worked with the metal piece in his hand, turning something with a ratcheting sound. He swore softly, dropped that wrench, and reached for another out of the nearby toolbox. The music appeared to be coming from the cube Travis called a Bluetooth, even though it was not blue and looked nothing like any tooth she had ever seen.

It thundered again, louder this time. Travis paused momentarily to touch his phone, increasing the volume, and advancing to the next song. He hummed while continuing to work the metal part in his hands. She thought he had a pleasant voice, wondering if she had ever heard him sing.

The humidity in the garage had risen with the rain, and a thin sheen of sweat covered the lean muscles of his shoulders and tattooed arms. She inhaled deeply, drunk on the combined scents of virile man, rain, soap, sweat, and machine oil. Powerless to leave, she inched several tentative steps closer, inadvertently bumping into the worktable and knocking over a spray can perched on the edge.

His head jerked in her direction, but he relaxed and smiled as soon as he saw her. "Hey, you."

"I am sorry, I did not mean to interrupt your work," she murmured, suddenly bashful.

He grabbed a rumpled bandana and rose to his feet, mopping his face. "You're not disturbing me," he explained, waving a hand toward the pieces on the floor. "I'm not making a lot of headway."

"What is that?" she asked, glancing past him.

He did not give an immediate answer. When he finally spoke, his voice seemed far away. "It's a motorcycle, belonged to my dad. We used to come out here on rainy afternoons, drink beer, listen to music, and work on it together, when he was alive. Never did get it running, but we always had hope, you know?"

"You miss him very much," Saoirse said firmly.

"Yeah, I do," he agreed with a soft chuckle. "Mom used to come out with us sometimes, but they'd always end up dancing while I worked." The current song, an early Bon Jovi tune, began to fade out.

A small crease appeared between her brows as she pursed her lips and frowned. "Dancing? I do not know this word."

At that moment, the sweet opening notes of *Wonderful Tonight* filled the garage. Rising to his feet, Travis wiped his hands on the rag and tossed it onto the bike. "Kind of hard to define. Let me show you." His smile widened as he held out his hand.

She gave him a wary look but took his hand, gasping when he pulled her close. "Easy now, I'm not going to bite," he chided gently, sliding his other arm around her waist. "Just listen to the music." He began swaying with the slow beat, smiling into her hair when he felt her body relax and mold into his. "Not so bad, right?"

After a couple of bars, he murmured against her ear. "Now we add a little more." He stepped out to the right, pulling her along in a gentle box step. She picked up on the pattern, mirroring his movements as she placed her hand near his shoulder for balance.

When he ventured a turn, she followed his lead as if they had been dancing together for years. Curling her hand into his chest, he pulled her closer and began singing softly:

We go to a party, and everyone turns to see
this beautiful lady, that's walking around with me

Her face flushed with heat, Saoirse turned her head so he would not see. When the song ended, he did not release her as she expected. Another song started, but she did not hear it. Travis curled a finger under her chin and lifted her face to meet his. His hungry expression struck her like a bolt of lightning, her lips parting in a soft gasp as he bent his head to hers. His lips brushed hers once, then twice, with a featherlight touch. Her fingers curled around his arm, and the kiss deepened in a whirlwind of sensations. The room began to turn in a slow spin. She could not catch her breath, but decided she needed him more than air.

The kiss ended far too soon, if her opinion counted for aught. Travis tightened his arm around her when she trembled and swayed, looking down at her in concern. "Are you okay?" he asked.

"I am not sure," she admitted. "I feel very odd."

He turned a skeptical glance toward the open garage door and the pouring rain. "Do you need to go outside and do that thing you do?"

"No, this is different," she explained. "I feel warm and lightheaded. My stomach is fluttery, and my limbs are weak. I have not experienced this before." She looked up to meet his gaze, confused by the myriad emotions she recognized in his eyes. He smiled down at her with tenderness, a sort of pride, and another she did not know. Her nostrils filled with the addictive aroma she had longed to smell again, the wild and musky male scent that meant he wanted her. "What have you done to me? Is this a kind of magick?"

"I guess in a way it is." His chest rumbled with laughter as he pulled her against his chest. "And as to what I'm doing, I don't have the first clue. I should be asking what *you* are doing to *me*."

Her lips curved in a secret, completely feminine smile. "I like your dancing very much. We could do more of this, should it please you."

The motorcycle lay forgotten as the hours passed. Saoirse proved a quick study, picking up the different dance styles intuitively. Darkness crept in while she got the hang of Shagging. "This is just the basics," he explained. "I'm not trying to do all that peacocking with the fancy steps. I think it's somewhere in the statutes that you have to learn it, being as it's the state dance." He gave her a double spin, making her laugh with delight. "It got dark on us," he noted with surprise. "I should probably clean up out here, and then we can eat. Did you dance up an appetite?"

She nodded and grinned. "Oh yes, m—Travis. I am always hungry."

He grunted as he lifted the bike upright and lowered the kickstand, giving her a sideways glance. "I sure wish I had your metabolism," he muttered.

"My what?" she asked, her eyes wide. "If you wish it so, it is yours."

He burst out laughing. "It's not something you can give away, although I do appreciate the gesture. If I ate every time I got hungry, I'd be as big as a house. You get to eat as much as you want, but..." He turned away, casting his face in shadow. "You still look amazing."

Her heart skipped several beats at his quiet words. Fighting the overwhelming impulse to hug herself with delight, she murmured, "Thank you," her voice barely audible over the rain. He began wiping off his tools and putting them away. When he did not say anything else, she cleared her throat. "I shall go prepare our food," she said, a little louder than necessary.

He jumped, startled. "Sounds good," he said. "I'll only be another few minutes."

She wondered if he had forgotten her presence so quickly, but dismissed the idea as he was clearly focused on his task. With a tight nod, she turned and disappeared into the kitchen.

Heart heavy with regret, Travis watched her go, his shoulders sagging when the kitchen door closed behind her. *I'm just a human, you know,* he thought. *I can only withstand so much temptation. What in the world am I going to do with you?*

You know what you'd like to do, his inner voice teased. *She's obviously attracted to you. You'd jump her in a New York minute if she gave you any kind of encouragement. She's living here; anybody in their right mind would be all over that—*

And it still wouldn't be right, he growled, and for once, his little shoulder demon didn't have anything else to say.

CHAPTER 19

Ansgar stalked through the forest for seemingly endless hours, the abundance of pine trees pungent but not unpleasant. The lunula vibrated in his hoodie pocket occasionally, working as a homing beacon to correct his course. *This is taking far too long; that old fool Pendaran Dyfed will arrive any day now.* He did not know if this passage of time and his were the same. There was so much he did not understand, and even more he had forgotten.

He almost had the fae last night, having found a mirror in an abandoned house. It was much finer in quality than he was accustomed to, making the simple spell even more potent. He had her in his control and moving toward his outstretched hand when the mirror suddenly exploded, giving him a deep gash across his bicep.

His arm throbbed as if in sympathy. He glanced down at his blood-soaked sweatshirt, sniffed once, and frowned. This clothing stank of the former owner, but in fairness, the dead needed no clothes. Although Ansgar would have enjoyed a good fight to vent his frustration, the prudent choice had been to kill the vagrant quickly and take what he needed.

This land was one of the strangest he had ever seen. Many green pastures held cattle, but only a scattering of horses. The few mounts he came across were old and on their last legs. He needed something strong and fast if he had any hopes of closing the great distance he sensed between him and his rebellious faery. He thought again of her unknown rescuer, cursing that he had not seen a face. The voice ordering her to change had been deep and male. His mind kept returning to the young warrior he encountered when he first arrived, that foolhardy whelp who called him by another's name and did not tremble with fear in his presence. He recalled the boy's look, but not his voice.

Darkness had fallen, cloaking his large form as he moved through the trees without a whisper of sound. He knew there were wild animals about, but they gave him a wide berth. He saw signs of boar, bear, and rabbit, and once he startled a young hind into flight. Eschewing the distasteful thought of hunting, he continued his journey, vowing to find food at the next settlement.

An unusual thunder rumbled in the distance, but the sky did not appear heavy with clouds. Intrigued by the strange sound, Ansgar decided to investigate. He reasoned that it was coming from somewhere directly ahead of him, still in the general direction he needed to travel. The noise grew louder as he closed in, raised voices and music mingling with throaty growls. There were women here, their irritating girlish squeals audible over the din. His cock stiffened even as his stomach grumbled, and the ghost of a sardonic smile curved his lips. He needed real food and a whore as soon as possible. On second thought, the whore might have to wait as he took care of his baser needs first.

He came to a large dwelling centered in a packed dirt clearing but hung back, watching from the woods. Several additions had been made to the original structure, but all were weathered from age and the elements. He squinted at the hand-painted sign over the door, puzzling over the letters he recognized as ancient Greek.

The approaching rumble caught his attention as a dozen or more strange vehicles rolled up to others like them and stopped. Men and women dismounted, talking and laughing as they disappeared inside the house. His eyes narrowed in speculation, realizing this place was the source of what he had thought to be thunder. He could drive one of these... the word *hogs* suddenly flashed, and he nodded, remembering. Several riders matched him in size, and his plan began to take form.

Carried by the light breeze, a tantalizing aroma caught his immediate attention, and his mouth watered. Easing around the treeline, he followed the smell to the back of the building. A lone woman stood near a fire pit where two suckling pigs hung suspended. A partially carved carcass covered in a transparent fabric rested on a nearby table. She held a small bucket in one hand, slathering a thick liquid over the cooking meat with a brush. The droplets sizzled as they hit the fire below, sending more delectable smoke his way. He watched with keen interest while she completed her task. Small and slender, she wore a scandalous sort of short pants that revealed the lower cheeks of her ass and the black sleeveless *léines* like the other riders. Hers had been cut in half to reveal her torso. A mass of unbound blond curls hung down her back. It swayed with her movements as she hung the bucket on a protruding hook, exchanging it for a long-necked bottle. Strange runes adorned her soft arms and stomach, visible below unbound, apple-like breasts. With a gentle touch like a summer breeze, his mind reached out to hers, searching for magicks but found none. *A simple beast, naught more*, he realized.

She was oblivious to him, tipping the bottle she held up to drink. Tables laden with bowls and boxes of food sat near boxes on the ground filled with ice, cans, and bottles. He glanced around to ensure they were alone and spoke, using the voice of compulsion. "Bring me food and drink, woman."

Startled, she whirled at his voice and then automatically began loading a paper plate with potato salad, slaw, baked beans, mac and cheese, and several large hunks of roasted pork. The plastic fork fell unused to the ground as he snatched the plate from her outstretched hands and began shoving the food into his mouth, barely slowing to chew. She popped the cap off a dark bottle and handed it to him, then, like a cornered animal, backed up slowly until her legs contacted the table edge. *Clever lass.*

He watched her in dark amusement, draining the beer with one continuous swallow and dropping the empty near his feet. With his hunger and thirst slaked, he tossed the plate away and exhaled with a loud belch, ready to indulge other appetites. "Come," he ordered, curling his fingers in an imperious beckoning gesture and releasing her from the spell of coercion. It was a game he oft played with himself. He found their futile struggles and fear much more exciting when his women were not compelled to obey his every command.

Even in the glow of the firelight, she paled, her eyes widened in abject terror. "You ain't one of the Own," she whispered. "We don't want no trouble here. Who are you?"

He was on her in two strides, his large hand seizing a handful of tangled ringlets to yank her head back. "I am not one to question," he hissed. Her mouth opened wide as she drew in a deep breath to scream, but he slapped his other hand over her lips and nose, pressing hard to cut off all the airflow. "Make no sound, and you may just survive this night. Do you understand?" Without waiting for a response, he dragged the struggling woman away into the looming darkness.

Half an hour had passed before he reappeared near the cooking pigs. The back door of the dwelling banged open, and a man exited. Clad in black jeans, a torn t-shirt, a leather jacket, and heavy, unlaced combat boots, he held another of those brown ale bottles in his hand. "Candy?" he called out, glancing around. "Where'd you get off to, girl? Them pigs gonna burn if you ain't watching after them."

Ansgar sized the man up, realizing he and the youth were close enough in size. "She is away," he said, stepping out into the light. "But you appear to have your wits about you. Is one of these yours?" He gestured toward the motorcycles.

In the split second that followed, a gun appeared in the man's hand. "Who the fuck are you?" he demanded as he stalked forward, pointing it straight at the druid's head.

Ansgar held up a hand and whispered a few words in a forgotten tongue. At once, the man's eyes glazed over. His face blank, the pistol slipped from his hand into the grass. "Now then," the druid ordered, stooping down to retrieve the weapon. He gestured with it toward the bikes. "Which of these motorcycles is yours?"

The young man smiled despite being under compulsion. "That one," he said with pride. "They just finished the paint today." The black Low Rider S gas tank had been decorated with those same Greek letters and an elaborate scene showing a dark avenging angel standing over a deep crevice from which thousands of locusts were escaping.

The druid nodded with approval and gestured toward the woods. "The woman went this way. I will take you to her while you explain how these things work. And remove your clothes—I have need of them."

Ansgar was on his way again in twenty minutes, astride the powerful Harley. The boots and strange clothing fit well, but smelled of sweat and smoke. The inevitable uproar would soon be miles behind him, assuming anyone cared to investigate the disappearances tonight. When he stumbled over Candy's body, the man saw his own death on Ansgar's face and attempted to run, to no avail. Ansgar's hands clamped around his throat, and the man fought desperately until the last drop of his life was squeezed out. He now lay next to what remained of the woman on the forest floor. Killing the boy proved as enjoyable as he hoped, and with all his needs satisfied, he was again ready to hunt.

CHAPTER 20

As promised, Mike and Geena came over a few nights later on their way out to dinner. Travis met them at the door, inviting them into the great room. With the TV off, he turned on the overhead lights for the artist. The pretty brunette brought a leather satchel, opening it to reveal a thick binder, her sketch pad, and various types of pencils and charcoal. She laid her tools out on the coffee table, working briskly and efficiently.

Saoirse joined them, bearing a tray of glasses filled with ice and sweet tea. She placed it at the opposite end of the table and sat next to Travis on the sofa. He took her hand and gave it a gentle squeeze of encouragement. When she offered him a tremulous smile, he leaned over to whisper directly in her ear. "If it gets to be too much, just slip out. They'll understand."

"Just to confirm—Michael hasn't told me anything about this case, so I have no idea what's happened or why you're looking for this person. Now then"—Geena smiled, holding the binder out to Travis—"I start by choosing a similar head or face and building from there. Look through these and see if any seem close."

Travis flipped through several pages of models with Saoirse peering over his shoulder. "There," they said in unison, pointing at the same photo.

She took the notebook back and laid it open on the coffee table. Her hand lingered over the pencils before making her selection. Long moments stretched while she sketched the outline of the face and head, the scratching of her pencil the only sound in the room. "Now, tell me as much as you can remember about him. Even the tiniest details will help."

When Saoirse hesitated, Travis quickly spoke up. "Maybe in his early forties, black hair, thin, salt-and-pepper beard. And a long scar that runs from the corner of his right eye down into the beard. Straight, like from a razor," he added.

Mike just sat quietly and listened while they discussed the druid. Travis gave a general description while Saoirse added the finer points. Geena nodded as she occasionally drew back to look at her unfinished work, tilting the pad toward her so the other couple could not see it. She frowned, then smudged and sketched more. "Describe his eyes for me."

Dead, Travis thought. "They're narrower, like this," he said, pointing to a photo in the binder. "And his nose is like this one, pointy and kinda hooked."

"Any jewelry or tats? Other scars?" she asked.

That was a good question, as Travis had only seen him wearing his druid robes. He glanced over at Saoirse, who glanced away to avoid his scrutiny. "He has runes painted all over his body," she admitted in a small voice. "He is strong and muscular but scarred from grave burns to his arm and chest."

"He's taller than me by a few inches," Travis added in a rush, wondering just how she knew what his body looked like under the heavy tunic. That quick flash of anger he had come to recognize as jealousy flared. "Stocky build. And he had some weird bones and feathers twisted up in his hair and beard."

Mike rolled his eyes. "Nothing says crazy faster than wearing body parts."

"He wears a metal amulet," Saoirse mumbled, "but I do not recall if he had it on when..." her voice trailed off.

"I like your ink, by the way," Geena commented, continuing to draw.

"Thanks," Travis said, casting a smug smile at Mike. "These took a while."

"He's an endorphin junkie," Mike snapped good-naturedly. "I get woozy from a splinter. They'd have to knock my ass out to do sleeves like those."

"Yours are nice, but I meant hers," she admitted with a smile, waving the pencil toward Saoirse. "I've never seen glitter tats like those, especially not on the face. It must have hurt, but they're very striking."

Saoirse touched her fingertips to the telltale markings and ducked her head shyly. "Thank you," she said.

"Don't let Mike kid you—he's a tough guy," Travis teased. "He's got a little ink himself."

Ignoring that, Mike sat up to look at the canvas and blew out a low whistle. "If this is your man, he looks like he just walked off a *Sons of Anarchy* set."

Geena turned the pad around and held it up for inspection. "Did I get him?" she asked.

Travis stared in stunned silence while Saoirse covered her mouth to catch the jagged gasp. Unable to speak, she nodded.

"We need to get that sketch out as soon as possible," Travis said, adding, "You did a fantastic job."

"Thanks," she said, holding out her pencil. "He's one scary-looking freak. Hopefully, this will help get him caught fast. Would y'all mind signing the back for me as witnesses?" When Saoirse hesitated, Travis put his signature at the bottom and added the date.

Everyone jumped as Mike's phone buzzed with two back-to-back incoming texts. "Well, that's never good," Mike quipped. He scanned the messages, paled, and stood. "Excuse us a moment," he said curtly. Striding toward the kitchen while dialing, he waved for Travis to follow.

Travis patted Saoirse on the knee as he stood. "You're doing great," he whispered as he stepped around her. By the time he reached the kitchen, Mike was already talking to someone, speaking in a rapid but hushed voice. It went on for another minute before Mike hung up. "That was my buddy in SLED. Major clusterfuckery just broke," he explained, pocketing his phone. "We have a problem."

Eyebrows raised, Travis did not have to wait long for clarification. "Somebody hit the Apollyon's Own clubhouse last night at a pig roast. Tore two of them into little pieces in the literal sense. Nobody saw anything or got a description, but at least one bike was stolen. They're going scorched earth on the other one percenters. Everybody's got smoke with everybody else as it is. Either way, bodies are going to start piling up if we can't get this sorted out fast. JDLR, man."

"What just doesn't look right?" Saoirse's cryptic words came floating back. *There is more than storm on this wind.* At once, Travis whipped out his phone and began searching for a state map, his finger blurring as he scrolled. "Where's their clubhouse?"

"Right smack in the middle of WishSomeone Woods. I don't remember the real name, but it's just outside Lake City," Mike answered. "Just a hunch, but I think we know where our guy is."

Travis stared at the screen for a few long, tense moments, plotting the course between the little motel and his house. Lake City sat just over halfway between the two, a mere hour and a half drive away. He looked up and met Mike's worried gaze, mirroring his own, then nodded in agreement.

"Headed here."

CHAPTER 21

O ver the years, Mike had often crashed in Travis's spare bedroom, considering it his home away from home. His roommate, a happy-go-lucky individual named Lebowski, frequently tagged along. Mike insisted Bo was a super-sized Labrador retriever and pit bull mix. Travis disagreed—his guess was an unfortunate pairing with a Cane Corso and Zuul from the first Ghostbusters movie. Whatever his lineage, the dog fell head over heels in love with Saoirse. He followed her everywhere, including into the bathroom if she wasn't quick enough to close the door behind her. The feeling was mutual, and they often found Bo and Search playing together in the backyard or splashing around in the portable kiddie pool.

"Are you able to talk to him? Like an actual conversation?" Mike asked, curious.

Saoirse pondered that, searching for the right words. "In a way, yes. He thinks more in images but feels deeply. He finds it frustrating when he tries to communicate, but no one understands. I did let him know that the hole digging must stop."

Currently, the digger-in-chief sprawled on the floor next to Mike's chair as they sat cleaning their weapons at the kitchen table. "I can't stress to you enough how dangerous this guy is," Travis explained, wiping the excess gun oil off his fingers. "He sized me up as soon as I walked into the motel lobby. Saoirse has told me stories about him that will raise the hairs on your neck."

"Have you given any thought to what exactly we're going to do when he shows up?" Mike wondered, reaching down to give Bo an ear scratch. "Can a jail even hold him, or would he just Harry Potter his way out?"

Travis said what they were both thinking out loud. "I don't see any way of stopping him that doesn't involve me getting brought up on manslaughter charges. No," he continued before Mike could object, "even if you're the shooter, I'm still taking responsibility. This is my mess."

"Our mess," Mike corrected.

"The mess is mine," Saoirse said firmly from the doorway. "I will not see either of you harmed for my sake." She nipped at her lower lip and straightened, throwing back her shoulders like a tiny warrior. "I will protect you, but should it become clear that I cannot, I will surrender myself."

Travis struggled not to smile. While he was sure she had a multitude of terrifying powers he knew nothing about, all he could see right then was a fierce little kitten hissing and spitting. "*We* will protect *you*," he assured her.

Mike nodded absently, reaching for the pieces of his firearm to reassemble it. "No offense, ma'am, but Trav and I trained for years in—"

Her gold eyes flashed in warning right before she vanished, empty clothing falling to the floor. Suddenly, an ear-splitting roar filled the kitchen, along with one very large, very pissed-off velociraptor.

A thunderous crash reverberated around the room as the table flipped, followed by a whooping yowl and a bang when Bo fled the scene through the doggie door, and loud thuds as all masculine dignity and bodies hit the floor. Only one sat back up. "You make a valid point, sweetheart." Travis laughed. "Why don't you get dressed while I get another ammonia ampoule for Braveheart here."

Weeks passed with no word of Ansgar, and the date of the police fundraiser crept closer. Travis wavered back and forth, trying to figure out how to take Saoirse without having to field a thousand questions from friends and coworkers. In the end, his desire to see her all dolled up for a night out overrode his reservations. This, however, opened up another set of problems, and no matter what scenario he envisioned, he finally conceded that he had just one way to make that happen.

As he finished up his regular overnight shift, he called and offered to buy Mike breakfast at the little pancake house near the station before he reported to work. Just opening the door to the bustling mom-and-pop restaurant brought back so many good memories. The aromas of savory sausage popping on the flat grill, old pleather booths, the clink of plates and glasses, and the scrapes of metal spatulas turning pancakes and eggs wrapped around Travis like a warm, familiar comforter. Bursts of happy chatter and laughter from the kitchen filtered into the dining room as the large metal doors swung open and closed.

At this time of day, the Salt Flat Diner's patrons mostly consisted of yawning officers, precinct staff, and a few tourists. Returning the shy waves of two preschool-aged children seated with a large group of vacationing adults, Travis slid into a booth to wait. His apology for leaving Saoirse to snooze in the car had been accepted, but only if he returned with a container of biscuits and gravy, crispy bacon, and scrambled eggs for her.

"Morning, Travis." The middle-aged hostess, in an orchid SFD polo, propped a plastic-jacketed menu in front of him, her wide smile revealing the gap in her front teeth. "Missy will be right along with some coffee. You coming or going?"

"Just finished up for the night, Mrs. Elsie," Travis said, turning his cup over and glancing out the plate glass window at his cruiser parked just on the other side. The owners had posted signs designating the row of spaces right next to the building as FIRST RESPONDERS PARKING ONLY. In addition, Mrs. Elsie let it be known that emergency personnel's coffee would always be hot, fresh, and free, ensuring that at any given time, cops, firemen, or EMS would be on the premises.

Less than a minute later, Mike's Jeep whipped into the parking lot and skidded to a stop next to Travis's SUV. He hopped out, playfully rapping on the tinted window. One ferocious bark sounded, followed by excited yipping as he waved hello to Saoirse.

"And there's the other half of the Hardy Boys now." Not missing a beat, Elsie dropped another menu and chuckled. "Y'all enjoy, now," she called back over her shoulder, moving down the row to greet another table.

Mike breezed in like a rock star, waving and calling out to the other officers. He dropped into his seat across from Travis just as the server arrived with two thermal carafes of coffee. "Yes, please," he said, turning his cup over. "I need all the high-octane I can get this morning. And please let Mrs. Ella Mae know I'm here. I'm starved near about to death and all about that home fry life this morning."

"I sure will." Missy laughed brightly as she poured both coffees, then positioned the brown Thermo-serv on the table between them. "She turned seventy-seven last week but said she still won't marry you until you put on some weight, no matter how much you beg. Have y'all about decided what you want?"

"I have," Travis answered. "Put it all on one check, please, ma'am."

With a brisk nod, Missy set down the unused carafe of decaf, pulling out her pad and pen. "Go," she said.

"I'm going to do two of the Salt Flat Specials, one to go. Scrambled eggs, wheat toast, regular bacon, home fries, and no butter on the pancakes for me. Biscuits and gravy instead of toast on the other one."

Mike folded his menu and pushed it to the end of the table. "Make that three, but I'll take his butter, please, and toast. As long as the regular coffee keeps coming, I think that's everything."

Nodding, the waitress pocketed her pad and turned, pausing to grab the unused decaf. Her blonde ponytail swung in wide arcs as she sped off for the kitchen.

Travis took in Mike's somewhat disheveled appearance. He raised his cup for a sip and grinned. "You look like you've had a long night," he said.

"And worth every minute of it." He laughed, raising his own cup in toast. "By the grace of caffeine, I will make it through this day. Although," he added, eyeing the carafe, "it may take a little more than that one pot."

"You know what they say about burning the candle at both ends," Travis warned.

"Yep, you gotta buy longer candles." He took another long drink and sighed with pleasure. "So what all you got going on this morning?"

Travis didn't waste any time. "You're bringing Geena to the thing at the convention center, right?"

Mike laughed, nodding. "Yeah, the way her eyes lit up when she heard about it, I just couldn't say no. She's already got her dress and everything."

"Do you think maybe—" He took a deep breath and started again. "Saoirse heard all the chatter about it in Dispatch, and she's got a million questions that I can't answer. I'd love to take her, but I don't know anything about dresses and shoes, makeup, or anything like that. I don't think she even needs makeup, but she's got it in her head that she does." Cradling his cup in both hands, he stared down at the ribbons of cream swirling inside the ceramic mug. "I think a fancy night out would be good for her after all she's been through. And I refuse to say *what could possibly go wrong*." He fell silent and took another sip of coffee.

"Say it. I need to hear these words," Mike wheedled in a startlingly good Yzma impression.

Travis smothered a smile as he blew out an exaggerated sigh. "I need your help. Please."

"Yeah, ya do." Mike chuckled. "How about I get with Geena and see what she can come up with? She adored Saoirse; I thought it might be that, uh, thing she throws off. Not that she's not adorable, of course," he added hastily. "I'll call her at lunch. I'm sure she can come up with a plan to get your faery princess ready for the ball. I imagine she'll need help getting a dress, too. If you want, we can drop by later today so the girls can do their online shopping. Your credit card is going to take a hit. Those dresses aren't cheap."

Travis waved that away. "Does she know? About Saoirse, I mean?"

"Just that wherever she's from is isolated with little to no connection to society. Does she suspect there's more to the story? Yes. Has she asked? No, but I expect she will at some point."

He nodded. "You and Geena are getting pretty serious, huh?" Travis asked, refilling both coffees. "Should I start worrying that you're changing your scandalous bachelor ways?"

Mike snorted with laughter. "I don't know, maybe. I'm not close to asking the big question, if that's what you're asking. We enjoy spending time together; we like the same weird stuff. You know, Disney, Monty Python, Hawaiian pizza, that kind of thing."

"Pineapple on pizza is a sacrilege. It's in the Bible or a state statute—one of the two," Travis snorted with disdain. "Same with anchovies. I can't even with fish on pizza or fish tacos. It goes against all the laws of nature."

"You are old and too set in your ways. You'd like it if you'd just—"

"No, I'm not old, I'm not set in my ways, and I'm not about to put that abomination in the temple that is my body."

"Speaking of big questions," Mike began, but stopped when Missy approached their table with a big tray.

"Here ya go. Butter..." she said, setting the steaming plate before Mike. "No butter and a carryout for you. Careful, everything's hot. Y'all good?" After assuring her they were, she moved on to the next table. "Just call if you need something," she said over her shoulder.

Travis grabbed the pepper mill and ground a little over his eggs. At the first forkful, he groaned. "Man, I needed this. I am *starving*." They ate in silence, wolfing down the delicious food.

Mike took his last piece of toast and wiped up the remaining egg. "So about that big question," he began, setting down his fork. "You haven't said anything, which I thought you would have, so I hated to ask, but... you know me. Has anything happened with you two?"

His mouth full, Travis lifted his eyebrows in question. *"Mmmph?"*

"You know."

Travis swallowed and took a sip of coffee. "I really don't. What are you asking me?"

"You know," he said again, balling up his fists and bumping them together, wiggling his eyebrows.

Travis coughed in surprise, banging his hand against his chest as he choked. "You're seriously asking me that?"

"That means no, then. Dude, what are you waiting for?" He counted the reasons off on his fingers. "She is crazy hot; she lives with you; she's sweet as the day is long; and she worships the ground you walk on. And she's hot."

"You said that already."

"So what's the holdup?" he asked. "Any idiot can see she's vibing on you."

A loud car horn's continuous blare broke the calm. Both men leaned over to look out the window for the source of the commotion. Saoirse had opened the partition between the seats and now sat posing as the driver with one paw firmly on the horn. They burst into laughter when she caught sight of their faces in the window and moved her paw. Her mouth spread into a wide grin, and she tilted her head in obvious question.

"Looks like your partner thinks you're taking too long," Mike joked as they both waved to her.

"We had a busy night. She said she wanted to nap while we eat," Travis explained. "She'll reheat hers in the microwave when we get home."

"She wasn't asleep when I pulled in. She lit up as soon as I banged on her window." Mike frowned, looking at his watch. "We haven't been here all that long."

"She talked about getting all the laundry done today. After she eats all this, she'll likely just want to sleep. I've explained until I'm blue in the face that the household chores aren't her responsibility. She catches naps in the car, but it's not the same as crawling into bed with no alarm clock."

Mike nodded sagely. "That's the absolute truth. There's nothing like—"

"Uh... did you just say your police dog does your laundry and cleans your house?" Missy stood next to the table, wide-eyed, with their check in hand. She placed it on the table next to Travis's coffee. "I've heard how smart she is, but... that's a joke, right?"

Travis recovered first. "Yeah, she's too smart for her own good. I'm teaching her how to drive next," he said with a self-deprecating chuckle.

"I think he should come out of the kennel and just admit she's his girlfriend," Mike said, adding a subtle Sullivan nod to sell the whole conversation as a joke between friends.

"I knew it had to be." Missy laughed. "I read somewhere that dogs are color blind, so she couldn't sort the colors from the lights. Y'all need anything else?"

Both men said no and called out their thanks as she moved away. Mike reached for his wallet. "You're getting that. I got the tip."

Travis nodded his assent and jerked his head toward the server station. "That was close."

"Yeah, it was." Dropping a couple of bills on the table, Mike scooted out of the booth and stood. "Are you feeling at least a little better about the benefit now?"

"Almost, but there's one other thing. Would you two mind coming over before we go? I'm kinda hoping I could impose on Geena again to help her get ready...?"

"She'd love to," Mike answered without hesitation. "It starts at eight—how about we show up around six? That will give them better than an hour to primp and fuss over each other. And you really should think about teaching Saoirse to drive. Honest to God, I'd pay good money to watch that."

"My last nerve is stretched far enough. You even suggest that to her, and they'll never find your body."

Mike smirked. "Challenge accepted."

CHAPTER 22

On the day of the benefit, the doorbell rang promptly at 5:55 p.m. "Wow—you both look fantastic." Travis grinned, stepping aside for them to enter. "Geena, your dress is beautiful. You even make him look good." He clapped Mike on the shoulder.

Mike smiled down at Geena, who flushed with pleased color. "Yeah, she does look amazing, doesn't she?"

"Thank you," she said with a laugh, hitching up her backpack. "Although this bag doesn't quite go with the overall look." The pearl-blue A-line gown, with its spaghetti straps, scoop neckline, snug bodice, and floor-length chiffon, flattered her slender figure immensely.

"Saoirse just got out of the shower. I've been banished to the den until she makes her appearance." He lowered his voice to a whisper. "She's been looking so forward to this, but I think she's a lot more nervous than she's letting on."

"Shoot, that girl could wrap up in a dirty beach towel and still be gorgeous." Geena took each man by the arm and gently pushed them toward the great room. "You have nothing to worry about, Travis. Y'all go do whatever boys do while they're waiting. I got this."

"That sounds like a drink to me," Mike said, carefully draping his tuxedo jacket over the back of a chair. He strode to the bar while Geena disappeared down the hallway with her bag, the skirt swishing quietly in her wake. "Beer, or are we going straight for the hard stuff?"

"I need whisky," Travis mumbled. "I think I'm more nervous than she is."

"You're looking a little pale," Mike said and nodded. "Calm down, brother, it's just a dance. Not like you're getting married or..." His voice trailed off as he noted the expression on his friend's face. "You're thinking about asking her, aren't you," he said, wonder coloring his voice. "Jesus Christ, McLean—are you thinking this one through? I mean, I love her to death too—" He spread his hands out in a holdup gesture as Travis lunged at him playfully. "In a very brotherly and nonsexual way, of course. But it's not like she's a girl from the next town over. She gives new meaning to the word tourist. Can y'all even do that?" He looked pointedly at Travis's tux and shrugged. "Well, I guess we're dressed for it."

"Feels more like the prom." Travis waved him off, filling two rocks glasses with ice and pouring a scant shot. "I can't do this right now. Distract me already. What kind of new cases do you have?"

They talked shop for a while, but the conversation meandered back around to Saoirse. "I still can't get over the transformation in your backyard. It's one thing to see the animals, but to see visible proof of real magic—it's beyond amazing. I didn't even know what half of those flowers were."

Travis snapped his fingers. "I'll be right back." He disappeared into the kitchen, rustled through the refrigerator, and returned with four small white boxes. After peering through the cellophane lids, he handed two to Mike. "These are yours," he explained. He set his on the bar, opened the smaller one, and removed the single burgundy rosebud nestled in dark green foliage. Finding the stick pin tacked to the inner box lid, he tried to secure it to his left lapel, using the mirror behind the bar. After several attempts, he managed to get it to stay on, albeit crooked.

"Jesus, you're mangling that—here, let me." Mike brushed his hand away impatiently, unpinning and repositioning the boutonniere. He drew back to look at his handiwork, made a slight adjustment, and then nodded with satisfaction. "That's better."

"Thanks," Travis said, taking and opening the other small box. "Let me get yours."

"You're a lifesaver. I never even thought of flowers. I guess this is like a prom after all," Mike admitted. "I couldn't for the life of me figure out why you asked about Geena's dress color; it kinda made me worry about you a little bit. Glad to see you did have an ulterior motive."

The girls used the entire hour, plus a little more, to get ready. Mike grumbled that they did it on purpose to keep them waiting, and Travis had to agree. When the bedroom door opened with a soft squeak, both men sat forward on the couch and listened for the soft footsteps that would announce their arrival.

Geena popped her head around first. "Get ready, both of you," she said and giggled. "Saoirse wants to make her entrance." Looking over her shoulder, she said something they could not hear, then stepped into the great room and dropped her voice to a stage whisper. "She got shy on me once she saw herself in the mirror. She's got it stuck in her head that she's not pretty enough to go with you, Travis."

"Well, that's just silly," he said, rising to his feet.

Geena waved at him to sit. "Trust me—you're gonna want to be sitting down when you see her. Y'all ready?"

When both men nodded, she stepped back into the hallway. "All right, Cinderella—time to go to the ball!" she called.

Travis heard the soft rustle of fabric moving up the hall and caught himself holding his breath. The moment stretched until he was ready to scream, and just when he thought he could not wait one second more, she appeared in the doorway. He had already braced himself, expecting her to be nothing short of breathtaking. At his first glimpse, he found that one simple word was woefully inadequate, but he did not have another that did her justice.

The dark hunter green lace gown hugged her torso to her waist, then fell in a wide sweep train. The neckline dipped in a heart-stopping plunge, exposing the barest hint of rounded breasts. The off-center front slit exposed one leg up to the top of her shapely thigh. Thanks to Geena, who had graciously shared some of her jewelry, Saoirse wore a dainty gold diamond pendant with matching ear wraps. Those finishing touches provided just the right amount of understated elegance.

Her hair was loose, the shining waves tumbling down her naked back. Travis suspected she had been practicing in the unfamiliar high heels, because he noticed the shiny shoebox appeared in a different location each day. The barely there gold stilettos laced becomingly across her feet and ankles, tied in small bows at the back of her calves. She took several slow, measured steps in Travis's direction, then stopped, her uncertainty clear. She cleared her throat. "Does my gown not please you?" she whispered.

It took him a moment to speak. "You are the most beautiful woman I have ever seen," he answered honestly, his voice tinged with awe. Belatedly remembering her question, he added, "And the gown is perfect."

A slow smile spread across her face, and for just a second, Travis went blind from the radiance. Mike wisely said nothing but gave Geena a discreet thumbs up.

"It starts at eight, so we should probably get going. I think we've waited long enough to make a fashionably late entrance." Geena gestured to the hallway. "Don't forget your purse. It's still on the bed." When Saoirse left to retrieve it, she whirled on Travis, speaking quietly and fast. "Don't you let her out of your sight even for one minute—you're taking a beautiful young swan to an old hen party. A bunch of those women will hate her on sight, and the men are gonna circle like sharks smelling blood in the water. Let me know if she needs to powder her nose, and I'll take her."

Mike nodded in solemn agreement. "You have your work cut out for you this evening, cuz."

Travis opened his mouth to respond but stopped as Saoirse returned with her clutch purse. She smiled, giving him an expectant look. With the confidence he in no way felt, he stood and offered his arm. "Your chariot awaits, my lady."

Placing her hand atop his, she dipped in a low curtsey. "You honor me, my lord." Tucking the bag, she slid her hand into the crook of his elbow and smiled up at him. "I am ready."

They took two cars but agreed to meet in the parking lot so they could walk in together. Saoirse was unusually silent on the ride to the venue, absently smoothing her dress or twiddling with her ear adornments. It did not take a psychic to realize the nervousness fast overtook her. "You're going to do just fine," Travis assured her. "I won't leave your side, so don't worry. Just relax." He winked. "You might even enjoy yourself."

She nodded and offered him a tremulous smile. "You will tell me if I do something wrong?" she asked.

"You won't."

"But will you?"

"I will." Keeping his eyes on the road, he took her hand, giving it a light squeeze. "But I won't have to because you won't."

CHAPTER 23

M ike and Geena walked into the crowded ballroom first and were met with a chorus of greetings. However, when Travis followed behind with Saoirse on his arm, he would have sworn everyone in the room stopped to stare. They paused at the first table with refreshments, accepting the plastic cups of fruity punch from a server clad in a tuxedo shirt, bow tie, and cummerbund for the dressy affair.

Up in the booth overlooking the dance floor, the DJ played a variety of music while everyone waited for the buffet to open. Later in the evening, a popular Beach Music band from nearby Charlotte would take the stage. Banquet tables loaded with gift baskets wrapped in colored cellophane, shiny electronics bearing oversized bows, glossy framed photos of vacation destinations, and other prizes donated by area businesses and philanthropists lined the walls.

Saoirse tried to take everything in all at once, riveted with excitement while Travis explained the fundraiser raffle. "You keep half of your ticket, and the other half goes into a

238

bowl. When the time comes, they'll pick one for each basket. If they call out your number, you win."

"They've got some good stuff this year," Mike said, gesturing to a large high-tech TV with a multi-speaker surround sound system. "I wouldn't mind having that at all." He leaned over to whisper near Travis's ear. "Can she twitch her nose or something to make that happen?"

Travis exploded with laughter. "Not sure if that's in her skill set, but I'll ask." At her inquisitive glance, he patted her hand, still tucked in his elbow. "I'll explain later."

Without missing a beat, Geena took Saoirse's other hand and announced, "We're going to go powder our noses while you two browse—be right back." And off they went, headed for the restrooms. The crowd parted to let the two women through, and Travis watched until they disappeared.

"Big turnout," Mike observed. "Looks like every agency in the state is here." He nodded in greeting to a group of what appeared to be SLED agents as they passed by on the way to get drinks. They were, to a man, big and athletic, with short hair and clean-shaven faces.

"Hey—aren't you McLean? From Cherry Grove?" one of them asked, stopping to talk. A few years older than the others, he exuded command and confidence as he extended his hand. "I'm Justin Meyers, SLED investigative services. Mike here has told us a lot about you. I'm tickled pink to finally put a face to the reports."

Travis shook the offered hand, chuckling. "I doubt any of what he's told you is true. He's been known to lie like a rug."

Justin shook his head. "Nope, I can read for myself. You and your dog have had some pretty impressive busts. Captain Bellamy has already warned me off you tonight, but if you're open, I'd like to talk to you sometime next week about taking your career up a notch or two. We can always use an experienced working team with a record like yours." Reaching into his jacket's inner pocket, he pulled out his badge wallet, withdrew a business card, and handed it to Travis. "All my info is there. Just give me a call or shoot me an email when you're ready."

"Thank you, sir." Travis accepted the card, tucking it into his jacket pocket. "I appreciate the opportunity."

"Well, we're supposed to be mingling and not recruiting," Justin said and finished with a laugh, "so I'll be on my way. Mike has had one of my cards for a while now. See if you can talk him into coming along with you." He shook hands with both men before moving to catch up with his friends.

Travis watched him melt into the crowd. "That was an interesting turn of events. What all did you tell him?"

"Nothing much, just how great a job you're doing. He sees your reports, too."

"Huh... SLED could be interesting. It's a big step up, for sure. I don't know about relocating, though. Are you considering it?"

Mike shook his head. "Not right now, but I'm not ruling it out altogether for the future. Too many variables right now to make a good decision."

"Variables?" Travis took a sip of punch and grimaced. "Man, this stuff is vile."

Mike sniffed his cup before drinking. "Reminds me of Vacation Bible School Kool-Aid. A little rum would improve it nicely, but I doubt this is the place to go spiking the punch."

"What variables?" Travis prompted.

He shrugged. "You know, my folks are getting on in years, you and Saoirse, Geena—the usual stuff. I need to stay put for a while."

"Your mama would whup your ass if she heard you say that, but I know what you mean. I couldn't even consider it, what with Saoirse's situation still up in the air. I'll keep the card, though, just in case," he agreed. "Stranger things have happened."

Mike scanned the large crowd, milling around as they socialized. "Incoming," he whispered, raising the plastic cup again to shield his mouth. "Nuclear meltdown in three, two—"

"Travis!" Lori Ann's bright voice cut through the boisterous chatter, nearly causing Travis to fumble his drink. "I'm so happy you came!" She pointedly glanced around, eyes narrowed in suspicion. "You know, I was sure you said you had a date. I came by myself tonight, too. Hello, Mike," she added flatly, as if it were an afterthought.

Travis turned to face the tall blonde, noting that she had unfortunately chosen a gown in the same dark green as Saoirse. The similarity ended there. Had he never met Saoirse, he might have thought her pretty in that color. "Lori Ann," he muttered, nodding once in acknowledgement.

Undeterred, she pressed on. "I'm just glad you didn't bring that dog with you," she said with a feigned shudder, lowering her voice to a confidential tone. "I've been meaning to tell you—that day I ran into you at the station, I think your dog... uh, had a... well, an accident in my purse. It wasn't one of my good ones or anything, but I wanted to—are you okay?"

"Yup, all good," Mike said with a straight face, hitting his chest with a balled fist. "Punch just went down wrong. Are you saying she peed in your purse?" His voice grew louder. "Travis, you've got to work on Search's manners if she's doing things like that. We can't have her randomly relieving herself in people's handbags. I hope you found it before it baked in the hot sun. I've heard tomato juice is good for getting the smell out. Although it's probably better that she didn't leave something more substantial."

"Michael..." Travis closed his eyes and shook his head, trying hard not to laugh. "It's been addressed."

Still scowling at Mike, Lori Ann looped her arm through Travis's and leaned in. "I've heard the band is excellent. You must promise you'll dance with me at least a couple—"

"McLean! Reynolds!" Captain Bellamy strolled up with his wife, Helen. "Glad you made it. Looks to be a good turnout, don't you think?"

"You boys look so handsome. You'll have to fight the girls off with a stick tonight," Mrs. Bellamy said, waggling a finger in warning.

The two men almost sighed aloud with relief at the welcome interruption. Travis extended the arm Lori Ann had been clinging to for a handshake, breaking her death grip. "Happy to see you, sir, ma'am," he said. "Mrs. Bellamy, you look positively radiant this evening."

"She sure does," Mike said, gesturing to the captain's wife. "You better keep an eye out that someone doesn't steal her away from you tonight."

"I suppose it's fortunate that I know where just about everyone here lives, so I reckon I could find her quick enough," the captain joked, watching as Lori Ann recaptured Travis's arm. He met the younger man's gaze, eyebrows raised in question.

"Our dates just ran to the ladies' room. They'll be right back," Mike explained, studiously ignoring Lori Ann, who gaped open-mouthed at Travis.

"Who—" Captain Bellamy's question was interrupted by a commotion near the back hallway as the crowd pressed in that direction. "What's going on over there?" He craned his neck to see, then turned a confused gaze to his wife. "I can't see—who is that?"

Travis and Mike exchanged a quick glance. Without having to ponder further, Travis suspected he knew the reason for the uproar and wondered if he'd have to rescue her. They all watched as the throng parted to let Geena and Saoirse through. *She's holding up great*, Travis thought, *walking through that crowd like a queen.*

Geena looked around as if searching. Saoirse saw Travis at once, and her face lit up in a brilliant smile. She pointed, and Geena waved as they began moving in the men's direction, slowed by random attempts to strike up a conversation with the beautiful women.

Travis watched their slow progress until he could no longer stand it. "Excuse me just a moment, be right back," he called over his shoulder, shaking Lori Ann loose again. He crossed the dance floor, meeting them halfway. "I thought y'all might need saving right about now," he joked, offering each an arm.

"Your timing is perfect," Geena said, laughing. "Honey, meet flies. I don't think there's a man here who hasn't tried his luck getting her attention."

Saoirse's lips curved into a smile. "But I told them no because I am already here with the most handsome man of all."

Travis ducked his head and flushed with her sweet words. "I don't know about that, but I'm sure glad you're here with me."

As they reached their small group, Geena released his arm to take Mike's. Travis lifted Saoirse's hand to press a soft kiss on her knuckles, then gently tugged her forward. "Saoirse, you remember Captain Bellamy and his wife, Helen."

Speechless, the captain's eyes went wide with astonishment. Mrs. Bellamy shot her husband a quizzical look at his uncharacteristic silence but nodded. "Yes—we met you in the grocery store. It's nice to see you again, dear, and oh my, what a gorgeous dress."

"Thank you most kindly, and yours is as well," Saoirse replied. Travis felt her begin to dip in a curtsey before catching herself. In that moment, he was so proud of her.

"And this is Geena," Mike said, taking her by the hand. "She's a sketch artist in the Criminal Justice program over at Tech."

Captain Bellamy seemed to snap out of his stupor and beamed. "It's a pleasure to meet you. I believe I've seen some of your work at the precinct. You're very good."

She gave him a bright smile. "Thank you very much, sir. I hope to join your agency as soon as I graduate."

The two couples began making small talk before a feminine throat cleared noisily. "I'm Lori Ann Sears," she interjected, extending her hand. She gritted out a smile as she waited.

"I've seen you before. You're dating Kendricks, correct? Is he here? I don't recall seeing him tonight," the captain said, absently shaking her hand.

"I was, but we're not together anymore," she answered, casting a coy glance at Travis. "I'm here all by my lonesome."

When Travis considered it later, he concluded that none of what followed could have been anticipated or prevented. Still, he would've paid a year's salary to have captured the moment on video.

Saoirse's gold eyes flashed as she slipped her arm through Travis's. She smiled up at the taller woman, baring small white teeth. "My name is Saoirse. I am with Travis."

Lori Ann's eyes narrowed. "Then you must know who I am," she said, voice dripping with saccharin sweetness. "Travis and I were together for a very long time."

"Your name is Lori Ann?" Saoirse's delicate brow furrowed as if in deep thought, and then her eyes widened in complete innocence. "No, I do not believe I have ever heard him mention you."

Mike coughed loudly to cover the first snort of laughter. Geena gave him a sharp elbow to the ribs, eliciting another cough.

"Well, I'm sure he has, Saoirse," she snapped, emphasizing the name. "I didn't catch your last name?"

"I have not yet decided, but I believe it might be McLean," she said with an angelic smile. Her warm gaze landed on Travis, and he beamed back at her, the corners of his mouth twitching with the superhuman effort not to laugh. Mike had to turn around in the opposite direction, his shoulders shaking convulsively.

Lori Ann's body stiffened with anger, but she kept the insincere smile glued to her face. "There's Lonnie— Lieutenant Adams; I must go say hello. Excuse me a moment, please," she clipped out, whirling on her heel. "Travis, I'll catch up with you later."

They all watched her exodus to the other side of the ballroom, but only Travis was close enough to hear Saoirse's teeth chatter behind her closed lips. He tightened his arm to squeeze her hand. "Now, now," he soothed.

Her whispered response came out as a hiss. "She needs biting. Hard."

"It's strange seeing you without your dog, McLean. What is Search up to this evening?" the captain asked.

Travis opened his mouth to speak, but Mike beat him to it. "She's guarding her territory, sir," he quipped.

CHAPTER 24

A clear bell chime sounded, and the crowd immediately moved toward the manned buffet tables. "About damn time," Captain Bellamy grumbled.

Helen patted his arm and looked at the younger couples. "I need to feed him before he turns grumpy," she explained. "Nice to meet you all. Enjoy yourselves tonight!" And with that, the older couple headed for the long line.

"Let's hang back so the dinner crowd can thin out some," Travis suggested, still holding Saoirse's hand hostage in his elbow.

"Works for us." Mike and Geena nodded in agreement.

Travis's gaze met Saoirse's and held it. "I'm glad you came tonight."

She glanced around the large room. "It is not as I pictured, but still, it is breathtaking. All the beautiful dresses, and so many colors. And everyone is so friendly," she added before her pert nose wrinkled with a sniff, "except for that Lori Ann person. I fear she has taken a strong dislike to me." She tossed her hair so that the waves bounced against her back. "Not that I care in the least, of course."

"I am Faery, hear me roar," Mike chortled. "Watching you brush Lori Ann back off the plate was worth the price of admission. You handled it like a pro; she didn't expect you to stand up to her." Visibly mortified at what he just let slip, he glanced at Geena, but she gave no indication she heard his blunder.

"Amen to that," Travis agreed, giving Saoirse's fingers a light massage. "What did you think it would be like?"

"I thought it would be more like the grand balls I have seen on TV, with large orchestras, servants running about filling glasses, that sort of thing. And maybe a monarch, although I have not heard you speak about one. Does a king reign over this land?"

"A long time ago, there was a king, but it didn't last," Travis explained. "Now we have one president over the whole country, elected by vote every four years."

"And it is a very large country." She shook her head. "I do not think I would like such a position as that."

"Me either," Mike said, jerking his head toward the buffet. "What *I* would like is some of that prime rib before it's gone. It's been calling my name for the last half hour."

With that, they took their places in line. Mike went first, then Geena, with Travis and Saoirse behind them. "So you can see how all this works," Travis whispered close to her ear as he picked up two plates, handing one to Saoirse.

Wide-eyed, she cradled it to her breast. "I will watch," she agreed solemnly.

The foursome moved through the various stations, making their selections. Mike scanned the room, found one of the circular six-top tables vacant, and waved for them to follow. An attentive server followed behind, filling the table goblets with water or sweet tea. Once seated, everyone compared selections. At the sight of Saoirse's mounded and nearly overflowing plate, he stage-whispered, "Does she have a family of refugees stashed in that tiny purse or—OW! That was entirely unnecessary." He rubbed the spot on his shin where both Travis's and Geena's heels had made contact.

"She wanted to try a little of everything," Travis explained. "Just wait until you've seen her at the dessert table. The girl has an Olympic-level sweet tooth and a metabolism like the Energizer Bunny. Burns everything off before it has a chance to stick."

"God, I wish I had that. I gain five pounds just walking down the cookie aisle," Geena groused, then squealed as Mike tickled her ribs.

"You don't need to change one thing. I like everything you got just the way it—"

"Is anyone sitting here?" a too loud, cheerful voice interrupted.

Oh, Christ on a cracker, girl—you gotta be kidding me. "No," Travis said succinctly.

Lori Ann beamed at her companion, resting her hand possessively on his chest. "We can sit here, Lonnie."

"So I heard," he said, his chagrined expression bordering on physical pain as he dutifully pulled a chair out for her. He nodded in greeting to the others at the table. "Ladies, Detective, Corporal."

Travis made the introductions. "Saoirse, Geena, this is Lieutenant Lonnie Adams with Horry County PD. Y'all already met Lori Ann."

"Just Lonnie, please," he began and laughed. "We're all friends here. Ladies, you are to be commended for putting up with these two knuckleheads."

Travis grabbed Saoirse's knee, preventing her from rising. "Oh, come on now. We have a few good qualities, too."

"That's true. I've seen some glowing reports about both of you. SLED is here, saying they're not recruiting, but we all know they are. Don't you let them sweet talk you away from here. If you're looking for a change, though, my unit would welcome you with open arms."

Travis smiled warmly at Saoirse and leaned over to brush a light kiss on her temple. "Nah, I have a good reason to stay put."

"Jesus Christ, you are flirting with disaster." Seated to Travis's right, Mike whispered behind his hand, "Look at Lori Ann's face; she's about to explode."

Indeed, the blonde's face had darkened like an impending thunderstorm. She slid a manicured hand under her hair and flipped it back off her shoulder, ensuring the sudden movement captured Travis's attention. Dragging her fingertips down Lonnie's forearm, she lightly squeezed his hand, then aimed a smug grin at Travis. Lonnie looked bewildered at the intimate show of affection from a woman he barely knew.

Keeping his expression deliberately blank to keep from laughing, Travis focused on his plate and sliced off several small pieces of the prime rib. "Did you try any of this yet?" he asked Saoirse.

"I did not," she admitted before dropping her voice to a whisper. "I was unsure which animal this rib came from."

"It's beef—cow. Here," he said, spearing one of the small bites and dipping it in the au jus, "try this." He held the fork so that a single drop of the thin broth fell onto her lips. "Open."

Her eyes lit with excitement as her tongue darted out to catch the savory gravy before it dribbled down her chin. "Oh my," she breathed, "I should like more of that, please."

"Then open." Like a baby bird, she allowed him to feed her, eyes rolling with pleasure over the taste. He didn't know if it was her faery vibe, but watching her chew with such obvious delight made him hard as concrete. He had thought to go get her a slice, but no way was he going to make that walk with a raging, and he was sure, visible hard-on. He nudged Mike with his elbow. "Would you do me a huge favor and get Saoirse some of that prime rib?"

Mike's cheeks bulged as he chewed, then swallowed. "Something wrong with your legs?"

"Right now, the one in the middle is giving me fits. I don't want to walk over there with my pants all tented up."

"Try thinking about baseball," he said, taking another bite.

"I'm picturing the holding cell floor on a Friday night. Not helping."

"Oh, to be fourteen again," Mike sang as he rose to his feet. "Yeah, I'll go. Anybody need anything?"

Geena shook her head no. "I'm good," Travis assured him as his friend left to complete his mission. Picking up his fork, a slight but steady vibration to his left seized Travis's full attention. He whirled around in his seat to find Saoirse pale and shivering. At once, he wrapped his arms around her and pulled her close. "Is it him again?"

She buried her face in his chest with a tiny whimper and nodded. "That's the third time today. Not good," he muttered, then whispered next to her ear. "You're safe, I've got you. Do you want to go home?"

She drew back and glared at him with steely eyes. "I do *not*. I will not allow him to ruin your evening for anything."

"It's your evening, too," he said.

"Then *our* evening. I will not miss a single moment of this night. And since you taught me, I want to dance when the music begins. But only with you."

"Of course we will," he soothed, pulling her close again for a tight hug.

Over the top of her head, his gaze met Lori Ann's. With a clearly fake sympathetic look, she mouthed, "Poor thing. Social anxiety?"

Travis glared at her and mouthed back, "NO. Mind your own business." He turned his attention back to Saoirse, relieved that her trembling had subsided for the moment.

Her soft voice was muffled against his chest. "I no longer feel him, but I like this hugging very much."

He heard the smile in her words and murmured against her hair. "We can do this whenever your little heart desires, faery girl."

She tipped her gaze up to meet his. "I shall remember you said that. Take heed of what you offer, my lord." His cheeks dimpled when he grinned back at her, and she gave a dreamy sigh. "You truly are very handsome."

"I don't know about that, but I reckon I'll do." He shrugged, but a flush of pleased embarrassment flooded his cheeks.

Mike returned with two plates of roasted meat and little ramekins of au jus, setting one plate in front of Geena and the other at Saoirse's elbow. "Good God—you two are making me blush, carrying on like that, and in public no less. You plan on getting a room or what?"

Saoirse giggled and gave Travis a playful push. "If you please, good sir—that meat smells delicious but will soon cool. And as Mr. Reynolds has just reminded us, we have propriety to observe."

Lori Ann dabbed the corner of her mouth daintily and rested her hand on Lonnie's forearm again. "Didn't I hear you were being promoted again soon? I think it's amazing how fast you're moving up the chain of command."

"I haven't heard anything, but I'm sure my CO would let me know if that were the case," Lonnie said offhandedly around a mouthful of baked potato. He washed it down with a long swallow of tea, then gestured at Saoirse with his half-empty glass. "I've been trying my best to pin down your accent, ma'am, but it has eluded me so far. May I ask where you are originally from?"

After a glance for Travis's approval, Saoirse answered. "Brú na Bóinne, in Ireland. I came here for a visit and liked it so much that I decided to stay," she added, anticipating the next question.

"I went to Ireland a few years ago. I remember seeing signs—it's near Dublin, right?"

"Yes, in County Meath. Do you have family there still?"

He shook his head. "I did one of those DNA ancestry kits, traced my family back to Dublin. I had a vacation coming up and thought seeing some of the places I read about would be interesting. It's a beautiful country, but the language was hard for me to understand."

Saoirse's merry laugh tinkled, and several nearby heads turned to find the source of the beautiful sound. "It is challenging for those not native-born. It has changed much over the years, easier now than was the ancient tongue."

With growing alarm, Travis realized Lonnie's eyes were getting that now familiar, glazed-over look. He cleared his throat and nudged Saoirse's knee under the table to get her attention and break the trance.

There was no shortage of conversation over dinner or dessert. After discussing the food, they veered into shop talk, current events, and local trends. Lonnie showed interest in Geena's criminology studies, offering his card if she wanted more cases to practice with. Saoirse's primary focus was trying the new foods, but she stayed engaged in the conversations, occasionally laughing or nodding at another's comment or joke.

Unable to contribute anything relevant, Lori Ann kept silent, eyes narrowed as she waited for another opportunity to shift attention back to her. At the sight of Saoirse's plate laden with sweets, she caught Mike's attention, then flicked her gaze over to Saoirse. "Is she pregnant?" she mouthed.

"Just stop," he mouthed back, rolling his eyes.

The piped-in music overhead abruptly stopped, and the increased activity near the stage caught everyone's attention. A small group of men and women clad in matching Hawaiian shirts and tan slacks mounted the steps leading up to the dais. Quickly strapping on guitars and checking their earpieces, the singer stepped up to the microphone and announced, "Ladies and gentlemen, we are so happy to be with you tonight. Coming at you from Charlotte, North Carolina—we are The Solo Cups. Now it's a party!" And with the introduction made, they launched into an infectious version of "You're More Than a Number in My Little Red Book." The dance floor filled quickly as couples rushed to show off their dance skills.

"Ooh, I love this song," Lori Ann gushed, grabbing Lonnie by the arm and dragging the disconcerted officer toward the stage. Mike and Geena followed close behind and started dancing before reaching the Marley flooring.

Travis started to rise, pulling Saoirse with him. She didn't budge, ducking her head shyly. "May I please just watch for a little while?"

Smiling, he sat back down. "Whenever you're ready, you let me know."

Her eyes glowed with excitement as she gripped his hand, watching the couples shag their way around the dance floor. "Some of these dancers are very good," she murmured, nibbling at her lower lip.

"They could be professionals," Travis explained. "The SOS—sorry, the Society of Stranders—do competitions all over. I believe they're based out of Ocean Drive. Most of these folks here aren't anywhere near that skill level."

She nodded. "Look at Mike and Geena," she commented as they spun by. "They are very happy."

"Seems so," Travis agreed. No one would mistake Mike for a great dancer, but he made up for his lack of skill with unbridled enthusiasm. Dancing with Geena, he managed to appear almost graceful as they negotiated the turns and twirls. On closer inspection, he realized Geena did most of the leading, which explained a lot. Still, from the smitten look on Mike's face, he didn't seem to mind.

They watched as the band ran through several more songs, all Beach Music classics, not speaking but hands still firmly clasped. When the sweet strains of "Unchained Melody" began, Travis decided he had waited long enough. "Come on," he ordered, rising out of his seat. "You love this one, and it's slow. No more excuses."

"But—"

"Nope," he said firmly, sliding her chair back from the table. "You're dancing. With me. Right now." Without waiting for an answer, he headed straight for the crowded dance floor with her in tow. They eased in, finding an open spot near the middle. Sliding his left arm around her waist, they began to sway in time with the music.

Saoirse sighed and laid her cheek against his lapel. "This makes me very happy. Thank you for tonight."

"The night is yet young," he said, pulling her even closer. His right hand entwined with hers, and he curled both against his chest. She made a soft purring sound and molded her body to his, lifting her head to meet his gaze.

Beautiful, he thought, struggling to find the right words to express how he felt. The inadequate compliment wasn't enough. Saoirse affected his entire being on a cellular level, and the carefully constructed psychological dam he built to keep his emotions under control had new, likely fatal fissures crisscrossing the broad expanse.

The music seemed to swell, and he lost all sense of self and surroundings. They moved as one, swaying and spinning in time with the slow, steady heartbeat of the song.

Feeling the building crescendo, Travis's self-control crumbled. He lifted Saoirse against him as they danced and claimed her mouth in a fierce kiss. She answered with a response that staggered him, parting her lips just enough to allow his questing tongue entry.

The jarring sound of thunder broke the spell. As the fog melted away, he realized they stood alone in the center of the dance floor, surrounded by the other couples who had stepped back to watch the striking couple. The applause resounded throughout the cavernous room.

Saoirse gasped in surprise. "I feel like a princess," she chirped, before throwing her arms around his neck and kissing him as if the world was ending. The applause grew even louder, mingling with whoops and wolf whistles of approval.

In all his life experiences, Travis had never encountered a situation remotely like this. However, not one to let a golden opportunity pass by, he pulled her tight against him and returned the kiss. To his relief, the band launched into another standard, and the dance floor began filling up again.

Saoirse broke the contact and gazed up at him with soft, guileless eyes. "I liked that very much," she murmured.

In that moment, the flood of heat left him breathless. He worried briefly that his heart might explode, but just as quickly decided he did not care. "Me too," he whispered near her ear, placing his hand near the small of her back as they exited the dance floor.

They passed Captain and Mrs. Bellamy, who reached out to touch Travis's arm. "That was absolutely beautiful," she gushed. "You two dance just like Gene Kelly and Cyd Charisse."

"You're telling your age, Helen," the captain scoffed with a laugh. "These kids don't know who those old-timers are."

Saoirse's brow furrowed in deep thought before she brightened. "Brigadoon. Heather on the Hills. Red dress."

Travis knew the surprise at her answer registered on his face. "What is that?" he asked.

"Only one of the most romantic movies ever made." Mrs. Bellamy sighed. "Honestly, Travis—you should watch it; you might learn something."

"Maybe I'll do that," he agreed, smiling down at Saoirse.

It took a while to return to their table, as they passed through the crowd of well-wishers who wanted a closer look or an introduction to the dark-haired beauty. Their server had been by with refills, and Travis reached for his glass. "That was some thirsty work." He laughed, taking a big swallow as he pulled out her chair.

Before Saoirse could respond, Lori Ann appeared at Travis's other side. She took his arm and gave him a demure smile. "My turn," she insisted, tugging him back toward the dance floor.

"Lori Ann," Saoirse purred in that soft, layered voice Travis had come to view as terrifying. She mimicked the blonde's old money Charleston accent flawlessly. "My dear, I do believe there is a spider in your hair."

Her deafening scream filled the room. Onlookers gasped as she tore wildly, destroying the perfect coiffure while she tried to shake the nonexistent pest free.

"You should go see for yourself," she added in the same voice of compulsion, lips twitching as she stifled a smile. "There are large mirrors in the restroom. Perhaps I am mistaken, and you will find nothing."

Without looking back, Lori Ann whirled and ran as the onlookers hastily parted to let her through. She blew past Mike, who yanked Geena back to prevent a collision. "What the hell was that all about?" he demanded, staring after the hysterical woman as she vanished into the crowd.

Travis didn't answer. Instead, he turned a narrowed gaze to Saoirse, who dissolved into a fit of giggles. "Was that necessary?"

Her shoulders shook as she tried to regain her composure. "She deserved it, and you cannot convince me otherwise."

"Couldn't you have just told her she didn't want to dance with me?"

She appeared to mull that over before answering. "I suppose I could have, yes."

"But you chose not to."

"Affirmative." Her eyes narrowed into a sly slant, confirming her mischievous mood. "I wearied of the wolf sniffing around my door each time my attention is drawn elsewhere."

"Just promise you won't ever use that on me," he pleaded.

"I would never," she assured him.

Their gazes locked for a long moment. "Are you being serious right now?"

"As far as you know, yes." She brushed her fingertips across his cheek and took on a serious expression. "But I have a pressing question of the utmost importance."

Travis stilled and braced himself, then nodded. "Go on."

"Do you suppose there is any cake left?"

CHAPTER 25

The evening progressed smoothly, with more dancing, sweet tea, and another dangerously overloaded plate of desserts for Saoirse, along with fun conversation. The cash bar had opened, and the spirits flowed freely. A constant parade of men found reasons to pass by their table, and occasionally a brave soul would stop and invite Saoirse to dance. She politely declined each offer, but one look from Travis had them moving on quickly to find another partner. Lori Ann did not make another appearance, and after making his apologies, Lonnie moved on to mingle.

When the band took their first break, the banquet staff moved a podium to center stage and set up a microphone for the speaker. Captain Bellamy climbed the few steps up to the dais and cleared his throat before beginning his speech. "I want to thank all of you for coming out tonight. I hope everyone is having fun—sounds like you are—but remember, some of us have to work in the morning."

A round of laughter and applause followed, and he waited for it to die down to continue. "This event is first and foremost a fundraiser for our law enforcement agencies here in Horry County. I don't have the final tally yet, but I can say that due to your overwhelming generosity, it has exceeded our wildest expectations, so thank you all." He went on to name some of the planned new resources going to various agencies, interrupted by bursts of applause.

Travis nudged Mike with his elbow, then leaned in. "I'm headed to the can. Keep an eye on her for me?" When his friend nodded, he waited until the next dignitary began speaking before leaning over to whisper in Saoirse's ear. "I'm going to the restroom, but Mike and Geena will be right here. Will you be okay for a few minutes?"

Her mouth full of chocolate cake, she nodded as he pushed back from the table. Reluctant to leave her side at all, his mission was to go, go, and get back in under five minutes. Keeping a low profile so as not to be disruptive, he skirted around the backs of the tables and made a beeline for the hallway. The men's room did not have a conventional door. Instead, it had an ornate stone wall blocking the view into the room, with entrances at either end. Travis disappeared into the empty restroom, took care of business, and washed his hands. As he turned to access the paper towel dispenser, the number of officers who slipped in unheard to fill the room startled him.

"Hey, McLean," a few said, nodding in greeting.

"Damn, I didn't hear any of you come in," he commented, drying his hands. Tossing the used paper towels into the trash, he made his way through the crowd to leave. "Excuse me," he said, but they began to close in a circle around him.

"Who is that woman you're with?" one of the men asked, and a murmur of agreement rippled as the interrogation began. "What's her name? Where'd you meet her? Are y'all together, like a couple? Does she have a sister? Is she a model? Does she swing?"

Ignoring that last question, Travis lifted his hands and laughed. "Her name is Saoirse. She's from Ireland, but we met over the summer in Columbia. She doesn't model, although she's most definitely beautiful enough, no sisters, and yeah, she is one hundred percent off the market. Sorry, gentlemen."

The sounds of despair mingled with more questions. "Sorry, I, uh—gotta get back," he said, disappearing around the corner. He rushed back to the banquet hall, entering right as a burst of applause filled the room, announcing the end of another speech. He noted a group of men clustered near one of the back tables. With a sinking feeling, he realized which table and quickened his pace.

Mike rose from his seat as Travis approached. "Thank God you're back," he whispered. "The piranhas moved in as soon as you left."

He looked at Saoirse, who gave him a cherubic smile. "I have had all I can eat," she said. "I did not think it possible."

She daintily dabbed the edge of her lips with the cloth napkin. "Will there be more dancing?" she asked, stifling a yawn.

"That is up to you. Think you've had enough excitement for one night?"

"I am not sure." She tapped her chin thoughtfully. "You still have the tickets in your pocket, and they have not given away the baskets we saw when we arrived."

He subconsciously felt around in the pocket where he had stuffed the string of tickets, relief washing over him when his fingers found the folded stack. "Okay, they should be doing that pretty soon." A server stopped by their table, carrying two carafes of coffee, but Travis declined. "Don't get your hopes up—I never win anything at these raffles."

Saoirse craned her neck to see the prize tables. "Is there something you would like?"

"Not really. I know Mike is lusting hard over that big TV, but his luck runs about the same as mine." He lifted her hand to brush a light kiss over her fingers. "I already won the best prize here, anyway."

Her eyes went wide. "You did? When did this happen?"

"When you agreed to come with me tonight," he murmured with a shy smile.

She turned a becoming shade of pink and opened her mouth to speak, but another round of applause interrupted her. Mrs. Bellamy approached the podium, carrying a large glass fishbowl filled with ticket stubs. "And now for your favorite part of the evening," she joked. "First, thank you to all the area businesses for donating these wonderful prizes and helping to make our fundraiser a success. Everybody got your tickets?"

She drew tickets one by one, reading the numbers. Shouts of joy mingled with groans of disappointment as the winners claimed each basket. When she announced she would be drawing for the enormous OLED TV with surround sound and all the electronic trimmings next, Mike leaned forward in his chair, studying his numbers. He held the ticket up in front of Geena's face. "Blow on it," he ordered.

"I think that only works with dice," she laughed, but did it anyway.

Travis did not notice at first when Saoirse began to hum, but when he glanced over, he saw her lips barely moving, her hands folded in her lap. "What are you doing?" he asked, suspicious.

She ignored him, focusing all her attention on the captain's wife, who stirred her hand around inside the fishbowl until she finally drew a single red ticket.

She squinted down at the numbers and blinked. "And the winner is...2-7-9-5-1-2..." Mrs. Bellamy paused for dramatic effect. "And 8."

Mike leapt to his feet. "That's me!" he whooped, fist-pumping the air. He grabbed Geena for an exuberant kiss, then rushed to collect his prize, accepting congratulations and fist bumps as he passed. When he held up the winning ticket, Travis, Saoirse, and Geena joined the room in another round of applause. Everyone laughed when Mike did something resembling an Irish jig upon reaching the stage, handing his ticket to Mrs. Bellamy with a short bow.

She took it with a big smile. "Many of you might not know this, but I retired as a teacher from Cherry Grove Elementary, and Michael here was one of my students. Once the class clown, always the class clown." She matched the numbers and nodded. "You are indeed the winner," she announced. "Congratulations!"

As Mike made his way back to their table, Travis turned to Saoirse. Her face was the very image of innocence. "Did you do that?"

"I know not of what you speak," she said primly.

"Mike's raffle ticket," he explained in a whisper. "Did you... you know... do some faery stuff?"

Her eyes rounded comically. "Are you suggesting I cheated?"

"Of course not," he assured her. "I just wanted to be sure everything is legit."

"It is most certainly legit." She smiled and took a big swallow of tea, choosing not to discuss the matter further.

Mike dropped down into his seat, flushed with excitement. Geena threw her arms around him in a tight hug. "Are you going to invite me over for movie night when you get everything set up?"

"Well, about that," he admitted. "I was kinda hoping you'd help me. As smart as you are, I figured you'd speak fluent electronics."

She gave him a knowing smile. "I saw your 'Do not use aluminum foil inside' note stuck to the front of the microwave, so I suspected you might need a little guidance. Good thing I know how to do all that. I work cheap, too. You can cook me dinner while I get it connected."

Travis leaned in again to whisper near Mike's ear. "You haven't gotten around to telling her you minored in Cybersecurity and Computer Science?"

"No, and neither will you. I know a good deal when I hear one."

Their attention shifted back to the stage as Mrs. Bellamy drew tickets for the last remaining prizes. As he predicted, Travis did not win anything. "It's just as well," he told Saoirse. "I already have everything I need." He took her hand and brushed her knuckles against his cheek. "Was there something special you wanted to win?"

When she finally spoke, he had to lean in to hear her soft voice. "Yes, there is."

Puzzled, Travis peered into her face. "You should have said something," he chided. "We could have gotten more tickets. One of the baskets?"

She shook her head. "There is only one prize I wish to win without using any... magickal, you say... abilities."

"What prize is that?" he asked, his interest piqued.

"Your heart."

CHAPTER 26

Travis felt like someone had just sucker punched him in the gut. The mix of overwhelming emotions—joy, love, fear, protectiveness, lust, awe—flooded his mind and body, rendering him momentarily incapable of movement or speech.

She tried to tug her hand free. "I should not have spoken," she whispered, turning her face away. "Pay my words no heed. It is not my place to want such things."

"Stop." He captured her hands in his larger ones and turned her to face him. "Look at me."

Reluctantly, she would not look directly at him but slanted her gaze to a side-eye. Even with her hands captive, she managed to shrink into herself as if trying to disappear.

"Saoirse, listen to me." His voice held a note of warning, enough to make her look up.

"Forget I even spoke, I beg you. I was unthinking, too much TV has made my imagination wild. My words, they mean nothing, just the—"

"I love you."

She stopped mid-word, her mouth open. "What did you say?"

Travis sucked in a deep breath and took a flying leap off that emotional precipice. "I said, I love you. I love *you*, Saoirse." And once that dam burst, the words just tumbled out one after another. "I've loved you from the moment I caught you eating my chicken in the dark. Since the day I carried you outside to do your earth thing. Since the day you gave me that pomegranate. And every day after that. I was just afraid to say anything. Our worlds are so different, and neither of us knows how it's all going to play out. You're the most beautiful woman I've ever laid eyes on, and you are so kind, and funny, and—and considerate, and I am in no manner, fashion, or form good enough for you. In fact, I—"

She touched a fingertip to his lips, a sweet smile curving her lips. "Is it time for my rose petals, champagne, chocolates, and strawberries?"

He blinked. "Do what now?"

"That is what you said to me. *Your first time should be special—rose petals on the bed, champagne, chocolates, and strawberries, that kind of thing. And with someone you love.*"

Realization slowly dawned, and even though every cell in his body reacted to her innocent words, he still needed to be sure. He needed *her* to be sure. Forget reasonable doubt—he had to be positive beyond the shadow of any doubt. "Saoirse, I—"

"I have thought much on this, so if you think to dissuade me, stop. I love you, my Travis McLean, and I want my first time to be with you. I do not know what I am supposed to do, so I hope you will be patient with me. You are a very good teacher, and I shall try my best not to disappoint you."

"Disappoint me?" he echoed, desperately hoping his erection wouldn't rip through his tuxedo pants. He tried visualizing the foul odor of the holding cell floor after a wild Easter weekend again, but it kept turning into his bedroom. With firm resolve, he gave up the struggle and grabbed her hand. "I want to take you home. Right now."

"And you will take me to your bed?" she asked, eyes wide.

Jesus, have mercy. "Please—I need you to stop talking about it, or we're not going to make it to the car, much less home."

She beamed. "Then, yes. I will go with you."

Travis leapt from his seat, pulling her chair back so fast that her feet flew up, and she had to grip the arms to hold on. Even Mike was startled by the suddenness. "You good?" he asked, at once concerned.

"Yeah—we gotta go," he hedged, holding out his hand to assist Saoirse. "Like now."

Mike began to rise from his seat. "You good?" he asked again. "Is everything okay? Do we need—"

"NO. Everything is fine. Just fine. We have to go."

Saoirse picked up her purse and waggled her fingers in a wave to Geena and Mike. "Thank you for helping me tonight. It has been a most memorable evening." And to Travis's abject horror, she placed her hand on his back, slowly sliding it down until it reached his butt cheek. She gave it a quick squeeze before grinning up at him. "I am ready to go now. Are you?"

Travis did not have Saoirse grabbing his ass on the evening's bingo card and wasn't quite sure how to react. He decided to pretend it did not happen, and that no one saw it not happen. He offered his arm, and she slid her hand in the crook of his elbow. He turned to Mike. "Y'all, uh—be, uh—going—uh, driving home."

"You don't say," Mike said, starting to laugh. To make matters worse, even Geena joined in.

The heat crept up his collar as he stopped and straightened his shoulders with a slight shake. "It's been fun, but we're heading home," he said, his words slow and deliberate. "Geena, thank you for all your help. Y'all be safe going home. Mike, I'll give you a call tomorrow."

Saoirse squealed with laughter, struggling to keep up as he whirled and bolted for the door. Mike's voice rang out, his parting advice cutting through the large room filled with noise from party chatter and music. "Go get 'em, tiger!"

Once out of sight of the small group gathered around the entrance of the convention center, chatting and laughing, Travis swept her up into his arms and ran to the Hellcat. Saoirse held on for dear life, giggling all the way. "I sense you are excited. Should I be afraid?"

"I don't expect to live through the night, but I plan to go out with a big smile on my face and hopefully on yours, too," he explained matter-of-factly.

"You will tell me what I need to do, how, and when? And what not to do. I do not—"

"Christ, girl—*relax*. We're not defusing bombs here. Don't overthink it. You do whatever you want, and I'll try my best to keep up."

As badly as he wanted to touch her on the drive home, he only allowed himself the modest pleasure of holding her hand. If he had to guess, the thirty-minute or so drive had taken them roughly fifteen hours so far. It took every ounce of his resolve not to pull over in the first dark parking lot and ravish her right there like some hormone-crazed teenager.

Neither spoke again, but the slight trembling in her hand was a testament to her nervousness. He gave it a reassuring squeeze. "Breathe," he soothed. "The pressure is on me right now. I only hope I live up to your expectations."

"You will be perfect, as in all things." She nodded once for emphasis and looked out the window, a mischievous grin on her face. "Are we there yet?"

CHAPTER 27

Travis had never been a religious man, but he had the distinct feeling this woman was about to take him to church.

He pressed the button to close the garage door before the car even rolled to a full stop and jumped out to open her door. Saoirse waited for him, offering a slender hand when he extended his own. She pressed against him as he typed in the alarm code with a trembling hand, miskeyed it, cleared his entry, and tried again. It took three attempts to disarm the system successfully. "I promise we do live here," he quipped in a desperate effort to get some semblance of control over his emotions.

Saoirse placed her hand on his arm. "Breathe," she suggested, her voice warm with a smile.

At once, Travis felt a calming wave pass over him, an almost drugging peace. His muscles relaxed, and the tightness in his chest eased. "Thank you," he whispered. "I'm sorry, I don't know—"

"Shush," she said, touching a finger to his lips.

His serenity lasted until they were in the kitchen. He reset the alarm, and a fresh blast of anxiety hit. *Are my sheets clean?* He tried to remember what condition his bedroom was in after rushing to get ready for the benefit. *Do I have any candles? It has to be perfect, everything has to be just—*

"No, it doesn't," she said with an impish smile. She grabbed his hand and tugged him down the hallway. "Stop dragging your feet—you have made me wait long enough." One shoulder lifted in a dismissive shrug. "Or if you are no longer interested, I suppose we could see what is on the TV, or—"

"Challenge accepted," Travis mock growled, pulling her against him. Sucking in a deep breath, he turned the knob and flung open the bedroom door. His heart sank. It was indeed a mess—the clothing worn earlier lay on the floor near the closet door, which sported a wet towel slung over the top. The dresser and nightstand tops were cluttered with various miscellany that had not found their proper places.

His shoulder demon chose that moment to speak up. *Since when have you ever cared about tidying up before bringing a woman over? Clean sheets? Really?*

This is different, he snapped. *Way different. Mind your business.*

"To whom do you speak?" Saoirse asked.

Jesus, tell me I didn't say that out loud. "Just my conscience, I guess," he said halfheartedly. "I wanted everything to be perfect for you. This isn't it." He pulled away from her and began rummaging through his nightstand drawer. "I think I might have some candles—"

"Stop." She crossed the room and cradled his face in her hands. "Close your eyes and show me what you envisioned."

Travis shut his eyes tightly and began to imagine. His bed, with pristine sheets and extra-soft pillows, was littered with soft rose petals. Scented candles provided a soft glow, and the light from a full moon overhead illuminated the room in an ethereal light.

"More."

Enjoying the game, he added a small table covered in a white tablecloth that swept the floor. A sterling platter with small pieces of cut fruit and a silver bowl of melted dark chocolate appeared, accompanied by two elegant crystal champagne flutes. The bottle of Dom Pérignon, chilled nearby in a wine bucket on a stand, completed the scene.

"More," she encouraged. "Is this room perfect?"

"Not yet." He moved his bed onto a white sand beach under a wooden pergola draped with sheer netting. He added hundreds of the strange flowers that had sprouted in his backyard, the vines twirling around the thick legs of the arbor.

She whispered close to his ear. "Do you smell them?"

"Uh-huh." He nodded, inhaling deeply. Their scent was pure intoxication—a potent combination of floral and spicy notes that weakened his knees.

"Keep your eyes closed—are you there now?"

He stood on the beach near the pergola's netting entrance, startled to find himself naked. A light breeze ran its fingers through his hair and caressed his bare skin. The warm sand beneath his feet was smooth like a fine powder. A loud splash caught his attention, and he turned in time to see a massive fish arc high into the air and disappear under the clear, blue waters. The snakelike leviathan was like nothing he had ever seen, its chameleon colors sparkling under the moonlight.

Moonlight. He looked up at the two moons overhead, one full and one crescent. "Where are we?" he murmured in awe.

Suddenly, Saoirse stood by his side. As naked as he, her hair fell in beguiling curls, shielding her breasts from his gaze. He slid his arm around to pull her close, her skin soft as the ocean breeze. "How did you know?" she asked, wide-eyed.

Eyes still closed, he shook his head in confusion. "Know what? Where are we?" he asked again.

"The Old Ones shared their memories with me." She smiled, looking around. "This was our home in the before time. You have brought us back."

"This isn't Earth," he said, his sentence ending with a slight lift. When she did not answer, he dropped a kiss on the top of her head. "What's it called?"

"You have no word for it in your tongue," she answered, shaking her head. Pulling away, she tugged his hand, leading him toward the water. "Come—I tire of talking. Let us swim."

Travis hesitated. "Is it safe?" he asked. "At home, nighttime is when the sharks come into the shallows to feed."

"Nothing will harm us here, and the sea is healing. Come," she ordered. "Take me into the water."

Without another word, he swept her into his arms and splashed through the gently breaking waves. Astonished at his suddenly fertile imagination, he felt the refreshing water on his skin, the current alternately tugging and gently pulling. He released her to float on her back when the water reached his waist. She stretched both arms overhead, extended her toes, threw back her head, and laughed. "This is perfect," she said with a sigh. "*You* are perfect, my Travis."

"Well, I don't know about all that..." He gave a self-deprecating laugh.

"I do. Open your eyes."

He did, and his mouth dropped open in disbelief. "This is all real? How did—"

"You talk overmuch." Without warning, Saoirse pounced on him, but he caught her easily and wrapped her long legs around his waist. She turned her face up to his with a serious yet earnest expression. "Teach me everything."

He turned and began walking toward the curtained pergola, cradling her body against his chest. "Yes, ma'am," he whispered.

The moons did not appear to change their positions. Travis could not measure time, but it hung suspended beneath the canopy. They made love for hours, taking occasional breaks to eat, talk, or play. He had never been accused of being a chatterbox in bed, solely focused on physical sensations. In his experience, pillow talk usually involved sharing feelings, something he avoided at all costs. Words uttered during the heat of passion, particularly the one starting with *L*, tended to bite him in the ass once the daylight came.

Saoirse was the exception. With no thought of what the new day would bring, he threw himself into the moment with complete abandon. Maybe it was the champagne or the erotic tension that had built between them over the months. Or perhaps it was how she looked at him like he was her entire world, moon, and stars. He paid tribute to her keen intelligence, quick mind, and sense of humor. He sang praises to her beauty, worshipping each part of her body. Beautiful words more worthy of a poet tumbled from his lips in a liturgy of love and devotion as they reached the pinnacle and were swept away in that dark tsunami over and over.

When they were both satiated, Travis lay on his back with Saoirse snuggled into his side, one shapely thigh resting atop his. He used his remaining strength to pull her closer still and kiss her forehead. "Now I understand," she said with a long, satisfied sigh.

At that moment, Travis was so relaxed he could not move anything but his mouth. "Understand what?"

Her fingers teased the wispy curls over his heart. "Why humans lie, or cheat, or even kill for this. It confused me before, watching television that shows people willing to die for it. For this feeling. For love. Why people do the craziest things to capture even the tiniest taste of this ecstasy. Now that I have experienced it for myself, all I want is more." She tilted her head back to see his face, her eyes heavy with drowsy contentment. "Is this what drugs feel like?" she said, yawning.

"I've heard people call love a kind of drug, so maybe. It has recently come to my attention that I have never been in love before, so all this is new to me, too."

"Oh? And may I ask who told you this?"

Jealous streak duly noted. He chuckled and pulled her tight. "You did, faery girl."

In the morning, Travis cracked one eye open when the first rays of sunlight crept through his bedroom window and smacked him full in the face. He stretched tentatively, and every muscle he had ached in response to the slight movement. The only thing that kept him from thinking he had the most vivid, brilliant, in-your-face dream was the diminutive woman in his bed. Saoirse curled into his side like a cat, sighing softly in her sleep. Her mussed hair tangled around her face, her lips still swollen from his kisses. She was the most breathtaking sight he had ever seen.

He moved slowly to disentangle himself without disturbing her. She made a chiming sound in protest when he broke contact and scooted into the warm spot he had just vacated. Once he was certain he had not woken her, he hobbled his way to the bathroom. *Feels like somebody beat me with a two-by-four*, he thought as he took care of business. He grinned and flexed his arms in the mirror. *Might be time to invest in a treadmill, cardio interval training, or something like that. Keeping her satisfied is a fitness challenge I can totally get behind.*

CHAPTER 28

Travis had mentioned Mike would be dropping by later that morning, so when the doorbell rang, Saoirse thought nothing of answering it while he puttered around in the garage. Without checking first, she threw open the door, then stopped short. "Who are you?" she blurted out, startled.

The elegant middle-aged woman wore a tailored pantsuit, a floral silk blouse, and a scarf emblazoned with the realtor's logo tied jauntily around her neck. Her mouth dropped open in shock before she expertly recovered her poise. "I'm Barbara Nielson with the realty," she replied, waving an elegantly manicured hand toward her scarf. "I just wanted to stop by and drop off some new listings for Officer McLean. And you are...?"

Saoirse hesitated before answering. "I am Saoirse. Travis is home. I shall let him know you are here."

As she began to turn, the realtor caught her by the arm. "You don't need to bother him, honey. Could I leave these with you?" She extended a folder Saoirse hadn't noticed, and her voice dropped to a conspiratorial level. "Are you two a couple? Oh, I do hope so. A bachelor his age needs to think about getting married, and if you don't mind me saying, you are just about as cute as a button. This big house needs to be filled with a family and lots of pretty babies."

"Yes, ma'am," Saoirse said carefully, taking the folder. "Are you sure you would not like me to—"

"Who's at the door?" Travis asked, stepping from the kitchen to the foyer as he dried his hands with a kitchen towel. He looked past Saoirse at the woman. "Oh—hi, Miss Barbara," he said, stepping closer and taking the folder. He opened it to scan the contents. "More listings?"

"Well, it doesn't look like you'll need to sell after all," she exclaimed. "I am over the moon delighted to meet you, Saoirse. You two make the cutest couple! Please let me know when you set the date. So exciting," she gushed. "You both are positively glowing." To Travis, she added, "Let me know if you need any assistance with venues or caterers, anything like that. I have many good connections in town." She winked and, with a wave, strode back to her Mercedes. "Y'all have a good day, now!"

They waved as the expensive sedan backed out of the driveway and drove away. Saoirse frowned in confusion. "We glow?"

"It's just a figure of speech," Travis assured her. "She's making a whole lot of assumptions, but it's better just to let her think what she wants." He affectionately chucked her under the chin. "Although I agree with her, you are as cute as a button." With that, he turned and headed back to the garage.

"Buttons are cute?" she murmured, but the frown remained. The other things the woman had said struck a new realization. It had never occurred to her that their relationship, as much as she adored him, would hold him back. *I cannot give him children*, she thought, suddenly miserable. *He speaks so often of his parents. Why would I think he does not desire children of his own? Does my presence keep him from that which he wants most?*

She wandered into the great room and grabbed a magazine, absently thumbing through the pages. By her estimation, every single page featured a baby. *Perhaps that Lori Ann woman would better suit*, she mused, but the mere thought of the blonde getting anywhere near Travis made her jaw tighten in anger. In a fit of pique, she threw the magazine back down and stamped a small foot, arms crossed. *He has made no mention of desiring children. Would he not have said if he did?*

Before she could talk herself out of it, she stormed through the house to the garage, where Travis stood looking for something on his workbench. "I must know," she began without preamble, "if children are something you most desire."

The look on his face was priceless. "Children? Like having kids, you mean?" He scratched his head. "Never much thought about it, I suppose."

This wasn't the answer she expected, but she would not be deterred. "Well, do." And with that, she whirled on her heel and disappeared into the kitchen.

Clearly, that was not the shot to fire and run. Travis quickly closed the distance between them, catching her arm. "Hold on," he ordered, dragging her to a halt. "Where did that come from? Did Miss Barbara say something to you?"

"She said to fill this house with pretty babies. This I cannot give you. Mayhap I am selfish for staying here with you as we have been. It is unfair that I distract you from finding the perfect mate. I should set aside my feelings and find you a lady wife to bear your children and make you happy. She will oversee your household and ensure it is properly run. Should I be fortunate, mayhap she will let me sleep under the sink if I promise to serve her." A loud wail punctuated the last words as Saoirse burst into inconsolable tears.

Flabbergasted at this appalling turn of events, Travis stepped back, raising his hands and enunciating each staccato syllable. "What. The. Actual. Hell."

This brought an even louder howl as she collapsed in a heap on the floor. She hugged herself tightly and began rocking back and forth as she keened. "And now I have made you angry on top of everything," she sobbed.

"Okay, this has got to stop." Moving slowly so as not to startle her, he knelt and wrapped her tightly in his arms. He held her for several minutes while she continued to cry. "Saoirse, I need you to listen to me," he finally said, stroking her hair. "The thought of having kids has never once crossed my mind. My life, liberty, and pursuit of happiness don't hinge on having babies. I'd rather have you, just you. And maybe adopt a bunch of dogs."

"But she said—"

"Her opinion doesn't matter. It's yours and mine that count. So, right now, I need you to dry your eyes. You don't need to worry one hair on your pretty little head about this one second more."

She drew in a deep, shuddering breath. "You mean that?"

"I do," he assured her.

"Lots of dogs?"

"Dozens."

"And candy?" she asked hopefully.

He burst into laughter. "All you can eat."

CHAPTER 29

The following Sunday found Travis tinkering with the motorcycle again, blasting tunes on the speaker. This time, Saoirse's interest was more than passing. She placed a folded shop towel on the floor near where he knelt. When his focus didn't waver from the bolt he struggled to reattach, she plopped down and sat cross-legged on the towel to wait. "Why does it not work?" she finally asked.

"I'm not sure," he answered, scratching his head. "Doesn't seem to be getting a charge."

She waited patiently until the bolt was firmly in place. "Are all the pieces back together now?"

He nodded, rising to his feet. Throwing a leg over, he turned the key, but the engine only sputtered a few times and died with a whimper. He swore under his breath. "I thought for sure that would be it," he muttered as he began to dismount.

Leaning forward, she touched her fingertip lightly to the engine. It roared to life with a throaty growl, startling Travis so severely he almost dropped it. The bike revved itself twice and settled into a low purring idle. She sat back with a pleased smile on her face. "I should like to go ride it now," she announced, scrambling to her feet. She disappeared inside the garage closet, the muffled thumps marking her search. Before long, she returned with two helmets, still in their original boxes.

Grinning, he took his father's helmet and pulled it on. "Climb aboard, milady," he quipped, patting the seat behind him.

Saoirse hopped on, chirping with excitement, and he adjusted her chinstrap. Snuggling up against his back, she threw both arms around his waist and squeezed him tightly. They coasted to the end of the driveway as the garage door rolled closed. Travis set his feet down to stop. "Where would you like to go?"

"I care not, sir, as long as we go somewhere I have not yet seen," she said, tilting her nose with an imperious air.

"I know just the place."

Located about twenty-two miles from neighboring Myrtle Beach, the little township of Cherry Grove is the northernmost point of the Grand Strand. For over eighty years, no vacation to the Grand Strand has been complete without time well spent "Cruising the Boulevard." Traffic creeps along at a snail's pace on the street lined on both sides with beachwear stores, snack bars, arcades, games of chance, bars, thrill rides, and tourists on the sidewalks striking up conversations with the drivers.

Travis turned onto Ocean Boulevard and merged into the line of cars, golf carts, and motorcycles traveling southbound. He watched Saoirse in the rearview mirror as she twisted and turned, trying to see everything. She chattered nonstop in a running commentary, pointing out the different attractions. Her excitement was infectious, and as soon as he found a good spot, he guided the bike into it and parked.

He offered his hand to help her dismount. "I have something very special to show you," he said mysteriously. Taking her hand, they walked up the street until they stood in front of a tall glass building that seemed much older than the other shops.

Saoirse shielded her eyes against the sun as she stared up at the sign. "The Gay Dolphin?" she asked. "What is this place?"

"It defies description—you'll have to see it to believe," he laughed, opening the door for her. "But I think you might like it."

Now *that* was an understatement. The Gay Dolphin remains a mainstay of touristy shopping, selling Myrtle Beach souvenirs from monogrammed ashtrays to faux zebra hides and everything in between. With ten split levels in the high-rise store, navigating can be a chaotic labyrinth.

Travis, a practiced GD explorer, made a fast decision and guided them up to the top level so they could work their way back down. As expected, Saoirse's love of the store did not adequately describe her reaction. Stunned and overwhelmed, her eyes widened like saucers.

He stopped walking when she still had not spoken by the second level. "All this quiet is scaring me—are you okay?"

She answered with a slow nod. "There is so much to see; I don't want to miss anything. There are so many colors..." Her voice trailed off.

"You've mentioned that before," he mused aloud. "Were there not a lot of bright colors where you were?"

"Butterflies and birds. People did not wear shades such as these," she said, indicating her burgundy sweater, jeans, and plum windbreaker. "But our clothing was not nearly so fine. I feel like a princess here with you, living in a palace and wearing beautiful clothes."

He put an arm around her shoulder and pulled her close. "You deserve all this and much more than I could ever afford."

A delicate blush stained her cheeks, but whatever she was about to say got tangled up in her gasp. "That is the most beautiful thing I have ever seen," she murmured.

Travis turned to see what had caught her attention. A necklace display sat on the glass counter, hung with dozens of enamel pendants in different animal shapes. "Which one?" he asked.

She didn't answer. With a trembling hand, she touched her fingertip to a butterfly charm. It seemed to capture every color in the rainbow, shot through with gold filigree on a dainty chain.

The man behind the counter sat on a wooden stool reading a tattered paperback. He looked up with interest, scenting a potential sale. When Travis waved him over, he didn't hesitate. "Can I help you folks find something?" he asked.

Travis turned away and lowered his voice. "Can I pay for this here?"

"Sure can." The man turned his attention to Saoirse. "Which one of these is your favorite, young lady?"

After an encouraging nod from Travis, she answered. "I find the butterfly most beautiful."

Todd, the man's name tag read, removed it from the display. "Would y'all want a bag for this?" he asked.

Saoirse's eyes widened. "This is far too much—"

Travis pulled out his wallet and exchanged his debit card for the necklace. "Turn around," he ordered.

She turned and lifted her hair, exposing the creamy expanse of her neck. He fastened the chain, then turned her to see for himself. It brushed the top of the hinted cleavage underneath her sweater. "It's perfect," he announced.

The clerk slid the countertop mirror over so she could see for herself while Travis completed the sale. "It is lovely on you, miss," he agreed.

Saoirse stared at herself in the mirror for a long moment before turning her gaze to Travis, her eyes bright with tears. "It is the most beautiful—" she whispered, but then changed her mind and enveloped him in a ferocious hug. "Thank you."

Travis's gaze met Todd's, and the older man gave him a cheeky grin and wink. "Y'all have a good day, now."

"We'll do our best—you too!" he called back, guiding Saoirse toward the decorative iron stairs separating the levels. The next floor held hats of all kinds, and she had fun modeling different styles for his approval. The section below that had t-shirts and beach towels. Travis spied the men's room sign and realized he'd have to leave her for just a minute. "I'm going to run to the restroom, but I'll be right back. You stay right here, and don't go anywhere, okay?"

She nodded, browsing through a rack of Hawaiian shirts. He was only gone for a few seconds before a deep male voice asked, "You here by yourself, gorgeous?"

Startled, Saoirse whirled around. "I am not," she said. Before she could resume shopping again, a large hand wrapped around her wrist. She tried to pull free, but the grip was firm. "Unhand me at once," she growled.

"Looks to me you're all by yourself," the man said. He looked like one of the miscreants she had seen on TV—big, slightly overweight, and wearing a denim jacket with the sleeves cut out. "Why don't you come along with Ol' Red here? I'll take real good care of you."

"I said unhand me," she snapped. "I am not alone, and I am not going anywhere with you."

"I say different," he said flatly, pulling her to his side and taking several steps toward the stairs.

"Stop," Saoirse demanded, dragging her feet. "Look at my face."

Surprised by her authoritative tone, he did and tilted her face up to look into her eyes. "You're a pretty little thing, that's for—"

For one brief second, she allowed him to see her true face, the one even Travis had not seen. Her eyes grew rounder, with vertical pupils, and when she blinked, the nictating membrane slid over and back slowly.

He dropped her arm like he had been burned. "What the fuck *are* you?" he gasped, stepping away from her.

The door to the restrooms opened. "I am not yours," she retorted, willing her human face to return. "And will never be. Best you leave now."

Ol' Red didn't need to be told twice. He blasted past Travis in his haste to escape, never bothering to look back. Travis stepped aside, looking startled. "Excuse you," he called after the retreating man, before noting Saoirse's body posture. She stood braced with feet apart, fists curled on her hips, scowling after the fleeing man as he disappeared around a postcard display. "What happened? Was that man bothering you?"

"He was, but I handled it," she said firmly.

"You must have, the way he lit up out of here," Travis said. "Should I ask how?"

"No. Probably not."

CHAPTER 30

The dispatcher's voice broke the extended silence. "842—are you available to assist state on a vehicle scan on westbound 22, mile marker three?"

Travis grabbed the mic. "Affirmative, let them know we'll be there in ten."

"Copy, 842."

He knocked on the divider door. "Wake up, Sleeping Beauty—we gotta work."

Saoirse yawned, stretched, and then shook fiercely from nose to tail. "Can we get food after? I am very hungry. Something sweet like doughnuts. And a pup cup."

Travis flipped on the lights and nodded. "We can do that after we help the staties with their stop."

It took just under ten minutes to get there. Highway Patrol had a luxury sedan pulled over onto the shoulder. Four people had been cuffed and were seated on the ground, loudly protesting their innocence. Two of the County cars also responded to the call for assist. Everyone stood around, talking and waiting for the K9 unit to arrive.

He parked on the shoulder and clipped Saoirse's leash to her harness. "Be careful," he warned. "I don't like the feel of this."

"I will," she assured him.

They exited the cruiser and approached the trooper who appeared to be in charge. Without preamble, the senior officer began to explain. "I stopped him for speed and left of center, but the car reeks of weed. Wouldn't give me permission to search, of course, but the smell is fresh. Would you run your dog to confirm?"

"Yes, sir." Travis nodded. Giving Saoirse a short whistle, they began walking around the rental car. Even though she knew her job inside and out, he still gave the commands for the benefit of their audience. As expected, she alerted on the interior and trunk almost immediately.

Travis nodded to the trooper. "All yours, sir," he said. He shortened the lead, bringing Saoirse close to heel.

Surprising him, she pulled on her harness, dragging him to a clearly miserable young woman seated cross-legged on the ground. "Get that thing away from me," she squealed, rearing back in alarm and trying to wiggle away.

"*Kemne*," he ordered, tugging her back toward their cruiser. He patted his thigh. "C'mon, Search. We're done here."

Saoirse parked her butt in front of the girl and refused to budge, no matter how hard Travis pulled. When he tried again, she whined softly.

Eventually catching on, he waved the female trooper over. "Have they all been searched?" he asked, keeping his voice low.

"Yeah, just as soon as they were cuffed," the officer answered.

"What are you trying to tell me?" Travis wondered aloud, then asked again. "Was this woman searched? My dog is alerting on her."

The trooper's tone was more than a little frosty. "Yes, I did it myself."

Saoirse whined again even louder. "Show me," Travis ordered. He stood behind Saoirse, who had jumped to her feet, staring straight at the woman like a pointer. "Show me," he repeated. She barked once and whined again.

"Ma'am, my dog seems very interested in you for some reason," Travis said, squatting down and directing his question to the seated woman. "Any idea why that might be?"

"I don't have anything," the girl snapped, jerking her head once at the female trooper. "That bitch over there told you already."

When Travis shrugged, Saoirse rolled her eyes and sighed heavily, ending in a soft whine. She flopped over on her back, exposing her belly, and chattered her teeth several times.

"You're acting mighty…" He stopped, studying the girl. A thin sheen of sweat coated her waxy face. At once, all the pieces fell into place, and he leapt to his feet. "Start EMS," he yelled back to the troopers. "Ma'am, what drugs did you swallow?"

She opened her mouth to speak, but no words came. Her entire body shuddered, wracked by violent convulsions. Travis held her upright, supporting her arms while she vomited up several small plastic bags of white powder. She collapsed like a rag doll, the whites of her eyes visible. He rolled her onto her side to clear the airway, placing two fingers on her carotid. "No pulse."

The female trooper dropped down beside him, tearing open a plastic package. She shoved the nozzle into the girl's nose and squirted. "Narcan administered, left nostril," she called out.

The piercing siren grew louder as the ambulance approached. Travis backed away, letting the troopers take over the scene. He took a knee next to Saoirse and hugged her close. "What a rock star," he whispered. "You saved her life."

The surrounding activity of loading the overdose victim onto the gurney and putting the arrested in the County cars masked her quiet response. "Two pup cups. And nuggies."

"Anything you want," he said, giving her a quick squeeze.

As the EMS unit left for the hospital and the other cruisers began to depart, Travis suddenly became aware of how quiet the evening had become. He turned to meet the hard stares from four sets of eyes. "How did your dog do that?"

"Do what?" He decided to play dumb, at least for the moment. "Oh, that... well, she's certified on narcotics."

The female trooper stepped forward with arms akimbo and planted her fists on her hips. "But that dog *told* you she swallowed those drugs. How did she know?"

Travis scratched his head and shrugged. "Seems logical she would have handled the bags before ingesting them. Search probably detected the odor on her hands."

The gathered officers made noises of agreement, but the remaining trooper wouldn't buy the simple explanation. "Your dog alerted on the woman. When you said *show me*, Search rolled over and gave you her belly. Now, I'm not a K9 handler, but it seems to me she was telling you the drugs were inside her stomach."

"You're McLean, aren't you?" one asked. "I've heard a lot about how smart your dog is."

"She's too smart for her own good," Travis agreed, laughing it off. "She flunked out of med school, so I think the appearance of her making any roadside diagnosis would have to be just a coincidence." As if to confirm, Saoirse flopped down and rolled onto her back, begging for a rub. "See, it was just a weird timing thing. She loves a good tummy scratch."

"She's a good girl," one of the County guys said, reaching for the exposed belly.

Travis caught the officer's arm before he got within biting range. "Ahhh... I wouldn't do that," he advised, guiding him back. "She runs a little spicy." Saoirse bared every tooth in a wide grin and rumbled deep in her chest. The officer hastened to pull away and step back.

"Well, I promised somebody a pup cup," he said, straightening. "You ready, girl?" Saoirse began pulling on the lead, and he used that excuse to make their exit. "Y'all have a good night, stay safe." He let her tug him back to their car and opened the door for her to hop inside.

Saoirse didn't speak until they were back on the highway. "I feel as if I did something wrong, but I do not know what," she whined, the cabin thumping as she scratched her ear with her back foot.

Travis thought a long while before answering her. "You didn't do anything wrong," he finally said. "You saved her life, and that's the important thing."

"I smelled death on her."

"That's right, and you alerted to tell me, which is what you're trained to do."

Saoirse snorted. "Then why did everyone stare and become hostile?"

"You did the right thing," he said firmly, "but a real dog wouldn't know how to communicate that the drugs were in her stomach. I'm pretty sure it freaked them out."

The inside of the car grew quiet as they traveled. "I saved her life, though?"

"Yes, ma'am, you did. I'm very proud of you."

"Are you so proud that I can have three pup cups, nuggies, *and* doughnuts?"

He burst into laughter. "Don't push your luck. I may have to get a second job or set up a GoFundMe just to support your dessert deficiency."

CHAPTER 31

Travis pulled the covers back and climbed into bed. "It's a lecture, sweetheart, and it'll be boring as hell," he insisted. "I'll be stuck staring at a whiteboard for hours, praying I don't doze off and start snoring. You'd be bored out of your mind in under five minutes. Stay here and relax. I'll be back before you know it." He snaked an arm underneath her pillow for a quick snuggle.

"I do not like this." Her lower lip pushed out in a pout. "I do not wish to relax when you are not here."

He blew out a deep breath and sighed. "It's just how it is. I can't explain why I'm bringing you in for a class not involving K9s." He drew her closer for a soft kiss on her temple. "It'll be fine. Now—I need sleep." He laughed as he reached behind him and turned off the bedside lamp. "You've worn me out, faery girl."

She stiffened in his arms, not yielding an inch.

"You're not supposed to go to bed mad, you know," he tried soothingly.

Saoirse huffed and gave him her back, scooting a few inches toward the edge of the bed.

He wasn't about to play that game. "Get back over here," he ordered. "Took me long enough to get you in my bed. I'm not about to let you camp out all the way over there."

She did not answer, but allowed him to pull her close again, her muscles still tense.

Thinking the battle won, Travis sighed and relaxed, settling into sleep. The first sign that the siege was far from over came in the form of a tiny sting on his cheek, followed by another, then another. He swiped a hand to his face, only to find his skin moist and his nose cold.

He turned on the light and gazed up at the ceiling. Tiny snowflakes drifted down, dusting the comforter in sparkling white. He blew out a deep, aggrieved sigh, his breath fogging in the chill. "Saoirse," he said carefully. "It's snowing. Indoors. In our bedroom."

A soft snore escaped her lips, and she snuggled deeper under the blankets.

"Saoirse," he repeated, a note of warning creeping into his voice.

When she still didn't answer, he gritted his teeth. "Saoirse!" There was no sign or movement to indicate she heard him, but he would have bet a paycheck she did. Disentangling himself, he eased out of bed and padded naked across the room to the dresser. He yanked one of the lower drawers open and, grumbling under his breath, yanked the knit cap down over his ears. Shaking out the waterproof mylar blanket, he fanned it out over the bedspread, climbed back into bed, and turned out the light. He pulled the covers up to his nose and exhaled deeply, determined to get some sleep. The last sound he remembered hearing was a soft but undeniably triumphant feminine giggle.

Travis was antsy, unable to pinpoint the source of his unease. When he arrived at the conference, most other attendees were already there and mingling in small groups before the lecture began. He grabbed a cup of coffee from the hospitality table and gave it the proper dosage of cream and sugar. Taking a cautious sip, he joined a group of officers laughing at an anecdote one had just shared. "What's going on?" he asked, looking around.

"Campbell was just telling us about his brother in the Myrtle Beach PD. He got a wild report from a tourist last week."

Travis blew on the coffee to cool it and took another sip. "What happened?"

"The guy flagged his cruiser down, screaming he had just seen an alien on the Boulevard. Inside the Gay Dolphin, of all places. He gave the dude the standard DUI tests, but he passed everything—stone cold, straight, and sober."

"That's different," he said with a bark of laughter. "Did he say what the alien looked like? Maybe little and green, flying saucer, that kind of thing?"

"Nah, man—he said she was drop-dead gorgeous. He hit on her, thinking she was there by herself. But when she looked straight at him, she had eyes like a snake. You know, with the vertical pupils and the third eyelid that comes up?"

Travis went very still. "What happened after that?"

"He said he saw a guy coming toward them and thought there might be more aliens, so he beat it out of there to find a cop and report it."

"Well, we all know the field sobriety tests don't pick up on crazy," Travis said, quickly brushing it off.

With perfect timing, the lecturer's voice rang out over the chatter. "If everyone could take their seats, we'll get started."

He sat in the packed conference room, notepad and pen at the ready, his eye on the clock. The lecture on the new policy and procedure dragged on for what felt like years. The short, bespectacled instructor spoke in a Sahara Desert dry, monotone voice, reading each slide aloud as if his captive audience could not read for themselves. The information was good, but could easily have been relayed in a mandatory reading email.

He hated leaving Saoirse at home, especially after her ire last night. He casually raised a hand to his face, remembering the sting of icy snowflakes. This morning, she seemed to have forgiven him, sending him off with a kiss and a flutter of long eyelashes, suggesting he not tarry long after class. Too late, it occurred to him that if she had shifted, he could have carried the proverbial mouse in his pocket for the duration of class. He smothered a smile at that, thinking how wide his world had opened.

After the slideshow, Travis readied to head for the door, but the instructor began a Q&A period for the class, which stretched on for another hour. Travis watched the second hand on the clock tick by, his sense of foreboding worsening with each passing minute. Trusting in the soldier's instinct that had kept him alive during combat, he swore under his breath, ready to throat-punch the next rookie who asked anything remotely asinine.

At the magic words—"Thank you all for coming today"— Travis slid his chair back and stretched, movements slow and measured. As soon as several others rose and the after-class chatter began, he bolted for the door and disappeared before he could be drawn into any conversations.

Once his car door closed, he blew out a long breath in a deliberate effort to relax. His recent life had been in a constant state of hyperawareness, acknowledging the imminent threat, but not knowing when or how it'd arrive.

Like living in a war zone, he thought, remembering his time in the Middle East. Still, to keep Saoirse safe, he'd do that and much more. He grinned, wondering when he fell so in love with the immortal fae, how strange his life had been since her arrival, and how he wouldn't trade a minute of it.

The officers who patrolled around his neighborhood all knew him and his personal car, but he wouldn't take the chance of getting stopped in his haste to be home. He kept it to a few miles over the posted speed, gripping the wheel with knuckles growing whiter by the minute. He kept an eye on the digital clock, watching more time creep by. Finally rounding the corner onto his street, he sighed with relief, seeing Mike's Wrangler parked out front.

As Travis began to turn into his driveway, he saw what the Jeep had blocked on his approach. The big motorcycle lay on its side, and just for a second, Travis couldn't breathe. Combat training kicked in with a massive rush of adrenaline. At once, he turned his car off and coasted into the driveway next to the bike. His front door was ajar, and without a conscious thought to do so, he switched his body camera on. Ducking low, he drew his weapon and slid out of the Charger, leaving the door open. He darted from the open door to the rear of the Jeep, listening. When he heard nothing out of the ordinary, he crouched down next to the bike and hovered his hand over the exhaust manifold. When he did not feel any residual heat, he grabbed the pipe and found it cold. Even in the mild, often overcast fall, a bike this big would still take an hour or more to match the air temperature. Using the azalea and viburnum planted around the house as concealment, he did a fast perimeter search of the sides and front, avoiding the windows.

Travis used his key to open the high gate to the backyard. Seeing it empty, he moved to the back door, which opened into the mudroom. *Locked.* He used his key again and slowly entered, holding his Glock down and close to his body. A sickening dread uncoiled in his stomach, but he steeled himself against the rising panic. His body cam vibrated, reminding him that it was still recording. Not knowing who else would see the video, he thought fast and instead of calling for Saoirse, he whistled as he would for his K9. No response.

"Mike? Where you at, man?"

Nothing.

The house sat quiet and still as the grave. He cleared the rear rooms quickly, working his way to the front. Nothing appeared out of place, but as he entered the great room, an unfamiliar hint of something reflective caught his eye. He saw the debris field of glass fragments in the foyer and frowned. The mirror had shattered into a million pieces, flinging the razor-edged shards a dozen or more feet away. The black king-sized flat sheets ripped from the destroyed mirror lay in a heap near the door.

As he drew closer, the pile shuddered with movement, and an unlaced high-top sneaker emerged from underneath. With a gasp of horror, he dropped to his knees, yanking the covering off with both hands.

Mike's eyes fluttered weakly, both hands clutched to his abdomen, where several large crimson stains bloomed. "'Bout time you got home. Thing's gone to shit 'round here," he mumbled.

Travis touched his shoulder to activate the radio. "Badge number 842, County Dispatch. I have an officer down, I repeat, officer down at—" He stopped, momentarily forgetting his own address. "1504 Marsh Way Drive, Cherry Grove. I repeat, 1504 Marsh Way. I need EMS trauma and a supervisor at my location ASAP."

"Affirmative, 842—all available units en route now."

Even as the dispatcher was speaking, he could hear approaching sirens in the distance. "Hang on, man, help's coming," he whispered, wadding up the sheet and applying pressure to staunch the bleeding. "Can you tell me what happened? Where is she?"

"Not—here," Mike wheezed out the words with great effort. "Wizard—took her through the m—mirror. S—sorry, Trav, I couldn't—" With a shudder followed by a soft exhalation, he closed his eyes and went still.

PART II

CHAPTER 32

Travis sat unmoving in the softly lit waiting room. In desperation, he stared at the doorway, willing someone—anyone—to tell him what was going on. He had never felt so helpless in his life, and he despised it. He replayed the too-short fact list over and over: Saoirse gone, Mike on an operating table fighting for his life, and Ansgar needed killing. *Took her through the mirror; what the hell does that mean? How can I even track that?*

Mike's large family began arriving soon after the unresponsive body had been rushed straight into the surgical theater. Travis braced himself as the statuesque older woman, who looked so much like his mother, wrapped him in a big bear hug. "He's going to be just fine," she assured him, whispering next to his ear. "Don't you worry. And they'll find Search, too."

"I know, Aunt Claire," he murmured, understanding she said it as much for herself as for him.

A middle-aged version of Mike crossed the room, put his arms around them both, and squeezed. When he relaxed a heartbeat later, he stepped back. "Do you have any idea what happened, Travis? All they've told us so far is that it happened at your house. Were you there? Did you see it?"

"Hey, Uncle Win," he answered. "No, sir, I had class today. I had just gotten home when I found him. He must've stopped by looking for me." He didn't know what else to say, and it went against his grain to lie. This was one of those rare situations in which telling the truth wasn't going to help anybody.

Hours ticked by with no word, and the waiting room filled to capacity. Officers came and went, each stopping to speak to the family and Travis, many offering to donate blood if needed. When an older Asian man in casual clothes and a hospital badge clipped to his belt finally appeared in the doorway, Mike's parents and siblings surged forward to get the full report. Travis hung back, listening.

"I'm Dr. Liu, the staff trauma surgeon," he said with a soft New England accent. "Your lucky young man is in post-op now. We removed one bullet from his abdomen, and I lost count of how many glass pieces. A second bullet passed through his side just above his kidney, so that's a blessing. He had several stab wounds to the chest, one of which punctured a lung. There's no damage to the major organs, but there has been massive blood loss; we're transfusing him as fast as we safely can. Fortunately, he got here quickly. Who found him?"

"That would be me," Travis answered, stepping forward, "but I wasn't there when the attack occurred. What's his status, Doctor?"

"Critical. All we can do now is wait to see how the next twenty-four hours go." He gestured toward the empty corridor and to the left. "We have a small chapel right down the hall, and a chaplain is there around the clock if anyone would like to offer up prayers. Might not be a bad idea, all things considered. It's out of our hands now."

"How soon can we see him?" Mike's father asked. "Is he awake?"

The doctor sliced his head left once in negation. "It won't be for a while yet. Once we feel it's safe to move him, he'll go to ICU. Right now, we have him under heavy sedation. He hasn't regained consciousness."

A young woman in crisp scrubs appeared behind the surgeon. She touched his arm gently to get his attention, murmuring something too quiet for Travis to hear. "Tell them I'll be right there," he said, turning back to the gathered family. "Different patient," he explained. "We'll keep you updated and let you know if anything changes."

With that, he turned and strode back through the double doors marked *Authorized Personnel Only*, the tech following close behind. They passed the two plainclothes officers just entering the waiting room. "Corporal McLean?" one of them asked formally, even though they both knew him. The younger of the two, Vic Edge, had joined the force right before Travis. The senior detective, Lambert Reeves, had just been promoted to head of the division.

Travis had expected them and appreciated that they waited until Mike's condition was known before questioning him about the day's events. "Here," he clipped out.

He turned to excuse himself just in time to catch another tight hug from his aunt. "I'll call you if anything changes," she whispered.

"Thank you, ma'am," he said and nodded. Wanting this part to be over as quickly as possible, he followed the two detectives into the hallway and asked, "Y'all want to do this at my house so you can see the crime scene at the same time?"

When they nodded, he asked the telling question. "Am I riding with you, or can I drive myself home?" When they didn't answer right away, he added, "One of you can ride with me if you want."

After a brief pause, Detective Reeves said, "We'll follow you, even though technically you're still being detained for questioning. We already know you didn't have anything to do with this; you and Mike have been joined at the hip since I've known you."

The drive home from the hospital took about thirty minutes, but moved much quicker after getting through the

Restaurant Row and Barefoot Landing tourist dinner traffic. He winced as he pulled up and parked on the street in front of his house. Mike's Jeep still sat in the driveway. A few investigators and uniformed officers lingered outside, snapping photos, taking notes, and discussing their findings. Several of the surrounding neighbors had chosen that time to do lawn work. Still, Travis understood the irresistible urge to rubberneck, especially when the object of interest happened to be a police officer.

At least they remembered to close the door. He sighed. His walkway and front porch had been sealed off with yellow crime scene tape. Even from the street, he could see the signs of fingerprint dusting on his front door. There were also markers where the motorcycle had been, but it was nowhere to be seen. Pressing the overhead remote, the garage door rolled open just as the unmarked car pulled in and parked behind him.

The time alone in the car had given him the opportunity to piece together a semblance of a story, sticking to the truth as much as possible. "I had class this morning," he explained, climbing out of the car just as the detectives reached him. "I saw the bike as I pulled in and knew something wasn't right."

"What was Mike doing here?" Edge asked.

"Not sure, but he's over here all the time. Him stopping by unannounced is normal." Travis continued his narrative as he moved through the garage. "I cleared the outside of the house and backyard first, didn't see any sign of forced entry. I came in through the back door," he said, gesturing. "Mike had to have turned off the alarm when he got here." He hated lying, knowing for a fact the alarm hadn't been set since Saoirse was at home.

Edge had retrieved a notebook from his pocket, scribbling quickly. "Did you have to use your key?"

"Yeah, the doors always stay locked," he repeated. They entered the kitchen, and all three men looked around. "I didn't see anything out of place in here, but the whole house seemed dead quiet."

"Where's your dog?"

The expected question cut Travis straight through the heart with a white-hot knife, and his knees almost buckled from the pain. "She's gone." He retraced his steps through the house, finally stopping in the foyer. Twinkling bits of broken glass littered the floor near congealing pools of blood. High velocity and castoff blood splatter on the walls marked the passage of recent violence. A partial print of a large male boot smudged one of the puddles, smearing it. The small yellow evidence markers were everywhere.

Lambert appeared to hesitate before speaking. "Given that this is your house and your K9 is missing, is it possible you were the intended target, and Mike was just in the wrong place at the wrong time?"

Travis nodded. "I'm sure of it."

"Any idea who you pissed off?"

He thought long and hard before answering. "Yeah, maybe. I was out of town near Columbia in August, ran into this creep who said he was looking for a missing girl. Seemed off to me. I suggested getting County involved, and he got pretty hostile. He took off through the woods, and I didn't see him again. Maybe he got my plate or something. I had my CGPD hat on, too." He left out the motel and welfare check parts on purpose, then threw them a distraction bone. "That bike left in my yard had colors on it. My guess is you run the VIN, it'll be the one stolen from the Apollyon scene."

Edge kept writing, so Travis kept talking. "I mentioned the guy to Mike. He had me do a suspect sketch just in case; it's around here somewhere." He walked back into the great room and started rifling through papers stacked in the wall unit bookcase.

"Why didn't you report this?" Lambert asked.

"Nothing to report. It was a brief exchange—he didn't threaten me, I didn't threaten him. I just didn't like his vibe. Here's the sketch," he said, holding out a copy of the original. "Didn't strike me as a local; he had a weird accent I couldn't place."

Lambert took it and frowned. "We'll post this around, see if anyone comes across him."

"If it's him and he took Search, he's likely not in the area anymore," Travis said, mentally adding *or in this century.* "Shooting a LEO and stealing a police K9 is some next-level shit, not the norm for your average scumbag with a grudge. Not sure how he'd be traveling; both the bike and Mike's Jeep were here."

"Could be he had help." Detective Reeves followed this with a snort. "If he did take your dog, we should check the hospitals. I'd like to know how he managed it without needing stitches. I've seen her in action. She's impressive."

Edge casually walked over to the wall organizer and skimmed the book titles before picking up the framed photo of Travis and Saoirse with arms around each other, taken at last month's Renaissance Fair. The strolling photographer's timing had been perfect, snapping the perfect picture of Saoirse in mid-laughter, wearing fake faery wings and glitter on her face. Travis's plastic crown tilted precariously as he looked down at her with a huge grin, the love shining clearly through his eyes. The detective continued his inspection of the room, his intent gaze landing first on a stack of Cosmo magazines piled on the couch, then on the small pair of sneakers under the coffee table. "Who else lives here with you?"

"Nobody," he lied. "My girlfriend moved out a couple of weeks ago. I've been boxing up her stuff."

"She around?"

"No." Travis shook his head, steeling himself against the sharp blade punching in again even harder than before. "She went back home to Ireland for a while."

"Y'all split on good terms?"

"Yes, definitely. We didn't break up or anything. She just had some unexpected family drama to deal with." He shrugged.

"When's she due back?"

Even Travis heard the misery in his voice. "I'm not sure, but I hope it's sooner rather than later."

"Is she the same one you took to the benefit?" When Travis nodded, Lambert smiled. "I didn't get the chance to meet her. You two had a crowd around you just about all night. She is one gorgeous lady."

The two detectives glanced at each other in silent communication, then Edge flipped the notepad cover and stuck it into a back pocket. "I believe that's all, but if you remember anything else, let us know."

Travis nodded and walked them out through the kitchen. "Do you know if the scene has been released yet? I'd like to get that glass up, if nothing else."

"I wouldn't touch anything just yet. I'll make sure someone calls you when it is."

CHAPTER 33

After three weeks, the doctors booted Mike out of the hospital to complete his recuperation at his parent's home. While on the mend, he worked the sympathy angle at every opportunity with his customary grin and twinkling eyes. Travis smiled—his best friend alive was a gift in itself, given the enemy he had squared off against.

He dropped in for a visit to find Mrs. Reynolds fussing over him as he lay on the couch in the family room. "Mom, I'm feeling like the Princess and the Pea here with all these pillows. I'm fine, I promise," Mike said.

She pulled the blanket up until the hem sat below his chin. "It's cold out. I don't want you getting the flu on top of all this." She waggled a finger at Bo, curled up on Mike's feet. "Get off my furniture, dog. Leave him be." Bo grumbled but did as he was told, flopping down next to the couch where Mike could scratch his ears.

"It's seventy degrees out, so mark me safe from frostbite today. Apparently, I'm not allowed to die before providing a bunch of grandchildren first," Mike joked, waving at Travis.

"That is correct," she said primly. "Travis, would you like a glass of tea?"

"Yes, ma'am—that would be real nice."

She disappeared into the kitchen but returned minutes later with a glass of iced tea and a plate of freshly made cookies. "I'll just leave you boys to visit. You call me if you need anything."

"Yes, ma'am," they both said. As soon as she left again and they could speak privately, Mike filled in all the missing pieces of the story. "Yeah, it was Ansgar. I knew you were in class, so I stopped by to check on Saoirse. I was raiding your fridge when this asshole just blew in the front door—which I one hundred percent know I locked behind me when I got there. Saoirse went to see what the noise was, and when she screamed, I dropped everything and came running." He shuddered. "Man, I expected magic wands and shit. Y'all didn't do him justice when you described how dangerous he is."

Travis nodded in sympathy. "I am so sorry this fell to you. I thought it would be me to confront him. What happened after he came in?"

"He had the leather jacket with the Apollyon colors, jeans, and combat boots. By the time I figured out who the hell he was, he was already on top of me, flashing a big-ass knife. Told Saoirse he'd skin me alive in front of her if she shifted." Mike grimaced and looked away. "I never even had the chance to draw. Saoirse kept begging him to stop, said she'd go with him if he spared me."

"That sounds like her," he murmured. Bo rose to his feet and stretched, then padded over to place his head on Travis's knee. He looked up with sad eyes and blew out a heavy sigh. Travis scratched behind the dog's ears. "I know, Buddy. I miss her too."

"I said she wasn't going anywhere. He grabbed me, so I tried to get him in a sleeper hold. The guy is too big and way too fast, with major Navy SEAL-level hand-to-hand skills. How he managed to shoot and stab me at the same time, I'll never know. When I hit the floor, he yanked the sheets off the mirror and fired the last shot into my chest."

Travis's eyes narrowed. "Ballistics said it was a .380 slug they pulled out of you. Do you remember how many shots were fired? Did it have an extended mag?"

"A bunch, maybe ten. Most of the shots went wild with us wrestling. You could probably count holes in your walls." Mike closed his eyes and frowned, then shook his head. "I don't think it was extended. Just your basic beat-to-shit pocket rocket."

Travis sat back and thought for a moment before speaking again. "The maximum rounds a .380 can carry is thirteen if it's a double-stack. I'll count holes, but if he fired ten and you caught two, he may or may not have another round left."

"That's what I thought, too."

"That's if he even kept the weapon. They didn't find anything but a few casings at the scene. The only prints on those came back to the Apollyon biker. IAFIS didn't get a hit on any of the others they found."

"Doesn't it strike you as odd that he knew how to use a firearm?" Mike wondered, scratching his head. "I mean, this guy is from over a thousand years ago. He should have been trying to hit me with a rock or something."

"I was trying not to say that out loud."

Both men fell silent for several minutes. "What happened after that?" Travis prompted.

"Saoirse put her hands on me and started singing in that Tinkerbell voice. Her palms got so hot I could feel them through my clothes. He snatched her up by the hair and shoved some kind of metal collar around her neck. Then he started chanting in a language I didn't recognize, and they both got fuzzy. I remember him kicking the sheet over me, Saoirse screaming, and then the mirror exploded. The next thing I remember is seeing you." His lips curved in a slight grin as he snorted with a laugh, then grimaced from the immediate pain. "Dude, I am never coming to your house without body armor again."

CHAPTER 34

Travis moved through his days like a robot, smiling when appropriate and frowning when not. His nights at home, however, were spent wandering from room to room like a sad ghost, unable to sleep. He avoided the things they did together, but every waking action sparked a memory of her smile, her laugh, even her exaggerated umbrage that always made him chuckle. She haunted his dreams, most ending with the nightmare image of her being snatched through the mirror and disappearing from his life forever.

One night after dozing off on the couch yet again, he wandered back into their—his—bedroom. His gaze landed on the enamel butterfly necklace near the lamp on her nightstand. Picking it up, he studied the delicate piece and smiled, remembering the day they bought it. He unclasped the chain and carefully slid the charm off. *I need this*, he thought, crossing to his side of the bed. With the solemnity of a priest administering the last rites, he slid the butterfly onto the chain to rest next to his parents' dog tags and smiled sadly. *Now you can protect me, too.*

Four weeks later, there had been no sightings of Ansgar, Saoirse, or Search despite a nationwide BOLO alert, but he knew there wouldn't be. He felt beyond guilty, wishing for the thousandth time he could tell everyone the truth and not waste the resources.

Travis fell back into bed and tugged the sheet over his naked body as a low roll of thunder sounded in the distance. *More rain*, he thought absently, his thoughts drifting back to a lifetime ago. The images of Saoirse dancing in the garage, holding her in his arms, and pressing his lips to hers replayed in his mind over and over—the hole where his heart used to be ached in response.

As the storm drew closer, he closed his eyes against the pain, and after a long while, finally dozed off in a fitful sleep.

The thunderstorm grew stronger, shaking the foundation with deep, echoing rumbles. Lightning cracked overhead, and tiny *pings* of hail pattered on the roof and windows. *That last clap sounded almost like a sonic boom*, he mused, caught on that otherworldly bridge between consciousness and dreaming. The scent of ozone filled his nostrils, clean and electric. *That's one hell of a storm ripping out there*. He rolled onto his back, determined to go back to sleep.

Travis...Travis...Travis...

Hearing his whispered name catapulted him into full wakefulness. A quick glance told him the alarm system had not been tripped, and he was alone in the room. He lay perfectly still, listening intently. When he didn't hear it again, he heaved a deep sigh and blamed it on yet another grief-riddled nightmare. He rolled onto his side and punched the pillow into a comfortable shape. Exhaling slowly, he forced himself to relax, hoping to catch another hour or two before the alarm went off.

Travis McLean...

He definitely heard it that time. He jerked upright, running through his options. The voice sounded distant, maybe coming from the kitchen. He eased out of bed without a sound, tugging on a t-shirt and a pair of baggy sweats. His duty belt sat in the usual spot on the nightstand. Winding it around his hips, he cupped the buckle between his hands and muffled the *snick* of the closing. He drew his weapon but held it loosely at his side, absently noting the torrent outside had quieted.

Travis...come here...

Easing the bedroom door open, he crept down the hallway, keeping his back to the wall and methodically clearing each room. The great room was as he had left it, the single pole light near the faux wood blinds still on—no signs of any intruder. By the time he reached the empty kitchen and found more nothing, he holstered his gun, dismissing it as another dream. With a start, he realized the strange storm had passed.

Travis McLean—COME HERE

He spun in the direction of the barked command coming from the training area and rushed to look out the back window. The motion sensor lights were not on, so he squinted into the darkness and froze. *Well, that's new.*

The granite dolmen loomed in the dark, shrouded in a light mist. Seated on the bench that also wasn't there earlier, he could make out the lone hooded figure turned away from the door. The stranger's face turned toward the stars, just beginning to peek out from behind the disappearing clouds. *Ansgar's come back to finish the job*, he thought.

Drawing his firearm again, he turned the alarm off with his other hand and brushed the sheer curtains aside to get a better look at his nocturnal visitor. Male, maybe. Impossible to get height, weight, or build with the dark robe.

"Is it your intent to just skulk in the doorway, or will you come out so that we may speak as men?" The figure did not turn around, but the voice was wise, male, and mature. It didn't sound like Ansgar at all. The broad shoulders trembled, and when he called out again, his voice shook with scarcely contained laughter. "I give you my word. I shall not bite."

With the element of surprise gone, Travis threw open the back door and turned on the porch lights. "Show me your hands," he snapped, pointing the pistol muzzle at the stranger.

The man rose slowly, lifting his arms out and away from his body. "This is quite unnecessary," he explained patiently. "I mean you no harm."

"I'll be the judge of that," Travis said, stepping forward. "Turn around slow and keep your hands where I can see 'em."

The robed man obliged, tilting his hands up in a greeting gesture. His lips moved as he whispered something too soft to hear.

Horrified, Travis reseated his weapon in the holster, snapping the strap closed. He couldn't imagine why he would be pointing a loaded gun at this nice old man. A shameful heat colored his face, knowing his mother would be appalled at his rudeness.

The stranger appeared in his sixties, still robust, tall, and broad across the shoulders. Narrow braids with shiny metal beads adorned his silver-streaked hair and beard that reached his chest. He bent to collect a long staff propped against the bench and leaned on it as he shuffled toward the porch. "Now then, Travis McLean—let us have a look at you," he said, moving closer to study his face. He nodded with approval. "She speaks true. You are indeed a handsome young man."

Travis froze. "She who?"

He pondered that for a moment and chuckled. "I believe you call her Saoirse. We can't pronounce her true name, of course. Our tongues were not meant to make those sounds."

It took him a moment to form the words and another to say them aloud. "Who *are* you?"

"Why, I am Pendaran Dyfed, of course."

CHAPTER 35

"**I**s she okay? Where is she?" Travis blurted out the first questions that came to mind.

"She is safe for the moment, although I must say I left her in quite a state," Pendaran said, one of his bushy white eyebrows arching in question. "Her concern was not for herself, but for you. She seems to believe you will suffer in her absence."

"Where is she?" he asked again in a rush of words. "How long have you been here? Can you take me to her?"

"I studied your stars while I waited for you to wake," the old man murmured, ignoring the questions as he looked skyward. "It is a great mystery how they are the same in this time." He shook his head to bring himself back to the present. "We leave at first light, but I have much to tell you before then." He stepped around the younger man, moved to the back door, and paused, waiting.

"Do I have to invite you in or something?" Travis hedged, remembering too many old vampire movies as a kid, then wondered where that random thought even came from.

"That would be the hospitable thing to do," Pendaran agreed with a sage nod. "Even in my more primitive time, one does not simply enter someone else's dwelling without invitation."

Travis opened the storm door and pushed the inner door open. "After you, sir," he said, waving the druid in. He flipped on the lights as he went, and the old man's eyes went comically wide.

"Oh my," he breathed. "This is wondrous, bright like the day."

His manners kicked in, and Travis opened the cabinet where he kept the everyday glasses. He paused, then bypassed those for the good ones on an upper shelf. "May I offer you a glass of tea?"

"Tea?" the old man echoed, confused.

I take so much for granted, he thought. Without waiting for an answer, he waved for Pendaran to take a seat at the kitchen table. He filled two glasses with ice and poured the tea from the pitcher in the refrigerator. Taking the seat opposite, he cradled his glass in both hands and braced for the worst. "Where is she?"

"Brú na Bóinne, and she is safe, at least for the moment." The high druid finished his tea in record time and held up the empty glass. "That is very fine indeed," he said, licking his lips. "Could I perhaps have more? I did not realize I thirsted so."

337

"Lot to be said for good Southern sweet tea." Travis nodded, rising to retrieve the pitcher and bring it to the table. He refilled the glass and sat back, crossing his arms as he waited expectantly.

Pendaran sat back, his weathered face appraising. The deep lines around his mouth were carved by good humor and smiles. Accordion-like folds appeared at the corners of his dark eyes, alight with amusement. "You took her to your bed," he said.

Shocked, Travis reared back in his chair but then slumped in defeat. "Damn, you're getting straight to the point. Yeah, I did. I mean, I resisted her as long as I could, but something about her, I don't know..." His voice grew soft, and he shook his head. "Never met anyone like her. She'd make me mad one minute and laugh the next. Her heart is so big and pure, you know? It didn't help that she's the most beautiful woman I've ever seen, plus that faery thing she throws off..."

"They mate for life, you know," the druid said quietly. "And hers is much longer than yours."

He sighed and looked away. "She never said, but I kinda figured."

"And pure is part of the reason I am here," Pendaran said. "How much do you know about her captors?"

"She told me enough. What y'all are doing to these women is criminal," he growled. "The whole bunch of you ought to be locked up."

The rebuke came swiftly and sharply edged. "Include me not in their number; I only just learned of this foolishness. They kept this hidden from me in past visits," Pendaran spat. "The druid's path is one of nature, science, healing, and truth. All life is sacred and must be protected. Ansgar thirsts for power, not knowledge. He dabbles in the dark and forbidden, believing it the true way. He thinks to replace me as High Druid. Even as we speak, he gathers his followers to him. May the gods have mercy upon us all should that happen."

Travis's patience began wearing dangerously thin. "He's a bad guy. I get it. What do I need to do to get her back? That's why you're here, isn't it?" Something the old wizard said earlier came rushing back. "Wait a minute, who is leaving at first light?"

"You and I. Once it became known that Saoirse is no longer pure—"

He exploded, unable to hold back his anger. "She is still pure! Are you saying just because we had sex, she's ruined?"

"Your relations with Saoirse gave us more time, at least a moon," the druid continued, ignoring the outburst. "I had the most troubling dreams and sought the wisdom of my yew sticks to discover their source. They told me I was needed at Brú na Bóinne and that I should go there with all haste. I was nearly there when I received the message summoning me, and had only just arrived when Ansgar returned with her. I wore the glamour of a servant to disguise my presence among them; I wanted to see what transpired in my absence. I heard the whispers amongst the slaves and asked Saoirse myself what had happened. It took a bit of coercion to get her to speak at all, but I thought her more likely to speak truth with a humble servant than with the high druid."

Pendaran took another long sip of tea and continued. "When Ansgar learned Saoirse was no longer virgin, he went mad. She escaped his immediate wrath, but some were not so fortunate. He whipped one slave to death in front of her before he calmed. He has her caged, awaiting her blood cycle to ensure she does not carry your child."

"And if she is?"

The older man frowned and paused before speaking again. "I do not know what she has shared of their origins, but I shall start at the beginning to give you a brief history. Thousands of years ago, the Tuatha dé Danann, or the children of the goddess Danu, came to Ireland in ships made of dark clouds. Wars ensued, and the Tuatha Dé ruled until they were defeated by another tribe. They went underground to live, and over time, became known as the Fae, or the Old Ones. They are magickal beings and not of our world. Our human eyes are unable to see them without their glamour. It would shatter the mind itself to view them in their natural state." He raised his eyebrows in expectation, waiting for Travis to piece the rest of the puzzle together.

A memory flashed through Travis's mind of Saoirse cradling an armload of squirrel kits, and suddenly, everything clicked. "She can't have a human child because she herself is not human," he said, understanding coloring his voice.

Pendaran smiled. "Exactly so, clever lad. Had Ansgar, in all his wisdom, asked any of the women he holds captive, they would have told him. The human form she wears is just that—a form."

Travis shifted uncomfortably in his seat. "What happens when he finds out she isn't pregnant?"

"He may continue with his plan of giving her to me, in which case I will release her to you. Or because she is no longer"—he caught himself and appeared to choose a different word—"untouched, he may keep her for himself, which presents another set of problems." He took another sip of tea. "Even if we somehow free her and escape, this does nothing to help the others being held prisoner. As a matter of pride, Ansgar would only fetch her back should she elude him again. No, I plan to end this folly once and for all, and in that quest, I ask for your help."

"I take her away from him and free the others." Travis began to see where all this was headed. *Good—war is something I understand.* He stood, resting his hands on the table. "I need to get ready."

Pendaran placed his wrinkled hand atop the larger one. "We have several hours before sunrise. There are things we must do, but we have a wee bit of time to spare. If you would be so kind, I should love to see some of these modern magicks Saoirse spoke of. I would also very much like..." He paused, searching for the word. "A sandwich."

CHAPTER 36

After the house tour and snack, Travis sat waiting on the new bench in the backyard, holding Grandmother McLean's old wooden mixing bowl, half-filled with water, on his lap. The old druid withdrew a leather pouch from beneath his robes, which contained small pieces of fabric folded into neat squares. Carefully opening each, he gathered a pinch or two of the dried herbs or powders they held and dropped them into the bowl. Once the leather bag was tucked away again, he collected the bowl from Travis and moved around the yard, gathering flower petals, singing, and chanting softly as he dropped them into the water. He paused several times, holding the basin up to be kissed by the moonlight or setting it on the ground while he used a small knife to cut away strips of vine. Longer pieces were bound together and frayed at the ends, forming a sort of brush.

After a time, he returned to the bench, hugging the bowl tightly. "Have you salt?" At the affirmative nod, he ordered, "Bring it all to me."

Travis returned moments later with two canisters of iodized salt and a half-full saltshaker, offering them to the old man. Pendaran turned them over, studying the containers with a quiet snort of amusement. "What a clever means of storage," he mused. "Now then—if you would be so kind as to remove your clothing."

"All my clothes? Like, get naked?" None of the neighbors would be awake at this hour, and no passerby could see over the fence, but it would not have mattered if they could. Travis stripped in record time, eager to get the rescue mission going.

"Stand still and do not speak until I say." Pendaran paced a slow circle around him, pouring a heavy ring of salt onto the ground. Once closed, he chanted in a strange language and sang softly, using the shredded vines as a paintbrush to cover Travis's body with the spelled water. The wind grew stronger, gusting with an icy cold that pierced his wet skin. Travis shivered but stood unmoving.

The druid set the bowl down and continued walking, hands lifted to the sky as he chanted. The winds increased, swirling grass clippings and leaves around the yard in miniature whirlwinds. Pendaran's long, silver-streaked hair writhed around his head, reminding Travis of a voltaic plasma ball. Heavy thunder rumbled in the distance once, then again. When lightning began crackling overhead in blinding spidery fingers, he forced himself to remain unmoving and not bolt for cover.

So involved in the weather overhead, it took a moment to register the electricity pulsing all over his body. He ventured a glance down, moderately horrified to find himself glowing with spreading patches of blue and greenish light. *Like blacklight paint*, he wondered, waiting for the druid to speak up and explain this weirdness.

The chanting increased in volume as the gathering storm intensified, the old man's face tipped up to the sky, his eyes closed. After a few more long minutes, the thunder and lightning abated, and the wind settled back into the usual light sea breeze. Pendaran opened his eyes, blinked several times, then burst into merry laughter.

"What?" Travis snapped, feeling somewhat foolish.

"It would appear," the druid said, clapping in delight, "that someone else saw to your protection before my efforts. Be at ease now," he added, sweeping his hand to indicate that they were exiting the circle.

"How long will I glow like this? Is it all over my body?" Travis asked, touching a finger to his face. Upon closer inspection of his forearm, he saw delicate designs of fern green Celtic knotwork, the complex, interlocking patterns winding around his arms, legs, and torso. The parts not covered by symbols were colored by swirling spirals of cobalt.

"It will fade in a moment but will be with you always. Saoirse saw to your armor, protecting you well. I but filled in the unmarked spaces."

Travis frowned, yanking his clothing on. "I don't remember her doing anything like that."

"You would not have known unless she told you. The green designs were drawn by her hand on your naked skin. I can see for myself," the old druid said with a chuckle, waggling his bushy eyebrows, "she touched you most thoroughly." He exhaled in a dreamy sigh. "She is a most winsome creature, but alas, not for the likes of most mortal men."

He kept his mouth clamped tightly shut, not trusting himself to speak. The glow began to subside to a faint light, then disappeared altogether. Thoroughly disconcerted, he glanced up into the dark skies. "Are we done out here?"

"I have helped you in all the ways I can. Oh, except for this," Pendaran said, removing his amulet. He gestured for the taller man to duck down and slipped the leather cord over Travis's head. "Worn under your clothing, it will shield you from many types of magickal attack. And I should like to have that back, once you are victorious."

Travis lifted the stone to inspect it more closely. The milky stone glowed with a soft white light, framed in a disc of gold metal. Arcane symbols etched around the circle were too tiny for him to read.

"We have rules, you see. Our order does not allow us to strike at each other directly, as it goes against our teachings of peace and the sanctity of life. Even so, such times arise that it becomes necessary to remove a druid from power. If he refuses to set aside his path willingly, he must be forced to accept the decision of his brethren. Thank the Gods, it is a rare occurrence. Have you ever killed a man, Travis McLean?"

When Travis cast his gaze downward and did not answer, Pendaran continued with a kind smile. "I can see that you have, but you took no joy in it. That tells me your heart is indeed good. She sang praises of your honor, courage, and worthiness." He began the trek to the back door, calling over his shoulder, "You should begin your preparations. Dawn approaches."

The ancient druid waited in the den, watching TV and flipping through magazines on the coffee table, while Travis went to change clothes and mentally prepare himself for the upcoming trial.

Travis studied his reflection in the full-length mirror. His own clothes hugged his frame too tightly to hide anything underneath, but he tugged on his usual long-sleeved wicking shirt to wear under the body armor. After a bit of searching, he found his father's faded fatigues and MOS 31K hoodie. The pants were looser around the waist than he would have liked, but his duty belt would hold them up. The OPC Scorpion pattern effectively camouflaged the outlines of the knee and shin guards. He pulled the sweatshirt over his head, greedily inhaling the ghost of his father's spicy aftershave still lingering in the folds. Tugging it down, he smoothed the wrinkles over the form-fitting riot vest. The long sleeves hid the body armor covering his forearms and elbows.

He ran through his weapon options, loading his pockets and concealing them wherever he could. He decided on three firearms: his service Glock in the drop holster, his Springfield tucked into the side of his vest, and a small Sig in an ankle holster. He tucked away at least a dozen fixed-blade knives, his collapsible baton, backup magazines, a can of OC spray, and a few flashbang grenades he thought might be helpful. He added a sharp wire coil that could be used as a saw or garrote, a tiny but powerful flashlight, and stuffed his fingerless sap gloves into a cargo pocket.

An urgent thought occurred to him. Snatching up his phone, he thumbed his favorites open and tapped the first on his list.

Mike's groggy voice answered before the second ring. "S'up," he mumbled.

Travis tapped *speaker*. "Mike, it's me," he said. "I'm leaving to go get Saoirse."

All sleep flew from Mike's voice. "Trav—do what now? How is it—what ha—what the hell are you even talking about?"

"Stonehenge and the high druid himself just showed up in my backyard, and he's taking me to her. The plan is to kill Ansgar, rescue Saoirse, and set the others free." Throwing open his closet doors, he turned on the light and pushed aside the pile of clothing concealing the safe. The combination dial clicked as it spun, and the heavy metal door swung open without a sound.

"Do you have even the slightest idea what the hell you're doing?"

"That's a negative."

Mike fell silent, but only for a moment. "I'm not even gonna try to talk you out of it. I can hear your mind is already made up. You better come back in one piece, you hear? And bring her home with you—she still owes me some garden juju. What can I do to help?"

Travis rifled through the documents on the safe's upper shelf until he found the single clasp envelope with his name scrawled across the front. "I need you to run cover and let somebody at the station know I'm not coming in. Maybe keep an eye on the house for me. I have no idea when I'll be back." Clutching the packet, he closed the safe again, spinning the dial. "I'm leaving my legal stuff in the top drawer of my nightstand. Everything you need is in there if it all goes sideways."

"Trav, I—"

"I have to," he interrupted. "There is no other option I can live with."

"I know. Just stay alive, okay? And kick his ass extra hard for me."

Travis smiled. "I have your cuffs. I promise I'll put them to good use."

His grin faded after the line went dead. The hard truth he had been trying to ignore reared its ugly head, and he wondered for the hundredth time what he was walking into. *He uses magick*, Travis considered, uncertain conventional weapons would even work. His thoughts turned to Saoirse, scared and alone, locked away inside a cage. A blinding rage flooded every fiber of his body as he donned his own talisman of protection.

You have to believe in yourself. The stern voice of Sergeant Major Dylan McLean rang out in his head, reminding him of the simple wisdom found in his father's dog-eared copy of *The Art of War*. He began a series of controlled stretches, forcing his breath and heart rate to slow. He cast one glance back into the mirror, then, squaring his shoulders, marched off to fight for his faery.

CHAPTER 37

"**M**istress, please—ye must eat," the servant begged, pushing a wooden trencher through the narrow slot opening. The small cup of thin broth sloshed onto the plate, greedily absorbed by the stale bread.

The aroma of cooked meat made her mouth water, but she remained where she was, ignoring the old woman. Saoirse did not look up. "Leave me," she ordered in a quiet voice, turning her face away. She sat huddled near the back of the iron cage, her arms wrapped around her knees, resting her head against them. "I do not hunger."

The loud *kerang* against the bars startled her into a crouch, ready to defend herself. "Yes, eat. Starving yourself will avail ye naught," Ansgar snapped, raising his staff again to strike the cowering woman. "Or shall I whip this slave until ye do?"

"Oh no, please, my lord, have mercy," the servant cried.

With no warning, he struck the old woman hard across the face with the back of his hand. The resounding *crack* drove her to her knees. "No one gave ye leave to speak."

Wisely staying down and bowing her head, the elderly slave held up wrinkled, clasped hands in supplication.

Saoirse met his gaze with open hostility, then reached for the platter. She tore off a chunk of gravy-soaked bread and shoved it into her mouth, chewing noisily. Starving, yes, but she refused to give him the satisfaction of knowing just how well his heavy-handed tactics worked.

He pointed to the full plate. "More," he ordered, watching her like a hawk. "Ye will finish all of that. I will not have ye weak of limb when Pendaran Dyfed arrives." His upper lip curled just a tiny bit at the high druid's name. "I have not yet decided what to do with you. Should you be carrying, mayhap I should let you whelp to study it. You have earned a beating for your defiance, that is certain, but I dare not mark you before the ceremony. If there is even to be one," he added caustically.

She looked away, the bread turning to dry sand in her mouth. Forcing it down with a sip of watery ale, she conjured the mental image of one of Travis's BLTs and ate another bite. When she thought she had eaten enough to satisfy him, she pushed the plate away and turned back to the wall.

Reaching down, he clutched the slave's shapeless brown robe between the shoulders and hauled her roughly to her feet. "See that she eats at least three more of these this day,"

Ansgar ordered. "If she becomes troublesome, send for me. I will force it down her gullet if need be."

"Aye, my lord." The servant bobbed a quick curtsey and fled.

He watched the old woman shuffle away, then stepped to the side of the cage. After a furtive glance around to ensure no one lingered nearby, he spoke softly. "Best that you make peace with your fate. No one is coming for you if that is the hope you hold. Your champion is dead." His voice turned oily, making her skin crawl. "Were you to submit and accept your circumstance, mayhap you would find life more agreeable." He stretched his hand through the bars and casually ran a callused fingertip down her cheek. "I can make it so."

Without hesitation, Saoirse turned her head and chomped down on the offending digit. Her K9 training now second nature, she let off the pressure for a split second, then immediately shifted forward so the finger rested across her back molars, reseating the bite. She bit down again even harder and felt something give with a soft *pop*.

"You foul bitch!" Ansgar howled in a mix of anger and pain as he tried to jerk his hand free. "You've broken it!"

A thick coppery taste filled her mouth. She smiled, her small white teeth stained crimson as a few drops of blood trickled past her lips. He struggled to free himself, but she held fast, giving a last squeeze of crushing force before releasing him. "Never. Touch. Me," she said, eyes blazing as she spat his blood out onto the cage floor.

"Make no mistake, I will touch you whenever and however I please," Ansgar snarled, spittle flying from his lips. "No one here dares stay my hand."

"He is not dead." Her soft voice was filled with savage resolve. "You are wrong."

"Oh aye, he is." He wrapped his other hand tight around his injury to stem the seeping blood. "I have killed enough men to know those last gasping breaths before death comes."

"You are wrong," she repeated, giving him a peppermint candy smile. "I gave of myself to spare him, else you would not have taken me so readily. And that man was not him. They both live." She took a sip of the ale, swished it around in her mouth, and spat again. "Your blood tastes of wasting sickness and death."

A fleeting look of uncertainty passed over his face before he could mask it. "You lie." He snorted with dark amusement, ignoring her last comment. "Even if it were so, your savior has no ability to reach you. And if by some miracle he did appear, he must defeat me to take you from your sacred purpose. Methinks you know how that would end." He cocked his head to listen as someone called his name from the great hall. "That doddering old fool will arrive any day now. Would that your blood come on you soon. I weary of this waiting." He spun on his heel and strode away, his long robe flapping in his wake.

Saoirse watched him go, her stomach knotted in misery. She relaxed back against the wall of the cage, her thighs shaking from the pressure of being held so tightly together. Another hard cramp seized her lower abdomen, and she bit down on her lower lip to stifle the whimper of despair. With a sickening sense of inevitability, the wet stickiness between her legs confirmed all her time had just run out.

CHAPTER 38

"This will pass. Had I given you warning, the effects would have been much worse," Pendaran said in a soothing voice, leaning against his staff. A gentle smile curved his lips. "Some swoon their first time, so you are very strong, if that helps your feelings at all."

Travis crouched on hands and knees, fighting to stay conscious under the overwhelming waves of nausea. Bitter saliva burned his mouth and throat as his gorge rose, then fell, only to rise again when he tried to move. He glanced up at the druid. "Is it always like this?" he rasped out.

"It will not be so bad next time," Pendaran assured him.

Travis struggled to his feet, taking a good look around for the first time. The dolmen still loomed overhead, but everything else... he shook himself violently. They stood in the middle of a stone circle in a large clearing, surrounded by thick forest. Encroaching on the millions of stars visible in the vast darkness, the first rays of dawn bled into the sky with wispy streamers of salmon, azure, and rose. Gone was the ocean salt-flavored breeze. The scents of ancient Scots pine, unusual blossoms, and unspoiled land filled the air.

"Where are we?" he asked, silently adding *not in Kansas anymore*.

"Brú na Bóinne," the druid explained, gesturing toward the trees, "is but a short walk in that direction. We must seek cover; our arrival will not have gone unnoticed." He turned and began striding briskly toward the eldritch forest, moving faster than a man of his apparent age should.

Travis fell into step alongside him, a long-legged lope to keep pace. "Is this the same portal Saoirse came through?"

Pendaran nodded. "She did not know the purpose of the stones, nor how to use them. Her intent alone opened the pathway to your time," he said, a note of admiration tinging his voice. "We study for decades to do what she did by accident."

They disappeared into the dense foliage as the forest began to wake. A chorus of birds trilled and chirped overhead, insects buzzed, and leaves rustled as small creatures prepared to meet the day. Travis did not need the druid's admonition to keep quiet; all his senses had been on high alert since they entered the woods. Pendaran moved with purpose, silent as the darkness. Travis followed close behind, careful to walk in the old man's footsteps to avoid any additional noises of breaking twigs or crunching the acorns littering the forest floor.

By the time Pendaran raised his hand to stop their trek, Travis could hear the waking sounds of a village or compound ahead. Cattle lowed eagerly, demanding to be milked and a choir of roosters gave lusty cock-a-doodle-doos to greet the dawn. Voices, male and female, began calling to each other but were too far away to be heard clearly.

"We shall wait here for a time, let the servants be about their morning tasks," the druid whispered, taking a seat near a fallen tree. He patted the ground next to him for Travis to sit. "Once morning devotions have begun, I will slip inside to procure clothing for you. I think the robe of an acolyte will do fine to hide your true form. You shall appear as my apprentice."

"What's the plan?" Travis asked, scanning the forest for movement. The tree sat next to a large pile of fallen rocks, framing a clear stream that ran down to the village. The soft bubbling sounds from the flowing water soothed his ragged nerves. A giant oak stood near the rocks, the branches forming a leafy canopy.

"Now that is an excellent question," the old man said and chuckled, his eyes brimming with amusement. "I suggest we expect nothing and prepare for anything." He leaned closer and lowered his voice. "I will try to see her while I am inside. Is there a word I may give, one that will alert her to your arrival without announcing you by name?"

He thought fast. "Tell her—" His voice wavered for a moment, then strengthened with resolve. "Tell her *Pozor*."

"Poe-zor," Pendaran repeated, rolling the word around. "This is not a word I know."

"It's Czech. She'll recognize it," Travis assured him. "It means be watchful."

"Ah. I suppose that is appropriate, given the situation."

Travis glanced around him, surveying the terrain. Old trees, thick brush, and thorny vines covered the ground, not unlike the woods he hunted in with his father. However, this ground was nowhere near flat, and there were large rocks lurking under some of the lichen. "How long will it take you inside?" he asked.

"Not long. It is on you to keep yourself hidden until my return." He looked up into the tall trees overhead. "I feel you are considering hiding above. That would be a good plan."

"How did—never mind," Travis said, shaking his head with a bemused smile.

"Druid," Pendaran said with a dismissive shrug. "And you have been gazing up there for the last quarter hour." He patted the younger man's hand kindly. "I remember the teachings of a wise man in my youth. He said, 'Great results can be achieved with small forces.' I am inclined to believe that is so."

Travis blinked in surprise. "You know Sun Tzu?"

"Aye," he nodded. "I read it often as a young man. I think it mistitled, as much applies to life as well as war."

They fell silent. The old man opened his leather pouch and seemed to take inventory of the items within while Travis used every sense to imprint on the unfamiliar place. The light breeze carried traces of smoke and the aroma of cooking meat from the direction of the village, mixed with the scents of farm animals and old dirt. They fell silent. The air seemed crisper, the colors more vibrant than usual. Newer. Brighter. More alive than Travis had ever known. *We went back before pretty much all the history I know.* He couldn't quite get his head around the mode of travel, but decided he would dwell on it later when lives were not at stake.

He shook himself, needing a distraction. "What can you tell me about Ansgar? What do I need to know going in?"

The druid leaned closer to whisper. "Ansgar came to us years ago as a broken warrior begging sanctuary, starving, and near death from fevered wounds. He claimed to be from a land unknown to us, in service to a cunning but foolish king who had sent his forces into certain death over an imagined slight. Ansgar's men were greatly outnumbered, and the battle claimed the lives of all but a few. Ansgar escaped and fled for his life."

"So the coward saved himself and left his brothers to die," Travis said flatly.

Pendaran pursed his lips before continuing. "We took him in to nurse his injuries and regain his strength. You have seen him; he is a tall, powerfully built man. He made himself useful to us, and we, in turn, provided succor. He seemed happy enough here. When he expressed interest in the druid arts, we taught him a few simple charms. We knew not how great were his appetites for knowledge and power. Before long, he was sworn into our order and began advancing into positions of more authority. You must understand, he was not always what you see now. I have oft wondered if the kind, gentle man we knew was but a mask hiding the evil lurking beneath."

"A wolf in sheep's clothing," Travis murmured in understanding.

"A fitting description," the druid agreed. "I fear he fooled us all, and we are only now seeing his true face. He must be stopped now before his power becomes too great to contain."

The sound of dry twigs snapping nearby startled them both into silence. Pendaran raised a wrinkled finger to his lips while tracing sigils in the air with his other hand. Travis did not dare move or even breathe, his attention laser-focused on assessing the potential threat.

A young woman shuffled into view, clutching the hem of her tattered apron as a makeshift basket. She bustled about picking up twigs, breaking the larger branches underfoot before adding them to her growing pile. She did not see them, so focused on her task. Some of her dirty russet hair was twisted into a bun, but just as much stuck to the grime and sweat glistening on her face and neck. Her nervous gaze darted around like a young doe feeling watchful eyes upon her.

Low crashing announced the approach of something larger. A dark shape formed into that of a man, moving through the thicket. He stepped into the clear area, and a bright smile lit his whiskered face. The spear he held fell to the ground. "Eilidh," he cried, opening his arms wide.

Her firewood forgotten, she dropped everything in her haste to join him in a tight embrace. "I feared ye would not come," she breathed. "They watch us with hawk's eyes."

"I would not miss the chance to see yer own beautiful eyes again," he said, lowering his head to steal a kiss. "Would that I could save enough to buy our freedom, and we could forever leave this accursed place."

"Ye dream, Uisnech," she said with a sad smile. "Not even the king himself has that much coin."

The clandestine lovers entwined in a passionate embrace, and Travis shifted uncomfortably, feeling like the worst kind of voyeur. It inflamed his sense of honor, this enslavement of people with the same rights to happiness as their so-called betters. He checked himself, remembering this to be a different time, and was grateful that this archaic system had long since disappeared from the modern world.

Memorizing their faces, he added them to his growing list of injustices to be addressed after he dealt with Ansgar.

The couple suddenly jerked apart and glanced in the direction of the compound. "Someone comes," Uisnech mouthed in an urgent whisper, snatching up his weapon. "Make haste." He glanced around, blew her a kiss, and melted back into the trees.

Eilidh rushed to gather the fallen firewood, securing it in her apron. Just as she tied her bundle securely, the man himself strode up the dirt pathway, using his staff as a walking stick. "Ye there—slave," Ansgar barked. "How long have ye been out here?"

The woman's shoulders hunched as she ducked her head, not meeting his intimidating stare. "Not long, my lord, only time enough to gather this wood." She held out her apron for him as proof, her hands trembling.

"Hmmm," he said, stopping in front of her. "Have ye heard aught unusual this morn? Any strange noises from that direction?" He gestured toward the stones in the clearing with the head of his staff.

She bobbed a fast curtsey. "Nay, my lord."

His keen gaze swept in a circle, pausing where Uisnech had disappeared, then coming to rest on the area where Travis and Pendaran sat motionless. He *harrumphed* with irritation, frowning. Shrugging off the apparent unease, he roughly grabbed the woman's chin to tilt her face upward. "What is yer name, girl?"

"Eilidh, my lord."

Ansgar said nothing, tilting her face from side to side in appraisal. He ran a large thumb over her lips, then dropped his hand. "Ye are a comely one. I shall remember yer name, Eilidh."

Visibly shaken at being touched so familiarly, the poor woman lowered her gaze again. "M—may I g—go, my lord?" she stammered. "They await this wo—wood in the ki—kitchen, sir."

Travis balled his fists at his sides, his anger near the boiling point. Pendaran placed a warning hand on his arm and shook his head, lips moving in a soundless chant. A sudden crack, followed by a loud crash, came from the deeper woods, nearer the clearing.

The woman forgotten, Ansgar's head jerked in that direction, eyes narrowed in interest. Without another word, he stalked off and disappeared into the trees. Eilidh clutched the sticks to her chest and fled, her cloth slippers making soft thuds on the dirt path. After a moment, Uisnech crept out from the thick brush and stared in the direction the druid had gone before following the woman, a dark scowl marring his rugged features.

The men did not speak, anticipating Ansgar's return. A short time later, the druid burst from the woods, brushing a few stray leaves from his robe. He glanced around again, his hard gaze searching the area. He took a few hesitant steps, then walked purposefully to their hiding spot. Pendaran's fingers flicked to the right, and Ansgar glided past them as if deflected, nostrils flaring as he inhaled deeply. It became clear to Travis that while Ansgar could not see them, he sensed their presence. And he did not like it one bit.

"I know not who ye are, but ye cannot hide from me," he growled low. "Show yerself that we may be done with this foolishness."

Pendaran's fingers tightened on Travis's arm, and both sat as still as the ancient rocks.

When nothing but the wind through the trees responded, Ansgar's lips pressed into a thin line of annoyance as a muffled shout drew his attention. With a final look around, he turned and stalked back down the path to the compound.

At least five minutes passed before Pendaran released his viselike grip on Travis's arm. "I thought he would never leave." He sighed. "That was too close for my liking. He has grown very powerful indeed in my absence. Would that he used it for the light instead of darkness."

"You have some amazing skills yourself," Travis said, admiration tinging his voice.

Flushing with embarrassment, the old druid made a *pshaw* noise and waved him away. "Illusion and misdirection. If he truly wished to find us, there are ways."

Heavy bells tolling in the distance sounded through the otherwise quiet forest, announcing the morning prayers. Leaning on his staff for balance, Pendaran rose to his feet. "Time for me to be off," he said, glancing toward the treetops. "I would see you safely hidden ere I leave. Up you go, my lad."

"Yes, sir." Travis hoped his tree-climbing skills as a boy still held. He had already selected the massive oak tree across the path with abundant leaves and low, gnarled branches. Tugging on his gloves, he jumped to grab the lowest limb and pulled himself up, mindful of the additional weight he carried. Quick as a wink, he climbed high and disappeared into the thickest foliage near the top.

Humming to himself, Pendaran walked three circles around the wide trunk, drawing strange symbols in the air with one finger. "Good, good," he murmured and began his slow trek into the village.

CHAPTER 39

Donning the glamour of an old serving woman, Pendaran shuffled through the main gate into the bustling village. The guard's glances flicked over him in passing, but one yawned while the other looked away. Spying an unused willow wood basket with a single handle, he snatched it up and tucked it near his body. The vendors, already set up for the day, called to each other in the busy marketplace. Moving about with the invisibility his shabby appearance afforded him, he chose items with care, adding small loaves of crusty bread, shiny apples, wedges of cheese, and wide strips of cloth to fill the small hamper. To the very few who noticed him, he murmured, "For the kitchen." They all responded with blank nods, making no effort to question him further.

He made it into the kitchen in time to add some dried venison strips to his stash, tucking a clean cloth over the top to disguise the contents. Glancing around, still unnoticed, he grabbed a pitcher and filled it with cool water from the huge pottery cistern, found a serving tray, and added a few wooden cups. Thus armed, he slowly made his way to where the prisoners were kept.

Pendaran made a point of eavesdropping on every conversation he passed, particularly those of the druids. With the morning devotions complete, they gathered in groups of twos and threes, going about their daily business and chores. He knew most of the elders by name, but not many of the newer brothers. He roamed up and down the hall, feigning great interest in a crack in the stone wall near two he recognized. They huddled close together, as if not wishing to be overheard.

"I do not like it at all, this plan of breeding. He claims melding the two races will enrich the future generations of both, but it is an indignity to the Tuath Dé, the very ones who taught us this magick. The High Druid will be most displeased, even more so once he learns Ansgar has not yet been successful in proving his theories. That poor youngling—" Brother Donnacha whispered.

"Which? The one he fetched back after she escaped?" Brother Ciarán asked.

"Aye. What a miserable creature. My heart is rent asunder each time I gaze upon her, sitting and waiting to be his broodmare. And it is all for naught."

The second man glanced around with a worried expression on his round face. "Best not to say that aloud, brother. Should word of your disapproval reach Ansgar's ears, I believe it would place you in grave peril."

"I will request a private audience with Pendaran Dyfed upon his arrival. He must be made aware of these vile deviations from our sworn path." He snorted with disgust. "Ansgar struts about as if he is already High Druid, and it sickens me."

Ciarán frowned. "What say you? Does he mean to seize control for himself?"

"That is a conversation best held elsewhere." Donnacha shrugged, dropping his voice lower. "But yes, he does. He makes no effort to hide his disdain for the High Druid. I know not how many followers he has behind him, but the few I overheard have loose lips, speaking openly when they should hold their tongues."

As one, they whirled to stare at the old servant woman. "Water, my lords?" she asked, lifting her tray.

When they waved in dismissal, Pendaran dipped in an arthritic curtsey and shuffled further down the hall.

Saoirse had given up trying to count the time passed in her accursed prison, caged like a beast with no thought for any privacy she might wish, and no window that she might see the passage of hours. It seemed that everyone gave her pitying looks but dared not speak. Huddled at the back of her enclosure, she became aware of another presence nearby. Venturing a peek, she saw the old servant pouring a cup of water.

"*Na Déithe duit*, Shining One," the old woman whispered, her eyes almost disappearing into the folds of wrinkles caused by her kind smile.

Saoirse's mouth quirked up on one side in a halfhearted response, but she made no attempt to move. "The Gods be with you also, Mother," she mumbled.

The servant set the cup down inside the cage and began rooting through her basket. She pulled out clean cloths, bread, cheese, and an apple, pushing everything through the bars.

Startled, Saoirse grabbed the rags first but gave her a quizzical look. "How—"

"I know you bear no human child. Eat now," the old woman interrupted.

"Thank you for your kindness, but I have no hunger." Saoirse sighed, looking away.

"But you should eat all the same to bolster your strength, my dear." Keeping her face lowered, she whispered again. "Come closer. I carry a message for your ears alone."

Her head jerked in response, expression sharp. She made no effort to mask her wariness but inched toward the slave in curiosity. "Who sends you to me?"

She turned in a slow circle to ensure no one lingered nearby before returning her warm gaze to the hapless prisoner. "No name, but a word—one it is said you will know—*pozor*."

Saoirse's eyes and mouth flew open wide. Before she could make a sound, the old woman quickly shushed her. "Do not speak. You are to remain watchful and await our signal."

She pushed to her knees and grabbed the bars with both hands, hissing at direct contact with the iron. "What say you—Travis is here? How is this possible?" When the servant nodded, she continued in white-faced panic. "'Tis utter folly—he walks into his death. You must make him understand. This battle cannot be won. Ansgar will never let me go."

"He is not alone. Look past what you see." Tilting her weathered face upward, she beamed at the confused faery.

Saoirse stared for only a moment before narrowing her eyes in suspicion. "Who are you?" she asked.

The old woman quieted her again with a dismissive wave. "Who I am is of no import. Just know I am a friend to you both, one who seeks to right this wrong." Looking around, she added, "Know you where I might find the laundry? I have need of a novice's robe."

Eyes wide, Saoirse pointed in the general direction. "What is this signal I should watch for?"

The servant pondered that a moment, then chuckled. "Now that I do not yet know, but I believe you will recognize it when it comes." And with those cryptic words, she shuffled off to the laundry.

From the top of the great oak, Travis sat still as the rough bark he hugged. From his high perch, he could see over the walls of the village. Fascinated with the activity, he tried to conserve his energy and not think about the upcoming challenges. Relieved that no one had walked the dirt path beneath him, he waited. *Maybe Murphy's Law came after ancient Ireland.*

No sooner had that acerbic thought crossed his mind than two small children appeared from the woods, taking their seats at the base of his tree behind some tall brambles. They spoke to each other in a strange language, their voices muted. From the furtive movements, Travis decided they were hiding and wondered why. Their whispered words were foreign and heavily accented, but from the few snatches drifting up, he recognized what he thought sounded like *Ansgar* and maybe *Mama*.

Wearing dirty clothing a step or two above rags, their narrow faces bore hard edges, signaling the beginnings of starvation. They glanced up once or twice into the trees where Travis crouched, but did not appear to notice him. He could not help but remember a time when his unit drove through a war-torn settlement on the way to an undisclosed location in the Middle East. Gangs of skeletal street children crowded their convoy whenever they paused, begging for coins or food. Unlike those memories, the children below him did not have that desperate, feral hunger for survival clouding their eyes and judgment.

A flicker of movement near his face drew his attention. He turned a fraction to see a large spider mere inches away, repairing a hole in her web. He froze so as not to jerk in revulsion. Years ago, he would have hurt himself trying to get away from it, but the US Army cured his arachnophobia for good. *Wake up all cozy with a camel spider in your bedroll a couple times. Now THAT'S terrifying. These little garden variety creepies are the minor leagues after that.*

Remembering that trip proved a good distraction. He recalled the sights and smells of the unfamiliar country, as well as the jokes and stories his buddies shared to pass the time between flights.

Traffic on the footpath picked up as the morning dragged on. He would have sworn he had been perched in the tree for half a day, but checking his watch revealed only an hour had passed. Farmers with hand carts piled full of vegetables, a boy driving two sheep, and several soldiers passed underneath while he watched. Each time footsteps announced someone approaching, the hidden children shrank down even further and held tight to each other.

Moving at a deliberate pace, an old servant woman carrying a basket came into view. She paused at Travis's tree, glancing around as if searching, then smiled and waved the children out from their hiding place. The woman spoke to them quietly while the little girl twisted her hands nervously around her apron hem, and the boy kept a watchful eye on the path. Gesturing for the child to hold out her skirts, she uncovered the full basket and deposited bread, apples, cheese, and some dark brown strips that might have been jerky in the fabric hammock. Even from his high perch, Travis could see the relief on their faces.

The children backed into the brush, bobbing their heads in thanks, and then disappeared with their treasure. With a lingering smile, the old woman set down her basket and glanced up and down the path to ensure no other travelers lingered nearby. Satisfied they were alone, she squinted into the oak branches directly at him. "I believe it is safe for you to come down now, Travis McLean."

She had called him by name, but didn't Pendaran warn him to stay hidden until his return? Torn with indecision, Travis didn't move or speak, waiting to see what the odd woman would do next.

"My stars—of course, you know me not," she said, and with a wave of her hand, her wrinkled façade melted into that of the High Druid.

Mouth agape, Travis began his slow ascent, jumping to the ground when he reached the lowest branch. "I—I'm sorry, I didn't recognize you," he said, brushing off the bits of bark and leaves clinging to him.

Pendaran's eyes lit with amusement, and he chuckled. "And for that, I am grateful. It would mean I have grown lax in my studies if you had. Learning to use glamour is a first year's lesson. Now come and eat," he said, indicating the basket. "I am certain a young man such as yourself has fierce appetites." Grunting with exertion, he sat and pulled out a battered wineskin. He tugged the stopper, then paused to sniff the contents. Nodding with approval, he squirted a small amount into his mouth. "'Tis good," he said, wiping his mouth afterward. "The brothers make an excellent wine that is flavorful but not over strong to steal away the mind." He dug around in the basket and tossed him a cup. "If you do not wish wine, the spring water is cool and clear."

Travis caught it with one hand. "Water it is," he agreed. Scanning up and down the path again, he took a few steps to kneel next to the stream and hold the cup under, filling it to the rim. He downed the contents in several large swallows, then refilled it several more times before wiping his mouth with the back of his hand. "I think this is the first time I've ever had untreated water," he mused. At the raised eyebrow, he explained. "Our drinking water has to be purified because of things you can't see in it that could make you very sick," he added for clarification, taking a seat on the other side of the basket. "Who were the kids?"

Pendaran glanced around in bewilderment. "Kids?"

"Children," Travis corrected. "The ones you gave food to. How did you know they would be here?"

"Ah." The druid nodded in understanding. "There are many in this land who starve while the higher feast. Where we sit is a common spot to find the less fortunate among us, begging for their day's bread. It would have been strange to return and not find at least one child. The adults do their best to forage and farm while they send their offspring out to beg, as it is harder to be unkind to a small child."

They ate in companionable silence. Travis chewed the dried meat slowly, washing it down with sips of the cool spring water. He didn't think he'd ever had plain cheese and bread this delicious before, and the apples, with their sweet juice, dribbled down his chin with every bite. When he had eaten as much as his nervous stomach would allow, he asked the looming question. "Do we have a plan?"

Pendaran pondered that for a moment. "In a fashion, aye. We will arrive as the High Druid and my attendant, received in all celebration and ceremony, of course. They will first show me to my chambers; a mat will be set out for you. Given the time, they will be readying the noon meal. I will explain that we have already eaten. While they are occupied, it would please me to show my new apprentice the libraries and gardens." He paused, then continued. "Ansgar knows your face, does he not?"

"He got a good look at me in the motel lobby, but not in connection with Saoirse."

"He is clever enough to recall faces upon one meeting," the old druid explained. "Even with Saoirse absent, he will remember where he saw you. That alone will rouse his suspicion." He reached for another bit of jerky and chewed it thoughtfully. "You will walk a step or two behind with your head bowed. Keep both eyes and ears open, but do not meet anyone's gaze. As your accent is strange to my ears, I suggest you be silent so as not to betray yourself. If you must speak, best try to affect the local accent. Also," he added, "keep your arms covered. While there are skin markings in this time, there are none so fine as what you wear."

"A tour of the grounds will allow me to get the layout of the place; I like knowing where my exits are." Travis nodded in agreement, then frowned. "Do I have to add 'my lord' after everything I say?"

"I would recommend doing so to avoid undue attention. I care not for such airs myself, but here they do. After the evening meal, we will discuss matters of our order. When the opportunity presents itself, I shall inquire about the talk I have heard of his plans for the *púca*."

Travis nodded but did not speak, waiting. Pendaran continued. "If I flatter him and show enough interest, his arrogance will no doubt run unchecked. He may even have her brought to the hall to display before us. It is then we will learn of his plans for her, and I shall confront Ansgar about his misdeeds in front of the brothers." He selected a small piece of cheese and popped it into his mouth, but said nothing more.

"And then what happens?" Travis prompted.

He chewed thoughtfully, his head tilting this way and that as he appeared first to consider, then dismiss, plan after plan. He swallowed, washing it down with a pull from the wineskin. "When I speak out against him, Ansgar will in all certainty react in anger. At this time, you shall reveal yourself. The two of you will battle, and you will emerge victorious. I confess I am at a loss for the finer points of how this will come about."

Finer points? How about no points. "So I will be ready to act when he reacts to you. Got it." He glanced away in thought, then back again. "Can I see her before all this starts?"

"I will try to take you to her," Pendaran said patiently, "but make no promises. We must proceed with all caution to stay undetected. Our situation could turn perilous at a moment's notice."

Travis didn't respond; he picked up the purloined robe and stood, shaking it over his head. The oversized tunic had few pockets, and he transferred what weapons he could keep hidden. The length fell to brush against his boot vamps, a good three inches from the ground. He turned from side to side, noting the gap. The quick movement made the heavy fabric swing out, exposing the modern footwear for all to see.

"Ah," the druid said, realizing the trouble. He lifted the bottom of the robe, and with a hard yank, broke and pulled out the single heavy thread holding the hem. This added a couple more inches, but Travis knew he would have to keep his movements slow and even just in case. Wearing thin leather boots like Pendaran's, or worse yet, going barefoot, left his feet unprotected. Not going to happen if he had any say in the matter. Nothing sidelined a fighter faster than a foot injury.

The older man rose and tapped Travis on the shoulder with his walking stick. "You are a big one," he chuckled. "Perhaps it best you walk a bit bent. With your size, you would have, without question, been trained as a warrior. Being a hunchback would explain why you sought the Druid's path." He tapped a long finger on his chin in thought. "Perhaps drag your foot a bit so as to appear clubbed. Aye, that should do it. And a name—you need a name." His gaze narrowed as he murmured to himself. "Ruaidri is common enough; that will do fine." He began searching around in the heavier brush inside the tree line. After several minutes, he produced a heavy cloth sack with a backpack-like strap. "I nearly forgot this; arriving without it would surely have raised an eyebrow or two. My traveling bag," he explained, handing it to Travis. "As my attendant, you are expected to carry it."

He accepted the bag with a nod, surprised at the weight. Without a word, he slung it over his shoulder, making sure to dip it slightly to appear hunchbacked. "How do I look?" he asked.

The old man grinned. "You'll do." He took a step onto the path and began striding toward the settlement, calling back over his shoulder. "Come along then, Ruaidri. Don't dawdle."

It took Travis a moment to realize *he* was Ruaidri and fell into a respectable step behind the high druid. They had only gone a short way before Pendaran stopped and whirled to face the younger man.

Travis went on immediate alert, scanning their surroundings. "Did you hear something?"

"Just one final warning," the elder intoned in a grave, hushed voice. "Do not underestimate Ansgar; he will use every weapon available to him, including magick and artifice. He will first attempt to intimidate you, and if he feels he has failed, will strive to make you cower before him. Should you prick his ego, it will bring his temper down like a tempest."

"Thank you." Travis nodded, then gave him an insouciant grin. "I'll be careful not to poke the bear until I have to. But I'm real good at poking." At the raised eyebrow, he added, "I don't go around picking fights, but I've ended more than my share. And I have to think that we have justice on our side."

Pendaran shook his head and chuckled, despite his growing concern. "Ah, the boundless bravado of youth. I imagine you have tricks of your own under that robe. Just take no unnecessary chances and do not let him catch you unawares. I will guard your back in as much as I am able and watch for undue trickery." With the final warning given, he turned back up the path, and Travis again fell in step behind. The two men made their way toward the village, toward Saoirse, and whatever evils awaited them there.

CHAPTER 40

The overcast skies blocked out the sunlight, and an ominous thunder rumbled in the distance. The threat of rain loomed heavy in the air by the time they reached the clearing. A shout went up from the guards at the outermost walls, announcing the approach of strangers. As the two men emerged from the shadow of the forest, curious faces appeared between the merlons of the high stone wall. Travis kept his shoulders hunched and head bowed, watching as well as he could with the hood shielding his face from view. Remembering to fake a clubbed foot proved challenging, but he managed to drag every other step, giving him an awkward, clumsy gait.

With a businesslike air, Pendaran strode to the high wooden gate and rapped smartly with the head of his staff. "Open in the name of Pendaran Dyfed, High Druid of Eire," he commanded in a loud voice.

The metal straps complained as the doors swung open to admit the travelers. "Hail and welcome, my lord," the guards murmured, bowing their heads with respect as the two men entered the grounds. They had only taken a few steps when the main doors to the keep flew open, hitting the stone walls with a loud bang. Brother Ciarán exploded through the doorway, his leather sandals slapping the packed earth in a breakneck rhythm as he rushed toward them. He fumbled around in his pockets as he ran, withdrawing a cloth to mop the sweat from his round, reddening face.

He skidded to a halt before the pair, out of breath and wheezing. He wiped his face again and drew up to his full height before bending over in a formal bow so deep his nose appeared to touch his knees. "We bid you welcome to Brú na Bóinne, High Druid Pendaran Dyfed. Your esteemed presence here at this time is most appreciated," he gasped out.

"Be at ease, my friend," Pendaran soothed, patting the brother's arm. Looking past the overexerted man, he asked the gathered crowd, "If someone would be so kind as to fetch Brother Ciarán a mug of water?"

A young maid scampered off, returning a moment later with a large wooden cup, the contents splashing over the rim. With a nod of thanks, the younger druid accepted her offering and drained it in several gulps. He wiped his mouth with the back of his hand and appeared to catch his breath again. "Your chambers have been made ready for you," Ciarán said, looking past Pendaran at the hunched figure standing close behind. His eyebrows raised in obvious question.

"My attendant and apprentice, Ruaidri," he explained with a casual wave. "You may have a pallet brought to my room for him."

"Then we bid you welcome as well." Dismissing the servant, Ciarán linked arms with the high druid and pulled him along, chattering with excitement. "You have arrived at a most opportune time, my lord. There have been interesting changes since last you were here, not all of them good, I'm afraid." His voice lowered in a conspiratorial whisper. "But there will be time enough to discuss those later when there are not so many eager ears about." His tone brightened again. "What news of the outside do you bring? Are the kings still warring, or have they reached an accord?"

Pendaran let out a short bark of laughter. "I trouble myself not with the machinations of kings and fools. They will do as they will, heedless of any good counsel they are given."

"A wise position, my lord." Ciarán nodded sagely. "As for us here, we have planted several new gardens and fruit trees. We are still working toward copying the sacred texts and..."

Travis quit listening when it became apparent that nothing important would be discussed. Head bowed, he shuffled behind the two druids, scoping out the surroundings as best he could with his limited vision. He made a point not to meet anyone's gaze but still managed to determine the hierarchy of the people in the bailey. The warriors were the easiest to identify, the largest men, armed with spears and wearing tunics marked with some sort of emblem. The other men were farmers or tradesmen. The women all fell under one heading—commodities.

He stifled a snort of disgust. No finery or alluring colors here—the women he saw wore the same drab long gowns, most long-sleeved, with an apron tied over some. Dirt did not appear to be a consideration for the very young and old, with varying states in between. Most were dark-haired, with a few redheads ranging from dark auburn to a flaming carrot top he saw lugging water buckets. *No blondes,* he mused, then remembered the Vikings would not start raiding regularly for a century or so.

The druids continued talking while Travis tried to acclimate to the alien surroundings. He wasn't a Ren Faire kind of guy, having gone only once with Saoirse. *She's somewhere in the middle of all this*, he thought, heartsick. It took every ounce of discipline he had not to rip off the robe and blast his way to her.

The food smelled amazing, if one could get past the underlying aroma of livestock, unwashed bodies, and, unless he was mistaken, open sewage when the wind shifted from the east. He glanced to his right to find an elderly woman beaming at him, her missing teeth giving her cheeks a cavernous look. She carried an empty basket, much like the one Pendaran had. He gave her a hesitant smile and nodded his head once in an automatic gesture of respect. Taken aback by his kindness, the woman's eyes grew comically wide as she bobbed in a slow curtsey. He caught himself before any more ingrained interaction followed, belatedly remembering Pendaran's warning not to make eye contact.

They mounted the steps and entered the large foyer. "We have you in your regular chambers upstairs," Ciarán continued, snapping his fingers at a passing servant. "Have a pallet brought to the high druid's chambers for his servant," he ordered, "and let the elders know he has arrived."

The young woman took off at a run to do his bidding, and they moved toward the stone staircase. Travis realized the building was much larger inside than he would have thought from his brief assessment outside. The spiral stairs curved to the right. He remembered reading about that years ago; curving to the right meant any attacker had to wield his weapon left-handed, giving him an almost certain disadvantage. *Innovative design*, he thought with a new respect for the forward-thinking ancient builders. Once on the second floor, they passed several closed rooms before arriving at the large wooden door at the end of the hall. Ciarán pushed it open without knocking and stood aside to allow the visitors entry. "I will have water brought up for you to wash away the dust from your travels. Our noon meal should be brought out soon, and you will, of course, join us?" His voice lifted in a slight question.

"We have eaten already." His tone was short, almost dismissive. "You go and enjoy what I am certain is a wonderful repast. Ruaidri and I will visit the libraries." He turned to Travis and added, "There is also a lovely pond stocked with fish nearby; a most serene spot should you have a moment for inner reflection. For now, see that my things are unpacked, and fresh clothing laid out for me."

Taking the hint, Travis turned away and busied himself removing items from the high druid's bag. He kept his head down and elbows tucked so his robe sleeves didn't slide back to expose his tattooed forearms. He tensed at the approaching footsteps in the hallway but did not jump when the door swung open. Two young boys wrangled a bulky straw mattress into the room and, at Pendaran's direction, positioned it on the floor near the foot of the bed. With bows to both druids, they disappeared back into the dark hallway. Travis nudged the mattress with the toe of his boot, stifling a rueful grin. *Still more comfortable than Afghanistan, but I doubt I'll get much sleep here.*

"...some of the younger men came to us lacking in even the most basic clerical—"

Travis's gaze darted around the spartan room before he paused, sobering. *How long is all this going to take?* His warrior's anticipation kicked in with a vengeance, making his palms itch to fill them with weapons and charge into battle. Realizing he had no control over the flow of events, an impotent snarl of rage escaped before he could catch it.

The abrupt noise startled the room's other occupants into silence, and they both stared at him. Travis ducked his head and barked a hoarse cough into his sleeve to explain the sound.

Pendaran jumped in with his response, again claiming Ciarán's full attention. "Then they must be instructed on how to handle the texts before being entrusted to copy them. Some of these scrolls are over a thousand years old and will crumble in unskilled hands."

Grateful for the diversion, Travis busied himself with laying out what he assumed to be the requested change of clothing. The bag, although heavy, held few personal items. The weight of a small eating knife, several rolled sheaves of paper, a small leatherbound journal, the half-full wineskin, various leaves, pieces of roots, small, folded squares of linen, a small piece of polished reflective metal, and what might have been a sort of rough comb made up the bulk of it. He found an additional robe at the bottom, much finer in quality than what they now wore and decorated with strange symbols painstakingly stitched in shiny thread.

A quick rap on the open door announced a young maid struggling with a bucket of water. Travis automatically moved to help her, but at a sharp glance from Pendaran, stopped short. "Place it by the basin there and close the door behind you," he ordered.

Without a word, she did as requested, pulling the thick door closed with a soft *thunk*. Pendaran whirled to face Ciarán. "Now then—do you tell me what weighs so heavy upon your mind."

Ciarán's round face went pale. "D—do you not think it b—best we spoke in private?" he stammered, casting a wary look toward Travis.

Pendaran flapped his hand in a dismissive gesture. "You may speak freely in front of him. He is simple and will remember naught."

Travis struggled to hold his face neutral at the slight, but ducked his head and said nothing as he continued to unpack.

"Tell me what plans this fool Ansgar has for the fae he holds captive."

The younger druid sagged with visible relief. "So you know, then," he said. "Make no mistake, there are few who support this travesty, but those few are indeed powerful. The rest of us dare not challenge him. He means to take your place as High Druid, my lord."

"I already have knowledge of this. But what of the fae, Ciarán?"

"I have heard it said he means to breed their magick into certain druid bloodlines." Ciarán twisted his hands together in a nervous tic. "His own. Again, I do not know this for certain."

The growing tension in the room suddenly flared, and without looking at Travis, the elder threw his arm up in a staying gesture. "In all his years of studying the *Tuath Dé*, how is it Ansgar does not know his goal is unattainable?"

"He believes," Ciarán's voice dropped to a whisper, "he has found the means to overcome that limitation."

Pendaran's face registered no change of emotion. "And does he say how this can be done?"

"He alone holds that secret, High Druid."

He made a dismissive noise. "How many of these poor creatures does he hold captive?"

"There were as many as a score once, but their numbers have dwindled. Maybe half of that now," Ciarán explained, "including one poor wretch that escaped. He crossed through the stones to retrieve her, and even now, she sits in an iron cage awaiting your arrival."

"My arrival? Whatever for?" Pendaran's bushy eyebrows lifted in surprise.

"I believe he had planned to gift her to you. Now I fear that has changed." Ciarán once again darted a worried glance at Travis and dropped his voice again to a hushed whisper. "He has become quite enamored of the girl, but first demands retribution for her flight. I have grave doubts whether she would survive his form of justice. They are all bound and unable to use magicks, but..." His voice broke, unable to continue.

Pendaran patted the younger man on the shoulder. "There, there, Ciarán," he soothed. "May I trust you will hold this in confidence?"

"Of course, my lord." He nodded, mopping his eyes with a worn cloth. "I shall guard your secrets with my very life."

"We mean to stop this madness once and for all."

"But how?" he cried. "Ansgar's thirst for power is boundless, and he has proven himself ruthless toward that end."

"We may have a few tricks of our own," Pendaran assured him, and raising his voice slightly for Travis's benefit, he added, "and I cannot help but think we have justice on our side. Now," he said, easing toward the door, "you should return before someone notes your absence and questions your whereabouts. And again, I should like to think that our conversation will be held in confidence, yes?"

"Of course, of course." Ciarán's head bobbed in agreement. He grabbed the metal handle and tugged the door open. "Enjoy your tour of the gardens, my lord," he said, a bit louder than necessary before entering the hall and pulling the door firmly closed behind him.

Travis moved away from the open window and tugged his hood back. "Do you think he'll keep his mouth shut?"

Pendaran's lips pursed in thought. "Hard to say," he admitted. "Ciarán is young and overeager to ingratiate himself. That being said, he also has a big heart and a small amount of common sense. I hope he keeps his silence, but if you have any last-minute preparations to make, I suggest you do so with all haste."

Travis didn't say anything. He shrugged off his robe and began reorganizing his weapons for easier access. As he made the necessary adjustments, a scene from an old movie kept playing through his mind: the crowd parting for Indiana Jones as the black-robed swordsman swung his weapon in wide arcs, inviting Jones forward to meet his death. Indy didn't hesitate; he withdrew his pistol and fired a single shot, dropping the swordsman where he stood. *You don't bring a knife to a gunfight*, Travis thought with an inner chuckle, then sobered. Making the conscious choice to take a life was never an easy task, even with your own at stake. His ingrained military and law enforcement training allowed no margin for error—you neutralize the threat until the threat stays neutralized, period.

Pendaran watched with interest as Travis withdrew the palm-sized Sig from his ankle holster, racked a round into the chamber, and replaced it. "I gather that is some fashion of weapon—what does it do?" he asked.

Travis reached into one of the pockets in the cargo pants, withdrew a loaded magazine, and handed it to the druid. He opted for the simplest explanation, figuring the technology of the Hydra Shok rounds would be information overload for the old man. "It fires these," he explained, tapping one of the jacketed hollow points with a fingertip. "A bow in capable hands can shoot an arrow that travels upward of one hundred per second. This weapon," he said, pointing toward his ankle, "can shoot that little chunk of metal over ten times that fast. It's designed to make a small hole going in and a great big one going out."

Pendaran blinked in surprise, staring down at the shiny bullets. "That is indeed a fearsome weapon," he murmured, handing the magazine back. "This could all be over in the blink of an eye."

After tucking it safely back in its hiding place, Travis turned to stare out the window. "I'm not an assassin," he said quietly. "It doesn't sit well with me to shoot an unarmed man in cold blood, no matter what he's done."

"And I would not ask that of you," the older man hurried to assure him, shaking his head. "I much prefer he surrender his power without violent coercion, but I harbor no illusions he will do so willingly. This would be the last resort to end his tyranny."

"There is something else," Travis added hesitantly. "It's possible Ansgar has one of these weapons. He used it to shoot my friend, but I'm not sure how many bullets he has left."

Pendaran took a wobbly step back and sat on the bed with a heavy *thump*. "That is grave news, indeed. Your friend—is he, ah..."

"Alive, thank God. And I promised him I'd deliver his retribution in person."

A timid knock halted further discussion. "My lords?" a feminine voice called.

Travis snatched his hood up again and turned away as Pendaran answered the door. A pretty young maid in her teens held a wooden tray with a jug and bowl of ripe fruit. He stepped aside for her to enter. She set the tray carefully on the table and turned, dipping a slight curtsey. "My lords, I am Brigid. If there be aught I can do fer ye, ye have but to ask."

From the winsome smile and sloe-eyed, inviting gaze turned his way, Travis knew her services would not be limited to a concierge nature if he gave her the slightest encouragement.

Pendaran grunted in both acknowledgment and dismissal just as the bells rang in deep, sonorous tones overhead, announcing the noon meal. The girl gave another quick bob, cast a backward glance at Travis, and scurried from the room. The old druid pushed the door closed behind her. "We shall give them a few moments to be about their meal, then you and I shall go exploring."

CHAPTER 41

The deserted hallway greeted them when, at last, they opened the door again. Pendaran's boots made no sound as he hurried toward the stairs, Travis hot on his six. Within minutes, they stood outside the back entrance of the keep, overlooking the tidy area with stone benches and shallow gazing pools scattered throughout the small gardens laden with bright flowers and ripe vegetables. *Mike would've loved this*, Travis thought with a sudden, sharp pang of homesickness.

"There," Pendaran whispered, using the head of his staff to gesture at what Travis realized must be the ancient equivalent of a Quonset hut. The hastily erected structure had clearly been built over something that had burned, evidenced by remnants of charred wooden planks lying nearby.

Two large men stood guard at the single door, straightening to attention at their approach. They inched almost shoulder to shoulder, barring the entryway. "This area is forbidden, my lords," one of the men announced, adjusting his sword belt in a blatant attempt at intimidation.

Pendaran looked from one man to the other in bemusement. "Know you not who I am?" he asked in disbelief.

The first man cast his companion an uncertain glance. "Nay, my lord?"

The old druid drew up to his full height, and his voice rang with authority. "I am Pendaran of Dyfed, High Druid of Eire and the Celtic Isles, lord of this keep and many others like it. Are you truly so foolish that you seek to bar my entrance?"

"But My Lord Ansgar said—" one of the men stammered.

"Ansgar is *not* the high druid, nor shall he ever be," Pendaran snapped, cutting him off. "Now, do you step aside so that we may enter?"

Still openly conflicted about the order, the two soldiers stepped in opposite directions, away from the closed door. In the distance, thunder rumbled again, the sound closer than before.

The gray skies overhead did not allow much light in through the high, narrow windows. A single lantern on a wooden table cast a feeble light throughout the large room, leaving most of it in shadow. At first, Travis thought the space was abandoned. The shadows merged into a feminine form as they moved forward. A young woman, perhaps in her thirties, clasped her hands together as she approached, her shoulders hunched. "My lords, it is unusual to see you at this time of day. The bells have rung for your noon meal."

Pendaran gently laid his staff down on the rush-strewn floor. "We mean you no harm, my dear. In fact, we intend to set you free," he whispered. "Come closer that I may see the collar you wear."

Travis snatched the single lantern and brought it to the old druid, holding it up for clearer viewing. Now that he could see her face, he caught the gasp before it escaped. Ethereally beautiful features graced her heart-shaped face, her eyes large and slanted like a cat. Her hair was long like Saoirse's, but fell in a riot of thick, honey-blonde curls. She gave a tremulous smile, lifting her chin for closer inspection of the lunula.

"This is indeed dark magick," Pendaran murmured, peering closely at the etched symbols. Straightening, he whirled to face Travis. "We must hasten to the library. I believe the spell can be broken, but its foulness does not just dissipate without consequence. We must learn how to be rid of this wickedness yet harm none in the process."

Travis jerked in alarm, forgetting not to speak. "We?"

"Aye—you will have your part to play," Pendaran replied and chuckled.

A chorus of soft gasps fluttered through the room as more women pressed forward. "You mean this? Free? How is this possible?" A few of the beautiful faces held shiny tracks where the tears had fallen as they hugged each other in utter exhilaration. "How can we help?"

Pendaran held up a hand for silence. "Wait, be ready, and say nothing of our visit. We shall return as soon as we are able." And with that, he retrieved his staff, turned, and strode for the door. "Come, Ruaidri. We have much work to do."

Hours later, Travis stifled yet another bout of sneezing triggered by the dust rising from the old leatherbound volumes. Glancing around, he kept his voice low so as not to attract attention from the library's other occupants. "Just how old are these books?"

Pendaran did not glance up from the yellowed pages of his current text. "Hundreds of years, some thousands." He dipped his quill into a nearby stone bowl filled with ink and scribbled something on his parchment. "Are you having any trouble reading?"

Still astonished, Travis admitted he did not, thanks to a quick incantation and a little hand gesturing from the old man, who explained that without that particular charm, they would be unable to read any of the older tomes. "Good. Then go fetch me—" He rattled off a title that sounded as dry as the dust inhaled with each page, and gestured with a wave. "You should find it in that section."

Remembering to move slowly, Travis went to the indicated area and began combing the shelves. He found it near the bottom, surprised by its heavy weight when he pulled it free.

"May I be of assistance?" a male voice asked.

Startled by the intrusion, Travis's head sliced once in negation. He moved around the unknown druid but had only taken one step before the man spoke again. "That is far too advanced for a novice," he explained, reaching to take the book away. His emphasis on the word *novice* lent a pompous air to his following sentence. "Allow me to suggest something more suitable for your level."

Travis hugged the book to his chest and shook his head again, trying to move past the presumptuous librarian. The man stepped in front of him again, blocking his path. "Give me the book," he ordered.

"No." Travis met the druid's arrogant gaze, giving him what he called the *LEO look*—a warning expression suggesting that the man reconsider whatever bad, life-changing decision he currently contemplated.

His hand shot out, grabbing a fistful of Travis's robe. "How DARE—"

"Brother Oengus, I see you have met my apprentice. Ruaidri, please take the book to my table." With a gentle but firm grip, Pendaran took Travis's arm and pulled him past the other man. "Just there," he said, giving a gentle nudge.

Red-faced, Oengus began blustering. "He defied my direct order to hand over that book—"

"Yet he fulfilled a direct order from me to procure it," the high druid snapped, his tone steely. "In the future, should you have a problem with any of my requests, you will bring it to me and not vent your frustrations on an underling."

The brother seemed to remember whom he addressed and paled. "Yes, my lord." Without another word, the frightened man bowed, turned, and fled back into the labyrinth of bookcases.

Pendaran's mouth twisted in a sneer as he stalked back to his table. "Witless fool," he spat, flopping back into his seat. "Ever ready to flaunt his meager authority."

Travis glanced around at the clerks working nearby, their eyes conspicuously riveted to their work, but more than one was stifling a smirk at the insufferable librarian's badly needed comeuppance.

The afternoon dragged on, and with each passing minute, Travis's frustration grew. He fidgeted in his seat, the heavy robe masking most of his furtive movements. He tried writing with the primitive tools provided, but succeeded only in smearing the ink on both the page and his fingers. The tightening of his facial muscles as he ground his teeth in aggravation did not go unnoticed. "Our research is near completion," Pendaran soothed. "Unless I am mistaken, your wish is to rescue your fae damsel and end this travesty once and for all, yes?" At the curt nod of assent, he continued. "Freeing her of captivity is the lesser of the two tasks, but from what I have discerned of your character, you will not rest until both are realized."

Travis nodded again. "You're right, of course. I'm sorry—all this waiting has me on edge," he grumbled, then gave the older man a thoughtful look. "Why hasn't he come looking for you? He has to know you're here by now."

"He perceives this as a show of power." The high druid chuckled. "He waits for me to present myself to him, which I shall not do. It is his place to come to me."

As if the mere thought conjured him, Ansgar skulked through the library entrance and stopped, scanning the tables as if searching. The air itself changed, becoming thicker and more oppressive, charged with an unseen current. The clerks huddled closer into themselves and ducked their heads lower, paying rapt attention to the pages in front of them. Seeing the man he was looking for at a rear table, he strode toward it with a fake smile plastered across his hairy visage. It did not dim the hostility in his black, flat eyes. "My Lord High Druid," he exclaimed, throwing his arms wide. "I heard of your arrival and have been searching for you high and low since."

"Then you are met with success, for here I am," Pendaran responded coolly, remaining seated.

Taken aback by the arctic tone, Ansgar's face registered confusion before he recovered enough to speak again. "I trust your journey here was uneventful?"

"Quite." The high druid bent his head to the text again and turned the page, dismissing the other man entirely.

Unready to admit defeat, Ansgar ran a long finger over the spines of the stacked books. "An interesting selection," he commented. "Is there something specific you seek?"

Pendaran lifted one shoulder in a casual shrug. "Nothing in particular, just reading."

When the silence stretched into minutes, Ansgar turned his attention to Travis. "And who would this be?" he asked, his annoyance making his voice loud enough to turn heads.

"My apprentice."

Travis sat unmoving, head bowed, fists balled up in his lap, the knuckles showing white. He did not speak, which angered Ansgar even further. "I asked you a question, boy."

He made no effort to hide his accent. "Ruaidri," he said softly.

Ansgar braced both hands against the tabletop and leaned forward. "Show me your face," he demanded.

Pendaran's knee pressed against his own in silent warning, but Travis tilted his head back enough to reveal the stone-faced expression of a soldier. By this time, his five o'clock shadow provided little disguise. He knew the greater wisdom in following the elder druid's plan, but he almost hoped he'd be recognized on the spot so they could get on with it.

Ansgar's head cocked to one side in a thoughtful pose. "You seem familiar to me. Have we met?"

"Doubtful," Pendaran interjected. "I came across his family during my travels to the West lands; peasants. The poor wretches were starving, of course. I gave them coin in exchange for this one." With a curt nod, he added, "He is big, yes, but lame and quite simple in many ways. I thought perhaps he could be of use to me. He has learned much these past years, haven't you, my lad?"

Travis gave a slight nod, and Ansgar seemed to lose interest in further questions. "After our evening meal, we have much to discuss. I shall leave you to your study, then." And without another word, he turned and left the library, his robes billowing behind him like a struggling sail.

Armed with a stack of books, they returned to their chamber and spread Pendaran's notes across the table. "In the event we are visited yet again, hide these away. The words written thereon would certainly raise eyebrows if not outright invite prying questions."

Travis studied the pages filled with elegant, crabbed script, but could not make out a single word. He nodded and took the chair closest to the door. He lifted the pitcher and peered down into it. Deciding it was water, he poured two cups but paused before drinking. "They wouldn't try to poison you, would they?"

Pendaran raised his cup and sniffed. "It is safe," he announced.

"That doesn't exactly answer the question."

"If Ansgar is successful in taking my place, rituals must be performed to shift the balance of power. It is unlikely he would jeopardize his plans by a careless act before that occurs." He wrote a few more words and laid the quill down. Anchoring several fingers to keep the page from flying away, he blew across the wet ink to dry it.

"Someone's coming." Travis leapt to his feet and stood by the door, listening. "One person, sounds like."

He swept the pages into a neat pile and tucked them inside his sleeve just as a soft knock sounded. Grabbing two of the books, he laid them open on the table. At his nod, Travis opened the door and stepped aside. A different woman bobbed in a curtsey and folded her hands. "My Lord Pendaran, the evening meal will be served anon. Shall I announce that you will join them?"

He pretended to study, following the text with a long finger. "No. Please have food and wine sent up to our chambers. I have traveled far this day and would relish a full night's sleep ere I meet with the others."

Travis managed to swallow the noise of annoyance before it escaped. He glanced up to see the woman stripping him naked with her eyes. Coloring with embarrassment, she looked away. "Then I shall have food prepared and sent up for you," she said, her tone businesslike.

Pendaran did not look up from his book. "Yes, thank you, and for my apprentice as well."

She looked shocked. "My Lord, his station dictates he should eat with the other—"

"No," he said, cutting her off. "Ruaidri is here to assist me. And do please offer the brothers my regrets. After all, I am an old man and need my rest."

"As you will, my lord." With that, she curtsied again and left the room.

Travis closed the door behind her with a firm *snick* and sat in the other chair at the table. "They really want you downstairs with them."

"You know what they say—wants and wishes are nothing without action. They will honor my wishes for this one night, but I doubt we will get a second. I must work with all speed." With that, he turned back to his reading. It wasn't long before another knock sounded at the door.

This time, it was a druid Travis had not seen before. Tall and broad, his blue eyes twinkled as he smiled. "My Lord Pendaran, I just heard you will not be joining us for the evening meal. Is aught amiss?"

"Nay, old friend. I would but finish my reading and rest from my long travels before meeting with you all. The Gods forbid I nod off like a doddering ancient in the middle of dessert." He chuckled and rose from the table to embrace the newcomer. "It is good to see you, Aiden."

Aiden chortled, the rich sound rolling from deep in his belly. "Doddering ancient? I think not. Wily old fox, more like."

"Quiet, lest you reveal all my secrets," Pendaran said with a laugh of his own.

Unnoticed, Travis engaged in some mental gymnastics as the happy reunion took place. This habit had served him well both in the military and on the force, keeping him alert and his mind engaged while waiting. It also, he remembered with an inner grin, had helped him on the night of his senior prom, when he mentally recited football statistics in the backseat of his car. Tonight, the multiplication tables worked their magic, keeping the maddening image of a caged Saoirse at bay.

"—doubt he will appreciate being thwarted, but your reason for not attending is valid."

"He dare not speak against me beforehand, as his opportunity for a peaceful transfer of power would be lost. Ansgar may have his own sycophants, but I do not believe that once exposed, they will remain by his side."

The bells tolled three times, their deep notes sounding throughout the keep. "The meal is served. Best you go before you are missed," Pendaran said, guiding his friend toward the door.

"I sense there is more here than you have revealed," Aiden said, glancing sideways at Travis.

"And that is because you are too clever by half. Be off now and be at ease. All is well, and I shall see you on the morrow."

"As you will, my lord." Aiden gave a short bow. "On the morrow, then."

Pendaran closed the door behind him and took his seat at the table again. Several moments passed before he spoke. "You would be wise to sleep now while you can," he whispered. "We've a long night ahead."

"What about you?" he asked.

The old druid chuckled. "Worry not about me. It is you who will need every bit of your strength to prevail."

CHAPTER 42

Filled with restless unease and deep in thought, Ansgar paced the halls after the evening meal. After such a lackluster reception from the high druid and his failure to appear for the evening meal, uncertainty gnawed at him. For the hundredth time, he wondered if Pendaran would see reason in stepping down in favor of a younger leader. The high druid's apprentice was another matter altogether. Of course, he would be compelled to defend his master should it come to that. Ansgar's brow furrowed as he racked his brain—*why should his face seem so familiar?* 'Tis obvious he had never before seen the great lout, but even so, something did not sit well with him.

Without realizing his destination, his steps led him to the hall where the fae waited in her iron cage. She sat cross-legged, arms folded across her chest, glaring daggers at him. Her insolence could not be tolerated, of course. Still, he couldn't help but feel a burgeoning sense of admiration for her courage and defiance. He would enjoy relieving her of those useless qualities.

He took a step toward her enclosure. The single posted guard straightened, stifling a bored yawn. She did not move, but a large smile spread across her impish face, showing every white tooth. At his second step, she chattered her teeth together with a loud *snap*. His injured finger throbbed in response, but he held his face impassive. "You shall not get that chance again," he muttered, then wondered aloud, "but perhaps removing them altogether would be the safest course of action. It would mar your beauty, of course."

The creature began to sing in a soft voice, barely audible at his distance. He did not know the language, but the cadence of her song raised the hairs on the back of his neck. His heartbeat quickened, and he knew the blood drained from his face. He raised his staff and pointed the tip at her, issuing the unspoken threat of a spell. "You will cease that noise at once."

She stopped but then chuckled, which was somehow worse than the song. "'Tis obvious I have frightened you. How sad—for you."

He said nothing but began pacing a slow circle around the cage, brows furrowed as if in deep thought.

She grinned at him through the thick bars. "Have you naught to say? I find that odd, given your need to have the final word in all things. Perhaps you should run along and find some other poor soul to torment..." She stopped, appearing to ponder her next word. "Gandalf."

Ansgar jerked in surprise at the name. He stared at her for a long time, and when his puzzlement gave way to a slowly widening grin, the triumphant expression on Saoirse's face turned to one of abject horror. He whirled and strode toward the door. Before disappearing into the hallway, he spun to face his prisoner and gave her a mocking bow. "You have my thanks for solving a most troublesome riddle. Sleep well knowing mine will be the last face he ever sees."

"Wake now."

It seemed as if only minutes had passed before the hushed whisper next to his ear made Travis jerk. He rested his body in that sweet place between slumber and readiness, perfected in the desert surrounded by unseen hostile forces. He focused on measured breathing to calm his stampeding thoughts and overactive imagination. So intently focused, he had not heard the old man move, and it unnerved him. "I'm not asleep," he snapped, his tone a little sharper than he intended.

Pendaran patted his shoulder. "Come—I have something to show you."

A single beam of light shone into the otherwise dark room. "What time is it?" he asked, rolling to his feet.

"Walk softly, as you do not want your footsteps overheard. The moon is now at its zenith. Some of the hallways are dark and narrow, but I fear using torch or lantern would make stealth impossible. I thought the moonlight could be of assist."

"I've got something," Travis said, feeling around in his pockets. He withdrew the penlight and clicked it on, directing the beam at the floor.

Pendaran jumped back and gasped. "This does not burn your hand?"

He handed it to the druid, who turned it from side to side, examining it closely. "'Tis surely a sort of spell to produce so much light without flint or tinder," he murmured.

"You said you have something to show me?" Travis asked, struggling to keep the impatience out of his voice. He didn't want to give a science lesson—he needed to get this show on the road.

"Oh, yes! With your permission, I should like to see that again when there is more time. But for now, we must hurry. Dampen the light." Pendaran eased the chamber door open and stuck his head out, checking both ways. "We should go now."

The two men moved down the hallway toward the stairway without a whisper of sound. Down the stairs, through the foyer, past another large room, and down another dark hallway they went, staying close to the walls. More than once, Pendaran stopped to listen, but when he held up his hand and turned to look behind them again, Travis couldn't remain silent. "Are we being followed?"

"I know not," the old druid said. "It is very odd. I sense both nothing and a deliberate nothingness, as if something is being hidden. Quite the puzzle. Still, let us keep moving."

The next hallway had the torches lit, and looking cautiously around the corner, they spied the lone soldier standing guard at a large door. Pendaran waved for Travis to stay put. Gathering his robes about him, he notched his chin up and marched directly toward the guard, who straightened to attention.

"Halt—my orders are to bar entry for everyone save Lord Ansgar," the man insisted, uncertainty tingeing his voice.

"Yes, he said I am to give you this." Pendaran fumbled around in his pouch. He withdrew his closed fist and held it up for the guard. When the man leaned over to look, the druid opened his hand and blew what appeared to be dust into the man's face. The guard slumped back against the door and slid into a sitting position, his eyes closing as his head lolled to one side. Pendaran watched him for a moment, then waved for Travis to come.

"What was that?" he asked.

"A strange powder from distant lands," he explained. "Ingesting it brings immediate sleep, but too much can be deadly. He will wake before long and remember nothing."

He clutched Travis's arm and nudged him toward the door. "Go—there is little time. I will stand watch."

Travis pushed the door, which opened with a complaining creak. A single lantern hung on a hook near the door, casting long shadows across the only other thing in the room—a large iron cage. A small figure was huddled inside, the blanket wrapped so tightly that only a tuft of dark hair was visible.

As he drew closer, it stirred. Saoirse's tousled head lifted, and her nostrils flared as she inhaled. She scrambled to her knees, extending her arm through the bars. "Do I dream?"

With an exhalation of relief, Travis rushed to take her hand. "You're not dreaming. I'm here."

She burst into tears and reached for him, pulling him against the bars. He crushed his lips against hers as she ran her fingers over his face and hair. "I thought never to see you again," she sobbed, covering his face with kisses.

"I've got help," he assured her. "We're going to get you out of here and set you all free."

"My Travis, you must listen," she choked, cradling her cheek against his hand. "Ansgar came to taunt me earlier. In my anger, I called him Gandalf, just as you did when you first met. The look in his eye and that terrible smile..." She shuddered. "I fear he may recognize you when you meet."

"Well, so what if he does? He's going to know me soon enough, anyway." He stroked his other hand over her hair to soothe her. "You're just going to have to trust me. We will win this thing, one way or the other."

"Then I shall send you all the magick I have," she said with a firm nod before her shoulders sagged again. She gave a halfhearted wave, her fingertips brushing her collar. "What is not restrained, anyway."

The door creaked as it opened, and Pendaran stuck his head inside. "We must away before the guard awakens from his slumber."

Travis took her hands in his, and she leaned closer for a kiss. "I love you," he whispered.

"I love you, too. Please come back safe to me."

"I'll do my best, I promise. We've got a whole lot more living to do yet."

She smiled through her tears. "Then I wish you all the good fortune in this world and beyond."

Despite his misgivings, he mustered his best cocky grin. "With all that luck coming our way, we can't lose."

The hooded figure shrank back into the shadows as the two men passed by silently. Once they disappeared around the corner, he walked quickly in the opposite direction. Even in the dark, he found the other stairs at the end of the dining hall and climbed them two at a time. Coming to a stop at one of the doors, he knocked once, then twice more.

"Enter," a deep voice said.

The man slipped inside, closing the door behind him. "The high druid and his apprentice went to her, just as you said."

"And?"

"I could not draw near enough to overhear, but they did not stay long," he admitted. "His hulking assistant went into the room while the old man stood guard. I believe he suspected they were followed."

"The apprentice went in while the master waited without. How very curious." Ansgar said, leaning back in his chair and smiling. "And has Pendaran taken you into his confidence?"

"Pendaran asked me to keep our conversations secret. I told him I would. He means to put an end to your plans, but did not say how he would accomplish this." He smiled. "I will question him further when the opportunity presents itself, and, of course, share what I learn with you."

"You have done well, Ciarán."

CHAPTER 43

Travis spent a fitful night on the thin pallet. The trumpeting crow of a rooster greeting the dawn jolted him from the few hours of sleep he had managed to get, and he could have cheerfully wrung its scrawny neck for five more minutes. It had been a long time since he had slept on what was essentially hard ground, and from the spasmodic cramps, his back did not appreciate the reminiscence. His face and neck itched from the day's beard growth, and his mouth tasted sour from last night's wine. He desperately wanted to peel off his dirty clothing and body armor to stand under a hot shower, but the icing on the cake was the marked absence of a fresh coffee aroma. In short, Travis woke up itching for a fight.

He opened his eyes to see Pendaran already up, dressed, and moving about the room. "'Tis about time you woke," he chided gently. "I feared you meant to lie abed until the noon meal." He gestured toward a full wooden bucket placed near his bed. "There is bread and cheese on the table."

Travis cupped his hands, raising the cool water to his lips. He gulped it down, parched from the night's alcohol.

When the dehydration felt manageable, he asked, "What are our plans for today?"

"I read far into the night. I believe the enchanted collars are bound to a single item, one I would suppose he keeps on his person at all times. If we can find and remove it, the curse should be broken. In theory," he added with an air of caution.

He thought back to the night Geena sketched Ansgar. "Saoirse mentioned he wears a metal amulet."

"Likely so, especially if he never takes it off. Something like that would have to be worn near the heart for potency, but magick that dark would leech strength from the body over time."

"One can only hope." He splashed water on his face and scrubbed the cobwebs away. Not seeing a towel, he dried using the sleeve of his robe. With a start, he glanced around the room and sighed. "Let me guess—chamber pot?"

Pendaran did not look up from his reading, but shoved another piece of cheese in his mouth and nodded.

"Spectacular," Travis muttered.

They spent much of the morning walking the grounds and gardens inside the walled compound. Whenever someone approached, Pendaran pretended to lecture about the different plants and their healing or magickal properties. Travis tried to appear attentive while mentally mapping their surroundings, paying particular attention to the castle layout.

The noon bells pealed, the sound reverberating through the courtyard. Pendaran pulled Travis close and whispered against his ear. "I have been absent from the last two meals and the dawn ritual. I must put in an appearance lest questions arise. You, however, need to rest."

When Travis protested, the old druid shook his head. "Exhaustion is etched upon your face, and I fear you will need all your strength and wits about you this eve. There is food left in our chamber. Eat all you care to and sleep. You may use my bed, which I warrant is much softer than your thin pallet."

The idea of a long nap did appeal to him, but not so much another meal of bread and cheese. He would have committed a first-degree felony for a big, juicy cheeseburger or one of Mrs. Ella Mae's Salt Flat Specials. His salivary glands kicked into overdrive at the mental image. Hell, even one of Mike's pineapple pizzas sounded good.

When he returned to their chamber, he saw room service had refilled the pitchers and buckets, emptied the chamber pot, and replaced the leftover breakfast tray with a new one filled with bread and soft cheese, strips of dried meat he now knew was wild boar, fresh berries, hazelnuts, and apples. "Oh, hell yeah," Travis groaned under his breath before polishing off half of the provided bounty.

With his hunger satiated, he dragged a side chair away from the table. He upended it, leaning it precariously against the door handle as a makeshift alarm against anyone entering while he slept. Tugging the thin blanket from the bed, he wrapped it around his shoulders like a cape and fell back onto the down-filled tick. His eyes fluttered closed, and within minutes, he fell fast asleep.

The clatter of the wooden chair hitting the floor jolted him fully awake. Pendaran stood in the doorway, looking first at the fallen chair and then Travis. He clapped his hands, laughing with delight. "You are indeed a resourceful lad. That is quite a good idea, and I shall remember it."

Travis sat up and rubbed his eyes. "What time is it?"

"You have been asleep for hours. The shadows grow long. I—"

A knock at the door interrupted his thoughts. Pendaran waved Travis off the bed and cracked the door open. "Aye?" He stepped back to allow Ciarán entry.

"My lord—I just wanted to ensure you are rested enough to join us for the evening meal." His voice dropped into a conspiratorial whisper. "I hear Ansgar means to share his plans with you after we eat. Have you found out any more? The only information I have of his intentions is vague at best."

"What I learned has naught to do with breeding. He thinks to replace the keep workers with fae believing they will not demand payment for their labor. Perhaps persuade some to teach here as well. How true this is, I cannot say."

Ciarán seemed taken aback. "I have not heard this, but it does not seem such a bad idea. Perhaps it could be mutually beneficial?"

"I doubt the fae will think it so," Pendaran said, snorting with derision.

The young druid studied his fingertips before asking another question. "Have you a plan on how to stop him?"

"No. In the spirit of fairness, I should hear what he has to say before making a judgment. Perhaps his suggestions will be valid and should be considered."

If it were possible for Ciarán to look even more startled, he did. He cleared his throat uncomfortably. "At any rate, I look forward to tonight's meeting. I feel it will be most enlightening." He began backing toward the open door. "At the evening meal, then."

"Aye," Pendaran said, closing the door behind him. He listened for the fading footsteps before heaving a deep sigh. "At least we know now which side he has chosen."

Travis had watched the other druid closely and reached the same conclusion. "He acted nervous, different from when you arrived." He scooped up water to splash on his face. "I don't trust him."

"Nor do I," the druid agreed, helping himself to a piece of cheese.

Rising to his feet, Travis began his stretching routine, starting from the top of his head down. His neck in particular needed attention to work out the lingering kinks, and he groaned with enjoyment as the pops assured him everything had found its proper place.

Pendaran watched with fascination. "Why do you do this?" he asked.

"I do this once or twice every day. It keeps me flexible and saves sore or pulled muscles later if I'm involved in something physical," he replied, bending over to stretch his hamstrings. "My dad got me in the habit, said it helped him get his mind straight for whatever lay ahead."

The druid gave a noncommittal grunt and reached for his dress robe, airing on a hook near the window. He shook it once to displace a few dried leaves and slipped it over his head. "We shall be called to the great hall very soon," he said, his voice muffled under the heavy fabric. "I would suggest you wear your full complement of weaponry as I have no way of knowing how this evening will progress."

"On it," Travis agreed. He had not removed any body armor since their arrival, but did tuck some of the edged weapons under his pallet while he slept for safety reasons. He caught a sweaty whiff as he removed his robe, refusing to think about his shower back home. *I got spoiled*, he thought, cringing inwardly at the stray thought.

The bells interrupted his musings, and he rushed to complete his preparations. The expected knock came as he smoothed his coarse robe into place. "The evening meal is served, my lord," came the loud call through the door.

Pendaran looked over to Travis, eyebrows raised in question. Without a word, he gave a thumbs-up gesture and forced a confident grin.

"Youth," he said with a chuckle. Before opening the door, he raised his hand and traced a symbol on Travis's forehead. "For luck. And remember to walk one step behind, and limp."

Exiting their chambers, the two men fell into step behind the other druids as they filed downstairs and into the hall, where the tables had been set for a meal. Travis got his first good look at the expansive room with its vaulted ceiling and large, smoothed stones forming the walls. Doorways leading to smaller rooms and fireplaces were scattered on each wall, and the floor appeared crafted from another flatter type of rock. During one of his dissertations, Pendaran proudly described the keep as a miracle of architecture, explaining that every modern convenience had been added.

Travis had wisely held his tongue about what he thought constituted modern convenience. For now, he followed the high druid, keeping his head bowed. A young brother approached and swept his arm toward the dining area where some in the order were already seating themselves. "Allow me to assist you, my lord." He pulled out the ornate wooden chair at the head of the table and waved for him to sit.

No sooner had Travis touched the chair to Pendaran's right than he found his wrist caught in a viselike grip. A different brother glared at him, lip curled in a smirk. "Out, you—apprentices eat in the kitchen with the servants. Not with us."

"And yet you will allow mine, at my request, yes?" Pendaran's tone was cordial but hinted at the steel beneath.

The man released the captive arm and stepped back. "Of course, my lord," he said stiffly, head tilted forward in a mocking bow. "As you wish." He moved away and disappeared into the crowd of women bringing rounded platters to the table.

The wafting aromas made Travis's mouth water. He did not recognize the foreign food or seasonings used, but decided the stewed fish might be salmon, and the wilted greens had something resembling field peas mixed in. Being a Southern man, his heart was all about the bread. When they set a basket of freshly baked goodness and a jar of honey down in front of him, his first impulse was to dive in face first. Glancing around, he saw everyone else had started eating. Not one to stand on ceremony, he snagged a chunk of bread and drizzled it with honey before raising it to his mouth.

"I think it rude to share a meal while hiding your face. Lower your hood." Ansgar dropped into the chair across from Travis, the intense glare on his face belying his cordial tone. His robe resembled the high druid's, with similar ornate stitching. A glint of metal peeked from the V-neck collar.

Travis glanced at his bread mournfully before placing it on the edge of the shallow bowl. He pulled the hood back and shook it with both hands, allowing it to lie smoothly on his shoulders. Without a word, he picked up the crust again and took a large bite, meeting the other man's stare with open hostility.

Ansgar appeared unruffled, helping himself to the fish. "My Lord Pendaran, it seems your apprentice—" he emphasized the word "—needs further instruction to comport himself in public." He speared a large chunk, stuffed it into his mouth, and spoke around it. "Far be it from me to criticize, but if we allow apprentices to eat at our table, they should, at the very least, show appropriate respect to their betters." As he ate, the sleeve of his dress robe slid up to reveal the horrific scarring on his right forearm. "And to stare at a disfigurement is rudest of all."

Travis's gaze snapped back to Ansgar's face, having been drawn to the malformed tissue, which looked like it had been carved away and cauterized. If he didn't know better, he would say there had once been color around the edges of the mutilation. "Looks like that might've hurt," he drawled, nodding at the scar.

"Ruaidri." Pendaran's single word carried a note of warning.

Further discussion paused as servants brought in the next course, a thick vegetable and barley soup, accompanied by bowls of hard-boiled eggs. Once the empty dishes were collected, they disappeared into the kitchen, and conversations began anew.

Travis's appetite fled with Ansgar's arrival, but he dutifully tried a bite or two of everything put before him. It all smelled heavenly, but he tasted nothing. The last thing he needed was a full stomach slowing him down if things got physical. *Ironic,* he thought, *that the people outside are starving while they feast in here.*

Ansgar did not look his way or speak to him again, joining in the various discussions up and down the table. He spent much of the time attempting to draw the high druid into conversation, but received only grunts of acknowledgment in return. When his attention turned to an animated discourse at the other end of the table, Pendaran nudged Travis's foot. When their gazes met, he tapped his neck, giving the younger man a meaningful look. Travis nodded in understanding.

By the time the last course, a blackberry compote, was served, Travis's nerves were stretched to the breaking point. It took all his reserve to sit still without his knee bouncing with nervous energy. He counted breaths to keep his heart from beating out of his chest, holding the mental image of Saoirse at the forefront of his thoughts, seeking her strength for the trials ahead.

"Tell us what news I have missed, and what studies you labor upon in my absence," Pendaran's voice rang out above the din, officially starting the meeting.

Everyone began speaking at once, and Pendaran raised his hand for silence. He swiveled in his chair to look directly at Ansgar. "I would hear you first."

"We have been quite busy, initiating the teachings of—"

"What plans have you for the captured fae?" Pendaran snapped. "That is what I wish to know." The room fell silent, but several chairs squealed against the stone as some brothers pushed away from the table, making hasty excuses to leave the hall. "I saw those miserable creatures and the conditions under which they are held. It is an abomination." His gaze skewered the younger man. "Explain yourself."

Ansgar cleared his throat. "My lord, I believe I have found the means to assimilate their shapeshifting abilities into our own training, and—"

"How?" The single word came out sharp as a razor.

Travis watched both men, recognizing what Pendaran meant to do—draw Ansgar into a confrontation where he would intercede on the old man's behalf. *Good plan*, he thought, *keep him distracted.* Moving slowly to avoid drawing unwanted attention, he turned his chair for a faster exit and perched on the edge to spring into action.

"You no doubt saw the lunulae," Ansgar rushed to continue. "It prevents them from taking another form, giving us time—"

"Giving you time, you mean. Go on."

"—to explore their abilities without unnecessary rushing. I am certain I have found the means to crossbreed them with human males, thus giving future generations this valuable—"

"You are the worst kind of fool! If you knew aught about these magnificent creatures you claim to study, you would know they cannot reproduce in the forms they assume. Do you have any considerations for their wishes in this travesty?" Ansgar opened his mouth to protest, and Pendaran raised a hand in warning as he rose from his seat. "You will not speak again. This madness will cease now, and I demand you release your prisoners at once. It was a regrettable mistake indeed, naming you head of this order in my absence."

When Ansgar stood, Travis took that as his cue to position himself behind the old man. Easing out of his seat, he rested his hands on the carved chair back and waited for the next move.

"Your time as high druid has reached an end, Pendaran Dyfed," Ansgar growled, slamming his balled fists on the table. "Your teachings are outdated. You ignore valuable opportunities with your nonsensical ramblings. Under my leadership, we have learned more about these beings than ever before. It is long past time you step aside and let another lead. Someone with the vision to look forward and embrace new ideas."

Pendaran let out a bark of laughter. "And you believe this to be you?"

"That is enough," Travis said, stepping between the two angry men and addressing Ansgar. "This is the high druid you're talking to. Show some respect."

A chorus of shocked gasps and a tittering of nervous laughter filled the room. "There is no need for—" Aiden began.

"No one gave you permission to talk, punk." The older man's eyes narrowed, and his lips twisted into a sneer. "Do you think I don't know who you are and why you're here? And the name's not Gandalf."

Travis barely had time to register the change in accent and speech before an invisible force flung him backward past Pendaran, who clutched his chair to keep from falling. He landed on his back and slid a short distance before coming to a stop. With a snarl, he leapt to his feet.

The room erupted into chaos as chairs were overturned or dragged out of the way to clear a space. Many gathered men shrieked in surprise or panic while others shouted encouragements to both combatants. Some continued eating as if nothing unusual was happening, while a few fled. Servants drawn by the commotion peeked cautiously around the doorways. Travis saw only the swish of Pendaran's robe as the old man disappeared through the hall entrance.

With no time to ponder the reason for the high druid's hasty retreat, Travis lowered his head and charged, intent on bringing his opponent to the floor. The shoving force hit him again, but he was ready for it and barely slowed when it came. He crashed into the taller man, wrapping an arm around his waist for the takedown.

With a loud grunt of exertion, Ansgar twisted and flipped Travis instead, slamming him backward onto the stone floor, then drove his full weight into his solar plexus with his elbow. With a loud whoosh, the air rushed out of Travis's lungs, and he wheezed, trying to claw it back. Ansgar lowered his face to whisper near Travis's ear. "That all you got?" he taunted.

Travis shoved with all his strength and wiggled out from underneath the heavy weight. He drew back and rained several blows on Ansgar's face and neck before the other man recovered enough to block. "Nah, I got more—you want some?" He jabbed again, connecting squarely with his nose, which gave a sickening crunch as it broke.

Blood splattered the floor in large, crimson drops. Ansgar stepped back, swiped once at the steady stream, and pinched his nose. He began pacing a slow circle around Travis. "You're a dead man," he snapped, voice muffled by his hand.

Travis lunged for him again, and this time, he successfully grabbed hold and threw him to the floor. He dove onto the prone body, twisting to get in position for a sleeper hold. A thick, coppery smell filled the air as a sudden burning flared above his eyebrow. His vision blurred from a rush of hot liquid. He raised a hand to touch his face, stunned to find it covered in blood.

Ansgar shoved free and stood, still clutching the knife in one hand. With the other, he crooked his fingers in a beckoning gesture and grinned. "C'mon. I'll make it quick; you won't feel a thing."

Struggling to see, Travis snatched up his robe, stepped forward and spun, landing a solid kick to Ansgar's ribs. He staggered and dropped to one knee, gasping. But before he knew what happened, Ansgar grabbed him around the knees and dumped him onto the floor again. Another searing pain tore across his throat, and he wondered absently if that cut hit his carotid artery.

Scuttling like a crab, Ansgar placed a knee in the center of Travis's chest and tore the apprentice robe off with loud rips of the coarse fabric. "Body armor," he muttered. "I fucking knew it. What are you—military?" He peered down to look more closely. "No, that's not standard issue. You're a cop or something." He grinned and spat a mouthful of blood in Travis's face. "A soon-to-be-dead cop. How does it feel, knowing you came all this way and still failed?"

Travis found himself growing dangerously lightheaded, both from blood loss and a lack of oxygen. *So this is how I go*, he thought dreamily. Awareness of the sharp pain from his good luck charms digging into his chest crept into his consciousness. *Dog tags... butterfly...* The concerned faces of his parents swam in his mind's eye, and blinking with amazement, he heard their words clear as a bell: *Get up, son—don't let him win, make him pay. Remember what Pendaran said—get the amulet.* Saoirse's smiling face appeared, speaking only the most wonderful three words—*I love you.*

Calling on his last reserves of strength, he broke free by sheer dint of will and struggled to his feet. With a loud cry, he launched himself at Ansgar and grabbed for the concealed amulet as they crashed to the floor. He wrapped it around his hand, jerked once, and the metal chain broke apart. Travis scrambled backward, clutching the pieces.

"What have you done?" Ansgar screamed, trying to snatch it back. "Give it to me now."

Travis rose to his feet and continued backing away. "Not until you tell me what it's..." He glanced down and froze, unable to wrap his head around what he held. Flashes and images of what had to be Ansgar's memories flooded his mind, dragging him under.

Corn. Rows and rows of corn in the middle of nowhere; get out of this dead-end place. Dad yelling, Mom cries. Hand raised, repeat the oath. A skinny kid with a buzz cut looking out from the mirror. Kicking ass in basic training. Deployed to the Middle East, desert and mountains, hotter than hell. Unit taking fire, burning pain, not dying out here. Running and running, feels like days. Harsh terrain, need food and water, wounds feel hot. Weird stones. Hiding in strange rock formation, need sleep. Wake up, still dreaming? Why is everything different? Can't understand anybody, gotta keep heading northwest. Stealing clothes, food. Stay hidden, blend in. Blinding pain, tattoos on arm and chest gone now. Traveling by boat, bad fever. Nothing is real. Cool cloth on my forehead, man cleaning my wounds—

Travis staggered against the onslaught, the images hurtling by too fast to fully process. The sheer rage at being shortchanged in what he felt the world owed him, the arrogant entitlement, and the palpable resentment coloring Ansgar's thoughts filled his mouth with the bitter taste of failure.

Faces in and out of focus, soft bed, men wearing robes—monks, maybe? Nowhere to go, days and days, healing. They don't know shit about growing food, fresh air, digging garden rows, feel stronger. Not monks—druids. Beautiful women don't see me, but these do. Wait, faeries are real? They have real magick, teach me. I want to know everything. They won't share; I'll learn how to take their power. Idiot treehugging druids, wasting a golden opportunity. I'll take it all and go home, then everyone will see—

All the intel is wrong, Travis realized, the truth hitting him like a bucket of cold water. Ansgar wasn't trying to create magickal children—he was sucking the faerie's life force dry for his own selfish gain.

The sound of a safety disengaging recaptured his full attention. "Give them to me," Ansgar said flatly, pointing the stolen semi-automatic handgun at Travis's head. "Now."

"Who are you?" Travis demanded, scowling.

"Last chance." Ansgar gestured to the necklace with the barrel, then raised it again.

"Wait! How—"

The screaming began anew as Travis threw himself down to avoid the shot that ricocheted around the room, creating wisps of dust where it struck the stones. *Maybe one shot left*, he remembered, seeing the slide lock open. Still somewhat dazed, he fumbled to draw his own weapon.

With the confidence of a trained marksman, Ansgar pressed the release button and shook it once to eject the empty magazine. Before it hit the floor, he slammed in a full one, racked a round into the chamber, and raised it to fire again.

"Hold!" A sudden fury of hurricane winds howled around the room, knocking Ansgar off his feet, overturning tables, and turning everything not nailed down into a flying missile. Instinctively, Travis shielded his head and face from swirling debris with his forearms, looking for the source.

Untouched by the chaos, Pendaran stood upright, his staff in one hand. Travis met his gaze, and the old man shook his head, dumbfounded. "This is not my doing," he yelled over the din.

The handgun ripped from Ansgar's hand, and he bellowed in rage as it caught in the cyclone and flew away. The fierce gale prevented him from regaining his footing, and he thrashed against the floor, attempting to break free.

The wind appeared strongest near Ansgar, so Travis stayed low and scooted backward until he reached the outermost edge of the room. Muscles straining, he braced against the wall to pull himself upright. Sweat and blood streamed down his face and body as he fought against the unseen force.

Once on his feet, he shoved the necklace in his pocket and stood staring at the man held captive on the floor. His plan to apprehend, subdue, and bring the offender to justice disappeared as his civilized mind went dark. The ancient warrior with testosterone overload inside him awoke and stepped up to the challenge, ready to defend his woman and crush his hated enemy. With two running steps, he threw himself forward and landed squarely atop Ansgar. His police and military training fused into the grappling skills learned from high school wrestling, and within seconds, Travis had him on his back, his knees pinning both arms. He closed his hands around his throat and pushed his thumbs into the horseshoe-shaped hyoid bone at the top of his neck. Gasping, Ansgar's face reddened as he stopped struggling.

It took every ounce of restraint he had, but Travis eased back on the pressure enough to allow a shallow breath. "I ought to just kill you right here and be done with it," he snarled, his face inches from Ansgar. "But I've got questions first. Are your dog tags what's holding the faeries?"

His gaze darted wildly, as if looking for someone, anyone to help. Travis leaned forward, putting more pressure on his arms. "Answer me," he hissed.

"Yes," Ansgar growled, trying to squirm free. Sweat from his effort dripped onto the floor, and he struggled to breathe with Travis straddling his chest.

"Where did you come from?"

"Iraq," he choked out, all European accent gone. "My unit was ambushed—I escaped, tried to make it back to the UK. Hid in some—standing—st—stones, B—Bu—Bulgaria, I think. Wound up here. I'm American, like you. Iowa."

"You're a low-life coward and a deserter—we are nothing alike. You let everyone think you were trying to breed the faeries, but you lied. Why?"

"Not breed—taking their power. Yours will be—last to drain. I soaked up their magick—" He paused to cough, then gagged from the pressure. "From a dozen or more of them. It's all inside me now, I can feel it. I—I had to lie—these fools would have strung me up if they knew the real reason. When I go back home, the whole world will—"

"Shut up," Travis said, tightening his grip into a killing vise. "You're not hurting Saoirse or anybody else ever again. Call whatever god you worship, tell him you're on your way."

At once, the entire room lit up with such brilliance that white spots danced before Travis's eyes, but he didn't let go. Soft hands petted and stroked his back, shoulders, and hair, tapping gently to gain his attention.

"He is not yours," a dulcet voice murmured. "He is ours."

Shaken by his uncustomary lapse in situational awareness, Travis glanced upward without releasing his prisoner. The hut faeries surrounded them, but the despised collars had vanished. Their smiles were radiant, tears of joy flowed freely, and a few laughed and blew him kisses of thanks.

The blonde fae spoke again. "He is ours," she repeated, "as is the means of his retribution. Release him."

Without hesitation, Travis rolled back and stood as several faeries tugged him away to safety. As soon as he was clear of the circle, the hypnotic chiming of their song began. Showers of gold sparkles erupted upward as the tattered gowns fell empty to the floor. Suddenly, the great room filled with massive, furry bodies, their eyes glowing yellow, and their slavering maws filled with razor-sharp teeth.

Ansgar did not have time to scream before the wolves fell on him, gnashing and tearing. A glittering fog descended, obscuring the horrific sight. Without warning, it exploded like a supernova and vanished, taking Ansgar and the fae with it. The room fell into an ominous silence. The only evidence of the great battle's passage and its outcome were the piles of discarded clothing, broken debris from the tables, and the pools of blood beginning to clot on the floor.

Travis staggered once and fell; from exhaustion or blood loss, he could not say. His eyes fluttered closed, and he breathed a relieved sigh. As consciousness began to slip away, a light touch on his cheek snatched him back. Saoirse bent over him, singing in a fierce whisper. He felt his wounds knitting themselves back together as her magick began working, and some of the wooziness faded away. He clutched her hand and pulled her close. "You're free," he rasped.

She gave him a tremulous smile, her tears flowing freely. "Aye," she agreed, brushing a kiss against his battered lips. "I love you, my Travis McLean. Always."

Before he could answer, she, too, dissolved into a cloud of golden sparkles, and just like that, she was gone.

CHAPTER 44

When the first rays of morning sun crossed his face, Travis awoke in the feather bed. Startled to find himself naked, he clutched the linen sheet to his chest as he sat up and glanced around. A young man he had not seen before sat near the window, quietly reading. "How did I get here?" he croaked, his voice raspy from disuse.

"Oh, thank all the gods—you are awake." He stood and set his book down on the empty chair. Crossing the room, he laid a cool hand on Travis's brow. "And your fever seems to have abated. Do you thirst?" he asked. Not waiting for an answer, he poured a cup of water from the pitcher on the bedside table and handed it to him. "Not too much at once, now. I will send for the high druid at once."

"No need," Pendaran said, pushing the door open. He smiled warmly. "Welcome back to the land of the living, Travis McLean."

He drained the cup and set it on the small table. "How long have I been asleep?" he asked, scrubbing at his eyes. The stubble on his face bespoke more than an hour or two.

"Two days. You had a raging fever, no doubt from a poisoned knife blade." He gestured toward the other man. "This is Lorcan, one of our most talented healers. The remaining brothers have worked many rituals to speed your return to health."

"I appreciate that, thank you," Travis said. "I think I was pretty banged up."

"It is our honor," Lorcan said, bowing his head respectfully. He poured another cup of water and pushed it closer to the bed. "They have broth simmering in the kitchen, waiting for you to awake. I'll fetch it for you now if My Lord Pendaran will sit with you?"

The old man nodded in agreement, and Lorcan slipped out the door, closing it quietly behind him.

Pendaran dragged a chair to the bedside and sat down with a grunt. "How fare you?"

Travis extended his legs and stretched, wiggling his toes and fingers. "Near as I can tell, everything seems to be working. What's been happening since I've been out?"

"Ciarán has been stripped of his status and banished, along with the rest of Ansgar's followers. The dark cloud blinding our order has lifted. We are once again on the right path, and the people are happier for it. You may be pleased to learn they are already composing songs in your honor. Travis McLean, the mighty warrior who descended from the clouds to free the Tuath Dé and deliver the people of Brú na Bóinne from the clutches of an evil tyrant."

He let out a bark of laughter but winced from the lingering pain in his ribs. "That's a bit much, don't you think?"

"No, it is how we remember that worth remembering. You bested a mighty foe and freed a people wrongfully enslaved."

"What about the fae? Have you heard anything?"

Pendaran sighed and looked away. "There have been no signs of them. We have left offerings of honey and wine, but they go untouched. Their memories are long, and this transgression is one they will not soon forgive or forget."

"And Saoirse?" The fact that he had to ask told him more than he wanted to know.

He shook his head sadly. "No. She has not returned." He reached into his pocket and pulled out Ansgar's dog tags, handing them to Travis. "There is engraving, but we are unable to make sense of it. Perhaps you can?" He hesitated, as if hating to ask. "I could not help but notice you wear a similar charm."

Travis turned one over to read the inscription: *Ainsley, Logan R.* "His name wasn't Ansgar—it was Logan. He said he was in the military, stationed in Iraq. If I remember right, you call it Mesopotamia. He deserted, trying to make it to England, and came here by accident."

"What do your charms say?"

He smiled, but there was no joy in it. "Mine belonged to my parents. When they died, I started wearing their tags, thinking that if I did, they'd watch over me. The butterfly is Saoirse's. I added it after Ansgar—Logan—took her." He straightened. "Keep putting out gifts for the faeries. The people who wronged them aren't here anymore. And sweets—they love sweets. Don't forget those."

"We shall not forget."

He lay back, staring at the rough-hewn boards of the ceiling. "What am I supposed to do now?" he asked, not expecting an answer.

Pendaran sighed again and patted his hand. "There is naught left for you here. 'Tis time you returned home."

PART III

CHAPTER 45

"I'm back."

The sheer volume of Mike's voice, even on speaker, made Travis's head pound. "It's only been an hour. How the hell did you manage to—"

"I've been gone for days," he said. "I don't know how the mechanics work, but I think Pendaran tried to set me back in the same place and time." He glanced at the clock, then out the bedroom window, where the first rays of sunlight began to peek in.

Mike went silent and waited for him to speak again. As the silence stretched on, he asked, "What happened? Is Sa—"

Travis cut him off, not wanting even to hear the name. "Gone. They're all gone. Ansgar's dead, the druids are back to doing normal druid stuff, and all the faeries vanished." He heaved a bone-weary sigh. "I'll tell you all about it later. Right now, all I want is a hot shower and my bed."

"Is there anything I can do for you?"

"No," he replied. "I just want to sleep all this off. I'll call you later when I get up."

Travis stood under the hot shower until the water began to cool, his forehead pressed to the wall tile. His mind ran in so many directions that he couldn't focus on any single thought. He turned the shower off when the cold reality of no hot water registered. The thick steam fogged everything, making it difficult to see, and the cool air coming from his bedroom raised goosebumps all over his overheated body. He grabbed a towel and began half-heartedly drying off, but after a minute, he dropped the towel and headed for bed. As he slid naked beneath the sheets, he caught a hint of Saoirse's unique spice and floral scent, and tears sprang to his eyes.

He closed them against the sudden burn and fumbled around for her pillow. Burying his face, he inhaled deeply. *I don't remember how to live in a world without you in it, faery girl.* His impenetrable emotional dam shattered without warning, and years of compartmentalized tears burst free. He wept for Saoirse, for the life they could have had, for the realization that he would never again see her bright smile or hear her infectious laughter at a corny joke. He wept for his parents, their dogs, and Reno. But mostly, he wept for himself, hating his selfishness.

She's free now. They're all free. Wasn't that the whole purpose? The mission had been successful—the hostages were released, and the bad guy dispatched straight to hell or wherever evil druids went. Why, then, did he feel like a failure? If he was such a big hero, why did this hurt so badly? *Too many movies*, he thought, suddenly too exhausted to move. *I thought the hero always gets the girl.* And with tears still streaming, he fell into a deep, dreamless sleep.

Hours passed before Travis roused again, slow to realize he was back in his own bed and time again. Alone. His body was sore, and his nose so stuffy he couldn't breathe through it. Checking the time, he grabbed his phone and punched in the number for Captain Bellamy.

The captain answered on the third ring. "McLean? What's the matter?"

"I'm sick, sir," he explained, his swollen sinuses making it sound convincing. "I've been in bed all day, but it's not helping much."

"It must be bad, you never call off. Hang on, let me find the schedule." Papers rustled in the background. "Shouldn't be a big night, I think we can spare you. And you're scheduled off for tomorrow," he reasoned. "You sound like shit. Drink lots of liquids and rest. If you're not better by tomorrow night, let me know quick as you can so I can get your shift covered."

"I will, sir. Thank you." Travis closed his eyes and had one last thought before exhaustion overtook him again. *But I won't be better tomorrow.*

Travis slept for twelve more hours before waking again, and another hour was spent just summoning the courage to get out of bed and be awake. He could have gone back to sleep, but his stomach had other ideas and rumbled loud enough to startle him. Grumbling, he threw on a pair of sweats and padded barefoot to the kitchen. He flipped on the overhead lights, and at once, Saoirse sitting at the kitchen table on that first night flashed in his mind. He shook his head hard to dispel the image but only succeeded in making it worse. The velociraptor, the teaspoon, the chicken leg... for a horrible moment, Travis was afraid this renewed pain wasn't going to kill him. *She asked if she could sleep on the kitchen floor,* he remembered, his appetite suddenly gone.

He gradually became aware of a dull throb at his temples, the beginnings of a hunger headache. Yanking a cabinet door open, he grabbed a frying pan and set it on the stove. "Fuel in the tank," he muttered aloud, reaching for the refrigerator.

Three eggs, some wheat toast and jam, a few strips of bacon, and a big glass of orange juice later, Travis started to feel almost normal again. Never one to procrastinate on the unpleasant, he grabbed a notepad and pen to begin his "get my life back together" to-do list.

The first order of business was packing up her things. He thought back to when his parents had died. A well-meaning great-aunt offered some wise advice—pack everything up right after the funeral so that it all would be handled by the time the shock wore off. *That's smart*, he supposed, *to do everything while you're still emotionally numb*. The older relatives had offered to help with the sad task, but he could not bear the thought of anyone else touching their things. It took him a week by himself, but he got the job done.

Travis pulled some empty storage tubs with locking lids from the garage and set to work. He carefully folded and smoothed each piece of clothing, pausing more than once to press a shirt to his face and inhale deeply before placing it in the box. Snagging the roll of paper towels from the kitchen, he wiped each shoe clean of dirt and dust before packing them away. When it came to the green dress she wore to the benefit, he stopped to wipe his face with a towel, surprised to find it wet.

He paused his packing and went into the garage to pull down the attic stairs. It had been forever since he had been up there, and the dust from the lowering door made him sneeze. He climbed up and began searching for the box of wrapping paper, bows, and related miscellany his mother used for birthdays and holidays. Upon finding it, he removed the lid to find what he was looking for right on top. He gathered the flat plastic pouches and tucked them under his arm for the climb down.

Back in the bedroom, he tore open each pack and laid out the thin, rectangular paper. With trembling hands, he removed the gown from the hanger, folded it into a neat square, and wrapped it in the decorative tissue. It was hard not to imagine her in the dress or the look on her face that unforgettable night. He shut his eyes against the fresh wave of pain and shook his head to dispel the provocative images. *She's gone. Really gone. And she's not coming back.*

Travis blew out a heavy sigh and forced himself to keep moving. Saoirse's bras and panties, socks, and pajamas went into the next box, along with the eclectic treasures she had collected during her stay with him. Ticket stubs from the Renaissance Fair, postcards of things or places she liked, tiny colorful seashells, a cheap plastic ring, a candy necklace—she had so few possessions, yet remained one of the happiest people he had ever met.

The attic dust kicked my allergies into overdrive. He paused again to wipe his face. This wasn't him crying over a woman, but even as that thought occurred, he already knew it to be a lie. *I've changed. She changed me. And yeah, it hurts, but I don't regret a single minute spent with her.* Raising the butterfly charm to his lips, he softly kissed it. *Not one single moment, my love.*

CHAPTER 46

B ecause everyone expected Search would be recovered, Travis continued working his regular shift in the K9 Unit cruiser. Well-meaning dispatchers and other officers asked daily if he had news about his dog. Every day, he had to lie and say nothing yet. He couldn't tell them the truth—that Search would never be found, and all efforts to find her were wasted. All these nice people showered him with reassurance that Search would be found and the perp would face his well-deserved justice.

He hated it.

He hated getting in the patrol car, knowing Saoirse wasn't in the back, bouncing with excitement for their next big adventure. He hated not having to remember which routes had drive-throughs offering fast chicken nuggies and pup cups for hungry K9s. Not being told to crank up the music or laughing at the silly lyrics she made up for songs she didn't know. No wet nose or soft muzzle nuzzling his neck at stoplights. And at the end of each shift, he felt like he had forgotten something when he exited the car alone. In short, he was miserable.

You are not your parents.

Travis had Saoirse's words reverberating around in his head all day. It played on an endless loop as he completed his watch, went home, and showered. He changed into his sweats and popped last night's leftover meatloaf into the microwave. Once the timer bell dinged, he put the plate and a cold soda on a TV tray and went into the great room to watch the local news. He had just found the remote when his phone rang.

"Whatcha doing?" Mike asked. The sound of bar chatter and clinking glass in the background sounded like the party was in full swing.

"Eating," he said, shoving a forkful into his mouth. "Just got home. Where are you?"

"Rockets. I'm trying to integrate back into society, thinking you should join me in that worthy endeavor."

Travis shook his head. "Nah, I'm good. I've got some work to do online tonight. 'Preciate the invite, though."

Mike groaned. "You are in desperate need of an evening of intoxication and overindulgence. You can't just stay entombed in your shrine."

"I'm not keeping a shrine. I cleaned out and packed most of her stuff right after I... got back," Travis retorted. "I'll come out soon, I promise. Just not yet."

"I'll hold you to that. You looking at puppies?"

"No," he hedged, "just some research I want to do."

"Alrighty then, Slim Shady. If you change your mind, I'll be here for maybe another hour or two. I'll let you buy me a cold one."

"Deal."

Once he finished eating, Travis pulled out his laptop and notebook to begin researching. He started with home defense websites before moving on to security systems, taking copious notes. He browsed through multiple sites offering high-tech surveillance equipment. Next, he searched the state code of laws and jotted down contact information for state and local veteran's outreach programs.

When he looked up again, he saw how late it was and realized he needed to sleep. Closing everything down for the time being, he got ready for bed. As he climbed under the cool sheets, he thought again about what Saoirse had said. He felt ashamed, remembering his anger with her for stating the obvious truth out loud.

You are not your parents.

He punched the pillow several times to plump it, then lay back and stared up at the ceiling. *Tomorrow is a new day, and I'm gonna have to get serious. I need to have an outlined model in hand before I bounce it off Mike.* Just thinking about the new plan lifted a great weight off his chest and shoulders, and he relaxed for the first night in a long time. He had one last conscious thought before drifting off into restful sleep, and it made him smile.

I am not my parents.

CHAPTER 47

Christmas came and went. Travis spent the holiday with Mike and his family, while Geena was in upstate New York, visiting her grandparents. Mike's mother went out of her way to make sure he felt at home, and in turn, he made sure she knew how much he appreciated the effort and all the love and concern behind it. He didn't let on or tell anyone the truth—that he felt more alone than ever.

On New Year's Eve, he reluctantly let Mike talk him into going out. Rocket's held their version of a party with hot hors d'oeuvres, drink specials, a guest DJ blasting loud dance music, balloons, and party noisemakers. The club was packed to over the posted fire marshal's capacity, but nobody seemed to mind. Travis forced a smile and nursed his drink while attempting to avoid inane small talk or, worse yet, dancing. He gravitated toward the back, further away from the rowdy partygoers. An hour before the stroke of midnight, he didn't have the heart for any more forced reverie. Making his way through the crowd, he found Mike at a corner table, chatting with a couple of local girls. He tapped him on the arm to get his attention. "I'm out," he said succinctly.

Mike stood and opened his mouth to speak but shook his head instead. "You look like hell," he said.

"Feel like it, too." Travis nodded at the girls and raised his voice just enough for them to hear. "You better be careful," he warned with mock seriousness. "Those women look mighty dangerous." They giggled in response.

"You want some company?" Mike asked.

"Nah—you stay and have fun. I'm just dragging all this down. I'll come out again soon, I promise."

"She wouldn't want you to be this torn up," he remarked. "She'd want you to be happy and have a great life, maybe eat something sugary for her once in a while."

"Yeah, maybe someday I'll get to that point. Just not yet." He forced a smile. "Give me a call tomorrow if your head isn't falling off."

"I will. And think about what I said. She'd be seriously pissed off at you for moping around."

Travis laughed bitterly. "Yeah, she would. Sad faces were definitely not allowed in our house." He waved and made for the door without looking back.

By the time Travis got in bed, the weariness had settled deep into his bones, and he fell into a restless sleep. His dreams were dark, filled with vague, disturbing images and shadowy wolves. Exhaustion blurred the line between awake and asleep, so when the disembodied female voice spoke, he thought himself still dreaming.

"Do not turn on your light, Travis McLean."

He turned over and mumbled into his pillow. "Oh...'k then."

Several minutes passed before the voice spoke again, the imperious tone penetrating his slumberous fog. "Awaken. Now."

At once, Travis jerked awake. "Who's there?" he demanded, reaching for the nightstand lamp.

The unseen visitor heaved a deep sigh. "No light," she admonished.

He hesitated and sat up, his gaze sweeping the room but seeing nothing amiss. "Where are you?" he asked warily, clutching the coverlet over his nakedness. The palladium window arch allowed the moonlight to bathe the room, but he saw no one. "Where are you?" he demanded again.

"We are but a projection. Your human eyes cannot look directly upon us."

He turned toward the sound of her voice. The space it came from shimmered like heat vapor rising from the highway in summer. He squinted and could almost make out a feminine shape, but without any detail. "Who are you, and what do you want?"

"You have done us a great service," she said, ignoring his questions, "and it is our pleasure to reward you."

"You're the Queen," Travis gasped, straightening. "Is Saoirse with you? Is she safe?"

She chuckled, her musical voice tinged with a bit of exasperation. "We are, and she is, although I must say she speaks of you without ceasing. As you undoubtedly know, we are immortal. Once grown, we no longer age as you do." The form drifted closer. "This is the gift I give you, Travis McLean. I will make her mortal to spend a human life with you and spare our ears from an eternity of her chatter."

Travis's heart leapt into his throat, the unexpected burn of tears clouding his vision. "You can do that?" His head spun from the possibilities, but he had another question. "What did she say when you asked her?"

"She said the choice would be yours, and she will accept whatever you decide."

The silence stretched out. "There was a time when I wouldn't have hesitated to say yes." He bowed his head, hating that there was only one answer he could live with. "She told me that being held captive is the only real memory she has. She has no idea what it even means to be a faery yet. I love her too much to take that away from her. It has to be her decision." He shook his head, a rueful smile twisting his lips. "My answer is no."

The shape gained more definition, and Travis could make out a diminutive woman clad in a gossamer gown of shifting colors. Her skirts and hair swirled as if she were underwater. She made a sweeping gesture with one hand. "We accept your answer, Travis McLean. You shall instead have a reward of our choosing." And with no further explanation, she winked out of sight.

Travis lunged for the lamp but cried out as a brief but blinding pain ripped across the undersides of his wrists. He fumbled for the switch, flooding the room with soft light. There was, as he expected, no one else there. He examined his wrists and found a tiny gold triskelion tattoo like Saoirse's at the base of each palm, the surrounding skin still pink from the sudden application. *And here's your lovely parting gift,* the game show host in his head announced. He switched off the light, but it was a long time before sleep came again.

CHAPTER 48

"Come again? You're doing what now?" Mike and Bo had dropped in for a visit and a glass of tea, and Travis seized the opportunity to make his pitch at the kitchen table.

"I'm quitting the police department and going into business for myself," he repeated patiently, opening the kitchen windows to let in the crisp March breeze.

Mike's expected overreaction did not disappoint. "Have you completely lost your mind? What kind of corkscrew-shaped critter is chewing on your circuitry to make you think this is a good idea? I know you're hurting, Trav, but you can't just make snap decisions like this."

"It's not a snap decision. I've been thinking about this for months now, ever since..." His voice trailed off before he continued. "Since I started doing the K9 work. Don't get me wrong, I love the job and working with the dogs. Knowing you're giving back to the community and getting dangerous people off the streets is great. I just don't love worrying if we'll live through it every time we're deployed."

"That's stretching it a bit, don't you—"

Travis cut him off. "You've read my reports?"

When Mike nodded, he continued. "Then you know what kind of risks she took every night we worked. We both had some close calls. I mean, she was immortal, but she could still be hurt. Did I ever tell you about the dog in Afghanistan?"

"Don't think so. What happened?"

"My unit was sweeping a deserted settlement, supposed to be just a formality, walking through it with Millie the Mal, our bomb dog. She was the sweetest girl, maybe three or four years old. Anyway, she ran ahead of us and triggered an IED. Survived the blast, but it tore her up. She died before we could get her back to camp."

"Damn. I can't even imagine," Mike whispered, shaking his head. "There's no way I could send Bo into danger, knowing he could get hurt or worse."

"I'm a decent handler, but it would destroy me to lose a dog in the line of duty, knowing I put her there. And I can't say with any degree of honesty that fear of loss wouldn't keep me from doing what I need to do in a bad situation."

"Feels like there's more to the story, though," Mike said.

"There is." Travis took a long sip of the iced tea as he stood and began pacing the kitchen. "I had a lot of time to think while I packed up... her stuff. It occurred to me that I'd spent my whole life living up to everyone else's ideas of who I was supposed to be—my parents, teachers, and coaches in high school, the army, the police department.

Hell, even Lori Ann. And not a single one ever asked me what I wanted. Not one. I think I fell so hard for Saoirse because she had no expectations at all. She just loved me, for me."

Travis sat back down and pushed the folder over. "So that's why I'm rethinking this—to figure out what I want to do with my life. I still want to work with dogs, and I like the law enforcement aspect. I'd also like to do something for the veterans and help educate civilians on how to stay safe. This is what I came up with."

"MST Elite Security, providing event, personal, and K9 services. What does MST stand for?" Mike thumbed through the paperwork, stopping on one page in particular. "Designing security systems?"

"I designed mine," Travis said defensively. "It covers the entire property with no vulnerabilities or backdoors."

"Yeah, but as I recall, you weren't the one who wired everything and programmed it."

Travis tapped his chin as if in deep thought. "I'd need someone who was a master in electronic technology to implement my designs. I bet if I put up flyers at the college, I—"

"Fine." Mike sighed and shoved the folder back. "I'm in."

Travis struggled to hold back a jubilant grin. "Wouldn't want to talk you into something you'd—"

"On one condition."

"Which is...?"

"You don't tell my mom until it's up and running. I think she'd be happier overall if I got out of policing, but your Auntie Claire will rain hellfire down on both of us if she thinks you roped me into some harebrained scheme."

He extended his glass, and Travis raised his own, clinking them in a toast. "Deal." They sat silently for another few minutes before he spoke again. "I'm really glad you said yes. Means I don't have to change the name or logo now."

"Pretty sure of yourself, aren't you?" Mike said with a laugh. "Mike, Saoirse, Travis. I didn't connect it until now."

"Just sure you'd know a good thing when you heard it," Travis said, "and doubly sure you couldn't resist seeing your name up in lights."

They discussed business plans and ideas for the next several hours. When Travis reached for his phone to check the time, Mike pointed to his hand. "Did you get some new ink? I don't remember seeing those before."

"Oh, I got these on New Year's Eve from the Queen," he answered, flexing his wrists to display the gold triskelions. "They fluctuate, sometimes dark or brighter—"

"You did WHAT?" Mike exploded. "THE Queen? You met her? And you're just now telling me this? Trav, your communication skills *suck*."

Soundly asleep and snoring under the table, Bo leapt to his feet with a yowl, knocked over a chair, and fled through the doggie door into the backyard.

Travis burst into laughter at the uproar. "You are traumatizing your dog."

"Dude, you have got to start leading with the big stuff. Tell me what happened."

"Sorry, I was sure I told you. After I got home from Rocket's, I went straight to bed. I was sound asleep when she came, thought I was dreaming at first. She said she was a projection because I couldn't look directly at her. Anyway, she offered me a reward for freeing the faeries and said she would make Saoirse mortal so we could live a human life together."

Mike glanced around the kitchen. "She's back?"

Travis shook his head. "She had never been free. I wasn't going to take that away from her. I told the Queen no."

Mike sat back and stared at him before an incredulous smile spread across his face. "You've changed."

"Yeah, I have," he admitted with a begrudging nod. "That wasn't a decision I was going to make for her. She's had no say in her own life up until now. I know how that feels."

They sat in silence, each lost in his own thoughts. "Do you think you'll ever see her again?" Mike finally asked.

"I have no way of knowing," Travis said, the words leaving a bittersweet taste in his mouth. "But wherever she is, I hope she's happy and there's lots of cake."

CHAPTER 49

"I like how you worded your narrative here. Very nice way of saying the guy was an asshat without coming right out and saying it."

Travis thought the world of his commanding officer, but at the moment, he wished he were anywhere other than in Captain Bellamy's office, going over reports at the end of his shift. "Thank you, sir. My instructors said never put anything in writing that you don't want to see on a poster board propped in front of a jury."

"Very smart, and it keeps you out of trouble with Internal Affairs," he agreed, but then his bushy eyebrows came together in a frown. "I've hated to ask, but are you looking for another dog? Given how long it's been, I'm not holding out much hope we'll get Search back."

He had known this would come up during their meeting, but it still hurt. "I'm not sure, sir," he answered honestly. "At this point, I'm—I am considering my career options."

A burst of loud noise from the lobby filtered into the closed room. Travis glanced over his shoulder, peering through the blinds to see what caused the uproar. "They've got their hands full out there today."

"Too early for the spring break crowd," the captain replied, frowning. Both men rose to their feet when the thunderous cheering and applause broke out. The older man reached the door first and flung it open wide. "What in the name of all that's holy is going—"

A sleek, chocolate brown shape blasted past him, body slamming Travis to the floor and covering his face in wet, sloppy kisses. Everything was moving so fast that his mind raced to catch up. He caught a whiff of that unique spicy scent, and eyes wide, he grabbed the dog to hold her still. "Is it you?" he whispered, staring into her eyes.

Her mouth opened wide on a yawn, but unless his desperate imagination played tricks on him, he would have sworn he heard "uh-huh" in the sound. She shook hard, the vibration rolling down her body from nose to tail, and began kissing him all over again.

"Looks like somebody missed you," the captain said, laughing. He stuck his head out of the office door. "Anybody see where she came from?"

A chorus of LEO voices answered. "No, sir—she ran up to the lobby doors and tried to Cujo her way in." Everyone laughed, agreeing. "She was going to tear those doors down if somebody didn't open them for her. She must have known McLean was inside."

Travis did not hear any of the comments or congratulations. He only saw the pair of limpid brown eyes looking back at him and knew her gaze went straight through to his soul. "Are you ready to go home?" he asked softly.

She licked both his cheeks, wet with more than saliva, and then put her head on his shoulder. "Yes," she breathed next to his ear.

He hugged her close, silently vowing never to lose her again. "I should get her home. She's probably hungry." After a quick squeeze, he rose and brushed himself off. "You ready?" he asked, patting his thigh.

She whipped around to his side in the heel position and looked up expectantly, making a soft whining sound.

Belatedly, Travis remembered where they were and what they were doing before Search's sudden arrival. "Sir, with your permission—"

"Dismissed," Captain Bellamy answered with a grin.

Knowing that being seen driving a police car with a naked woman in the front seat would be difficult to explain, Travis asked her to wait until they got home before shifting. The garage door was halfway down when the sparkles began.

Fully materialized, she leapt into his arms and wrapped herself around him, squeezing tight.

He gently squeezed back, scared he would break her in his exuberance. "I didn't think I would ever see you again," he murmured against her hair. "Where have you been for so long?"

Saoirse pulled back to look at him. "I just saw you yesterday," she said with a confused frown.

"Honey, it's been months," he said. "I didn't think you were ever coming back. I even—"

"Packed up my things?" she shrieked, pointing to the clear storage tubs. "Did you not want me to return?" She relaxed her hold and slid down his body until her feet touched the floor. Her eyes filled with tears as her gaze met his, and her bottom lip trembled.

Travis recognized the warning signs and knew a meltdown was imminent unless he took swift action. "Come here to me," he said, pulling her tight. "Now you just simmer down and listen. Every day since I came back, I've tried my best to live in this house without you. I've had to look at clothes hanging in the closet that smell like you, and your fifteen bottles of shampoo, and your five million refrigerator magnets, and I trip over your shoes lying all over the place. Every day, my soul died a little bit more because you were not here. It was either pack everything up or go stark raving insane."

"I suppose that is a good enough reason," she murmured against his chest, and with that, all the tension fled.

Crisis averted, they stood locked in their embrace for the longest time, swaying gently to and fro. Travis was just about to suggest they take it to the bedroom when she pulled away again, inhaling deeply. She frowned, a bewildered expression on her face as she sniffed his arms and chest. "Yeah, I need a shower, I know," he said, suddenly self-conscious.

"It is not that," she whispered. She stepped back and shook her head, then returned to sniff him again. "Why do you smell different?"

"I do? Is it bad or something?"

"No, it's just..." Her head tilted slowly and deliberately as she puzzled it out. "You smell... not like before."

Travis lifted an arm to check the status of his deodorant and nearly hit the deck when she exploded with a deafening shriek. She grabbed his hands and turned them over to see the small symbols etched there. "Where did you get these?" she demanded.

"The Queen came by to say thanks and offered to make you mortal to be with me. I told her it had to be your decision, not mine. I couldn't live with myself, taking that away from you." He froze, suddenly suspicious. "You're still the same, right? You didn't give all that up, did you?"

"I would have, but no. Instead, she gave me an elixir to make me age with you. She has given you—us—the most wonderful gift!" She clapped her hands together and squealed, bouncing up and down with excitement.

"Tattoos?" He looked at them, bewildered by her excitement.

"The Queen did not reveal all this to you?"

When he shook his head, she took his hands in hers and explained it like he was five years old. "I took an aging elixir, so now I will age at the same rate as you. When we die after long and happy lives, we will come back as we are now, but you will be fae too, immortal, like me."

He blinked. "Come again?"

Saoirse blew out an exasperated sigh and tapped his wrist. "When we die, we both come back as fae."

"I'll be immortal?" he asked numbly. "Like you? Will I be able to shift, too?"

"I do not know what abilities you will have." Her shoulder lifted in a nonchalant shrug. "We shall have to wait and see. There are any number of—"

Travis shook his head violently. "We'll have to unpack that at length later. Right now, I have only one thing on my mind, and we need to get to it before I lose sanity." With a loud whoop, she leapt into his arms. He caught her easily and spun around. "Welcome home, faery girl."

"You talk too much. Take me to bed already."

Breathless with laughter, he kicked open the kitchen door and sprinted for their bedroom. He had almost made it when she fired the expected warning shot directly over his bow, and his heart knew with a joyful certainty that it was impossible to love her more than he did at that moment.

"I absolutely do *not* have fifteen bottles of shampoo."

EPILOGUE

Three months later

"Pizza?" Mike pushed the cardboard box across the kitchen table.

"Hell yeah—it smells amazing," Travis said and nodded. Lifting the lid for inspection, he selected a slice of the Hawaiian pizza and took two large bites. "Damn, that's good."

Mike sat back with a smug smile. "I told—"

"—you so," he finished. "Everybody is allowed to evolve. Look at you—settling down with one woman and getting all domestic. Your folks must be over the moon happy."

"They are. I'm pretty sure they love Geena more than me, anyway. Mom's got wedding magazines strategically placed for optimal viewing whenever we come over. Your dear auntie is anything but subtle." He shook his glass to settle the ice and took a swallow. "I never told you, but they straight up panicked when I announced we were going into business. None of us knew we'd get this much business right out of the gate. At this rate, we'll have to hire another team in a month or two."

"I've got cards in every VA office in the Carolinas, and their main website just listed us as a resource. Geena said we're getting an insane amount of email. She's started dropping hints about needing help."

"She mentioned it to me, too. We'll need to hire somebody to help with the background checks and tax stuff, too. Might be time to start looking for a bigger office."

"Enough shop talk. What is this super secretive op you called about?" Travis took another bite, rescuing a chunk of pineapple that had fallen off and popping it into his mouth.

"I wanted to—"

The back door flew open, and Saoirse breezed into the kitchen, her flowered sundress swirling around her. "Why did you not let me know the pizza has arrived? I toil away in your garden, and you think to starve me?" When Mike began to bluster apologies, she waved him off as she removed her wide-brimmed gardening hat. "I but tease," she laughed, helping herself to a slice as he poured her a glass of tea.

"What's the verdict, Doc? Are my tomatoes going to live?"

She chewed thoughtfully, then swallowed. "I think you shall find it vastly improved by the morrow."

Mike sighed with relief, placing a hand over his heart. "That is the best news I've heard this week."

"Do you like your neighbors?" Her sudden subject change came from far left field.

"I guess so—they're kin, so I kinda have to," Mike drawled, but then frowned. "That was a pretty random question—why do you ask?"

"The hornworms, slugs, and beetles will be moving their colonies for the remainder of this day. The other pests have already gone." She shrugged, taking another bite. "I but suggested the fare might be better on the other side of the fence. Those bad-tempered fire ants are also moving. The two black snakes live near the trees, but I asked them to stay. They do not like your vegetables and prefer to hunt the larger pests. The voles and the..." she paused, trying to remember the word, "tick-tocks said they would also leave."

Travis burst into uproarious laughter while Mike just looked confused. "You sent all the pests to my cousin's garden?"

Saoirse nodded and took another bite. "Aye. They have no remorse for eating your vegetables, but they promised to leave them alone from now on. The butterflies asked for more flowers, and the squirrels want another bird feeder, please." She took a long swallow of tea, then daintily used a paper napkin to dab at her mouth. "Were you aware of the rabbit warren and the underground stream?"

Mike's brow furrowed. "I've seen a few bunnies near the trees, but I didn't know about the stream. I've been thinking about having somebody out to check if I can dig an irrigation well."

"Their tunnels run deep, and they tell me their home is very old. They wanted to know if they must leave, but I told them no as long as they stay out of your garden." She gave a tentative smile. "I mentioned that you might be persuaded to donate your excess and spoiled vegetables to them. But their main concern is if you will dig up the warren to collect the bodies."

Mike choked on his mouthful of pizza. "Bo—bodies?" he stammered.

"Oh yes," she said, nodding. "They showed me images of what they see at the deepest levels, far below ground. Only bones remain now, of course, but there are other things that must have been buried with them. Swords and shields, helmets, such as that."

"But the Native Americans didn't..." Mike began, meeting Travis's intent gaze.

"...use weapons like that," Travis finished for him. He shook his head as if to clear it. "I'm sorry, but we'll have to unpack that another time. Mike here was just about to make a monumental announcement."

Saoirse immediately pulled out a chair and sat, primly folding her hands. "I am ready."

"One sec." Mike hopped up and jogged out of the kitchen, returning moments later clutching a small package. With a magician's flourish, he popped the small velvet box open to reveal the sparkling engagement ring. "I'm going to ask her tomorrow night," he announced, "and I'd like it if you both are there to hold my hand when she turns me down."

"She will not say no," Saoirse said, stating it as fact. "She is expecting it. She also—"

"Well, now—that just takes all the suspense out of it," Mike interrupted, then laughed. "Whoever would have thought I'd be getting married. My mom was convinced that I planned to be a bachelor forever."

"I'm happy for you," Travis assured him. The two men shook hands and shared an awkward congratulatory hug. As they separated, he asked, "What were you going to say, sweetheart?"

"Only that she has a surprise for you as well. She hopes you will ask for her hand before the babe starts—" She clapped a hand over her mouth, eyes wide in mortification. "I should not have spoken."

The transition was startling—Mike paled as the blood drained from his face before rushing back to color it a deep scarlet. "Geena is pregnant?" he asked, his tone lodged firmly between hopeful and terrified.

She placed a reassuring hand on his arm to steady the slight sway. "You must act surprised when she tells you," Saoirse insisted. "She is unaware I know her secret."

Travis gave Mike a celebratory clap on the back. "Husband and Daddy. My oh my, how your world is achangin'. I guess that would make me an uncle to be," he mused aloud, turning to Saoirse. "That means you'll be an aunt."

"No." She looked at him thoughtfully before she laughed, her smile so happy and bright. "I'll be her faery godmother!"

THE END

AUTHOR'S NOTES AND GLOSSARY

Ansgar (*AHNNS-gar*): Old Norse masculine name meaning "spear of God"

Apollyon (*ah-POLL-yon*): The Destructor, king of locusts and fallen angel of the abyss from the biblical Book of Revelations.

Art of War, The: This is widely acknowledged as the first manual on military strategy, dating back to the fifth century BC, written by Chinese military strategist Sun Tzu. The valuable lessons found in this small book have influenced millions, military or otherwise. Worth reading and re-reading, in my opinion.

Brigadoon: This is truly one of the most romantic movies ever made. An MGM musical from 1954, it tells the story of two modern American hunters on holiday in the Scottish Highlands who come across a little village that only appears for one day every hundred years.

Brú na Bóinne *(Brew Nah Boin)*: This World Heritage Site is located in the Boyne Valley, County Meath, Ireland. It is home to three of Ireland's most ancient passage tombs—Newgrange, Knowth (*NOW-th*), and Dowth (*DOW-th*).

Cherries and Berries: The red and blue lights on top of a police cruiser

Ciarán (*KEER-awn*): Irish Gaelic masculine name meaning "dark-haired one"

Crenet (*KREN-net*): One half of the "toothy" architecture is found on high medieval castle walls. The merlons (the tooth or raised part that provides cover during battle) alternate with the crenets or gaps, which allow soldiers to fire arrows or other missiles with a clear view.

Cuff and Stuff: To make an arrest or collar, the suspect is handcuffed and stuffed into the back of a police car.

Cujo: From the 1981 Stephen King novel of the same name. Cujo was a friendly St. Bernard who transformed into a vicious killer after being bitten by a rabid bat. One of the more famous scenes depicts Cujo attacking a car window to reach the terrified people cowering inside.

Donnacha (*DONE-acka*): Irish Gaelic masculine name meaning "dark chief"

Duck cloth: A heavy canvas material used in K9 training aids, (hopefully) preventing damage to the costly scents in cases of enthusiastic, overexcited chewing. If you want to learn more, https://www.rayallen.com/ is a good place to start.

Dutchie: The Dutch Shepherd is a herding breed of dog often used in police or security work. They weigh between fifty and seventy-five pounds and are intelligent, affectionate, independent, and driven to work. Despite their unique brindle coat, they are often confused with German Shepherd Dogs and Belgian Malinois.

Drz (*drush*): Czech K9 command for bite.

Eilidh (*AY-lee*): Scots Gaelic feminine name meaning "radiant one"

EOW: End of Watch, used when a police officer has passed away.

Flash Bang grenade: Unlike an actual grenade, this non-lethal, handheld explosive device temporarily disorients an enemy's senses and causes confusion. Upon detonation, it produces a blinding *flash* of light and an extremely loud *bang*, hence the name.

FAFO: Fuck Around and Find Out

FIDO: Law enforcement shorthand for "Fuck It, Drive On," meaning not worth investigating.

FST: Law enforcement shorthand for "Field Sobriety Test," which could include the Horizontal Gaze Nystagmus test, walking a straight line with a turn, and balancing on one foot.

GSD: German Shepherd Dog

Hail Mary: In football terminology, this refers to a long-range pass toward the end zone, usually done in desperation by the losing team near the end of a game. The quarterback throws the pass, and all eligible receivers run downfield, praying someone will catch it for a touchdown.

Hardy Boys: Fictional brothers and amateur sleuths who were the main characters in a popular series of children's/teen mystery books, counterpart to the female heroine Nancy Drew mysteries. Debuting in 1927 and winding up in 2005, there are 190 books in this long-running series.

HMTD: Hexamethylene Triperoxide Diamine, a highly explosive organic peroxide compound. Despite its inherent instability, it is a common ingredient in homemade explosives.

Hot N Pop™: This special computer monitors vital components inside the K9 police vehicle, including temperature sensors and vehicle battery voltage. If an alarm condition is detected, the unit will activate a SOS car horn honk signal, siren and light-bar activation, and dual window drop. The K9 Door Popper™ releases the K-9 partner from the vehicle to be by the officer's side in an emergency situation. This feature is disabled when the vehicle is in gear.

To learn more about these life-saving products, go to https://acek9.com/

Hydra Shok: A bullet created for close-range, immediate defense situations. A small post in the middle of the hollow point is designed to reduce the collateral damage caused by the slug passing through the intended target.

IAFIS: The FBI's national Integrated Automated Fingerprint Identification System (IAFIS) provides finger and latent print search capabilities, electronic image storage, and electronic exchange of prints and responses.

IED: Improvised Explosive Device. In other words, a homemade bomb. These can be concealed within objects or buried, placed inside a vehicle (VBIED, or Vehicle Borne IED), or carried by a suicide bomber.

J. Reuben: Short for J. Reuben Long Detention Center, a minimal-level security facility located about forty-five minutes from Travis's house, depending on traffic.

JDLR: Law enforcement shorthand for "just doesn't/didn't look right"

Jump Out Boy: A member of a SWAT or a police unit on a stakeout, often hidden inside a sound van listening to wiretaps, wired informants, or in unmarked cars. When the signal is given, these officers *jump out* of their vehicles and take the surprised suspects into custody by a sudden show of force.

Kemne (*come-en-ye*): Czech K9 command for come, summoning the dog.

Kong: Hands down the best dog toy/training tool ever made. Their rubber toys are color-coded for the type of chewer or age. As a puppy, my dog chewed metal cans open for fun—the black Extreme Kong Classic is his favorite, and the only toy he has not destroyed in under ten minutes. You can get your own here: https://www.kongcompany.com/

Léine *(LANE-yuh):* Irish Gaelic for shirt

LEO: Law Enforcement Officer

Lunula (*loo-NEW-lah, pl. Lunulae loo-NEW-lay*): A type of hammered gold collar necklace shaped like a crescent moon. Dating back to the Bronze Age (2200 to 2000 BC), most of these archaeological treasures were discovered in Ireland, although variants have been found in other Celtic nations such as Scotland and Wales. The ancient Romans wore a similar pendant shape. In medical terminology, the lunula is the white crescent area on a fingernail.

Magick: Throughout the story, the words magick and magic both appear. This isn't a typo or error. Adding the *k* is attributed to Aleister Crowley (1875–1947), founder of the

Thelemic religion, twentieth century occultist, explorer, and inspiration for a great Ozzy Osbourne tune. The additional letter distinguishes stage or performance magic (such as Criss Angel or Harry Houdini) from the arcane arts of the metaphysical, will-driven spellwork, and ritual.

Merlon (*MER-lohn*): One-half of the "toothy" architecture is found on high medieval castle walls. The merlons (the tooth or raised part that provides cover during battle) alternate with the crenets or gaps, which allow soldiers to fire arrows or other missiles with a clear view.

Mess: a Southern unit of measurement, meaning an amount sufficient for a meal. The size of the mess can vary, depending on how many folks are coming over to eat.

Miranda: From the 1966 Arizona Supreme Court decision in *Miranda v. Arizona*. At the time of arrest, officers must read the Miranda Warning: *"You have the right to remain silent. Anything you say can and will be used against you in a court of law. You have the right to an attorney. If you cannot afford an attorney, one will be provided for you. Do you understand the rights I have just read to you? With these rights in mind, do you wish to speak to me?"* The suspect must give a clear Yes/No answer to both questions before they can be interrogated. If the suspect invokes his/her rights at any time, all questioning stops.

MOS 31K: US Army Military Occupational Specialty Working Dog Handler

NAPWDA: North America Police Work Dog Association. For more information about the K9 certification process, go to https://www.napwda.com/

Narcan (Naloxone): This life-saving drug quickly reverses opioid/narcotic overdoses. It is now standard issue equipment for police and first responders, packaged as a single-use nasal spray.

Nesting: This term is usually associated with pregnancy. In the South, it is often used to describe a young woman actively seeking marriage.

Nuggies: slang term for chicken nuggets. My dog's favorite nuggie source is Chik-Fil-A. He recognizes the sign and complains loudly if I pass by the restaurant without stopping.

OCP Scorpion: Operational Camouflage Pattern is a military camouflage designed to reflect surrounding colors in different environments, seasons, and weather conditions. It uses a green base color with no beige/brown slug patterns, as it has no vertical elements.

OC spray: A non-lethal and very effective means of incapacitating an opponent. OC is short for Oleoresin Capsicum, a compound that irritates the eyes to cause tears, pain, and even temporary blindness. Capsicum is found naturally in peppers, ranging from the mild bell pepper (0 Scoville Heat Units, or SHU) to the Carolina Reaper (2,200,000 SHU) that makes you question your life choices. Police grade OC spray measures 500,000 to 2 million SHU, with some brands measuring up to 5.3 million SHU.

Oengus *(EN-is):* Irish Gaelic masculine name

Ogam (*AGH-um*): The ancient version of *Ogham* (*OH-um*). This runic alphabet appears in writings and inscriptions dating back to the fourth century AD, used to write in Primitive Irish, Old Welsh, Latin, and Pictish.

One Percenter: This term came from a statement made by the American Motorcycle Association after the Hollister Riot in 1947, saying 99 percent of motorcycle riders are good, decent, law-abiding citizens. The "outlaw" clubs engaged in (allegedly) criminal activity immediately seized on that, branding themselves as the other one percent. A few well-known OMGs (Outlaw Motorcycle Gangs) or 1 percent clubs are the Hells Angels, the Outlaws, the Bandidos, and the Pagans.

Perp: Police slang for perpetrator, a person who commits an illegal, criminal, or evil act

Playlist: If you'd like to hear some of Travis's favorite classic rock and metal tunes or Saoirse's Beach Music, their playlists can be found under my profile on Spotify.

Pozor (*PO-zor*): Czech K9 command to watch, be alert and on guard

Prey Drive: A dog's natural hunting instinct, hardwired for finding, chasing, and ultimately capturing their next meal. K9 work that involves chasing down motivated to escape criminals requires a dog with a high prey drive because, you know, they love fast food.

Púca (*POO-kah*): A Celtic caste of dark fae or Unseelie, known for their shapeshifting abilities and general mischief-making.

Purpose, single or dual: Some K9s are trained for one purpose or area of expertise, such as tracking, narcotics, explosives, apprehension, riot control, etc. A K9 trained for dual or multiple purposes undergoes extensive additional training. Note: K9s are not trained to detect both narcotics *and* explosives, Search/Saoirse being the exception to that rule. Searching for narcotics often employs an <u>active</u> alert, barking or pawing at the suspect area. However, with explosives, they are trained to give a <u>passive</u> alert, meaning to sit quietly in front of the suspect area. Increased activity, sound, or motion could unintentionally set off a lethal charge.

Revir (*rah-VERE*): Czech K9 command for search

Ruaidri (*RUA-r'i*): Irish Gaelic masculine name meaning "red king"

Saoirse (*SER-shah*): Irish Gaelic feminine name meaning "freedom"

Scentcasting: When a K9 or other type of scenting/hunting dog lifts its head, turning it from side to side while sniffing. This often happens when the ground scent weakens or goes in multiple directions.

Shag: the state dance of North and South Carolina, performed to Beach Music. It has been described as a slower Jitterbug, essentially a one and two, three and four step dance. The male partner tends to do the more complicated or flashy moves, hence the term "peacocking."

Shot across the bow: This phrase originated during the days of tall ships and naval warfare. It was used to describe a warning shot fired from one ship to another. These shots were usually aimed at the front or bow, with the intent of expressing displeasure and indicating the possibility of dire consequences.

Simmer Down: a unique Southern US expression meaning to unbunch your panties and calm yourself.

Six: When not used for the number, the six refers to the position behind someone else. When someone says, "I've got your six," it means they "have your back" or are watching your back (or blind spot) in case of trouble. Using a clock face, if the person "on point" or in the lead is at twelve o'clock, the person behind them would be at six o'clock.

SLED: South Carolina Law Enforcement Division

So What Had Happened Was: A mostly Southern US phrase, and how all the best "you're not going to believe this, but..." stories start.

SOS: Society of Stranders, a fun group of dance aficionados devoted to Beach Music and The Art of the Shag. You can learn more about them at their official website https://shagdance.com/

Sullivan Nod: This sales technique uses a subconscious suggestion to influence the customer to choose a particular item when multiple options are available. It is very common in food/beverage service: "Do you want well (house) vodka or Grey Goose (top shelf)?" Several slight yes nods accompany the suggested upsell. Done correctly, it's a powerful Jedi mind trick.

TATP: Triacetone Triperoxide, a highly explosive organic peroxide compound. Despite its inherent instability, it is a common ingredient in homemade explosives. This one bears the ominous nickname "The Mother of Satan."

Tuath Dé *(TWO-ah day)* or *Tuatha Dé Danann (TWO-ah-ha day DAWN-nan)*: Tribe of the Gods and Children of the Goddess Danu, respectively. This is the Irish name given to the Fae, who ruled in Ireland from 1897 BC to 1700 BC. They were defeated in battle by the invading Milesians. The victors allowed the Tuatha Dé Danann to remain in Ireland, but only if they went underground to live. Check out the *Irish Book of Invasions* or *The Annals of the Four Masters* for more historical information.

Uisnech (*ISH-nack*): an Irish Gaelic masculine name. The origins of this name are unknown, but they may relate to the Hill of Uisneach, an ancient and sacred place now being considered for listing as a World Heritage Site.

University of South Carolina Gamecocks vs. Clemson University Tigers: the biggest rivalry in SC collegiate football. It's hard to find anyone who isn't firmly on one side or the other, wearing the orange/purple/white of Clemson or the much more regal garnet/black/white of USC (not that I'm biased or anything, but USC *is* my alma mater). Many people plan their business trips, vacations, weddings, surgeries, and even funerals around whichever day this falls each year.

Velociraptor: a dinosaur from the late Cretaceous period, weighing around 100 pounds, close to an adult wolf in size, and feathered. However, after deciding this was not scary enough for the Jurassic Park blockbusters, the film moguls tweaked their basic design to terrorize moviegoers even more. When Travis presented the picture of one to Saoirse, he searched for the movie and showed her the Hollywood version.

VIN: a unique vehicle identification number etched on an auto in eighteen places, two or three on a motorcycle.

WishSomeone Woods: A play on "I wish someone would" such as in "I wish someone would (bad action) and I'll (reciprocal bad action)." This phrase is often viewed as overcompensating smack talk.

Wonderful Tonight: A sweet ballad by guitar master Eric Clapton, from his album <u>Slowhand</u> released in 1977.

Yzma (*EEZ-ma*): the female villain in Disney's animated classic *The Emperor's New Groove,* voiced by the eternally fabulous Eartha Kitt.

Zustan (*ZOO-stan*): Czech K9 command for stay.

"Real heroes die serving the law, not resisting it."

— Unknown

If you would like to help our heroes:

Throw Away Dogs Project –

https://throwawaydogsproject.com/

Project K9 Hero – https://projectk9hero.org

K9s of Valor – https://www.k9sofvalor.org/

Project Paws Alive – https://www.ppak9.org/

Vested In K9s – https://www.vik9s.org/

Brady's K9 Fund – https://bradysk9fund.com/

GA Police K9 Foundation –

https://www.gapolicek9foundation.org

National Police Dog Foundation –

https://www.nationalpolicedogfoundation.org/

Mission K9 Rescue – https://missionk9rescue.org/

Warrior Dog Foundation – https://warriordogfoundation.org/

Universal K9, Inc. – https://www.universalk9inc.com/

Joint Task Force K9s, training and providing service dogs for veterans, active-duty military, and active/retired LEOs – http://www.jtkf9s.com/

Protection 4 Paws – https://www.protection4paws.com/

Category 5 K9 – https://www.cat5k9.org/

Vested Interest in K9s – https://vik9s.org/

ABOUT HERSELF

Shannon MacLeod lives next to an abandoned theme park. A proud member of Romance Writers of America and PAN, her Celtic romantasies include *Embrace the Lace, Rogue on the Rollaway, The Celtic Knot: Suit of Cups (Arcana Love I), The Gypsy Ribbon: Suit of Wands (Arcana Love II),* available now from Kensington Books. Her tales are filled with strong heroes and equally strong heroines, interesting locales, colorful characters, a touch of magick and mystery, loads of quirky humor, a hint of snarkiness, a body count, and absolutely no sparkly vampires.

Writing as her evil twin, *The Celtic Cross Tarot Spread: Cutting to the Chase* and the companion book for the *Shadowfox Tarot* (as Jennifer Shadowfox) are currently available from Schiffer Publishing.

When not writing, she lives a life of servitude to three spoiled cats, and one entitled German Shepherd Dog. She enjoys rainy days, good music, and spending long hours gazing at her beloved ocean. An avid wearer of boots regardless of the season and dangerously high heels, she watches Lord of the Rings more than any sane person should and can, in fact, reenact entire battle scenes using interpretive dance. Her spirit animals are the Honey Badger and Gordon Ramsay.

If you'd like to hear more about the music mentioned in K9 Mine, check out Shannon's profile on Spotify. There you'll find Travis's 80's Rock and Hauling Ass playlists, as well as Saoirse's favorite Beach Music tunes.

Shannon loves to hear from her readers.
Email her at Shannon@shannonmacleod.com or find her at
http://www.shannonmacleod.com/

The Bear, Shannon's ride-or-die housewolf

ALSO BY THE AUTHOR

The Celtic Knot: Suit of Cups

The Gypsy Ribbon: Suit of Wands

Rogue on the Rollaway

Embrace the Lace

Writing as Jennifer Shadowfox:

The Celtic Cross: Cutting To the Chase

The Shadowfox Tarot (companion book)